Even Cowgirls Get the Blues

Books by Tom Robbins

Another Roadside Attraction

Even Cowgirls Get the Blues

Even Cowgirls Get the Blues

by Tom Robbins

Houghton Mifflin Company Boston

A portion of this book has
appeared in *American Review.*

Library of Congress Cataloging in Publication Data
Robbins, Tom.
Even cowgirls get the blues. I. Title.
PZ4.R636Ev [PS3568.0233] 813'.5'4 75-46633
ISBN 0-395-24305-X *hardbound*
ISBN 0-395-24510-9 *paper*

Printed in the United States of America

c 10 9 8 7 6

To Fleetwood Star Robbins, the apple,
the pineapple, the mango, the orchard of my eye.

And, of course, to all cowgirls, everywhere.

The lust of the goat is the bounty of God.
The nakedness of woman is the work of God.
Excess of sorrow laughs. Excess of joy weeps.

— William Blake

I told Dale, "When I go, just skin me and put me on top of Trigger." And Dale said, "Now don't get any ideas about me."

— Roy Rogers

Author's Note

THROUGHOUT this book I have used third person pronouns and collective nouns in the masculine gender. To those readers who may be offended by this, I apologize sincerely. Unfortunately, there are at this time no alternatives that do not either create confusion or impede the flow of language; which is to say, there are no acceptable alternatives. Here's hoping that when and if I publish again, there will be.

No novel ever has been written by one person alone. Among the people who contributed, in one way or another, to the writing of this one are Paul Dorpat, Lorenzo Milam, Darrell Bob Houston (who *is* the great American novel), Michael St. John Smith, Tiny Terrie, Leonore Fleischer, Phoebe Larmore, Holly Henderson (sweetest pissant I know), Libby Burke, Aurora Jellybean (no kin to Bonanza), Keith Wyman, Gigi Carroll, Thomas G. Gregg, Roland Kirk (on nose flute), James Lee Stanley (on guitar and vocals) and the Paul Winter Consort (on everything). Yes, and let's not forget Wendy the Typist, who managed to get through a whole year of teaching Biz Ed without yelling out something obscene in front of the pupils of Mount Vernon High.

T.R.

Even Cowgirls Get the Blues

Single Cell Preface

AMOEBAE leave no fossils. They haven't any bones. (No teeth, no belt buckles, no wedding rings.) It is impossible, therefore, to determine how long amoebae have been on Earth.

Quite possibly they have been here since the curtain opened. Amoebae may even have dominated the stage, early in the first act. On the other hand, they may have come into existence only three years — or three days or three minutes — before they were discovered by Anton van Leeuwenhoek in 1674. It can't be proven either way.

One thing is certain, however: because amoebae reproduce by division, endlessly, passing everything on yet giving up nothing, the first amoebae that ever lived is still alive. Whether four billion years old or merely three hundred, he/she is with us today.

Where?

Well, the first amoeba may be floating on his/her back in a luxurious pool in Hollywood, California. The first amoeba may be hiding among the cattail roots and peepers in the muddy shallows of Siwash Lake. The first amoeba may recently have dripped down your leg. It is pointless to speculate.

The first amoeba, like the last and the one after that, is here, there and everywhere, for its vehicle, its medium, its essence is water.

Water — the ace of elements. Water dives from the clouds without parachute, wings or safety net. Water runs over the steepest precipice and blinks not a lash. Water is buried and rises again; water walks on fire and fire gets the blisters. Stylishly composed in any situation — solid, gas or liquid — speaking in penetrating dialects understood by all things — animal, vegetable or mineral — water travels intrepidly through four dimensions, *sustaining* (Kick a lettuce in the field and it will yell "Water!"), *destroying* (The Dutch boy's finger remembered the view from Ararat) and *creating* (It has even been said that human beings were invented by water as a device for transporting itself from one place to another, but that's another story). Always in motion, ever-flowing (whether at steam rate or glacier speed), rhythmic, dynamic, ubiquitous, changing and working its changes, a mathematics turned wrong side out, a philosophy in reverse, the ongoing odyssey of water is virtually irresistible. And wherever water goes, amoebae go along for the ride.

Sissy Hankshaw once taught a parakeet to hitchhike. There is not much in that line she could teach an amoeba.

For its expertise as a passenger, as well as for its near-perfect resolution of sexual tensions, the amoeba (and not the whooping crane) is hereby proclaimed the official mascot of *Even Cowgirls Get the Blues.*

And to the *first* amoeba, wherever it may be, *Even Cowgirls Get the Blues* would like to say happy birthday. Happy birthday to you.

Welcome to the Rubber Rose Ranch

It is the finest outhouse in the Dakotas. It has to be.

Spiders, mice, cold drafts, splinters, corncobs, habitual stenches don't make it in this company. The hands have renovated and decorated the privy themselves. Foam rubber, hanging flower pots, a couple of prints by Georgia O'Keeffe (her cow skull period), fluffy carpeting, Sheetrock insulation, ashtrays, an incense burner, a fly strip, a photograph of Dale Evans about which there is some controversy. There is even a radio in the outhouse, although the only radio station in the area plays nothing but polkas.

Of course, the ranch has indoor facilities, flush toilets in regular bathrooms, but they'd been stopped up during the revolution and nobody had ever unstopped them. Plumbing was one thing the girls were poor at. Nearest Roto-Rooter man was thirty miles. Weren't any Roto-Rooter *women* anywhere, as far as they knew.

Jelly is sitting in the outhouse. She has been sitting there longer then necessary. The door is wide open and lets in the sky. Or, rather, a piece of the sky, for on a summer's day in Dakota the sky is mighty big. Mighty big and mighty blue, and today there is hardly a cloud. What looks to be a wisp of cloud is actually the moon, narrow and pale like a paring snipped from a snowman's toenail. The radio is broadcasting "The Silver Dollar Polka."

What is young Jelly thinking, in such a pensive pose? Hard to say. Probably she is thinking about the birds. No, not those crows that just haiku-ed by, but the birds she and her hands are bamboozling down at the lake. Those birds give a body something to think about, all right. But maybe she is thinking about the Chink, wondering what the crazy old coot is up to now, way up yonder on his ridge. Maybe she is thinking about ranchly finances, puzzling how she's going to make ends meet. It is even possible that she is pondering something metaphysical, for the Chink has more than once subjected her to philosophical notions: the hit and miss of the cosmic pumpkin. If that is unlikely, it is still less likely that she is mulling over the international situation — desperate, as usual. And apparently her mind is not on romance or a particular romantic entity, for though her panties and jeans are at her feet, her fingers drum dryly upon the domes of her knees. Perhaps Jelly is thinking about what's for supper.

On the other hand, Bonanza Jellybean, ranch boss, may just be looking things over. Surveying the spread from the comfort of the privy. Checking out the corrals, the stables, the bunkhouse, the pump, what's left of the sauna, the ruins of the reducing salon, the willow grove and cottonwoods, the garden where Delores teased a rattlesnake on Monday, the pile of hair dryers still rusting among the sunflowers, the chicken coop, the tumbleweed, the peyote wagon, the distant buttes and canyons, the sky full of blue. Weather's hot but there's a breeze today and it feels sweet, swimming up her bare thighs. There is sage smell and rose waft. There is fly buzz and polka yip. Way off, horse lips flutter; she hears the goats at pasture and the far, faint sounds of the girls tending the herd. The bird herd.

A rooster clears his sinuses. He's loud but absolutely nothing compared to what those birds can do if the hands don't keep them quiet. They'd better!

Still sitting, Jelly focuses her dreamy gaze on the rooster. "Someday," she says to the empty seat next to her, "if that Sissy Hankshaw ever shows up here again, I'm gonna teach her how to hypnotize a chicken. Chickens are the easiest critters on Earth to hypnotize. If you can look a chicken in the eyes for ten seconds, it's yours forever."

She pulls up her pants, shoulders her rifle and ambles off to relieve the guard at the gate.

Welcome to the Rubber Rose. The largest all-girl ranch in the West.

Part I

Nature's got a hankering after experiments.

— Trader Horn

1.

IT IS NOT a heart: light, heavy, kind or broken; dear, hard, bleeding or transplanted; it is not a heart.

It is not a brain. The brain, that pound and a half of chicken-colored goo so highly regarded (by the brain itself), that slimy organ to which is attributed such intricate and mysterious powers (it is the self-same brain that does the attributing), the brain is so weak that, without its protective casing to support it, it simply collapses of its own weight. So it could not be a brain.

It is neither a kneecap nor a torso. It is neither a whisker nor an eyeball. It is not a tongue.

It is not a belly button. (The umbilicus serves, then withdraws, leaving but a single footprint where it stood: the navel, wrinkled and cupped, whorled and domed, blind and winking, bald and tufted, sweaty and powdered, kissed and bitten, waxed and fuzzy, bejeweled and ignored; reflecting as graphically as breasts, seeds or fetishes the omnipotent fertility in which Nature dangles her muddy feet, the navel looks in like a plugged keyhole on the center of our being, it is true, but O navel, though we salute your motionless maternity and the dreams that have got tangled in your lint, you are only a scar, after all; you are not it.)

It is not a ribcage. It is not a back. It is not one of those bodily orifices favored for stuffing, nor is it that headstrong member with which every conceivable stuffable orifice somewhere sometime has been stuffed. There is no hair around it. For shame!

It is not an ankle, for her ankles, while bony, were ordinary, to say the least.

It is not a nose, chin or forehead. It is not a biceps, a triceps or a loop-of-Henle.

It is something else.

2.

IT IS A THUMB. The thumb. The thumbs, both of them. It is her thumbs that we remember; it is her thumbs that have set her apart.

It was thumbs that brought her to the clockworks, took her away, brought her back. Of course, it may be a disservice to her, as well as to the Rubber Rose, to emphasize the clockworks — but the clockworks is fresh and large in the author's mind right now. The image of the clockworks has followed the author through these early sentences, tugging at him, refusing to be snubbed. The image of the clockworks tugs gently at the author's cuff, much as the ghost of Duncan Hines tugs at the linen tablecloths of certain restaurants, little that he can eat now: *long time no cheese omelet.*

Still, as is well known, our subject's thumbs brought her to myriad other places besides the clockworks and to myriad other people besides the Chink. For example, they brought her to New York City and, there, before the gentleman Julian. And Julian, who looked at her often, looked at her well, looked at her from every angle, exterior and interior, from which man might look at woman — even Julian was most impressed by her thumbs.

Who was it who watched her undress for bed and bath? It was Julian. Whose eyes traced every contour of her delicate face and willowy body, invariably coming to rest on her thumbs? Julian's. It was Julian, sophisticated, sympathetic, closed to any notion of deformity, who, nevertheless, in the final analysis, in the sanctuary of his own mind's eye, had to regard her thumbs as an obtrusion on the exquisite lines of an otherwise graceful figure — as though Leonardo had left a strand of spaghetti dangling from the corner of Mona Lisa's mouth.

3.

THE NORMAL rectal temperature of a hummingbird is 104.6.

The normal rectal temperature of a bumblebee is calculated to be 110.8, although so far no one has succeeded in taking the rectal temperature of a bumblebee. That doesn't mean that it can't or won't be done. Scientific research marches on: perhaps at this moment, bee proctologists at Du Pont . . .

As for the oyster, its rectal temperature has never even been estimated, although we must suspect that the tissue heat of the sedentary bivalve is as far below good old 98.6 as that of the busy bee is above. Nonetheless, the oyster, could it fancy, should fancy its excremental equipment a hot item, for what other among Creation's crapping creatures can convert its bodily wastes into treasure?

There is a metaphor here, however strained. The author is attempting to draw a shaky parallel between the manner in which the oyster, when beset by impurities or disease, coats the offending matter with its secretions, thereby producing a pearl, a parallel between the eliminatory ingenuity of the oyster and the manner in which Sissy Hankshaw, adorned with thumbs that many might consider morbid, coated the offending digits with glory, thereby perpetuating a vision that the author finds smooth and lustrous.

The author did not choose Sissy Hankshaw for her thumbs per se, but rather for the use that she made of them. Sissy has provided this book with its pearly perspectives, just as the clockworks — where there is tick and tock enough for everyone — has supplied its cosmic connections; just as the Rubber Rose has generated its rather warm rectal temperature.

4.

SISSY HANKSHAW arrived at the Rubber Rose — and, subsequently, the clockworks — as she had always arrived everywhere: via roadside solicitation. She hitchhiked into the Rubber Rose because hitchhiking was her customary mode of travel; hitchhiking was, in fact, her way of life, a calling to which she was born. Regardless of what luck her other eight digits grabbed onto, her thumbs carried her to many wonderful times and places and finally they carried her to the clockworks as well.

Even had she been common of thumb, however, she might have bummed a ride into the Rubber Rose, for she was without private transportation, and no train, bus or plane goes near the ranch, let alone the clockworks.

A woman came hitchhiking into a remote region of the Dakotas. She rolled in like a peach basket that had swallowed a hoop snake. It was nothing. She made it look easy. She had the disposition for it, not to mention the thumbs.

That woman did not come to stay. She meant to leave no more tracks in the hills of Dakota than a water bug might leave on a double martini. She rolled in effortlessly, her thumbs wiggling like the hula hips of Heaven. She planned to leave the same way.

But plans are one thing and fate another. When they coincide, success results. Yet success mustn't be considered the absolute. It is questionable, for that matter, whether success is an adequate response to life. Success can eliminate as many options as failure.

At any rate . . . Just as there were ranch hands, politically oriented, who objected to the 8 x 10 glossy of Dale Evans in the Rubber Rose outhouse on the grounds that Miss Evans was a revisionist, a saddlesore (as they put it) on the long ride of cowgirl progress, there were interested parties who objected to Sissy Hankshaw's being identified with the Rubber Rose on the grounds that Sissy is not a true cowgirl and that, despite her friendship with Bonanza Jellybean et al., despite her presence during the revolt, she was only temporarily and peripherally involved with the events that took place on that hundred and sixty acres of lipstick criminal moonlight. Their contention is not without merit. How we shape our understanding of others' lives is determined by what we find memorable in them, and that in turn is determined not by any potentially accurate overview of another's personality but rather by the tension and balance that exist in our daily relationships. That the axis around which Sissy's daily involvements revolved was a result of her physical condition is obvious, and it is equally true that whatever memorable or epiphanic impact this singular woman has had on us occurred in a context quite removed from the Rubber Rose — or, at least, as the cowgirls themselves saw the Rubber Rose. It cannot be denied, however, that Sissy Hankshaw came not once, but twice, to the ranch, as well as to that place that, because therein occurs both a measuring and a transvaluation of time, we are obliged to call the "clockworks." She came in different seasons and under different circumstances. But on both occasions she hitchhiked.

5.

SISSY'S EARLIEST MEMORY was of a day when she was four or three. It was Sunday afternoon and she had been napping under sheets of funnies on a horsehair sofa in the living room. Believing that she was still asleep, for they were not intentionally unkind, her daddy and a visiting uncle were standing over her, looking down at her young thumbs.

"Well," her uncle said after a while, "you're lucky that she don't suck 'em."

"She couldn't suck 'em," said Sissy's daddy, exaggerating. "She'd need a mouth like a fish tank."

The uncle agreed. "The poor little tyke might have a hard time finding herself a hubby. But as far as getting along in the world, it's a real blessing that she's a girl-child. Lord, I reckon this youngun would never make a mechanic."

"Nope, and not a brain surgeon, neither," said Sissy's daddy.

" 'Course she'd do pretty good as a butcher. She could retire in two years on the overcharges alone."

Laughing, the men went out to the kitchen to fill their glasses.

"One thing," Sissy heard her uncle jest from a distance. "That youngun would make one hell of a hitchhiker . . ."

Hitchhiker? The word startled Sissy. The word tinkled in her head with a supernatural echo, frozen in mystery, causing her to stir and rustle the funny papers so that she failed to hear the conclusion of her uncle's sentence:

". . . if she was a boy, I mean."

6.

THE SURPRISE of Sissy Hankshaw is that she did not grow up a neurotic disaster. If you are a small girl in a low-income suburb of Richmond, Virginia, as Sissy was, and the other kids jeer at your hands, and your own brothers call you by your neighborhood nickname — "Thumbelina" — and your own daddy sometimes makes jokes about your being "all thumbs," then you toughen up or shatter. You do not merely stretch rhino leather over your own fair skin, for that would deflect pleasure as well as pain, and you do not permit your being to turn stinking inside a shell, but what you do is swirl yourself in the toughness of dreams.

It is all you care about. When the other kids are playing hopscotch or kick-the-can you go off alone to a woods near your home. There are no cars in the woods, of course, but that does not matter. There are cars in your dream.

You hitchhike. Timidly at first, barely flashing your fist, leaning almost imperceptibly in the direction of your imaginary destination. A squirrel runs along a tree limb. You hitchhike the squirrel. A blue jay flies by. You flag it down. You are not the notorious Sissy then; just a shy Southern child at the edge of a small forest, observing the forward motion of your thumbs, studying the way they behave at different velocities and angles of arc. You hitchhike bees, snakes, clouds, dandelion puffs.

In school you learn that it is the thumb that separates human beings from the lower primates. The thumb is an evolutionary triumph. Because of his thumbs, man can use tools; because he can use tools he can extend his senses, control his environment and increase in sophistication and power. The thumb is the cornerstone of civilization! You are an ignorant schoolgirl. You think civilization is a good thing.

Because of his thumbs, man can use tools etc., etc. But *you* cannot use tools. Not well. Your thumbs are too immense. Thumbs separate humans from the other primates. Your thumbs separate you from other humans. You begin to sense a presence about your thumbs. You wonder if there is not magic there.

The first time . . . You'll never forget it. It's a frigid morning and a thin snow is filling the chinks in the wind. You don't feel like walking the five blocks to school. Over your shoulder you see — Oh you can barely speak of it now! — a Pontiac stationwagon approaching at a moderate speed. How you suffer through those false starts before your hand takes the plunge. Your bladder threatens to overflow. The sweep of your skinny arm seems to last for minutes. And even then you are passed by. But no — brake lights! The Pontiac skids ever so slightly on the snowflakes. You run, actually sweating, to its side. Peer in. Your face, beneath your stocking cap, is a St. Vitus tomato. But the driver motions for you to get in . . .

After that you never walk to school. Not even in fine weather. You catch rides to the movies on Saturday afternoons (your first exposure to cowgirls); catch rides into downtown Richmond just for practice. You are amazed at the inherent, almost instinctive, precision with which your thumbs move through air. You marvel at the grace of those floppy appendages. That there were ever such instruments as thumbscrews bring tears to your eyes. You invent rolls and flourishes. During your thirteenth summer you hitchhike nearly a hundred miles — to Virginia Beach to see the ocean.

For one reason or another, you look up "thumb" in a dictionary. It says "the short, thick first or most preaxial digit of the human hand, differing from the other fingers by having two phalanges and greater freedom of movement."

You like that. *Greater freedom of movement.*

7.

THEY CONTINUED TO GROW, the first or most preaxial digits of Sissy's hands. They grew while she ate her grits and baloney; they grew while she slurped her Wheaties and milk. They grew while she studied history ("As the settlers pushed ever westward, they were threatened constantly by hordes of savage Indians"); they grew while she studied arithmetic ("If a hen and a half can lay an egg and a half in a day and a half how long will it take a monkey with a wooden leg to kick the seeds out of a dill pickle?"). They grew in the sour-smelling room where she slept with two brothers; they grew in the small forest where she played all alone. They grew in the summer when other things grew; they grew in the winter when most growing had stopped. They grew when she laughed; they grew when she cried. As she inhaled and exhaled, they grew.

(Yes, they grew even as millions of young Americans under social pressure and upon the instruction of their elders, struggled to cease growing; which is to say, struggled to "grow up," an excruciatingly difficult goal since it runs contrary to the most central laws of nature — the laws of change and renewal — yet a goal miraculously attained by everyone in our culture except for a few misfits.)

They continued to grow, the first or most preaxial digits of Sissy's hands, and not quite in direct ratio with the rest of her growing-girl self.

If Sissy was fearful that they might grow on forever, that eventually they might reach a size that would put them beyond her control, that they might cause her to end up in a roadside zoo, third geek from the left, just across the pit from the Gila monster, she did not let on.

With no mental effort, she was expanding her breasts from bottle-stoppers to mounds that required material restraint. Without any help from her brain, she was beginning to sprout velvety hairs over that area between her legs that heretofore had been as bare and ugly as a baby bird. Lacking reason or logic to guide her, she nevertheless maneuvered her bodily rhythms into perfect synchronization with those of the moon, at first merely spotting her panties and then, after only a few months' practice, issuing a regular lunar flow. With the same calm and expert innocence, she pumped up her thumbs, ever lengthening the shadows they dropped on schoolwork and dinner plates.

As if intimidated by this rank and easy spectacle of growth — which, because they shared her room, they must witness in intimate detail — her brothers all but halted their own physiological progression. They remained their whole lives short and peanutlike, with baby faces and genitals of a size that women don't really mind but that other men often feel compelled to mock. Believing that old wives' tale about the correlation in scale of the thumb and the penis, locker-room anatomists sometimes suggested to the brothers that it was a pity they hadn't shared in their sister's digital largess.

Jerry and Junior Hankshaw would have been horrified had their thumbs assumed sisterly proportions; would have been horrified, for that matter, if their peckers had so enlarged. But a *slight* increase, a *reasonable* enlargement, would have been welcome, and indeed, after numerous clandestine consultations in the same scrubby forest where Sissy had learned her business, the brothers decided actively to seek it.

Junior, whose mechanical skills were to lead him in his daddy's gritty footsteps (in the tobacco warehouses of South Richmond there is always a dryer, a humidifier or an exhaust fan that needs repair), began work on a secret apparatus. After no less than three used innertubes had been ripped and stripped in vain, and following the theft of both rawhide laces from Mr. Hankshaw's boots, Junior finally produced a gadget that resembled a mix between a vise, a slingshot and the center tube from a toilet tissue roll. For reasons of discretion, the thumb-stretcher could be used only late at night, and the brothers spent many a sleepy hour in the dark taking turns at the agony dispensed by the device they had fastened to their imitation maple Sears and Roebuck bedstead.

Their endeavor was not without historical precedent. Around 1830, when he was twenty years old, the composer Robert Schumann subjected the fingers of his right hand to a stretching machine. Schumann's purpose was to escalate his progress toward piano virtuosity, his pianist-sweetheart Clara having expressed dismay over the length of his reach. In the sugar-frosted elegance of a nineteenth-century Leipzig drawing room, Schumann would sit stiffly, sipping *kaffee,* while his stubby fingers suffered growing pains in the grips of a contraption that resembled a nightingale harness, a rack for heretic elves. The result was that he crippled his hand, terminating his performing career.

All that happened to Jerry and Junior Hankshaw was that, with thumbs too red and raw to disguise, they soon were questioned by their parents and ridiculed by their peers. Thanking Jesus that he and Jerry had gone through digital intermediaries and not subjected their peckers directly to his invention, Junior threw the device into the James River. Poor Schumann threw himself into the Rhine.

Only one set of thumbs was destined to grow — and glow — in the rickety house of the Hankshaws. One set of thumbs destined to soar and bow, as if that set of thumbs was the prematurely shortened performing career of Robert Schumann, continuing now in a Rhine-soaked frock coat upon the cement stages of America's freeways, O Fantasia, O Noveletten, O Humoreskes, Gas Food Lodging Exit 46.

8.

South Richmond was a neighborhood of mouse holes, lace curtains, Sears catalogs, measles epidemics, baloney sandwiches — and men who knew more about the carburetor than they knew about the clitoris.

The song "Love Is a Many Splendored Thing" was not composed in South Richmond.

There have been cans of dog food more splendiferous than South Richmond. Land mines more tender.

South Richmond was settled by a race of thin, bony-faced psychopaths. They would sell you anything they had, which was nothing, and kill you over anything they didn't understand, which was everything.

They had come, mostly by Ford from North Carolina, to work in the tobacco warehouses and cigarette factories. In South Richmond, the mouse holes, lace curtains and Sears catalogs, even the baloney sandwiches and measles epidemics, always wore a faint odor of cured tobacco. The word *tobacco* was acquired by our culture (with neither the knowledge nor consent of South Richmonders) from a tribe of Caribbean Indians, the same tribe that gave us the words *hammock, canoe* and *barbecue.* It was a peaceful tribe whose members spent their days lying in hammocks puffing tobacco or canoeing back and forth between barbecues, thus offering little resistance when the land developers arrived from Europe in the sixteenth century. The tribe was disposed of swiftly and without a trace, except for its hammocks, barbecues and canoes, and, of course, its tobacco, whose golden crumbs still perfume the summer clouds and winter ices of South Richmond.

In South Richmond, smelling as it did of tobacco, honky-tonk vice and rusted-out mufflers, social niceties sometimes failed to make the six o'clock news, but one thing the citizens of South Richmond agreed upon was that it was not fit, proper or safe for a little girl to go around hitchhiking.

Sissy Hankshaw hitched short distances but she hitched persistently. Hitching proved good for her thumbs, good for her morale, good, theoretically, for her soul — although it was the mid-fifties, Ike was President, gray flannel was fashionable, canasta was popular and it might have seemed presumptuous then to speak of "soul."

Parents, teachers, neighbors, the family minister, older children, the cop on the beat tried to reason with her. The tall, frail, solitary child listened politely to their pleas and warnings, but her mind had a logic of its own: if rubber tires were meant to roll and seats to carry passengers, then far be it from Sissy Hankshaw to divert those noble things from their true channel.

"There's sick men who drive around in cars," they told her. "Sooner or later you're bound to be picked up by some man who wants to do nasty things to you."

Truth was, Sissy was picked up by such men once or twice a week, and had been since she began hitching at age eight or nine. There are a lot more men like that than people think. Assuming that many of them would be unattracted to a girl with . . . with an affliction, there are a lot of men like that, indeed. And the further truth was, Sissy allowed it.

She had one rule: keep driving. As long as they maintained the forward progress of their vehicles, drivers could do anything they wished to her. Some complained that it was the old rolling doughnut trick, which even Houdini had failed to master, but they would take a flyer. She caused a few accidents, taxed the very foundations of masculine ingenuity and preserved her virginity until her wedding night (when she was well past the age of twenty). One motorist, a tanned athletic type, managed an occasional French lick while keeping his Triumph TR3 on a true course in moderate traffic. Normally, however, the limitations imposed by her steadfast devotion to vehicular motion were met with less dexterity.

Sissy neither solicited nor discouraged, but accepted the attentions of random drivers with calm satisfaction — and insisted they keep driving. She would eat the cheeseburgers and Dairy Queen sundaes they bought for her while they fished in her panties for whatever it is men fish for in that primitive space. Personally, she preferred gentle, rhythmic trollings. And automatic transmissions. (No girl likes to be molested by a party who is always having to shift gears.) Being molested was, in a sense, a fringe benefit of her craft, a secondary pleasure pulled like a trailer behind the supreme joy of the hitchhike. In honesty, though, she had to admit that it was also an avocational hazard.

Since the brain has such a high susceptibility to inflammation, there were occasional hotheads who would not or could not abide by her rule. In time she learned to recognize them by subtle symptoms — tight lips, shifty eyes, and a pallor that comes from sitting around in stuffy rooms reading *Playboy* magazine and the Bible — and refused their rides.

Earlier, however, Sissy dealt with would-be rapists in another way. When pressured, she placed her thumbs between her legs. Usually, the man simply gave up rather than try to remove them. The very sight of them there, guarding the citadel, was enough to cool passions or at least to confuse them long enough for her to leap out of the car.

Sissy dear. Your thumbs. HOLLYWOOD SPECTACULAR. LAS VEGAS. THE ROSE BOWL. Larger than any one man's desires.

(Incidentally, Sissy's mama never noticed any olfactory traces of her daughter's adventures. Perhaps that is because in South Richmond even a young girl's damp excitement quickly assumed the fragrance of tobacco.)

9.

SHE WAS TAKEN to a specialist once. Once was all that her family could afford.

Dr. Dreyfus was a French Jew who had settled in Richmond following the unpleasantries of the forties. On his office door it was proclaimed that he was a plastic surgeon and a specialist in injuries of the hands. Sissy owned some toy automobiles made of plastic — she used them to set up theoretical problems in hitchhiking. Unlike some children, she took excellent care of her playthings. The notion of a *plastic* surgeon seemed silly to her. The suggestion of injury puzzled her further.

"Do they ever hurt?" asked Dr. Dreyfus.

"No," replied Sissy. "They feel *goo-ood.*" How could she explain the tiny tingle of power she had begun to perceive in them?

"Then why do you flinch when I press?" inquired the specialist.

"Just because," said Sissy. Again the schoolgirl could not elucidate the true emotion, but throughout her life she would refuse to shake hands for fear of damaging those digits that were to be to hitchhiking what Toscanini's baton was to a more traditional field of motion.

Dr. Dreyfus measured the thumbs. Circumference. Length. He gave them eyeshine treatment although their skin was not lacking in shine. He tapped them with tiny hammers, registered (without hint of aesthetic preference) the various tints and shades of their coloration, milked them with syringes, pricked them with pins. He placed them one at a time upon the scales, cautiously, as if he were the Spanish treasurer and they musical hot dogs brought from America by Christopher Columbus to amuse the queen. In a hushed voice he announced that they comprised four percent of the girl's total body weight — or about twice as much as the brain.

The x-rays had a go at them.

"Bone structure, apparent origin and insertion of musculature, and articulation are properly proportioned and normal in every aspect but size," the doctor noted with a nod. The ghost-thumb in the negative nodded back.

Mr. and Mrs. Hankshaw were summoned from the waiting room where *Saturday Evening Post* fantasies had clouded their instinctive parental concern the way that Norman Rockwell's sentimental ideas cloud the purity of a blank canvas.

"They are healthy," Dr. Dreyfus said. "There is nothing I could do that would not cost you a year's salary."

The doctor was thanked for his consideration of Hankshaw finances. ("But a kike's a kike," Sissy's daddy told the swing shift the next time he was sober enough to work. "Iffen he thought we had the money he'd a tried to squeeze us dry.") Parents and child rose to leave. Dr. Dreyfus remained seated. His heavy black fountain pen remained on the desk. His diploma from the Sorbonne remained on the wall. And so forth.

"When he was asked by the French government in nineteen thirty-nine how to design parachutists' uniforms for maximum invisibility, the painter Pablo Picasso replied, 'Dress them as harlequins.' "

The physician paused. "I don't suppose that means very much to you."

Mr. Hankshaw looked from the specialist to his wife to his high-top Red Wing work shoes (in which stolen laces had recently been replaced) to the specialist again. He laughed, half in embarrassment and half in irritation. "Well, shee-ucks, Doc, it sure enough don't."

"Never mind," said Dr. Dreyfus. Now he stood. "The girl has, of course, a congenital abnormality. I am sorry but I do not know the cause. Giantism in an extremity is usually the result of a cavernous hemangioma; that is, a vein tumor that draws excessive amounts of blood into the extremity affected. The more nutrients an extremity gets, the larger it grows, naturally, just as if you put chicken, how you say, manure around one rose bush, it will grow larger than the bush that has no manure. You understand? But the girl has no tumor. Besides, the odds of hemangioma in *both* thumbs is like billions to one. She is, if I may speak frankly, somewhat of a medical oddity. Due to impaired dexterity, her life activities and career potentialities will be reduced. It could be worse. Bring her back to me if there ever is pain. Meanwhile, she will have to learn to live with them."

"That she will," agreed Mr. Hankshaw, who, since having been "saved" at the Moore's Field Billy Graham Rally, had begun to look with bitter resignation upon the gnomish blimps moored to his only daughter's hands. "That she will. The Lord made them things big for a purpose. God don't never git tired of testing *our* kind. It's a punishment of some sort, for what I don't rightly know, but it's a punishment and the girl — and us — got to bear that punishment."

— Whereupon Mrs. Hankshaw began to whimper, "Oh Doc, if you should git a boy in here, if a young man ever shows up here with, a young man with *ugly fingers,* you know, something similar, a similar case, Doc, would you please . . ."

— Whereupon the plastic surgeon remarked, "Remember the words of the painter Paul Gauguin, dear lady. 'The ugly may be beautiful, the pretty never.' I don't suppose that means very much to you."

— Whereupon Mr. Hankshaw pronounced, "It's a judgment. She's gotta bear the punishment."

— Whereupon Sissy, like the Christ in the lurid picture that hung above the TV set at home, beamed serenely, as if to say, "Punishment is its own reward."

10.

OH YES. She was taken, also, to a specialist of a different discipline.

Commercial practice of the persuasion of palmistry was forbidden by ordinance in the city of Richmond, but in the surrounding counties of Chesterfield and Henrico it was entirely legal. Around the scuzzy edges of the town, where pine groves and truck gardens bumped against roadside honky-tonks and low-bid developments, there were to be found six or seven house trailers and three or four conventional homes within whose confines the testimony of the hands was daily given.

It was simple to recognize the lair of a palm-reader. Outside her trailer or bungalow there would be a sign on which a silhouette of the human hand, wrist to fingertips, palm outward, was painted in red. Always in red. For some reason, and for all the author knows there may be a tradition here whose origins stretch back to the Gypsies of Chaldea, it would have been less surprising to find flesh-colored tights in General Patton's laundry bag than to find a flesh-colored hand on a palmistry sign near Richmond. Every hand was red, and directly below the red wrist joint, where on an actual hand a watch or bracelet might cling, the sign-painter would have rendered the title "Madame" followed by a name: Madame Yvonne, Madame Christina, Madame Divine and others.

Madame Zoe, for example. "Madame Zoe" was the name under the red palm that was passed almost weekly by Sissy's mama when she rode the bus out to the end of Hull Street Road to visit her friend Mabel Coffee, the plumber's wife. Mrs. Hankshaw must have passed that sign two hundred times. She always looked at that sign as if it were a deer in a meadow, it was that real to her and that elusive. But it was not until Mabel Coffee had a cyst removed from her ovary and nearly croaked — the same week of the same autumn that President Eisenhower's heart went kablooey — that Mrs. Hankshaw (moved, perhaps, by the drama of events) impulsively pulled the buzzer cord and got off the bus at Madame Zoe's. An appointment was made for the following Saturday.

When Mr. Hankshaw was informed of the date with the palmist he snorted and cussed and warned his wife that if she wasted five dollars of his hard-earned money on a goddamned fortuneteller she'd find herself moving in with Mabel, her plumber and her one good ovary. During the week, however, Sissy's mama used the vaginal wrench to slowly, gently turn her husband's objections down to a mere trickle. Mabel's plumber, with his full set of tools, could not have done better.

On Palm Saturday, Sissy was made to dress as if for church. She was coaxed into a plaid wool skirt whose every pleat was as fuzzed as the romantic dreams of its former owners; she was helped into a cousin's hand-me-down long-sleeved sweater (once white as dentures, now smoking three packs a day); she had her fair, naturally wavy hair combed out with tap water and a dab of White Shoulders cologne; her mouth (so full and round in comparison to the rest of her angular features that it seemed a plum on a vine of beans) was smeared lightly with ruby lipstick. Then mother and daughter took the Midlothian bus to Madame Zoe's, Sissy pouting the full distance because she wasn't allowed to hitchhike.

By the time they wobbled their worn heels on the palmist's walk, however, the girl's petulance had given way to curiosity. What an inspiring drill sergeant curiosity can be! They marched straight to the door of the house trailer and gave it a self-conscious thunk. Moments later it opened to them, releasing odors of incense and boiled cauliflower.

From the vortex of competing smells (This was outside the tobacco zone), Madame Zoe, in kimono and wig, asked them in. "I am the enlightened Madame Zoe," she began, stubbing a cigarette in one of those enlightened little ceramic ashtrays that are shaped like bedpans and inscribed BUTTS. The trailer was cluttered, but not one knick-knack, chintz curtain or chenille-covered armchair seemed to have come from the Beyond. The floor lamp was powered by electricity, not *prana;* the telephone directory was for Richmond, not Atlantis. Even more disappointing to the girl was the absence of any physical reference to Persia, Tibet or Egypt, those centers of arcane knowledge that Sissy was certain she would hitch to someday, although it should be made clear, here and now, that Sissy never really dreamed of hitching *to* anywhere; it was the *act* of hitching that formed the substance of her vision. It turned out that there was nothing the least bit exotic in that house trailer except for the smoldering incense, and although in the dead air of the Eisenhower Years in Richmond, Virginia, incense seemed exotic enough, that particular stick of jasmine was in the process of being kicked deaf, blind and dumb by a pot of cauliflower.

"I am the enlightened Madame Zoe," she began, her voice an uninterested monotonous drone. "There is nothing about your past, present or future that your hands do not know, and there is nothing about your hands that Madame Zoe does not know. There is no hocus-pocus involved. I am a scientist, not a magician. The hand is the most wonderful instrument ever created, but it cannot act of its own accord; it is the servant of the brain. (Author's note: Well, that's the brain's story, anyhow.) It reflects the kind of brain behind it by the manner and intelligence with which it performs its duties. The hand is the external reservoir of our most acute sensations. Sensations, when repeated frequently, have the capacity to mold and mark. I, Madame Zoe, chiromancer, lifelong student of the moldings and markings of the human hand; I, Madame Zoe, to whom no facet of your character or destiny is not readily revealed, I am prepared to . . ." Then she noticed the thumbs.

"Jesus fucking Christ!" she gasped (and this in an era when the expressive verb/noun *fuck* did not, like a barnyard orchid, like a meat bubble, like a saline lollipop, did not bloom, as it does today, upon the lips of every maiden in the land).

Mrs. Hankshaw was as shocked by the fortuneteller's epithet as the fortuneteller was startled by the girl's digits. The two women turned pale and uncertain, while Sissy recognized with a faint smile that she was in command. She extended her thumbs to the good madame. She extended them as an ailing aborigine might extend his swollen parts to a medical missionary; madame showed no sign of charity. She extended them as a gentleman spider might extend a gift fly to a black widow of fatal charm; madame exhibited no appetite. She extended them as a brash young hero might extend a crucifix to a vampire; madame recoiled rather nicely. At last, Sissy's mama drew a neatly folded five-dollar bill from her change purse and extended it alongside her smiling daughter's extremities. The palmist returned immediately to her senses. She took Sissy by the elbow and led her to sit at a Formica-topped table of undistinguished design.

Apprehensively, Madame Zoe held Sissy's hands while with closed eyes she appeared to go into trance. Actually, she was trying desperately to remember all that her teachers and books had taught her about thumbs. At one time, as a young woman in Brooklyn, she had been a serious student of chiromancy, but over the years, like those literary critics who are forced to read so many books that they begin to read hurriedly, superficially and with buried resentment, she had become disengaged. And like those same dulled book reviewers, she was most resentful of a subject that did not take *her* values seriously, that was slow to reveal itself or that failed to reveal itself in a predictable manner. Fortunately for her impatience, the hands submitted to her by the rubes of Richmond read easily: their owners were satisfied with the most perfunctory disclosures, and that is what they got. Now here was a skinny fifteen-year-old girl wagging in her face a pair of thumbs that would not accept "You have a strong will" as an analysis.

"You have a strong will," muttered Madame Zoe. Then she fell back into "trance."

She grasped the outsized members, first timidly, then tightly, as if they were the handlebars of a flesh motorcycle that she could drive backward down memory lane. She held them up in the light to scrutinize their plump muscles. She placed the right one of them against her heart to register its vibrations. It was then that Sissy, who had never before touched a woman's breast — and Madame Zoe's forty-year-old mammaries were well formed and firm — lost control of the situation. She grew warm and scarlet and retreated into adolescent awkwardness, permitting the enlightened Madame Zoe, who could sense a latent tendency as readily as she could spot a broken life line, to regain some of the gelid composure from behind which she was accustomed to listening condescendingly to those pathetic proletarian palms whose little stories were always aching to be told.

Still, Madame Zoe was awed by the blind babes in her grip, and Sissy, despite a fluster that was doubled by the fact that she feared her mama might notice it, was to leave the house trailer in a sort of triumph.

The palmist began hesitantly. "As d'Arpentigny wrote, 'The higher animal is revealed in the hand but the man is in the thumb.' The thumb cannot be called a finger because it is infinitely more. It is the fulcrum around which all the fingers must revolve, and in proportion to its strength or weakness it will hold up or let down the strength of its owner's character."

The snake soup of memory was cooking at last. It could almost be smelled above the cauliflower and the incense.

"Will power and determination are indicated by the first phalanx," she continued. "The second phalanx indicates reason and logic. You obviously have both in large supply. What's your name, dearie?"

"Sissy."

"Hmmm. Well, Sissy, when a child is born it has no will; it's entirely under the control of others. For the first few weeks of its life it sleeps ninety percent of the day. During this period the thumb is closed in the hand, the fingers concealing it. In other words, the will, represented by the thumb, is dormant — it has not begun to assert itself. As the baby matures, it begins to sleep less, to have some ideas of its own and even to show a temper. When that happens, Sissy, the thumb comes from its hiding place in the palm, the fingers no longer closed over it, for will is beginning to exert itself, and when it does, the thumb — its indicator — appears. Idiots, however, or paranoiacs either never grow out of this thumb-folding stage or revert to it under stress. Epileptics cover their thumbs during fits. Whenever you see a person who habitually folds his thumb under his fingers, you'll recognize that they're very disturbed or sick; disease or weakness has displaced the will. As for you, Sissy, you're healthy, to say the least. Why, I bet even as a baby . . ."

An electric toaster, which shared the table top with the forearms and hands of the palmist and her subject, and whose shiny chrome was dusted with the crumbs from the morning's slices much as cathedrals are dusted with the crumbs from eternity's pigeons, an electric toaster, manufactured in Indiana (for in those days Japan was still flat on her *tatami*), an electric toaster, whose function it was to do to bread what social institutions are designed to do to the human spirit, an electric toaster reflected — like a cynical impersonation of the crystal ball Sissy thought would be there and wasn't — the tremors that ran through this little scene.

"Now, as to the shape of your thumb, it is, I'm not pleased to say, rather primitive. It's broad in both phalanges, attesting to great determination, which can be good; and the skin is smooth, attesting to a certain grace. Because, furthermore, its tip is conic and the nail glossy and pink, I'd say that you have an intelligent, kindly, somewhat artistic nature. However, Sissy, *however,* there is a heavy quality to the second phalanx — the phalanx of logic — that indicates a capacity for foolish or clownish behavior, a refusal to accept responsibility or to take things seriously and a bent to be disrespectful of those who do. Your mama tells me that you're pretty well behaved and shy, but I'd watch out for signs of irrationality. All right?"

"What *are* the signs of irrationality," asked Sissy, rationally enough.

For reasons known only to her, Madame Zoe chose not to elaborate. She pulled the young girl's thumb to her breast once more, breathing with relief as Sissy sweated and swallowed, unable to pursue her questioning. The palmist's house trailer was neither wide nor tall, but oh it was rich in odors that day.

"Your thumbs are surprisingly supple, flexible . . ."

"I exercise 'em a lot."

"Yes, well, um. The flexible thumb personifies extravagance and extremism. Such people are never plodders but achieve their goals by brilliant dashes. They are indifferent to money and are always willing to take risks. You, however, have a pretty full Mount of Saturn and, here, let me see your head line; hmmm, yes, it's not too bad. A long sharp head line and a developed Mount of Saturn — that's the little pad of flesh at the base of the middle finger — will often act as a sobering influence on a flexible thumb. In your case, though, I'm just not sure.

"I guess the most important aspect of *your* thumbs is the, ahem, overall size. Uh, what was it, do you know, that caused . . . ?"

"Don't know; doctors don't know," called Mrs. Hankshaw from the couch, where she'd been listening.

"Just lucky, I guess," smiled the girl.

"Sissy, dang you, that's what Madam Zoe means when she tells you about 'irrational.' "

Madame Zoe was anxious to get on with it. "Large thumbs denote strength of character and belong to persons who act with great determination and self-reliance. They are natural leaders. Do you study science and history in school? Galileo, Descartes, Newton, Leibnitz had very large thumbs; Voltaire's were enormous, but, heh heh, just pickles compared with yours."

"What about Crazy Horse?"

"Crazy Horse? You mean the Indian? Nobody that I've ever heard of ever troubled to study the paws of savages.

"Now, I must tell you this. You have the qualities to become a really powerful force in society — God, if you were only a male! — but you may have such an overabundance of those qualities that they . . . well, frankly, it could be frightening. Especially with your primitive phalanx of logic. You could grow up to be a living disaster, a human malfunction of historic proportions."

What had she said? With some effort — for they seemed to hold her even as she held them — Madame Zoe let go of Sissy's thumbs. She wiped her palms on her kimono: they were red like the sign. It had been years since she'd given such a deep reading. She was more than a little shaken. The toaster, for toasterly reasons, sat with endlessly bowed back, its flank mirroring her wig, which now hung slightly askew.

"So accurate a revealer of personality is the thumb" — she was addressing Mrs. Hankshaw now — "that the Hindu chiromancers base their entire work on it, and the Chinese have a minute and intricate system founded solely on the capillaries of the first phalanx. So, what I've given your daughter amounts to a complete reading. If you want me to consider the palms separately, it'll cost you an extra three-fifty."

Confusion had the better of Mrs. Hankshaw. She wasn't sure whether too little had been revealed or too much. Her eyes looked like a fire in a Mexican nightclub. She felt she should be outraged but she wanted more information.

"How much for one question?"

"You mean one question answered from the palm?"

"Yes."

"Well, if it's simple, only a dollar."

"Husband," said Mrs. Hankshaw, withdrawing a bill from her ratskin bag. (*The blaze, which started in a pot of paper flowers, spread quickly to the dancers' costumes.*)

"Beg your pardon?"

"Husband. Will she find a husband?" (*The bandleader bravely led the orchestra in "El Rancho Grande," even as his pet Chihuahua was being trampled in the panic.*)

"Oh, I see." Madame Zoe took Sissy's hand and gave it the old tall-dark-stranger squint. But she was in too deeply now to be deceptive. "I see men in your life, honey," she said truthfully. "I also see women, lots of women." She raised her eyes to meet Sissy's, looking for an admission of the "tendency," but there was no signal.

"There is most clearly a marriage. A husband, no doubt about it, though he is years away." And feeling expansive, she added at no extra charge, "There are children, too. Five, maybe six. But the husband is not the father. They will inherit your characteristics." Since it is impossible to tell these last two things from the configurations of the hands, Madame Zoe must have been operating on psychic powers long dormant. She might have said more, but Mrs. Hankshaw had heard plenty.

Mother ushered daughter from the trailer as if she were leading her from the burning El Lizard Club. (*At the height of the inferno, a battery of overheated tequila bottles began to explode in the flames.*)

The elder Hankshaw female had difficulty speaking. "I'm gonna take the bus on out to Mabel's, sweetie," she said, giving Sissy a rare embrace. "You can catch a ride home iffen you want, but you promise me, word of honor, you won't git in a car with no man alone."

Then she thought to add, "And no lady alone, either. Just a married couple. You promise? And don't you worry none about the stupid stuff that woman said. We'll talk it over when I git home."

Sissy wasn't worried at all. Confused, maybe, but not worried. She felt somehow — *important* — in an obscure, off-center fashion. Although she knew nothing of such things then, she felt important in the sense that the clockworks is important. The clockworks is a long way, in every way, from the White House, Fort Knox and the Vatican, but the winds that blow across the clockworks always wear a crazy grin.

Inside the house trailer, behind the red palm, where once again only jasmine incense and boiled cauliflower battled for olfactory supremacy, Madame Zoe crouched at a window, watching her young subject hitch a ride.

(The conic tip led the way, cutting through the atmosphere like the bowsprit of a ship, pulling after it the slightly bent phalanx of logic, followed by a fairly gliding phalanx of will and, quivering and rolling at the end of the procession, the ever-voluptuous Mount of Venus.) Suddenly, Madame Zoe recalled a sarcastic saying, a bon mot, that she had not heard in years. It made her laugh pointedly and with little humor; she bit her lipstick and shook her wig. The saying concerned the first or most preaxial digit of the human hand, although it had nothing to do with palmistry. It went like this:

"If you only had a thumb you could rule the world."

Cowgirl Interlude (Bonanza Jellybean)

She is lying on the family sofa in flannel pajamas. There is Kansas City mud on the tips and heels of her boots, boots that have yet to savor real manure. Fourteen, she knows she ought to remove her boots, yet she refuses. A *Maverick* rerun is on TV; she is eating beef jerky, occasionally slurping. On her upper stomach, where her pajama top has ridden up, is a small deep scar. She tells everyone, including her school nurse, that it was made by a silver bullet.

Whatever the origin of the extra hole in her belly, there are unmistakable signs of gunfire in the woodwork by the closet door. It was there that she once shot up one half of an old pair of sneakers. "Self-defense," she pleaded, when her parents complained. "It was a outlaw tennis shoe.

Billy the Ked."

11.

So Sissy lived in Richmond, Virginia, in the Eisenhower Years, so called as if the passing seasons, with their eggs hatching and rivers rising, their cakes baking and stars turning, their legs dancing and hearts melting, their lamas levitating and poets doing likewise, their cheerleaders getting laid at drive-in picture shows and old men dying in rooms over furniture stores, as if they, the passing seasons, could be branded by a mere President; as if time itself could toddle out of Kansas and West Point, popularize a military jacket and seek election to Eternity on the Republican ticket.

In the croaked air of the Eisenhower Years in Richmond, Virginia, she must have been a familiar sight. In clothes that were either too big for her or too small — floppy coats whose hems rubbed the cement, summer slacks that disclosed everything anyone might wish to know about her socks — she moved through the city (the city of which it has been said, "It is not a city at all but the world's largest Confederate museum").

At all hours and in every weather the girl could be seen, if not admired.

Her soon-to-be-lovely features were still getting their sea legs and at that unsteady stage of their development must have clung clumsily to the bleached deck of her face (which, due to unusually high cheekbones, appeared as if it were pitched aslant in rough waters).

Her long, svelte body, as eloquently as it might assert itself, could not have been heard above the funky din of the clothing she wore.

Certainly her mind didn't count for much: in the sotweed suburb of South Richmond, no mind did. Few were the schoolmates to notice the headlight shine of her eyes and wonder who was driving around inside there.

When they said, "Here comes" (or "there goes) Sissy Hankshaw," they meant "not a thumb more, not a thumb less."

For wherever she went those wads of meat went with her; those bananas, those sausages, those nightsticks, those pinkish pods, those turds of flesh. She smuggled them around town in her baggy duds, launching them on appropriate corners and regarding them always as if they were manifestations of some secret she alone understood — although in the bank-vault air of the Eisenhower Years in Richmond, Virginia, they must have stood out like sore . . .

(It is surprising that she was so faintly remembered in Richmond in later years. When the author asked the late Dr. Dreyfus about that, the surgeon replied: "According to the artist Michelangelo, 'The human figure is the ideal ornament for the niche.' I don't suppose that means very much to you.")

If, like the cat that looked at the world through mouse-colored glasses, she was rather insular, let it not be supposed that she was immune from indulging those heightened hormone flows and colored thoughts that, of all the trillions of visceral/cerebral reactions triggered by the limbic system of our trigger-happy brains, we single out to honor as "true human feelings."

One day, one spring Thursday near the end of a semester, more than three years after she had been examined by Dr. Dreyfus and a few months after Madame Zoe's special knowledge had come her way, she was invited to a party. It was to be a costume party, given by Betty Clanton, a druggist's daughter and one of the more privileged kids in that roach-gnawed, white-trash school.

All day Thursday Sissy thought she would not attend Betty's party. All day Friday and Friday night (when she lay awake on three, yes, three pillows) she thought she would not attend Betty's party. But late Saturday afternoon, with an overtime sun nosing into everything and green froggies peeping and honeysuckle affixing a sweet faint hem to the golden pungency that hung like a curtain over the tobacco warehouses and a typewriter of birds banging out sonnets in the dogwood buds (*And wilt thou have me fashion into speech* Ding! Line space. Carriage return. *The love I bear thee, finding words enough* Ding! The birds hacking it out) and spring in general coming on like a geometric progression, she began to get ideas. For the first time in her life, perhaps (although Sunday school had occasionally moved her and although Madame Zoe's bosom and the by-now-customary mobile molestings had certainly stirred her), she felt directed by forces other than her thumbs. She heard music that was not road music; her head swayed to rhythms that were softer and lighter than the rhythms of the hitch. Something in the springtime had telephoned something in her limbic system and reversed the charges. Something had touched Sissy Hankshaw and it doesn't matter what.

Sissy went out back and gathered feathers where her mama had recently deplumed a hen. Using electrical tape, she fashioned them — slowly and sloppily — into a kind of headdress. With Jerry's old watercolor kit, she painted herself as best she could, not neglecting at the last moment to paint her hands.

She went to Betty's costume party. She went as Chief Crazy Horse. She drank two bottles of Coke, munched a package of Nabs, listened to the new Fats Domino records, smiled at some jokes and left early. Only two thin rivulets streaked her warpaint to reveal how she felt when Billy Seward, Betty's boy friend and the most popular guy in school, bounded through the door, amid shrieks of laughter, wearing giant papier-mâché thumbs. Ach! Billy had come as Sissy Hankshaw.

12.

"When you grow up with somebody you just sort of accept them, even if they are odd," said Betty Seward née Clanton. She checked the coffeepot. It was still perking. Over and over the coffee turned in the pot. Its wheels sang in the interviewer's nostrils. They were singing a song of the past.

"I mean, she wasn't a freak, exactly, or a loony; she was a right smart girl and right polite and nice, but you know, she did have this peculiar development; but what I'm saying is, we got pretty used to it over the years, except that every now and then . . .

"I remember the night we graduated from junior high. When your name was called you were supposed to get up and walk across the stage and take your diploma from the principal with your left hand

and shake hands with him with your right hand. But Sissy wouldn't shake hands. Not even with the principal. It wasn't that she *couldn't;* she just wouldn't. Mr. Perkins was pretty irritated. And a lot of the kids complained that Sissy was making a mockery of our graduation.

"There's an old abandoned rock quarry in South Richmond, all filled up with water, you know, and we used to swim there when we got the chance. The day after graduation our class was gonna have a picnic there — unchaperoned, weren't we devils? all on the sly — and some older kids who drove cars were gonna pick us up and take us. We were supposed to pick up Sissy, but just for spite we decided not to. We left her. Well, about noon somebody saw her out on the road catching a ride, hitchhiking like she did, big as life, not scared or ashamed but getting into any car that would stop for her, but she never showed up at the picnic. All day long she hitched up and down the road that runs near the quarry, up and down, back and forth, passing again and again. But she didn't ever stop; she just kept passing it by.

"And, you know, most of us at the picnic got sunburned, and a third of us got poison oak, and a bunch of us got drunk and sick off beer the older kids bought us and we caught the dickens from our parents, and one boy got bit by a watersnake and somebody sat on broken glass. And I thought to myself, hmmm, that Sissy's the only one that came out of that day okay; nothing happened to her 'cause she just kept moving. You know what I mean?"

Mrs. Seward left her chair to unplug the coffeepot.

"Right off, I don't remember how old she was when she found out she was part Indian. Her mama's family, a lot of them, had lived out West, in the Dakotas, and one of them had married a squaw, I don't recollect the tribe . . .

"Siwash? That's right. That sounds like it. So one time Sissy's aunt — her mama's sister — came here for a visit from Fargo, and there was a lot of fuss about integration here then; everybody was all upset about the Supreme Court telling us we'd have to go to school with the colored, and I guess the Hankshaws were discussing it like everybody else when the aunt let the cat out of the bag about Indian blood in the family. Well!! Sissy's daddy got furious. I don't know why; a Indian's not the same as a nigra. But I guess he just about divorced his poor wife. Sissy, though, was right pleased. She figured out she was one-sixteenth — what was it? — Siwash. She talked about it at school. We'd never seen her so excited. She showed a lot of interest in Indians after that, although not as much as she showed in hitching rides. Of course, she didn't look a bit Indian. She was as fair as an apricot. But for a while about then she started putting designs on her poor thumbs. Mercy! Her own brothers had to hold her down and wash them off."

Having perked sufficiently, coffee made the short trip from pot to cup. It traveled direct. There were no other stops on its route. Betty Clanton Seward produced a box of Saltines and a brown and yellow aerosol can.

"This stuff is the latest thing in the stores," she said, brandishing the can. "You spray a regular old soda cracker with it . . ." zzzzt zzzzt ". . . and it makes it taste like a chocolate chip cookie. Here."

The interviewer declined. He wished to ask clear and concise questions concerning a former classmate of Mrs. Seward's. He didn't want his mouth full of soda crackers, even if they did taste like chocolate chip cookies. (What won't those Japanese think of next?)

"There were times, I'll admit, when I'd look at her sitting in school, sitting so straight and smiling so secretively and all, and I'd think that maybe there was something special about her, something other than her physical condition, I mean; something positive. She couldn't take the secretarial program because she couldn't use a typewriter; she had good ideas in art class but she wasn't able to bring them off; heck, she only got a C in Home Ec 'cause she couldn't sew, and *everybody* got A or B in Home Ec. Just the same, and even though her future looked hopeless, I had this feeling that she could teach us others something. Only I never figured out what it was, exactly. And I guess I was as, ah, insensitive to her as the rest. One evening after dark when she thought nobody would see her, she brought a whole armload of yellow jonquils that she'd picked — kicked out by the roots, actually — alongside some road or other and left them on my front porch. She kinda liked me, I think." Betty Clanton Seward tugged at a strand of her hair as a preoccupied milkmaid might tug at a teat in the dawn. "She was real quiet, but I heard her anyway. I was upstairs putting in curlers and I looked out the window and saw her. I could tell who it was because the moon was shining on her . . . her abnormality.

"Well, I couldn't keep my big mouth shut. I told the kids at school about it and they teased her pretty hard.

"That wasn't the worst time, though. The worst time was when I gave a costume party and I invited Sissy, partly because I felt sorry for her but also because she was, I don't know how to put it into words, she fascinated me, in a sense. At any rate, Bill — he's my husband now, he's a chemist at the Philip Morris plant, you oughta talk with him — Bill made himself a huge pair of thumbs outta paper and chicken wire and that was his costume. He didn't really mean to be cruel, but you know how young folks are. Thoughtless."

She sighed. She milked another half-pint from her hair. Then, as had the coffee before her, she perked.

"Goodness, it's nearly two. I've gotta start getting my face on. Can you excuse me? Young Willie has to be at the doctor's at three. He's gotta have a wart burned off today."

Whereupon the ten-year-old boy who had been loitering on the edges of the interview glomming crackers by the dozen presented his unshod foot — washed, thank God, in recent times — and sure enough, there was a wart atop it the size of a burr. The interviewer wondered why Mrs. Seward simply didn't spray the wart until it tasted like a chocolate chip cookie and let Willie eat it off.

The interviewer didn't tell Mrs. Seward that.

There was something else the interviewer didn't tell Mrs. Seward.

He didn't tell her that the next time persons adorned themselves with fraudulent thumbs in imitation of Sissy Hankshaw, it would be an act of homage.

Mrs. Seward would have thought it ridiculous, an homage of tree-bark thumbs waving impertinently in the face of the twentieth century like a forest of prehistoric diplomas that expect no handshake in return. As a matter of fact, it *was* a bit ridiculous. But because it was ridiculous, we know it must be true.

Cowgirl Interlude (Venusian)

On Venus, the atmosphere is so thick that light rays bend as if made of foam rubber. The bending of light is so extraordinary that it causes the horizon to tilt upward. Thus, if one were standing on

Venus one could see the opposite side of the planet by looking directly overhead.

Perhaps it is best that we on Earth resist the temptation to thicken our atmosphere. Maybe we should give second considerations to those leaders who insist we learn to think of smog as our friend.

Imagine that you are a cowgirl, trotting your pony in the grassy hills of the Dakotas. Suddenly you hear a wild trumpeting cry. You rear back in the saddle and look aloft — expecting to see a flight of whooping cranes, dancing in midair to their own loud music. Instead, you gaze upon a bugler blowing reveille on the other side of the world. The Chinese army is bivouacked all over the sky.

13.

ONE JUNE, Richmond, Virginia, woke up with its brakes on and kept them on all summer. That was okay; it was the Eisenhower Years and nobody was going anywhere. Not even Sissy. That is to say, she wasn't going far. Up and down Monument Avenue, perhaps; hitching up and down that broad boulevard so dotted with enshrined cannons and heroic statuary that it is known throughout the geography of the dead as a banana belt for snuffed generals.

The old Capital of the Confederacy marked time in the heat. Its boots kicked up a little tobacco dust, a little wisteria pollen, and that was it. Each morning, including Sundays, the sun rose with a golf tee in its mouth. Its rays were reflected, separately but equally, by West End bird baths, South Side beer cans, ghetto razors. (In those days Richmond was convoluted like the folds of the brain, as if, like the brain, it was attempting to prevent itself from knowing itself.)

In the evenings, light from an ever-increasing number of television sets inflicted a misleading frostiness on the air. It has been said that true albinos produce light of a similar luminescence when they move their bowels.

Middays, the city felt like the inside of a napalmed watermelon.

Whenever possible, men, women, children and pets kept to the shade, talked little, stirred less, watched the blades of fans go 'round as is the nature of fan business. Only Sissy Hankshaw voluntarily frequented those places where tar was sticky, where fried gravel sparkled, where weeds wilted, where asphalt crumbled (the Devil's leftover birthday cake), where worn concrete translated into Braille long bitter arguments between the organic and inorganic levels of life. (If you have ever licked nickel or kissed steel, you know the arguments.)

Some say excessive sunshine softens the brain (repulsively soft already) and maybe that's what made her do it. Maybe it was the yellow gloves of hydrogen boxing her ears; maybe solar radiation caused her atoms to whirl a trifle coocoo. On the other hand, her action may have been merely an indication of the scope of her ambition, and while remarkable, should hardly be considered any more strange than little Mozart's impulse, at age nine, to compose a symphony.

In any case, and whichever the ever, upon a sweaty but otherwise nondescript afternoon in early August 1960, an afternoon squeezed out of Mickey's mousy snout, an afternoon carved from mashed potatoes and lye, an afternoon scraped out of the dog dish of meteorology, an afternoon that could lull a monster to sleep, an afternoon that normally might have produced nothing more significant than diaper rash, Sissy Hankshaw stepped from a busted-jaw curbstone on Hull Street in South Richmond and attempted to hitchhike an ambulance. As a matter of fact, she tried to flag it down twice — coming and going.

Squalling, its red lamps flashing as if in frenetic, amateurish imitation of that summer's quietly professional sun, the ambulance was on an errand of mercy. Naturally, it did not stop. Had she expected it to? Would she have boarded it, joined its bleeding or gasping cargo if it had? Had she successfully hitchhiked an ambulance, would she next have tried a hearse?

Conjecture. The meat wagon rolled on, and Sissy, unlike young Mozart, was rewarded by not so much as a lump of sugar for her experiment. However, the ambulance crew had not failed to notice her hailings. Before Sissy had gotten many blocks away, she was, for the first time in her career, arrested.

Her appearance at the station house created a minor stir. On the one hand, the girl seemed pathetic; on the other, she was Buddha-belly serene, and to the cop mentality, serenity smacks of disrespect. She was underage, her crime difficult to classify, the procedure uncertain. A police reporter from the *News Leader* became the first journalist to be intrigued by her; he telephoned his city editor to send over a photographer. File clerks were sneaking around corners to get a glimpse of her; other prisoners were making remarks. Finally, the desk sergeant lectured her against interfering with emergency vehicles and had a policewoman hustle her home.

The photographer arrived too late to get a picture and the reporter was peeved, but for the others involved, a hasty release was ideal: the police got her out of their crew cuts; Sissy got back to work. Early that humid evening, as a roaring warehouse blaze sent the makings of a billion Pall Malls up in premature smoke, she was arrested again — for trying to flag down a fire engine.

This time she was booked and held for twenty-four hours at the juvenile detention center, although the authorities once more found it expedient to set her free. Not the least of the reasons for her release was the frustration she caused the fingerprinter.

14.

RICHMOND, VIRGINIA, has been called a "depression-proof" city. That is because its economy has one leg in life insurance and the other in tobacco.

During times of economic bellyache, tobacco sales climb even as other sales tumble. Perhaps the uncertainty of finances makes people nervous; the nervousness causes them to smoke more. Perhaps a cigarette gives an unemployed man something to do with his hands. Maybe a pipe in his mouth helps a man forget that he hasn't lately chewed steak.

In times of depression, policy-holders somehow manage to keep up their life insurance premiums. Life insurance could be the only investment they can afford to maintain. Perhaps they insist on dignity in death since they never had it in life. Or is it that the demise of one of its insured members is the only chance a family has of getting flush?

Each autumn for many years Richmond has celebrated its depression-proof economy. The celebration is called the Tobacco Festival. (Somehow "Life Insurance Festival" didn't set any leather to tapping.)

Sissy Hankshaw liked to watch the Tobacco Festival parades. From a Broad Street curb, where she would secure an early position, it was her habit, once her courage climbed, to try to hitch the open convertibles in which the various Tobacco Princesses rode. The drivers, Jaycees one and all, never noticed her; they kept their gaze straight ahead for the safety that was in it — tobacco gods would cough lightning should a Jaycee drive up the hindquarters of a Marlboro Filters float — but the waving Princesses, projecting eyebeam and toothlight into the multitudes, ever on the alert for kinfolk, boy friends, photographers and talent scouts, the Princesses sometimes would catch sight of a pleading pod, and for a crowd-puzzling second — Oh the perils of innocence in the service of nicotine! — lose their carefully coached composure. We may wonder what thumbtales — thumbfacts evolving into thumbmyths — those beauties carried home to Danville, Petersburg, South Hill or Winston-Salem when that year's Tobacco Festival had burned down to a butt.

In 1960, the Tobacco Festival parade took place on the night of September 23. The *Times-Dispatch* reported that there were fewer floats than the previous year ("but they were fancier, and wider by six feet"); even so, it took ninety minutes for the procession to pass a given point. There were twenty-seven Princesses, from whose company Lynne Marie Fuss — Miss Pennsylvania — was the next day named Queen of Tobaccoland. The parade grand marshal was Nick Adams, star of a TV series called "The Rebel." Adams was a perfect choice since "The Rebel" had a Civil War theme and was sponsored by a leading brand of cigarettes. The actor became piqued at one point in the parade when he discovered, rather abruptly, that his horse's flank was the target of a gang of boys armed with peashooters. There were marching bands, clowns, military formations, drum majorettes, dignitaries, animals, "Indians," a few temporary cowgirls, even, their reptile-shiny shirts loaded down with embroidery and udders; there were hawkers of souvenirs and the aforementioned gang of evil peashooters. City Manager Edwards estimated attendance at the "noisily lavish extravaganza" at close to two hundred thousand, by far the largest crowd in festival history. Sissy Hankshaw was not among the throng.

Miles across town from the thousands (who, according to the newspaper, "yelled, giggled and clapped"); across the James in South Richmond, where, economic theories to the contrary, it was always depression time; in a dim, dinky house, frescoed with soot and some termites' low relief; before a full-length mirror merciless in its reflection of thumbs — Sissy stood naked. (Never say "stark naked." "Naked" is a sweet word, but nobody in his right mind likes "stark.")

Sissy was making a decision. It was a point in life that could not hold still for ninety minutes' worth of bright-leaf boosterism to pass it by.

In the seven weeks since her arrest a lot had happened to the girl. First, an assistant commonwealth attorney, encouraged by the policewoman who had driven Sissy home, was pulling strings to have her shipped to reform school. The public defender was using those terms "incorrigible," "wayward," "curfew breaker" and "beyond parental control," that, when applied to a young girl, mean simply "She fucks." As late as 1960, the large majority of juvenile females behind bars were there because they had acquired an early taste for sexual intercourse (early in the eyes of civilized society, that is, for by nature's calendar the twelfth or thirteenth year is precisely correct).

That our Sissy remained free on that September evening when animated cigarettes pranced in glittery goosesteps down Broad Street was owing in part to the efforts of a social worker who had been assigned to her case. However, if Miss Leonard had helped keep Sissy out of reformatory, insisting that the girl's hitchhiking was a chaste idiosyncrasy that offered no threat to society, she herself had been an upsetting factor. A few weeks back she had nagged Sissy to go to a dance with her, a "special" dance where the girl would "feel comfortable." At last the limbic telephone had jingled again — *"Ready on your call to Romance. Please deposit sixty-five micrograms of estrogen for the first three minutes"* — and Sissy found herself throbbing into a formal gown that a cousin had worn to a distant prom and with which some moths had recently been dancing cheek to cheek. Repairs to the gown had caused Sissy and Miss Leonard to arrive late at the community hall where the soirée was in progress. When Sissy read the poster that said GOODWILL INDUSTRIES BALL, she began to suspect that they should not have arrived at all. Once inside, she was sure of it. The dance floor glistened with drool as over it there limped, staggered, slid and dragged the crab toes and chicken heels of a score or more splayed, spindly and rickety organisms; while in the red glow of homemade Chinese lanterns cleft palates, harelips, slack jaws, tics, twitches, frothings, popped eyes, dripping nostrils and skull points bobbed at various tempos, inspired by a Guy Lombardo record and the kinetic examples of their partners in the dance. When Sissy froze in alarm, Miss Leonard lectured her. "Listen, honey, I realize how it is with you people." She smiled knowingly at the remarkable creatures who were either shuffling vacantly or flying apart at every joint to the "sweetest music this side of heaven." "I'm aware of how it is in here. The polios can't stand the cerebral palsies, the cerebral palsies snub the birth defects and all three hate the retardeds. I'm aware of that, but you've got to overcome it; the handicapped have got to stick together." She was gently pushing Sissy toward the stag line, where the chair-pilots were spinning their wheels, when the girl, for the first time in her life, heard her own voice rise above a wispy phosphorescence. Sissy screamed. "I'M NOT HANDICAPPED, GODDAMN IT!!" The cry turned Guy Lombardo's sugar to lumps. The dancers stopped, some taking longer to wind down than others. They stared at her. A few of them giggled and cackled. Then, one by one, they began to applaud her (some of them clapping with one hand, in flailing and unintentional illustration of Zen Buddhism's most famous proverb). Growing uneasy, almost afraid, the chaperones called for quiet, and Miss Leonard, in an effort to cast a more reasonable light on the scene, began tearing the red paper away from bald bulbs, but the applause flopped to an unsteady end when Sissy ran from the hall. Sissy wore that strange applause like a corsage of swampflowers as she hitchhiked home in her first formal gown, waltzing the waltz of the cars.

Now she stood before the mirror. She couldn't hear the bands blaring "Dixie" as the talking cigarette package kicked up its silver slippers over town on Broad Street, but she could still hear the noise of the Goodwill Industries Ball, though weeks had passed. Perhaps sound carries farther across time than across space. No matter. There was a more pressing noise: the voice of her daddy in the adjoining room. Sissy's daddy was speaking in his Carolina voice, his booze voice, the voice that sounded as if it had been strained through Daniel

Boone's underwear. He was speaking about the Colonel, the elderly man in the yellow sport coat who for years had petitioned to manage Sissy's show biz career. "We'll begin with my carnival, of course," the Colonel would purr, and then he would chart a path up the golden staircase that led all the way to Ed Sullivan. The Hankshaws were embarrassed by the Colonel's overtures. They had discouraged his interest. Recently, however, Mr. Hankshaw had had a change of mind. For two reasons: Sissy was starting to cause him trouble, and the Colonel had doubled his offer. Mr. Hankshaw was a working man, after all, and in his breast, as in the breast of working men everywhere, there beat the fatty heart of a profiteer (Could Marxist stethoscopes be so universally faulty? Do all socialist heart specialists have gum in their ears?). Sissy's daddy and mama were arguing at that moment about the contract, already signed by the Colonel, that lay like a freshly ironed pillowcase atop the TV set.

Her brothers were not home to defend her. Junior was watching the parade with the girl he was soon to marry. Jerry was in traction (no wonder the Hankshaws needed the Colonel's money) at the Medical College of Virginia. Refused enlistment into the paratroopers because of his size, Jerry had stood up in a ferris wheel seat at the Atlantic Rural Exposition — he had to do *something* — and gravity, that old scene-stealer, had once more gotten into the act.

Other things were bothering Sissy. Things as minor as her inability to locate information pertaining to the Siwash Indians, about whom she wished to write a paper in school. Things as annoying as the fact that teen-aged boys in the neighborhood had begun to follow her whenever she set out to hitchhike, burning to halts beside her, trying to coax her, as much out of malice as lust, into their vulgar Fords.

Many things had changed in Sissy Hankshaw's world, including her own physical image. Suddenly, in the seventeenth year of a life that had begun with a doctor's doubletake and a nurse's gasp, she had become lovely. A perfect compromise finally had been worked out between her predominantly angular features — high cheekbones, classically fine nose, fragile chin, peaceful blue eyes — and her decidedly round mouth — a full, pouty mouth that the Countess was later to compare to a mink's vagina at the height of the rut. Her figure had come to correspond to the average measurements of the high-fashion model: she stood five-nine in her socks, weighed 125 pounds and taped 33–24–34; one of those bony beauties of whom wags have said, "Falling downstairs, they sound like a cup of dice."

She had given herself completely to the hitchhike because heretofore she had nothing else nor any hope of else. Ah cha cha, but now there was a choice. Or the possibility of a choice. She was pretty. And a pretty girl can always make her way in a civilized society. Perhaps she should somehow find a job, work and work and save her money — even if it took years — so that she could return to Dr. Dreyfus for that complex operation; so that she could lead a normal human female life.

Every time she said it to herself, however (there before the mirror), every time she thought "Dr. Dreyfus" or "normal life," her thumbs talked back to her in thumbtalk: tingles, throbs and itches. Until at last she knew. Accepted what she had always sensed. She had been correct when she had howled at the dance. They were not a handicap. Rather, they were an invitation, a privilege audaciously and impolitely granted, perfumed with danger and surprise, offering her greater freedom of movement, *inviting her to live life at some "other" level.* If she dared.

Well, about the time the steam calliope was wheezing like emphysema through the lungs of Tobaccoland, Sissy decided to dare. And about the instant she decided to dare, she commenced to laugh. She was laughing with such abandon, such secret delight, she could scarcely wiggle into her panties, even though her daddy stalked in from the living room and took a long, granite look.

Her parents warned her not to go out, but their attentions were on the TV screen when she stood at the refrigerator and coaxed a package of Velveeta cheese into her coat pocket. Some olives jumped in also. An apple joined up. A half-loaf of Wonder Bread said, what the hell, it'd go along, what was there to lose. "Nothing," said Sissy.

She made it out the back door during a shootout on "Gunsmoke." Silently, she thanked Marshal Dillon for the cover, but it didn't occur to her then to lament for Miss Kitty, ever a saloonkeeper, never a cowgirl.

On a dead run, olives bouncing out of her jacket, she reached the corner where Hull Street was intersected by U.S. Route 1 — in 1960 still the principal north-south interstate highway.

By the time she got her arm in the air, the light had changed and the first car, a boatish, blue Lincoln with Jersey plates, was already passing. For a second, it appeared as if she were late, as if the driver had missed her gesture. But no, some aspect of it — a glint of neon on the nail, perhaps — snagged the hem of his vision. He glanced back in time to see the entire appendage, immense, scrubbed, lubricated, zeppelinlike, looking as fresh and newborn as an egg, invoking a strange interplay between the joyful and the ominous, as it swam at eye-level past his opposite rear window.

He braked.

What else *could* he do?

"Going north?" asked Sissy for openers as the door swung toward her like a slab of candied sky. Were it any other direction she wouldn't have cared.

"You bet your raggedy white ass I am," said the driver, grinning sardonically. He was black-skinned and beret-topped, and it was difficult to ascertain which there were the more of, saxophones in his back seat or gold teeth in his mouth. Sissy hesitated. But what the hell? In imitation of the Wonder Bread, she said to herself, "This is it; what is there to lose?" She boarded.

Actually, there was a fine style about the driver, about the tingle of treasure when he grinned, about the billow of marijuana smoke in which he sat (how different from the celebrated smokes of Richmond!); about the gardenia in his lapel and the flask by his side, about the degree to which his cameoed fingers turned up the volume on the radio, about the speed at which he made that big Lincoln rocket out of the tobacco slums, forever and forever, bearing Sissy Hankshaw up to the heights.

And Sissy Hankshaw, knees knocking with thrill and fear, and not knowing what else to do, reached into her scrawny coat and offered the black man a slice of cheese.

Cowgirl Interlude (Chuck Wagon)

Fire is the reuniting of matter with oxygen. If one bears that in mind, every blaze may be seen as a reunion, an occasion of chemical joy. To smoke a cigar is to end a long separation; to burn down a police station is to hold homecoming for billions of happy molecules.

Beside a marshy lake in an obscure sector of the Dakotas, a campfire was smiling its head off. Around it, however, there arose from a group of cowgirls several flares of discontent. Some of the girls were complaining that their stew was tasteless and bland.

"This stew is bland," said one girl.

"It's like milk from a sick cow," said another.

Debbie, on cook duty that day, was defensive. "But spices aren't good for you," she said. "Spices burn the tummy and inflame the senses," she went on, using two metaphors improperly inspired by the fire.

The dissatisfied diners scoffed, and because little Debbie looked so near to tears, Bonanza Jellybean spoke in her behalf. "It's a well-known fact," said Jelly, "that the reason India is overpopulated is because curry powder is an aphrodisiac."

Delores del Ruby flicked an ember out of the reunion with a sharp crack of her whip. "Bullshit," said Delores. "There isn't but one aphrodisiac in the world.

"And that's strange stuff."

15.

"Hitchhiking is not a sport. It is not an art. It certainly isn't work, for it requires no particular ability nor does it produce anything of value. It's an adventure, I suppose, but a shallow, ignoble adventure. Hitchhiking is parasitic, no more than a reckless panhandling, as far as I can see."

Those were the words of Julian Gitche, spoken in exasperation to Sissy Hankshaw. Sissy did not bother to answer Julian's charges, and the author, who is ambivalent about the whole matter of hitchhiking, certainly is not going to answer them for her.

From Whitman to Steinbeck to Kerouac, and beyond to the restless broods of the seventies, the American road has represented choice, escape, opportunity, a way to somewhere else. However illusionary, the road was freedom, and the freest way to ride the road was hitchhiking. By the seventies, so many young Americans were on the road that hitchhiking did take on, Julian to the contrary, characteristics of sport. In the letters column of pop culture magazines such as *Rolling Stone,* hitchhikers boasted of records set for speed and distance, and whole manuals were published to advise those new to the "game."

Oddly enough, Sissy was almost indifferent to this cultural phenomenon. To approach her for practical advice on the subject of hitchhiking would have been virtually futile. For example, she could not have told you, as did Ben Lobo and Sara Links in their booklet *Side of the Road: A Hitchhikers Guide to the United States,* that Montana laws strictly forbid hitchhiking in the vicinity of mental institutions. And it is difficult to say how she might have reacted to this piece of advice in *Hitchhikers Handbook* by Tom Grimm: "Don't use your thumb to hitchhike. Use a sign instead."

And at *this* Grimm observation, "I doubt whether most girls could safely hitchhike long distances alone," Sissy would have had to laugh.

Because by that day in the New York clinic when Dr. Goldman administered to her the "talk serum," many years after the black musician's Lincoln had transported her away from home and family, Sissy could say:

"Please don't think me immodest, but I'm really the best. When my hands are in shape and my timing is right, I'm the best there is, ever was or ever will be.

"When I was younger, before this layoff that has nearly finished me, I hitchhiked one hundred and twenty-seven hours without stopping, without food or sleep, crossed the continent twice in six days, cooled my thumbs in both oceans and caught rides after midnight on unlighted highways, such was my skill, persuasion, rhythm. I set records and immediately cracked them; went farther, faster than any hitchhiker before or since. As I developed, however, I grew more concerned with subtleties and nuances of style. Time in terms of m.p.h. no longer interested me. I began to hitchhike in something akin to geological time: slow, ancient, vast. Daylight, I would sleep in ditches and under bushes, crawling out in the afternoon like the first fish crawling from the sea, stopping car after car and often as not refusing their lift, or riding only a mile and starting over again. I removed the freeway from its temporal context. Overpasses, cloverleafs, exit ramps took on the personality of Mayan ruins for me.

Without destination, without cessation, my run was often silent and empty; there were no increments, no arbitrary graduations reducing time to functional units. I abstracted and purified. Then I began to juxtapose slow, extended runs with short, furiously fast ones — until I could compose melodies, concerti, entire symphonies of hitch. When poor Jack Kerouac heard about this, he got drunk for a week. I added dimensions to hitchhiking that others could not even understand. In the Age of the Automobile — and nothing has shaped our culture like the motor car — there have been many great drivers but only one great passenger. I have hitched and hiked over every state and half the nations, through blizzards and under rainbows, in deserts and in cities, backward and sideways, upstairs, downstairs and in my lady's chamber. There is no road that did not expect me. Fields of daisies bowed and gas pumps gurgled when I passed by. Every moo cow dipped toward me her full udder. With me, something different and deep, in bright focus and pointing the way, arrived in the practice of hitchhiking. I am the spirit and the heart of hitchhiking, I am its cortex and its medulla, I am its foundation and its culmination, I am the jewel in its lotus. And when I am really moving, stopping car after car after car, moving so freely, so clearly, so delicately that even the sex maniacs and the cops can only blink and let me pass, then I embody the rhythms of the universe, I feel what it is like to *be* the universe, I am in a state of grace.

"You may claim that I've an unfair advantage, but no more so than Nijinsky, whose reputation as history's most incomparable dancer is untainted by the fact that his feet were abnormal, having the bone structure of bird feet. Nature built Nijinsky to dance, me to direct traffic. And speaking of birds, they say birds are stupid, but I once taught a parakeet to hitchhike. Couldn't speak a word, but he was a hitchhiking fool. I let him get rides for us all across the West, and then he indicated that he wanted to set out on his own. I let him go and the very first car he stopped was carrying two Siamese cats. Tsk tsk. Maybe birds are stupid at that."

16.

THE SO-CALLED TALK SERUM is essentially racemic methedrine with a pinch of Sodium Pentothal. It is not to be confused with the controversial "truth serum," which is wholly Sodium Pentothal. Indeed, according to Dr. Goldman, the talk serum may cause a subject to exaggerate. Clearly, he believed Sissy Hankshaw guilty of overstatement while under the influence of the injection.

The author frankly doesn't know. The author isn't altogether certain that there is any such thing as exaggeration. Our brains permit us to utilize such a wee fraction of their resources that, in a sense, everything we experience is a reduction.

We employ drugs, yogic techniques and poetics — and a thousand more clumsy methods — in an effort just to bring things back up to normal.

So much for that. And so much for Sissy Hankshaw's testimony on hitchhiking, whether distorted or exact. There is something else to get at here. Listen.

Suppose you awoke one morning with the uneasy feeling that the world had, while you slept, somehow slipped a-tilt and rose to find that your dresser drawers were mysteriously open a fraction of an inch and that prescription bottles had tipped over in the medicine cabinet (although neither you nor anyone else in your household had ventured since bedtime to get an aspirin, a condom or a Tums) and that pictures on the wall, shades on the lamps and books in the case were askew. Outdoors, the taller buildings were posing à la Pisa, or, should you live in the country, streams were running slightly outside their grooves as fruits dropped like gargoyle ganglia from the uniformly leaning trees. What would be your reaction to such a phenomenon? Honestly, now, and seriously, too. How would you feel? Would you be scared? Confused? Puzzled and anxious? Would you telephone the police? Would you pray? Or would you numbly await an explanation, refusing to attempt to analyze the event or even to experience it with your full emotions until you had read the papers, tuned in the news, heard how experts from the universities were explaining the tilt, learned how the Pentagon planned to deal with it, were reassured by the President, who might insist, as Presidents will, that nothing really nothing had gone wrong? Or instead of fear, bewilderment and anxiety, or in *addition* to fear, bewilderment and anxiety, or instead of a hard impulse to dismiss the happening and get back to business-as-usual, or in *addition* to a hard impulse to dismiss the happening and get back to business-as-usual, do you imagine that a bright trace of delight, unnamable and indefensible, might tickle your spine; could you feel in an odd way elated — elated, perhaps, because, in a rational world where even disasters are familiar and damn near routine, something of almost fairytale flavor had occurred?

Another try. Suppose that upon a late evening with thirsty guests in your home your supply of beer runs dry. You slip out and aim your car in the direction of the only store in the area open after midnight, a half-case of Budweiser your goal. Well, a couple of blocks from your house, the store not yet in view, you are subjected suddenly to an intense sensation of being spied upon. You scan for patrol cars but spot none. And then you see it, in the sky (its altitude and size indeterminable due to lack of reference points), a whirling disc outlined by concentric circles of white and green light with a scattering of rapidly blinking purple lightpoints in its center. It hovers — you are positive it is interested in *you* — beyond and above the hood of your car, whirling all the while, occasionally darting to the left or right with incredible speed. Before you gain the presence of mind to decide whether to brake or accelerate, the outer rings of white and green are extinguished and the small purple lights arrange themselves in a recognizable pattern — a pattern of a duck's foot — against the starless sky. Seconds later, the whole craft disappears. You drive on to the store, of course, because there's nothing else (for the moment) you *can* do. A while later, stunned and excited, you arrive home with the beer (you forgot Rick's cigarettes), where you are faced with the problem of what, if anything, to tell your friends. Maybe they won't believe you; they'll insist you're drunk or lying or worse. Maybe they'll blab too much; word will get to the press; you'll be hounded by skeptics and nuts. Should you call the radio station to ascertain if anyone else saw what you saw? Do you have a moral obligation to notify the nearest military installation? The way you handle these questions, as well as how much thought you eventually devote to the meaning of the UFO's visual message — why, you might wonder, a duck's foot? — would be determined by your basic personality, and with all tender respect, that is of small concern to the author. The significant query here is this: would you not, sooner or later, no matter who or what you are, feel a rise in spirit, a kind of wild-card joy as a result of your encounter? And if this elevation, this joyousness, can be attributed in part to your contact with . . . Mystery . . . cannot it equally be attributed to your abrupt realization that there are superior forces "out there," forces that for all their potential menace, nevertheless might, should they elect to intervene, represent salvation for a planet that seems stubbornly determined to perish?

Take now the clockworks. Both the clockworks, the original and the Chink's. The clockworks, being genuine and not much to look at, don't generate the drama of an Earth-tilt or a flying saucer, nor do they seem to offer any immediate panacea for humanity's fifty-seven varieties of heartburn. But suppose that you're one of those persons who feels trapped, to some degree, trapped matrimonially, occupationally, educationally or geographically, or trapped in something larger than all those; trapped in a *system,* or what you might describe as an "increasingly deadening technocracy" or a "theater of paranoia and desperation" or something like that. Now, if you are one of those persons (and the author doesn't mean to imply that you are), wouldn't the very knowledge that there are clockworks ticking away behind the wallpaper of civilization, unbeknownst to leaders, organizers and managers (the President included), wouldn't that knowledge, suggesting as it does the possibility of unimaginable alternatives, wouldn't that knowledge be a bubble bath for your heart?

Or is the author trying to ease you into something here, trying to manipulate you a little bit when he ought to be just telling his story the way a good author should? Maybe that's the case. Let's drop it for now.

But look here a minute. Over here. Here's a girl. She's a nice girl. And she's a pretty girl. She looks a bit like the young Princess Grace, had the young Princess Grace been left out in the rain for a year.

What's that you say? Her thumbs? Yes, aren't they magnificent? The word for her thumbs has got to be rococo — rococococototo tutti! by God.

Ladies. Gentlemen. Shhh. This is the way truth is. You've got to let those strange hands touch you.

. . . the Eskimos had fifty-two names for snow because it was important to them; there ought to be as many for love.

— Margaret Atwood

17.

NEWSPAPERS keep photographs of famous persons in their files. When one of the famous dies, a staff artist (the same guy who draws the circles around fumbled footballs) borrows the dead celebrity's photo folder and with an air brush obliterates the highlights in his eyes.

It is standard procedure on most American newspapers. By thus visually distinguishing those with us from those gone, the press shows its respect for, or its fear of, death. Whenever you see a picture of a deceased notable in the papers, chances are his eyes will be dull and flat — as if the sparkle of his living had been divided among his next of kin.

In the official Postal Service photograph of the President of the United States, the process seemed almost to have been reversed. Eyes that originally had been inert and shallow had been made with the retoucher's brush to twinkle warmly and project volleys of paternalism and health.

Sissy Hankshaw was standing beneath that very portrait of the President, in the lobby of the LaConner, Washington, post office. She looked at the President's portrait as if it were the benign fantasy of some Jehovah's Witness cartoonist — while she waited at the counter for her mail.

LaConner, Washington, was one of a half-dozen places around the country where Sissy received letters. The other places were Taos, New Mexico, Pine Ridge, South Dakota, Cherokee, North Carolina, Pleasant Point, Maine, and one other town. What these post offices had in common was that they all were on or adjacent to Indian reservations.

The President in the picture on the LaConner, Washington, post office wall that morning was not Ike. Oh no, Ike had led the people during Sissy's childhood and, except as to how they might best grip a golf club, had never thought of thumbs at all. Sissy had fled Richmond just as the Eisenhower Years were dying. (Dying of boredom, we might say — although the Eisenhower Years and the fifties were perfectly suited for one another; they went together like Hi and Lois. It was when the Eisenhower Years *returned,* in 1968 and, worse, in 1972 — times too psychically complex, technologically advanced and socially volatile to endure simple-mindedness on such a grand scale — that a civilization already green around the gills began to flip-flop in earnest.)

More than ten years had passed since Sissy made her move; a decade during which she hitchhiked obsessively, constantly, solitarily, marvelously. Among people who pay attention to such things, she had become a legend.

Being a legend is not always financially gainful. There is no United Federation of Legends union to ensure that members be compensated for their legendary labors at a minimum wage of $5.60 an hour. Legends have no lobby in Washington, D.C. There isn't even a Take a Legend to Lunch Week. Consequently, Sissy had to rely on something other than her legendary hitchhiking for eats (for Tampax and toothpaste and repairs to her shoes). That is why she occasionally worked for the Countess. And it was because the Countess had to have a means of contacting her that Sissy checked post office general delivery whenever she was near LaConner, Taos, Pine Ridge, Cherokee, Pleasant Point or that other place. Certainly, nobody *but* the Countess ever wrote to her. Sissy had neither heard from nor contacted her family since she had hitched off into the sunset. (Actually, of course, it was night when Sissy made her getaway, but in remembering South Richmond it is easy to confuse the memory of old brick with the memory of sunsets, as it is easy to inadvertently mingle in one's recollections the odor of toasting tobacco with the odor of blood: another of the brain's little practical jokes.)

Sissy wished quite hard for a message from the Countess that day, because there was less than a dollar in her pockets. Wishing made it so. As the President beamed upon her, the postmaster returned to the counter with a slinky mauve envelope, addressed in puce-colored ink and smelling (even as it snuggled against the postmaster's hand) of the boudoir. "Thank you," Sissy said, and she carried the missive out onto the sidewalk.

Hitchhiking into LaConner, Washington, had been like hitchhiking down a mossy old well. Dark, damp and very green. There were puddles in the street and the smell of mushrooms everywhere. The sky was a crock of curdled cloud. Mallards swam within quacking distance of the village post office and, as if in welcome, ten thousand hitchhiking cattails pointed their fat thumbs in the air.

She could hear foundations decaying as she stood there, and every horizon she tried to focus upon was mysteriously blurred, as if licked by the tip of the tongue of the Totem. Snails advanced upon the woodpiles. Fir trees stood their ground.

Directly across the slough from the village was the Swinomish reservation. Indeed, several Indians walked past Sissy at the post office, distracting her, for the moment, from the Countess's letter.

At last, however, she ripped it open and was surprised to read just this:

> Sissy, Precious Being,
>
> How are you, my extraordinary one? I worry so. Next time you are near Manhattan, do ring me up. There is a man to whom I simply must introduce you. Thrill!!
>
> The Countess

Refolding the sheet of expensive notepaper, Sissy warmed it for a while between her palms, as if, like the dirty old man who sat on a Girl Scout cookie hoping to hatch a Brownie, it might metamorphose into a work order. When she read it again, alas, it was the same pointless message.

"You'd think the Countess would know me better than that," she mused. "I haven't had a paycheck in half a year and all the Countess can come up with is an introduction to a man. Crimineyǃ"

Just then, on the slough, some Indians tore by in a long canoe (an antique shovel-nose war canoe), chanting furiously in the Skagit language. They were Swinomish bucks, mostly high school ballplayers or young unemployed veterans, practicing for the annual Fourth of July longboat race against the Lummi, Muckleshoot and other Puget Sound tribes. Sissy flung the scented letter into a waste can.

On television once, she had seen a cheapo Western called *Reprisal.*

Guy Madison played a half-breed who passed. In the end, however, he soured on the System and went back to the wild old ways. "I deny that part of me that is white!" he cried

Sometimes Sissy had considered following Guy Madison's example. Ah, to wahoo in the fir-shadowed streets of LaConner and deny that part of her that was civilized and pale!

But that would be denying fifteen-sixteenths of her.

What would it be like, living life as a one-sixteenth?

(a) Like that part of the moth the candle burns last.

(b) Like a "slow dance on the killing ground."

(c) Maybe not so bad at that: in the land of rotting grapes a raisin could be queen.

(d) Like a pair of thumbs to which there is no brain, no heart, no cunt attached.

18.

THAT HER PLEASURE in Indianhood and her passion for car travel might be incongruous if not mutually exclusive never occurred to Sissy (as it was to occur to Julian and Dr. Goldman). After all, the first car that ever stopped for her had been named in honor of the great chief of the Ottawa: Pontiac.

Perhaps Sissy was one of those who believed that nature and industry could sleep between the same flowered sheets. Perhaps she entertained visions of a future wilderness where bison and Buicks would mingle in harmony and mutual respect, a neoprimitive prairie where both pinto and Pinto would run free.

Perhaps. The visions of a woman in motion are difficult to gauge.

Visionary beliefs were neither expressed nor implied as Sissy, provisioned with Three Musketeers bars, thrilled LaConner's municipal cattails by the manner in which she hitched out of town. As previously suggested, Sissy made it a general practice never to plan an itinerary nor fix a destination — but could she help it if the only road out of LaConner, Washington, ran directly to New York City?

Just as Chief Pontiac's beseeching question, "Why do you suffer the white man to dwell among you?" arrowed straight to the soul of his people, so the only road out of LaConner shot straight to Park Avenue and the Countess.

"I honestly don't know how I got here so fast," Sissy told the Countess. "When I walked into the LaConner Food Center to buy candy, some Indians at the beer cooler snickered at my hands. I freaked out and the next thing I knew I was approaching the Holland Tunnel. I woke up in the front seat of a convertible. The top was down and my first impression was that we'd been scalped."

19.

The Countess had a smile like the first scratch on a new car. It was immanently regrettable. It was a spoiler. It was a stinging little reminder of the inevitability of deterioration.

As if further vandalizing a marred surface, an ivory cigarette holder periodically pried apart the Countess's prickly jowls. Ashes from French cigarettes sifted onto the white linen suit that he wore daily without respect to season; ashes sifted upon the month-old bloom in his lapel. His monocle was fly-specked, his ascot was steak-sauced, his dentures thought that they were castanets and the world was a fandango.

The Countess didn't give a damn. He was rich, and not a penny less. You would be rich, too, if you had invented and manufactured the world's most popular feminine hygiene products.

The Countess had built a fortune on those odors peculiar to the female anatomy. He was the General Motors of body cosmetics, the U.S. Steel of intimate fresheners. As any genius might, he obsessively directed every phase of his company's activities, from research to marketing, including advertising campaigns. That was where Sissy came in. She was his favorite model.

He had discovered her years before in Times Square, where a crowd had gathered to watch her cross Forty-second Street against the lights. In a rare concession, he had wiped off his monocle. She had an ideal figure for modeling, she was blond and creamy, her demeanor was regal — except for her mouth: "She has the eyes of a poetess, the nose of an aristocrat, the chin of a noblewoman and the mouth of a suck artist in a Tijuana pony show," announced the Countess. "She's perfect."

"But my God in holy Heaven," protested the vice president of the Chase Manhattan Bank, with whom he had just lunched. "What about her hands?"

Bookkeepers should know better than to argue with genius.

The Countess had a fine photographer in his employ. Background was essential to the dreamy, romantic yet slightly suggestive tableaux with which he appealed to potential consumers of Dew spray mist and Yoni Yum spray powder, so he frequently sent his cameraman on location, as far away as Venice or the Taj Mahal. He spared no expense to get the image he wanted, and he learned to wait patiently for Sissy to hitchhike to her assignments.

He never photographed her hands.

Now, in the days when Lucky Strike cigarettes sponsored "Your Hit Parade" on television, the program featured a singer named Dorothy Collins. Miss Collins invariably appeared in blouses or dresses with high collars. Eventually, the high collars led to the rumor that Miss Collins was hiding something. She was said to have a scar or a goiter or one hell of a mole. Perhaps a vampire had given Dorothy Collins a permanent hickey. There were all sorts of stories. After several years, however, the vocalist abruptly appeared on "Your Hit Parade" (singing "Shrimp Boats Are A-Coming" or something like that) in a low-cut gown — and her throat was as normal as yours or mine. Of course, someone in Dr. Dreyfus's profession could have worked a little plastic magic. We'll probably never know.

At any rate, what with Sissy Hankshaw posing for so many picturesque Yoni Yum and Dew ads, it didn't take more than about a year for sharp eyes to ascertain that her hands were never in the picture. They would be behind her back, or cropped out, or some tropical foliage or gondola prow would be obscuring them. And rumors à la Dorothy Collins spread along Madison Avenue. The usual stories — she had warts or birthmarks or tattoos or six fingers where five would do — came and went; but one version, that when she had once accepted an engagement ring from another, a jealous lover had lopped off her hands with a fish knife, persisted. The Countess, of course, wouldn't say. He kept Sissy's identity a secret and paid his photographer extra to develop lockjaw. It was the kind of game the Countess loved. Listening to the rumors about his mystery model, he would probe his nasty smile with his cigarette holder and his dentures would clack like a goose eating dominoes.

Years afterward, when he was no longer using Sissy exclusively, the Countess posed a female impersonator in a Dew ad. He was not above that sort of trick. But he truly was taken with Sissy Hankshaw. Among other things, he believed her responsible for the jumpsuit interest that seized Western womanhood in the late sixties, and he placed her in the avant-garde of fashion. Well, it is true; Sissy wore jumpsuits long before any editor at *Vogue,* but it is also true that she continued to wear them after they passed out of style. Zippered jumpsuits were, in fact, the only garb Sissy *could* wear — because she hadn't the facility to button her clothes.

Sissy never complained about the censorship of her hands, although as a matter of pride she would have preferred them in plain view. To the Countess's credit, he often expressed a desire to get Sissy's thumbs into the photo, simply for their phallic counterpoint, but he feared the American public wasn't ready for that.

Maybe he'd test a thumb shot in Japan, he said, for among the Japs his firm already had grossed millions with an ad that paraphrased a haiku by the eighteenth-century poet Buson:

The short night is through:
on the hairy caterpillar
little beads of Dew.

Cowgirl Interlude (Moon Over Dakota)

The moon looked like a clown's head dipped in honey.

It bobbed ballishly in the sky, dripping a mixture of clown white and bee jelly onto the Dakota hills.

Coyote howls (or were they crane whoops?) zigzagged through the celestial make-up like auditory wrinkles.

Moonlight fell on Bonanza Jellybean as she bent over the horse trough, still scrubbing out her panties. (A warm day in a bouncing saddle can really stain a girl's underwear.)

Moonlight spilled in the bunkhouse windows, competing with the lampshine that illuminated the pages of Mary's *Holy Bible,* Big Red's *Ranch Romances* and Debbie's *The Way of Zen.*

Moonlight ghosted the cheeks of girls sleeping and girls pretending to sleep.

A single moonbeam quivered timidly on the stock of Delores del Ruby's blacksnake whip, where the stock protruded from beneath the sack of peyote buttons that nightly served as her pillow.

Moonlight lured Kym and Linda outdoors in their nightgowns to lean against the corral fence in silent rapture.

Our moon, obviously, has surrendered none of its soft charm to technology. The pitter-patter of little spaceboots has in no way diminished its mystery.

In fact, the explorations of the Apollo mechanics revealed almost nothing of any real importance that was not already intimated in the Luna card of the tarot deck.

Almost nothing. There was one interesting discovery. Some of the rocks on the moon transmit waves of energy. At first it was feared that they might be radioactive. Instruments quickly proved that the emissions were clean, but NASA was still puzzled about the source and character of the vibrations. Rock samples were brought back to Earth by astronauts for extensive laboratory testing.

As the precise electromagnetic properties of the moon rocks continued to baffle investigators, one scientist decided just for drill to convert the waves into sound. It's a simple process.

When the moon vibrations were channeled into an amplifier, the noises that pulsed out of the speaker sounded exactly like "cheese, cheese, cheese."

20.

"SIT DOWN, DEAR, do sit down. Take a load off those lovely tootsies. Yes, sit right there. Would you fancy some sherry?" The decanter the Countess lifted was dusty on the outside, sticky empty inside; a stiff fly lay feet-up on its lip. "Shit O goodness, I'm all out of sherry; how about a red Ripple?" He reached into the midget refrigerator beside his desk and removed a bottle of pop wine. After a shameful amount of effort he tore loose its cap and filled two sherry glasses.

"You know what Ripple is, don't you? It's Kool-Aid with a hard-on. Tee hee."

Sissy managed a polite smile. Shyly, she gazed at her glass. It was impastoed with so many fingerprints it should have been buried with J. Edgar Hoover. (At FBI headquarters in Washington, D.C., there is an agent who can go through the fingerprint files and pick out all the trumpet players. Perhaps he is the same agent who kept returning Sissy's file card to the Richmond regional office demanding to know why there were no thumb marks. He was in good shape and didn't know it. There once was a family in Philadelphia that went through four generations without fingerprints at all: they were born without prints, the only known case in history. "This could present quite a problem for law enforcement," said one public official. "No way," replied another. "If the police ever find a murder weapon in Philly with no prints on it, we'll know immediately that one of *them* did it."

The Countess lifted his glass in salute. "To my own special Sissy," he toasted. "Cheers! And welcome. So my letter brought you flying, eh? Well, I may have a little surprise for you. But first, tell me about yourself. It's been six months, hasn't it? In some circles that's half a year. How are you?"

"Tired," said Sissy.

He stared at her sympathetically. "That's the very first time in the eons that I've known you that I've ever heard you complain. You *must* be tired. You've endured the greatest hardships without a whimper. I've always said, 'Sissy Hankshaw never has any bad luck because nothing seems bad luck to her. She's never been disgraced because there is nothing which she'd acknowledge as disgrace.' And now you're tired, poor darling."

"Some folks might say I had my hard luck at birth, and after dealing with that everything else was easy. A born freak can only go uphill."

"Freak, schmeek. Most of us are freaks in one way or another. Try being born a male Russian countess into a white middle-class Baptist family in Mississippi and you'll see what I mean."

"I understand that. I was being facetious. You know that I've always been proud of the way nature singled me out. It's the people who have been deformed by society that I feel sorry for. We can live with nature's experiments, and if they aren't too vile, turn them to our advantage. But social deformity is sneaky and invisible; it makes people into monsters — or mice. Anyway, I'm fine. But I've been steady moving for eleven years and some months, you realize, and I guess I'm a tad fatigued. Maybe I should rest up for a spell. Not as young as I used to be."

"Shit O goodness, you won't be thirty for another year. And you're more beautiful than ever."

Her jumpsuit was patterned with robins and apple blossoms. It bore sweet testimony to recent laundering, but there were creases where it had been folded in her rucksack. Her lengthy blond hair fell straight; it would have been more convenient to travel with it in braids, but, alas, how could her fingers braid it? A mask of grime and road filth that no rinsing in service station ladies' rooms could adequately remove clung to her face. In the pores of her crisp nose and high forehead was the residue of various fossil fuels as well as flea's-eye particles of Idaho, Minnesota and western New Jersey: clay, sand, loam, mud, pollen, cement, ore and humus. The dirty veil with which hitchhiking draped her features was one reason why her identity as a model had been fairly simple to conceal. If the Countess wanted her to pose, he'd have to steam her for a day or two in his private bath. Still, the sunshine that was projected in the office windows, having first passed through the green filter of Central Park, showed the Countess to be no snaky flatterer: Sissy was beautiful, indeed.

"Does that mean you might have an assignment for me?"

There was a long pause, during which the Countess tapped his monocle with his cigarette holder, during which a squirrel successfully crossed Park Avenue, during which the twentieth century flicked its pea under another shell, catching a few million more suckers with their bets in the wrong places.

"You were the Yoni Yum/Dew Girl from, let's see, from nineteen sixty-two through nineteen sixty-eight. That's a long time in this business. It was a brilliant campaign, if I do say so, and it was a good association. But it can't be repeated. One can't repeat oneself. Not and dredge any flavor out of life. Now, I've been using you two, three times a year, in trade magazine ads only, ever since. And I may use you again. I probably shall. You're my eternal favorite. Princess Grace herself couldn't be better, not even if she had your personality, which she doesn't; I am by proclamation official feminine hygienist to the Court of Monaco and I know, but that's telling tales out of school. Anyway, dear, I'm out of photography now and into watercolors. Whole new campaign about to start, built around incredibly lyrical watercolor paintings. Ah, how circuitous conversation is! We're back at the beginning. The exact man I've wanted you to meet is my artist, the watercolorist."

Sissy dared a sip of Ripple. "If I'm not going to pose for him, why do you want me to meet him?"

"Purely personal. I believe you might enjoy one another."

"But, Countess . . ."

"Now now. Don't get exasperated. I realize that you've always avoided all but the most rudimentary involvements with men, and, I might add, you've been wise. Heterosexual relationships seem to lead only to marriage, and for most poor dumb brainwashed women marriage is the climactic experience. For men, marriage is a matter of efficient logistics: the male gets his food, bed, laundry, TV, pussy, offspring and creature comforts all under one roof, where he doesn't have to dissipate his psychic energy thinking about them too much — then he is free to go out and fight the battles of life, which is what existence is all about. But for a woman, marriage is surrender. Marriage is when a girl gives up the fight, walks off the battlefield and from then on leaves the truly interesting and significant action to her husband, who has bargained to 'take care' of her. What a sad bum deal. Women live longer than men because they really haven't been living. Better blue-in-the-face dead of a heart attack at fifty than a healthy seventy-year-old widow who hasn't had a piece of life's action since girlhood. Shit O goodness, how I do go on."

The Countess refilled his glass. The squirrel started across Park Avenue again but didn't make it. A uniformed chauffeur got out of a limousine and held the crushed animal up where it could be seen by the elderly woman passenger, who next week would make a twenty-five-dollar donation to the SPCA.

"But here you are, still a virgin — you *are* virginal yet, aren't you?"

"Why, yes, technically. Jack Kerouac and I came awfully close, but he was afraid of me, I think . . ."

"Yes, well, what I'm getting at is that there comes a time when it is psychologically impossible for a woman to lose her virginity. She can't wait too long, you know. Now, there's no reason why you *must* lose yours. You're so much better off than most women. You've remained on the battleground, center stage, experiencing life and, what's more important, experiencing yourself experiencing it. You haven't been reduced to a logistical strategy for somebody else's life-war. I'm not suggesting that you capitulate. But maybe you should pause — now in your weariness is a perfect opportunity — and consider if perhaps you aren't missing something of magnitude; consider if perhaps you wouldn't want to experience a romantic relationship before, well, frankly, before it may be too late. I mean, just ponder it a bit, that's all."

"What makes you think this watercolorist and I would develop a romantic relationship?" Sissy's brow was spaghettied.

"I can't be certain that you would. Furthermore, I can't imagine why I would want you to. I mean, you've always *smelled* so nice. Like a little sister. The irony has just killed me." The Countess's teeth began a faster clack. "You, the Dew Girl, one of the few girls who doesn't *need* Dew. I loath the stink of females!" The clatter grew louder. "They are so sweet the way God made them; then they start fooling around with men and soon they're stinking. Like rotten mushrooms, like an excessively chlorinated swimming pool, like a tuna fish's retirement party. They *all* stink. From the Queen of England to Bonanza Jellybean, they stink." The dental flamenco hit a delirious tempo, a *bulería,* a Gypsy flurry of too many notes too soon.

"Bonanza Jellybean?"

"What? Oh yes. Tee hee. Jellybean." As the Countess's jaw muscles calmed down, his dentures eased into a samba. "She's a young thing who works on my ranch. Real name is Sally Jones or something wooden like that. She's cute as a hot fudge taco, and, of course, it takes verve to change one's name so charmingly. But she stinks like a slut just the same."

"Your ranch?"

"Oh my dear yes, I bought a little ranch out West. Sort of a tribute to the women of America who have cooperated with me in eliminating their odor. A tax write-off, actually. You'll have to see it sometime. Meanwhile, back to business at hand. Why don't you consider meeting my artist? You admitted you needed a rest. I'm going out to East Hampton to gossip with Truman for a few days. You can light at my place and relax. I'll put Julian in touch with you there. Perhaps you can go out together, have some fun. Come on, Sissy love, give it a try. What have you got to lose?"

The Countess was a genius, all right. He asked the one question that Sissy could never answer: what have you got to lose?

"Well, okay. I'll try it. I don't see the point in it, but I'll try it. Just for you. It's kind of silly, actually, me going out with an artist in New York City. However . . ." (Was that old limbic telephone purring on its hook again? After all, she had *asked* for an unlisted number.)

"Good, good, good," the Countess cooed. "You'll enjoy it, you'll see. Julian is a gentleman."

Suddenly, the Countess swiveled in his desk chair and leaned forward. Lowering his wine glass, he focused directly, intensely into Sissy's blue eyes. His rip of a smile widened until it was a job for a body-and-fender shop. He had been waiting for this moment.

"By the way, Sissy," he said very slowly, accentuating every syllable, clacking one beat at a time. "By the way. He's a full-blooded Indian."

21.

SHE HAD MADE Mack trucks rear back on their axles, caused Mercedes-Benzes to forget about Wagner, stopped Cadillacs as cold as a snowman's heart attack. Torpedoes changed their courses for her, planes dived, submarines surfaced, Lincoln Continentals straightened their neckties. Wherever traffic flowed she had fished its waters, hooking Barracuda and Stingrays, throwing back Honda minibikes and garden tractors. At her signal, Jeeps and Chryslers fell over one another, Mercurys and Ramblers went into trance, VW's halted with a Prussian exactitude, Chevies executed the shim sham shimmy and toddlers begged to pull her to San Francisco in their little red wagons. Once she made a Rolls-Royce brake so abruptly they had to fly a man in from the factory to scrape up the rubber. While stickers peeled off bumpers, Confederate flags wrapped themselves around radio aerials and exhaust pipes farted the overture from "My Fair Lady," she had commandeered every vehicle manufactured by man in his manic horsepowerphilia, from a Stutz Bearcat to a Katz Pajama — but she could not seem to attract an elevator.

"Maybe you have to call on the phone to get an elevator to come up to the penthouse. Maybe the buzzer is broken. Maybe I'm doing something wrong."

Sissy had been waiting ten minutes. She felt trapped. Where was the elevator? Why wouldn't it respond? Teardrops were poking their bald heads out of her ducts.

It was more than just the elevator. Three days before, the Countess had procured a dress and buttoned her into it. She had agreed that it looked very nice. Then he went off — monocle, cigarette holder and everything — to Long Island, leaving her alone. The first evening, the watercolorist hadn't phoned. Sissy couldn't unbutton the dress, and to sleep in it would have left it geriatrically wrinkled. So she had sat up all night. She had watched TV, sipped red Ripple (the only beverage her host had in supply), read the *New York Times* and chanced pleased looks in the mirror. Alone on a June night in a seven-room penthouse. It had been strange.

At approximately ten in the morning the telephone rang. A voice that might have belonged to a Grecian urn, so soft and round and cultured it sounded, identified itself as belonging, instead, to Julian Gitche. Would Sissy Hankshaw please have dinner with Julian Gitche and friends on Friday next? Yes, Sissy Hankshaw would. The Countess's phone (a Princess — royalty sticks together) and, presumably, Julian Gitche's, had been replaced in the cradle. Dinner on Friday. It was then Wednesday.

As through the second TV-humming night she sat upright in the yoga position known as the *dress-protecting asana,* she reminded herself of Betty Clanton and the other girls of South Richmond High, setting their hair, combing it out, painting their lips, rouging their cheeks, washing their sweaters, pressing their skirts, primping away the hours and days of their youth in the peahen hope that for one blushing moment they could distract a boy from football. Nature had spared

Sissy that as a teen-ager — but, mama, look at her now! Every hour or so, she became angry at herself, sprang up and announced to whatever television personality happened to be facing her that she was going to bed. She did not.

Thursday night was much the same, except that she was sleepier, angrier, more nervous. Newspapers, with their quaint accounts of politics and economics, TV, with its heroic policemen, could no longer amuse her. Red Ripple in hand, she fled to the balcony. She had passed the point where fresh air was of much use in reviving her, but she felt less confined pacing a patio in the New York sky.

"This is stupid, really dumb," she told herself. "But if I'm going to do it I might as well do it right. I can't go to dinner in a good New York restaurant wearing a wrinkled sack. I'm used to skipping sleep on the road. I can make it." Serenity once again illuminated the corners of her mouth, although her eyes, over which the lids drooped like detectives' bellies, failed to notice.

It was a cloudless night with only moderate smog. A furry northeaster was blowing in over Coney Island and Brooklyn, bringing to the upper East Side a teasing sniff of the ocean. Trembling with energy, unable to contain itself, Manhattan was popping wheelies beneath her. In every direction, her tired eyes saw flashing lights, lights that caromed off the horizons and joined with the stars in the sky. The city seemed to be inhaling Benzedrine and exhaling light; a neon-lunged Buddha chanting and vibrating in a temple of filth.

It was difficult for her to imagine that an American Indian was at home somewhere down there. Where exactly did he live, she wondered; which lights shone in his windows? What was he doing at this moment? Sleeping? (Sleep was bright on her mind.) Drinking — the way the Indians drank in LaConner, Taos, Pine Ridge, etc.? Performing a clandestine ghost dance or chanting to his private totem as prescribed in the dreamer religion? Watching "Custer" on TV? Painting watercolors? Until the dawn, she paced and pondered.

The day that followed had been a blur of boredom and misery; she was more asleep than awake. She found a loaf of Wonder Bread and wadded the soft individual slices into balls, as she had done when a kid, eating the bread balls on the balcony while watching traffic. Mostly, she sat around. (Were it not such an obvious understatement, we might say that she twiddled her thumbs.) When, however, at 7:45

P.M., Julian Gitche called to announce that he was downstairs, her central nervous system treated itself to a double adrenalin on the rocks. She flashed into consciousness, inspected herself — wrinkle-free! — in the mirror, took a pee and headed for the elevator. She had arranged to meet him in the lobby. Somehow it had seemed inappropriate to her to receive Mr. Gitche in the Countess's penthouse, with its frilly, sloppy and decidedly un-Indian décor.

Now Sissy was waiting for an elevator. She waited with a fatigue-induced approximation of that combination of stoicism and anxiety with which people wait for the Big Event that will transform their lives, invariably missing it when it does occur since both stoicism and anxiety are blinders.

At last, as she was on the brink of weeping, she heard a ping and saw a wink of green. A door slid open with a mechanical slur, to reveal a uniformed elevator operator looking sheepish and not altogether unafraid. Having suffered the Countess's ire on previous occasions, he was on the alert for a walking stick that might be mistaking his skull for a grand promenade. Relieved at seeing Sissy alone, he expressed her to the lobby at maximum speed.

The carpet felt like meadow to her hallucinating feet. The bronze fountain sounded like a mountain creek. Her redman glided from behind a tree (so what if it was a potted palm?). He was wearing a plaid dinner jacket and a yellow cummerbund. Of medium height, his shoulders were narrow, his face babified and puddingish. Approaching her, he smiled shyly. He reached to shake her hand — and fell immediately to his knees with an asthma attack.

Cowgirl Interlude (Love Story)

Some of the younger ranch hands — Donna, Kym and Heather; Debbie, too — have wondered aloud why *Even Cowgirls Get the Blues* couldn't be a simple love story.

Unfortunately, little darlings, there is no such thing as a simple love story. The most transitory puppy crush is complex to the extent of lying beyond the far reaches of the brain's understanding. (The brain has a dangerous habit of messing around with stuff it cannot or *will* not comprehend.)

Your author has found love to be the full trip, emotionally speaking; the grand tour: fall in love, visit both Heaven and Hell for the price of one. And that doesn't begin to cover it. If realism can be defined only as one of the fifty-seven varieties of decoration, then how can we hope for a realistic assessment of love?

No, the author has no new light to beam on the subject. After all, though people have been composing love songs for at least a thousand years, it wasn't until the late 1960s that any romantic ballad expressed a new idea. In his song "Triad" (*"Why can't we go on as three?"*), David Crosby offered the *ménage à trois* as a possible happy remedy for the triangularization that seems to be to love what hoof-and-mouth disease is to cattle (to employ an analogy that any cowgirl can understand). Bold David (Grace Slick of Jefferson Airplane recorded his song) sought to transport love beyond its dualistic limits; to accept the three-sided configuration as an inevitability, perceiving it as positive, building upon it, expanding it, drawing lines in different directions (*". . . in time there may be others"*). But Crosby's Euclidean approach complicates love rather than simplifies it. And it is doubtful whether many lovers could endure further complications. As a visitor to the clockworks once heard the Chink say, "If it's sloppy, eat it over the sink."

So trot your ponies, honeys, and accept the tangled facts, knowing that your author would prefer to write a simple love story if it were possible. How refreshing to deal with something subjective, intuitive or, best of all, mystical! But the serious writer, like his brother the scientist, has been reduced to dealing with the mere objective.

22.

JUST AS a piece of shell can take all the fun out of an egg salad sandwich, just as the advent of an Ice Age can poop a million garden parties, just as a disbelief in magic can force a poor soul into believing in government and business, so can a fit of asthma rather spoil the first date between a young woman and an Indian.

Sissy didn't know what to do. Initially, she thought Julian was reacting to the sight of her thumbs, although the Countess had sworn that he had made his watercolorist fully cognizant of Sissy's anatomical embellishments. At one time or another, folks had sniggered at her, pointed, blanched, blinked, clucked, snapped hurried snapshots, bitten their tongues and fallen off barstools, but this reaction took the cake, and the pie, too. They weren't *that* big.

Should she try to assist him, or flee?

Conveniently, from the other side of the lobby Julian's friends came to the rescue. They were two well-groomed couples, white, mid-thirtyish and middle-class. The younger of the men took charge. He broke an inhaler of epinephrine under Julian's nose. The epinephrine hormone relaxed the smooth muscles in the small bronchi of the victim's lungs, allowing air to pass more freely in and out. Within moments his breathing had improved. However, the attack was severe and Julian continued to whistle and wheeze. His chest sounded like the trombone section of the old Stan Kenton orchestra. His chest was playing "Stars Fell on Alabama." Nobody danced.

"We'd better take you home," the man in charge said to Julian. As it turned out, he and Julian had once been roommates, so that's why he knew how to handle the attack.

Embarrassed, and in the red of embarrassment looking more Indian than he had previously, Julian begged Sissy's pardon. In wheeze-ventilated and cough-derailed speech, he managed to tell her:

"I've been enthralled with your photographs for years. When the Countess hinted that you might like to meet me — he never explained why — I was ready to paint for him free of charge. And now I had to go and spoil it."

It was Sissy's turn to redden. Her one-sixteenth came swimming to surface, matching Julian's full measure of uncompromised blood. Although uncomfortable, she was moved by his lament. The emotions she felt were almost counter to the ones she had imagined this talented Indian would inspire in her. Once again (as in Madame Zoe's trailer), she found herself on top of a situation that she had expected would dominate her. Through the blush, her mysterious calm smile stirred and slowly beat its wings, a seabird ascending through a spray of tomato soup.

The man who took charge was named Rupert, a salesman for a publishing house. His wife was Carla, a homemaker, as they say. The other couple broke down into Howard and Marie Barth, both copywriters for an ad agency. While Rupert helped Julian to the street, Howard hailed a cab and Carla and Marie fluttered around Sissy. "This is dreadful," Marie said. She lowered her voice, becoming confidential. "You know, asthma attacks are brought on by emotional stress. Poor Julian is so high-strung. The excitement of meeting you — my dear, you look so stunning! — must have upset his chemical balance." Carla nodded. "It'll be all right, dear. It isn't as serious as it sounds." She started to pat Sissy's hand, then thought better of it.

The six of them squeezed into a taxi. Can you guess how humiliating that was for our Sissy, ushered insensitively into a vehicle that she had not snared in her net of meat and gesture? Can you appreciate that she must have felt like a hummingbird stuck in the bubblegum of pedestrianism? Would you invite Thelonius Monk to your house and not let him play your piano? Would you shove an arthritic nanny goat into the ring with El Cordobes? Lord! She sat upon that taxi upholstery in frosty revulsion, like a queen compelled to squat over a ditch latrine; and why not? For she was Sissy Hankshaw, who had carved out an identity for herself in the vast realm of personal idiosyncrasy instead of carving it out of someone else's flesh, as is normally the case; Sissy Hankshaw, who, following a suggestion from nature, had created herself and then paraded her creation before ye gods and planets that whirl above our daily routine; Sissy Hankshaw, who proved that grandiose ambition need not be Faustian, at least not for a woman in motion. Einstein had observed motion and learned that space and time are relative; Sissy had committed herself to motion and learned that one could alter reality by one's perception of it — and it was that discovery, perhaps no less a one than Einstein's, that finally allowed her to smile away humiliation just as a short while earlier she had smiled away fatigue.

The taxi, having no free will, rolled downtown.

23.

New York City. June 21, 1972. Eight-thirty in the evening, according to the position of two mechanical hands on an arbitrary dial. Mars is in the House of Virgo, Jupiter is in the House of Values and Venus is in the House of Pies. The weather: hot hokey puppy poopie with billows of industrial paranoia at 600 feet. Manhattan smells like the litter box for the Kitty of the World. It has twisted its body into the *dog-shit asana.* Close by but far away, in a world beyond odors, ghosts of the original inhabitants are laughing their feathers off, remembering how they'd stuck the white devils with this doomed piece of real estate for some very chic beads and a box of Dutch Masters. The Big Apple, polished with Rockefeller spit and wiped on the tight pants of a multitude of Puerto Ricans, is ready for the chomps and nibbles of Friday-nighters from everywhere. Junkies are stirring in their warrens, pizzas are primping in their ovens, Wall Street is resting its bloody butthole and the Statue of Liberty wears a frown that won't quit. As City College professors, disgruntled over martinis, talk about dropping out and farming rhubarb in Oregon, neon signs all over town rejoice because it's the shortest night of the year. Headline on the front page of the New York *Daily News:* THE CHINK SUMS IT UP, SAYS LIFE IS HARD IF YOU THINK IT'S HARD. New York City. In progress. Not a cowgirl in sight.

Taxi cabs are pulling up in front of restaurants and theaters, and one pulls up in front of a remodeled tenement on East Tenth Street, between Third and Second avenues, three blocks west of where young Latins have all but taken away Tompkins Square Park from old Ukrainians and winos of indeterminate age and national origin. This block of East Tenth, freshly painted, maintains some class: behind its barred windows and triple-locked doors with chains à la mode, professional people, some with a creative bent, are holding their own against the constant onslaught of soot, cockroaches and burglars. In this block Hubert Selby, Jr., wrote *Last Exit to Brooklyn,* and a famous art critic ponders hourly the problem that inherent pictorialism presents to the ongoing mainstream of modernism. The taxi has stopped in front of the building where the wheezy Julian Gitche resides. It discharges its passengers, all too slowly for the taste of Sissy Hankshaw, who holds exhaustion and revulsion at bay only with the aid of the Great Secret (which, as we've determined, is this: one has not only an ability to perceive the world but an ability to alter his perception of it; or, more simply, one can change things by the manner in which one looks at them).

As tired as she is, Sissy has a single flame-edged longing — to get on the road and hoist her thumbs in the wind. However, she is buttoned into an expensive linen dress, is hemmed in by four persuasive people and is held by fine threads of curiosity and sympathy to this *Gentleman's Quarterly* parody of an Indian who curds up with mucus every time he tries to speak to her. So she employs the Great Secret to turn her predicament into an educational, if not entertaining, experience.

Julian's apartment is second floor front. It's neat and clean, with waxed hardwood floors, a wall of exposed brick, a white piano, books and paintings everywhere. There is a blue velour sofa upon which Julian is made to lie. While Howard mixes Scotch and sodas, Rupert fills a syringe from a vial of aminophylline he has taken from its place behind a gelatin salad mold in the refrigerator. He gives Julian an injection.

"There, that ought to beat them bronchial buggers into submission," he says to Julian. Then, to Sissy, "I was a medic in the Army. I really should have become a doctor. Sometimes, though, I feel that pushing books is a whole lot like pushing medicine. Think of books as pills. I have pills that cure ignorance and pills that cure boredom. I have pills to elevate moods and pills to open people's eyes to the awful truth: uppers and downers, as it were. I sell pills to help people find themselves and pills to help them lose themselves when they require escape from the pressures and anxieties of life in a complex society . . ."

"Too bad you don't have a pill for bullshit." Carla smiles as if she were joking, but she'd said it tartly. Rupert glares and takes a big bite of Scotch.

"Where do you live, Miss Hankshaw," asks Howard, trying, perhaps, to change the subject.

"I'm staying with the Countess."

"I know," says Howard, "but where do you reside when you aren't visiting New York?"

"I don't."

"You *don't?*"

"Well, no, I don't reside anywhere in particular. I just keep moving."

Everyone looks a bit astonished, including the recumbent Julian.

"A traveler, eh?" says Howard.

"You might say that," says Sissy, "although I don't think of it as traveling."

"How *do* you think of it?" asks Carla.

"As moving."

"Oh," says Carla.

"How . . . unusual," says Marie.

"Mmmmm," mumbles Howard.

Rupert bites into his Scotch again. Julian issues a watery wheeze.

The silence that follows is soon broken by Carla. "Rupert, before you get too engrossed in your research on Scotch as a cure for aging, don't you think you'd better phone Elaine's and cancel our dinner reservations? We'll never get in again if we just don't show up."

"What would we do without you, Carla? Without our little efficiency expert, Carla, everything would just go to hell. Carla is thinking about running for mayor next year, aren't you Carla?"

"Up yours, Herr Doktor Book Salesman. Will the demands of your medical practice allow you to call Elaine's or shall I?"

"Oh let me do it," pipes Marie. The short, vivacious brunette lifts herself out of her platform shoes and glides in stocking feet to the telephone.

"Speaking of running for office," says Howard pleasantly. "Does anybody think McGovern has a chance?"

"Do you mean a chance to be canonized or a chance to be assassinated?" asks Rupert.

"If Rupert needs a bullshit pill then Hubert Humphrey needs two," says Carla. "And that might be McGovern's role. If he can turn off Humphrey's fountain of corn then McGovern has done the sensibility of America a great favor, even if he forces his party to nominate a jingoist creep like Scoop Jackson in Miami Beach."

Like many of their liberal counterparts, the friends of Julian Gitche are disillusioned with politics, but also like their counterparts they have failed to discover an alternative to politics in which to place their faith, channel their humanism or indulge their penchant for conflict and speculation. Thus, the conversation around the red patient on the blue sofa drifts to the upcoming national political conventions. When Marie returns from phoning the restaurant, she joins in.

Sissy leaves her chair and wanders about the apartment. Its full bookshelves remind her of public libraries in which she has napped.

Wandering, she holds her thumbs close to her side, lest she nudge an antique, totter an objet d'art, smear a picture glass or agitate the pet poodle. She is intrigued but suffers no illusions; she knows she is in an alien environment.

Eventually her explorations lead her into the bedroom, where there is a covered birdcage of Florentine design. She wishes its inhabitants were not sleeping, for she "has a way" with birds. She recalls Boy, the runaway parakeet who for a time was the sole exception to her rule to go always alone. Boy's owners had clipped his wings, but once Sissy taught him how, he hitchhiked as well as some birds fly. That Boy is a cinch to go down in the Parakeet Hall of Fame.

Hoping to hear a cheep that might indicate insomnia in the cage, Sissy sits upon the double bed. Gradually, she reclines. "No Indian blankets," she notes. "No Indian blankets." And that is the last thought she has before she blacks out.

Two hours pass before she is awakened — by a sound softer than a cheep. It is the sound of buttons passing through buttonholes. Buttons that have not breathed freely in three days are sighing with relief, their yokes lifted, their nooses loosened. One by one, button necks are freed from the trap that is the fate of most buttons the way that compromises are the fate of most men. Soon Sissy cannot only hear button liberation; she can feel it.

Someone is undressing her.

And it is not Julian Gitche.

24.

"WHERE ARE THE OTHERS?" asked Sissy, in a voice webby with sleep.

"Oh, Rupert and Carla had a little hassle and went home," said Howard.

"Julian fell asleep on the couch; we covered him up," said Marie.

"We thought that we should make you comfortable, too," said Howard.

"Yes, dear," said Marie. "We've been watching you here sleeping and you looked so sweet. We thought we should help you get comfy for the night."

Sissy thought that quite considerate of the Barths. They were a couple as amicable as they were handsome. She did wonder, however, why they were both in their underwear.

Between the two of them, they had her out of her dress in no time.

"There, isn't that better?" inquired Marie.

"Yes, thanks," said Sissy. She did feel more comfortable, but she also felt as if she should apologize for not having on a brassiere. Bra hooks can test the most agile of thumbs, as many a frustrated boy will testify, and Sissy had been unable to wear that garment whose name in French means, enigmatically, "arm protector," since she had left her mama. Light seeping in from a crack in the bathroom door gave a strawberry sheen to her gumdrop-shaped nipples. She hoped she wasn't embarrassing these nice people.

Oh my goodness, she must have been, for in a second Marie slipped out of her own brassiere — in an effort, obviously, to make Sissy feel less conspicuous.

Marie moved her bare bosom close to Sissy's. The two sets of nipples stiffened in formal greeting, like diplomats from small nations. "Mine are fuller but yours are more perfectly shaped," observed Marie. She leaned closer. The envoys exchanged state secrets.

"Highly debatable," said Howard. "I'll wager they're the exact same size." Judiciously, in the spirit of fair play that characterizes his profession, he cupped his left hand about a Marie breast and his right about one of Sissy's.

He weighed them in his palms, squeezed them the way an honest grocer squeezes excess water from a lettuce, let his spread fingers sample their circumference. "Hmmm. Yours *are* larger, Marie, but Miss Hankshaw's — Sissy's — are more firm. You'd think they would have started to droop; I mean, from not wearing a bra."

"Howard! Watch your manners. You've made her blush. Here, Sissy, let *me* compare." Marie seized Sissy's free breast, quickly, like a monkey picking a fruit, rolling it about in her hungry little fingers, rubbing it against her chin and cheeks.

Now, Sissy became more awake. Consciousness returned and when it unpacked its bags, there was suspicion in them. She shouldn't be staying, uninvited, in the bedroom of an ill man with whom she'd scarcely spoken. She ought to get back to the Countess's. Did Mr. and Mrs. Barth have her best interests at heart? She had been so relieved to get out of that dress that she hadn't considered hanky-panky. She wondered if this friendly couple could be up to something?

Her question was answered by a hand — she was not sure whose — creeping into her panties. She tried to turn away from its probings, but her cunt, without her knowledge or permission, had grown quite slippery, and a finger fell into it almost as if by accident.

Lowered steadily, like a flag at sunset, her panties were soon below her knees. She thought she felt a second finger slish into her pussy, but before that could be confirmed, still another finger muscled up her asshole . . . and . . . ohhh. It was like her early days as a hitch-hiker. It was nostalgic; it was disgusting; it was . . . ohhh.

Philosophers, poets, painters and scholars, debate all you want on the nature of beauty!

Tropical plums. Wine in a rowboat. Clouds, babies and Buddhas, resembling one another. Bicycle bells. Honeysuckle. Parachutes. Shooting stars seen through lace curtains. A silver radio that attracts butterflies; a déjà that just won't quit vuing. Han-shan wrote, after a moment of ecstasy, "This place is finer than the place I live!"

Across Sissy's lips passed Marie's tongue, then Howard's tongue, then Marie's titty, then Howard's . . . then Howard's . . . Howard's . . . !!! One by one, like apartments in a new high-rise, orifices were being filled.

Anima mixed with animus. It was Marie who was climbing her, sliding around on her, pulling down her own panties with a wild hand. Marie nuzzled Sissy's calves, then her thighs. Marie's mouth, oozing hot saliva, apparently had a destination. But before it could be reached, Howard entered his wife from the rear.

Ah, sir penis, that old show-stopper! Chalk up another stolen scene for the one-eyed matinée idol. Marie could not suck for groaning.

Like a disc jockey from Paradise, Howard flipped Marie over and played her B side. Every now and again, he reached for Sissy, attempting to include her, but certain laws of physics insisted on being obeyed. Over and over, Marie called Sissy's name, but her eyes were half-closed and her caresses blind and scattered.

The Barths were really going at it. It would tax a day's output at the Countess's factory to quell the spreading funk in that room. Marie was kind of yowling, sounding so much like a cat that the poodle in the kitchen began to grrr. God knows what the birds in their cage were thinking.

"So this is what it's like," thought Sissy. Fascinated, she propped herself up on her elbows to observe. Often she had imagined the act, but she was never entirely sure she imagined it correctly, not even after that evening of embracing Kerouac in a Colorado corn field. "So this is what it's *really* like." The Great Secret could be returned to its bottle. Perceptual transformations were no longer necessary. This truly *was* educational.

In truth, Sissy found it more interesting than the canoe races at LaConner, Washington, more interesting than the San Andreas Fault, or Niagara Falls, or Bonnie and Clyde State Park, or Tapioca State Pudding — of course, Sissy never was one for sightseeing. She even found it more interesting than the Tobacco Festival, although not so much a challenge to the wiles of her thumbs.

Before the performance was over, however, and to Howard and Marie's dismay, Sissy debedded on a particularly high bounce and walked out. She pattered to the living room couch and crawled under the cover with Julian. There she stayed three days.

25.

THEY HAD a lot to talk about.

Julian was still in his formal trousers, cummerbund attached, while Sissy was nude as she had ever been, and was smeared, besides, with those feminine juices, both her own and Marie's, that gave the Countess nose trouble — but the sofa-mates refused to let those differences stand in their way; they had a lot to talk about and there were larger differences than dress.

It would seem that Julian Gitche had dealt with the world by combining pigment with water in varying viscosities and making it spread, leak, splash, pour, spray, soak or fold onto a chosen paper format in selected tones, hues, volumes, shapes and lines. Sissy Hankshaw had dealt with the world by hitchhiking with a dedication, perspective and style such as the world had never seen. It was as befuddling to Sissy that an Indian would spend his life painting genteel watercolors in a bourgeois milieu as it was mind-wrenching to Julian that a bright, pretty, if slightly afflicted, young woman with a promising modeling career would spend hers endlessly hitchhiking.

"You have a romantic concept of Indians," said Julian. "They are people, like any other; a people whose time has passed. I see no virtue in wallowing in the past, especially a past that was more often miserable than not. I am a Mohawk Indian in the same sense that Spiro Agnew is a Greek: a descendant, nothing more. And believe me, the Mohawk never approximated the glory that was Greece. My grandfather was one of the first Mohawks to work as a steel-rigger in New York City; you know Mohawks are used extensively on skyscraper construction because they have no fear of height. My dad helped build the Empire State Building. Later, he founded his own steeplejack service, and despite prejudices against him by the unions and so forth for being an uppity redskin, he made a great deal of money. Enough to send me to Yale. I have a masters degree in fine arts and fairly good connections in Manhattan art circles. Primitive cultures, Indian or otherwise, hold a minimum of attraction for me. I cherish the firm order of symmetry that marks Western civilization off from the more heterogeneous, random societies in an imperfect world."

In the limited space of the sofa, Sissy turned over, dinging one of her Howard-and-Marie accentuated nipples against one of Julian's shirt studs. "I don't know anything about this order and symmetry business. I'm a high school dropout from a race — the Poor White Trash race — that has done nothing for ten centuries but pick up rocks, hoe weeds, sweat in factories and march off to war whenever told to; and each generation has begot a smaller potato patch. But I've spent some time in libraries, not all of it asleep, and I have learned this: every civilized culture in history has discriminated against its abnormal members. 'Schizophrenia' is a civilized Western term, and so are 'witch' and 'misfit' — terms used to rationalize the cruel and unusual punishments doled out to extraordinary people. Yet the American Indian tribes, as you ought to know, treated their freaks as special beings. *Their* schizoids were recognized as having a gift, the power of visions, and were revered for it. The physically deformed were also regarded as favorites of the Great Spirit, welcome reliefs to the monotony of anatomical regularity, and everybody loved them, enjoyed them and paid them favor. In that ancient Greece that you find so glorious, somebody like me would have been killed at birth."

"Now, Sissy, you're being overly sensitive and defensive. You saw how you were treated last night by my highly civilized friends. Why, not one of us even looked at your . . . your . . . your . . . thumbs."

"Exactly my point," said Sissy.

And so that argument went. The other one went something like this.

"Aside from everything else, Sissy, I fail to see how you've even survived. My God! A girl, alone, on the roads, for years. And not killed or injured or outraged or taken sick."

"Women are tough and rather coarse. They were built for the raw, crude work of bearing children. You'd be amazed at what they can do when they divert that baby-hatching energy into some other enterprise."

"Okay, that may well be true. But what an enterprise! Hitchhiking. Bumming rides. I think of hitchhiking I think of college kids, servicemen and penniless hippies. I think of punks in oily denims and maniacs with butcher knives hidden in their wad of rumpled belongings . . ."

"I've been told that I looked like an angel beside the highway."

"Oh, I'm sure you are a beautiful exception to the rule. But why? Why bother? You've traveled your whole life without destination. You move but you have no direction."

"What is the 'direction' of the Earth in its journey; where are the atoms 'going' when they spin?"

"There's an orderly pattern, some ultimate purpose in the movements of Nature. You've been constantly on the move for nearly twelve years. Tell me one thing that you've proven."

"I've proven that people aren't trees, so it is false when they speak of roots."

"Aimless . . ."

"Not aimless. Not in the least. It's just that my aims are different from most. There are plenty of aimless people on the road, all right. People who hitchhike from kicks to kicks, restlessly, searching for something: looking for America, as Jack Kerouac put it, or looking for themselves, or looking for some relation between America and themselves. But I'm not looking for anything. I've *found* something."

"What is it that you've found?"

"Hitchhiking."

That stopped Julian for a while, but on the second day, long after Howard and Marie had tiptoed out of his apartment, he returned to the subject. He could not appreciate Sissy's accomplishments. So what if she had once flagged down thirty-four cars in succession without a miss? What merit in the feat of crossing Texas blindfolded in cyclone season with a parakeet on her thumb? He viewed such deeds as pathetically, sophomorically, wanton. He shook his unpainted and featherless head sadly when he considered the police record (arrests for vagrancy, illegal solicitation of rides and, ironically, suspicion of prostitution) of an essentially respectable woman.

So effectively did he chide her about it that a vaguely guilty gloom arrived in her eyes, its cold feet shuffling in the dampness there. He wrung sniffles out of her, and when she was appropriately unhappy, he comforted her. He held her tightly in protective arms, built a castle around her, dug a moat, raised the drawbridge. Only her mama had ever held her like that, cooing in her ear. He petted her with poodle-petting hands, hands so soft they could get splinters from eating with chopsticks. He cuddled her as if she were an infant. He insulated her bare wires. And she, Sissy, who had slept in the excesses of every season, uncared for and without a care, snuggled down deeply in Julian's paternal tenderness and let herself be coddled.

It was at this point — Julian cooing, Sissy purring — that the magic that had attended her thumbs from the moment in her youth when she first made her commitment to a life less shallow, safe and small than our society demands of us, excused itself, tiptoed out of the apartment like Howard and Marie and strolled down to Stanley's Bar on Avenue B for a beer.

Beer does not satisfy magic, however. So the magic ordered a round of Harvey Wallbangers. But it takes more than vodka to fuel magic. It takes risks. It takes EXTREMES.

Cowgirl Interlude (Delores del Ruby)

Some folks said she had scaled a convent wall in San Antonio and run away with a Mexican circus. Others claimed she had been the favored daughter of a prominent Creole family in New Orleans, until she got mixed up with an alligator cult that practiced peyoteism. Still others said she was Gypsy, through and through, while one source insisted that — like so many "Spanish" dancers — she was actually Italian or Jewish, and had picked up her routines watching Zorro on television in the Bronx.

One thing all the cowgirls agreed on, however, was that their forewoman flicked an educated lash, so none disputed the story that she had acquired her first whip when she was five years old, a gift from an uncle who had said, upon presentation, "Spare the rod and spoil the child."

The day Delores del Ruby arrived at the Rubber Rose, a snake crawled across the dusty road that led to the ranch, carrying a card under its forked tongue. The card was the queen of spades.

26.

EACH TIME HE GOT UP, whether it was to go to the bathroom or feed his pets, Julian had removed an article of clothing, so that now, on the third day of their sofaing, he was nearly as naked as she.

The smack of kisses sounded with increasing frequency in the room; discussions and naps were of shorter duration. After she had broken down and surrendered to his protective ministrations, the last faint traces of his asthma evaporated like moth pee off a sixty-watt bulb and he found himself host to an erection.

Sissy knew just how to entertain it. She had been recently educated. She stroked it. She pushed its hood back. She ringed its rosy. She let it throb alongside her thigh, and better yet, alongside her thumb. She maneuvered herself beneath it and guided its crabapple noggin through the seam in her being. Like a bullet of thick fish meat, it went to target.

Alas, Julian's chimes rang before the appointed hour. He was subjected to a sudden attack of the old premature. And Sissy was left with her virginity intact, throttling a sticky wicket. Gitche *Goo*mee!

The watercolorist apologized with downcast eyes. It was Sissy's turn to comfort. She reassured him so convincingly that he soon cheered up and began to chatter again about such wonders as Shakespeare and Edward Albee, Michelangelo and Marc Chagall. "It is the measure of Western civilization," said he, "that it can encompass in harmony, balance off, as it were, such divergent masterworks as *A Midsummer Night's Dream* and *The American Dream,* as the dome of the Sistine Chapel and the ceiling of the Paris Opera."

Sissy sat up. Her eyes moped about the apartment, looking at but not seeing the macramé wallhangings, the volumes of Robert Frost.

"What's the matter?" asked Julian.

After a while Sissy answered. "I'm cold," she said.

"Here. I'll turn down the air conditioner."

"It's not the air conditioner that's making me cold."

"Oh . . . Well, what is it? Is it . . . me?" Eyes downcast again.

"It's the piano."

"The piano? You don't like my white piano? Well, if you'd prefer, I mean, if you'll be coming here often — and I hope you shall — I suppose I can have it removed. Might as well. I play badly. I've studied for years but I'm rotten. The Countess says I'm the first Indian in history to be scalped by Beethoven. Ha ha."

"It's not the piano."

"Oh . . . What is it then? Me?"

"It's the books."

"The books?"

"No. It's the paintings."

"The paintings? My watercolors? Well, I do use lots of blues and greens."

"No, it's not your paintings."

"Not my paintings?"

"It's the *stillness.*"

"My home is too quiet for you?" asked Julian incredulously, for he could plainly hear Puerto Ricans beating garbage cans in the next block.

"Not quiet. *Still.* Nothing moves in here. Not even your birds."

Sissy stood. The Countess had sent a flunky by with her rucksack, and now she walked to it.

"What are you doing?"

"Getting dressed. I've got to go."

"But I don't want you to leave. Please stay. We can go to dinner. I owe you a dinner. And tonight . . . we can . . . really make love."

"I have to go, Julian."

"Why? Why do you have to go?"

"My thumbs hurt."

"Oh, I'm sorry. Is it something usual? What can we do for them?"

"I've made a mistake. I've been negligent. I haven't exercised. I have to hitchhike a little bit every day, no matter what. It's like a musician practicing his scales. When I don't practice, my timing gets off, my thumbs get stiff and sore."

To that, Julian could not respond. Sissy Hankshaw was one of those mysteries that drop onto Earth unasked, and perhaps undeserved, like grace — like clockworks. His ancestors might have known what to do with her, but Julian Gitche did not. All of a sudden her presence seemed completely outside his frame of reference. His apartment was no longer static when she moved about it; tall, jump-suited, globs of air orbiting her like planets of musical roses. She caused sculptures to sway on their pedestals. The bedroom birdies came alive and flitted in their cage. It was incomprehensible to Julian that he had presumed to be her consoling daddy a few short hours before.

Julian had a poodle named Butterfinger, named for the candy bar that F. Scott Fitzgerald was eating when he fell dead of a coronary surprise. Julian called him Butty for short.

Butty had every fault known to dog. He was a face-licker and crotch-sniffer, a hair-shedder and corner-crapper, a shoe-chewer and guest-nipper, a garden-digger and cat-intimidator, a nylon-snagger and chair-muddyer, a scrap-begger and lap-crawler, a car-chaser and shrub-defiler, a bath-hater and air-polluter, a garbage-raider and leghumper and, moreover, a yapper in that shrill, spoiled, obnoxious yap-style to which poodles alone may lay claim.

(Sissy, unlike most humans who travel on foot — subject to the bites and barks of canine fancy — was not a dog-hater per se; the wild dingo of Australia had her sincerest respect.)

Butty was yapping as Sissy left Julian's apartment. For once, it may have been a tolerable sound. Because of the yapping, Julian could not hear her hurrying, almost sprinting, down the stairs; Sissy could not hear the wheeze that struggled out of Julian's lungs like a wimpy wind that blew between their worlds.

The magic caught up with her on Fourteenth Street as she headed for the George Washington Bridge.

27.

THE COUNTESS was practicing dental karate. Chop chop chop. His Princess telephone was in imminent danger of being incapacitated by a blow from the teeth.

"So she left town," he said — chop chop. "Well, that shouldn't surprise you. Leaving town is what Sissy is all about. But tell me, how did she strike you?"

"Extraordinary!"

"She's obviously that. Jesus! Which would you rather have, a million dollars or one of Sissy's thumbs full of pennies?"

"Oh you! I'm not talking about her hands. They're difficult to ignore, I confess, but I'm speaking of her whole being. Her whole being is extraordinary. The way she talks, for example. She's so *articulate*."

"It's high time you realized, honey babe, that a woman doesn't have to give the best years of her life to Radcliffe or Smith in order to speak the English language. What's more, those intellectual college girls have got the odor as bad as any others. Worse, I suspect. One healthy waitress probably uses more Yoni Yum each week than the entire dean's list at Wellesley." Chop!

Julian sighed. "I wouldn't know about that," he said. "But she *is* extraordinary. I don't understand her in the least, yet I'm helplessly attracted. Countess, I'm really in a dither. She's turned my head."

"Ninety degrees to the left, I hope." Chop clack click. "How does she feel about you?"

Another wheezy sigh. "I think she's disappointed that I'm not more, ah, sort of atavistic. She's got some naïve, sentimental notions about Indians. I'm sure she liked me, though; she gave me many indications that she liked me. But . . . then she left town."

"She *always* leaves town, you dummy. That doesn't mean anything. What about in bed? Does she like it in bed?"

Evel Knievel's motorcycle could not have jumped over the pause that followed. Finally, Julian asked, "How did she like what in bed?"

"Like *what?*" Chop!! Clack!! "What do you think?"

"Well . . . er . . ."

"Shit O dear, Julian. Do you mean to tell me you spent three days together and you didn't get it on?"

"Oh, we got it on. But you might say we didn't get it *all the way* on."

"Whose fault was that?"

"I suppose it was mine. Yes, it definitely was my fault."

"In a way I'm relieved it wasn't hers. I've been worried about her psychological virginity. Only now I'm concerned about *you.* What do they do to you boys in those Ivy League schools, anyway? Strap you down and pump the Nature out of you? That's what they do, all right. They can even press the last drop of Nature out of a Mohawk buck. Why, send a shaman or a cannibal to Yale for four years and all he'd be fit for would be a desk in the military-industrial complex and a seat in the third row at a Neil Simon comedy. Jesus H. M. S. Christ! If Harvard or Princeton could get hold of the Chink for a couple of semesters they'd turn him into a candidate for the Bow Tie Wing of the Hall of Wimps. Oogie boogie."

"You needn't stoop to reverse snobbism just because Ol' Miss was the only university in the nation that would take you in. If we Ivy Leaguers aren't earthy enough to suit you hillbillies, at least we don't go around indulging in racist terms such as 'Chink.' Next thing I know, you'll be calling me 'chief.' "

" 'Chink' is the guy's name, for Christ's sake."

"What guy?"

"Aw, he's some old fart who lives in the hills out West. Gives my ranch the creeps, and the willies, too. But though he be old and dirty, he's alive, I'll bet, clear down to his toes. They don't have his juice in a jar in New Haven. That prissy alma mater of yours could pluck the hair off a werewolf. Better Sissy keep her virginity than lose it to the strains of 'The Whiffenpoof Song.' "

"Sex isn't everything, just because it keeps you in business. And speaking of your business, you'd *better* be concerned. Because that mysterious model of yours has got me too upset to paint."

"You'll paint, all right, sweetie-poo. You'll paint because you're under contract to paint. Moreover, you'll paint better than you've ever painted before. Nothing like a little suffering to put some backbone into art. Has she got you smoking and drinking? Good! Creativity feeds on poisons. All great artists have been depraved. Look at me! As sure as Raoul Dufy is peeing over the side of Eternity's sailboat, this little affaire is going to inspire the finest watercolors of your career. Now, tell that goddamned poodle of yours to quit whimpering and you get in there and paint!"

"That's not the poodle."

"Oh," said the Countess. "Well shit O dear. Just hold on, you hear. Don't go getting asthmatic. We can write her a letter, if you'd like. Send copies to Taos, LaConner, Pine Ridge, Pleasant Point, Cherokee and that other place. I'll pick up some Ripple and come right over."

The eyes of the sky's potato have seldom looked down on such a frantic epistolary collaboration as occurred that night.

28.

THE CHINK is right: life is essentially playful.

Of course, it plays a bit rough at times.

Maybe life is like a baby gorilla. It doesn't know its own strength.

Life was mashing the big fat drops out of Julian Gitche and Sissy Hankshaw. They had chipmunk festivals inside their stomachs and the fillings in their teeth were picking up signals from sentimental radio. Life is forever pulling this number on men and women, and then acting surprised and innocent, as it it didn't realize it was *hurting* anybody.

On the surface, to the untrained eye, Sissy was hitchhiking as well as she ever had. She had even developed some new wrinkles. Such as using both thumbs at once, addressing one appendage to the far lanes of traffic while causing the other to beckon wittily to the cars passing closest to roadside. She had also perfected a high bouncing roll to the left, comparable to the "American twist" service in tennis. It was flashy but there was no real joy in it, no substance or spontaneity. It was what is known as a virtuoso performance. It lacked soul. You know. Show biz is teeming with performers like that, all of them with more tiles in their swimming pools than you or I have.

A sense of urgency had crept into her style. Whereas in the past Sissy had kept up her astonishing pace out of sheer exhilaration at being unique and being free, she now kept going because she was afraid to stop. For when biological necessities did force her to stop, time and space, which she had heretofore held in abeyance (as if she were some clockworks personified), fell in on her in a gravitational rush. Time and space fell in on her like a set of encyclopedias falling off a missionary's shelf onto a pygmy. And time brought along its secretary, memory, and space brought its brat, loneliness.

In the past, she had been subjected to ridicule, pity, awe and lust. Now, she was being subjected to tenderness and need. It was better and worse. As do many strong people, she had fallen victim to the tyranny of the weak.

As for Julian, he took to swilling Scotch. In the mornings. Before he had even had his Mother of God Wheat Flakes (or was it his Joyce Carol Oats?) One night he went to Max's Kansas City and created a minor ruckus by yelling, in a wheezy voice, "Jackson Pollock was a fraud!" A sculptor, hardly making an effort, bloodied his nose; and a perverted biology student followed him home because he thought Julian had said Pollock was a *frog.* (In New York, my dears, there are all kinds.) He listened to Tchaikovsky and stopped combing his hair.

Sometimes one gets the idea that life thinks it's still living in Paris in the thirties.

29.

JULIAN GITCHE's letter caught up with Sissy Hankshaw in Cherokee, North Carolina, on Christmas Eve. She picked it up at 11:00 A.M., just before the post office closed for the holiday. After reading it twice, she escorted it into a honky-tonk (where aghast drunks reacted to her thumbs as if they were the hellish little reindeer of some kind of anti-Santa Claus) and read it again. The Countess had advanced her four hundred dollars when she got to New York back in the summer and she had enough left to buy a bottle of wine. She chose red Ripple, for old times' sake, and promptly spilled some on the letter. While a jukeboxed Bing Crosby crooned "I'm Dreaming of a White Christmas," a postage-stamp Ike grinned his I-made-it-all-the-way-to-the-top-but-I-still-don't-understand grin through a puddle of wine. Under the plastic mistletoe, pool balls kissed. Blue lights winked from a metallic silver tree. Vulgarity called, and was answered.

Halfway through the Ripple, Sissy got up to go to the toilet and went to the phone booth instead.

Julian, holding back wheezes with a herculean effort, told her that he loved her. She protested that he didn't even know her. Abandoning all that he'd been taught at Yale, he replied that feeling was superior to knowledge.

"I love you," Julian said.

"You're a fool," said Sissy.

"I'm offering love and you're rejecting it. Maybe *you* are the fool."

Well!

A week after New Year's, she hitched into Manhattan. With the Countess, who despised the way men behaved and women smelled, as their sarcastic witness, Sissy and Julian went to the Little Church of the Positive Thought and were married by a protégé of Dr. Norman Vincent Peale's.

Thus ended for all practical purposes what the author knows to be one of the most remarkable and least understood careers in human history.

But a career, however unusual, is not a story. And Sissy's story, dovetailing as it does with the stories of the Rubber Rose cowgirls and the clockworks Chink, and disclosing as it does the possible pancake beneath the sluggish syrup and slippery butter of life, is far from ended.

Cowgirl Interlude (Bing)

Under an orchard tree, drooping with cherries, cowgirls lay in the shade. They fed each other fruit. Dark juice dribbled into dimples. Cherry meat stained smiles and nostrils.

Kathy was embroidering a rainbow on the back of Heather's work-shirt. Inspired, Linda rendered an all-red rainbow on Debbie's bare waist, and Kym, dipping slightly below the belt, added the pot of gold. Cherry paint.

Fruit goo began to attract flies, so the cowgirls imitated their hobbled horses and brushed them away by flinging their hair. A cloud chugged by. If it was not gone by sunset, it would be painted, too.

The forewoman, Delores del Ruby, was away from the ranch on a peyote run. Big Red was acting forewoman, and she was permitting the hands a very extended break. The goats in their charge were straying far and wide, and as for the birds, they could not be seen from the cherry tree.

Placing her New Testament back in her saddlebag, Mary asked, "Pardners, do you think this is honest, goofing off like this?"

"I don't care if it's honest if it's fun," said Big Red.

"I don't care if it's fun if it's real," said Kym.

"I don't even care if it's real," said Debbie. Not everyone knew what she meant.

30.

If you could buckle your Bugs Bunny wristwatch to a ray of light, your watch would continue ticking but its hands wouldn't move.

That's because at the speed of light there is no time. Time is relative to velocity. At high speeds, time is literally stretched. Since light is the ultimate in velocity, at light-speed time is stretched to its absolute and becomes static. Albert Einstein figured that one out. There's no need to hang around the clockworks and bug the Chink about it.

Assuming that our brains will get off their fat butts, for a change, and play cosmic ball with us, allowing us to fully comprehend *no time,* then we might try to picture (if "picture" is the right word) what Einstein meant when he defined "space" as "love."

Einstein knew a lot about space — he determined, for example, that beyond the expanding volume of the universe space ceases to exist, and so we have *no space* to contend with as well as *no time* — and he may have had some special insights into love, as well. The first of his two marriages was a mess, however. Einstein wed a girl with a physical defect.

It was some sort of crazy limp that plagued Mileva Marić, some eccentricity of the foot. A few days after the civil ceremony in Zurich, one of young Einstein's friends confessed, "I should never have the courage to marry a woman unless she were absolutely sound." Well, for all that fellow might have known, it could have been the daily contemplation of Mileva's wild toes that led Einstein to perceive the wondrous workings of Nature in a way that no other scientist ever had.

But never mind. We know for a fact that it took more than a sardine of courage for the watercolorist Julian Gitche to marry the "unsound" Sissy Hankshaw. The union altered his life almost as drastically as it altered hers.

Good-by to dinner parties. Sissy was clumsy with silverware and, as previously noted, had a tendency to slosh the wine. Invitations were routinely refused, never extended. Julia Child was overtaken by dust. They gnawed Colonel Sanders drumsticks and Big Mac burgers in their apartment, alone. Julian began to complain of his stomach. Grease was giving him ulcers, he said. Sitting at the kitchen table, beneath the paper imitation Tiffany lampshade, he would peer into the hot slit of a taco and wonder who was dining that night at Elaine's.

While her husband painted, Sissy would stare out the windows at traffic. Or she would leaf through the motoring magazines that she brought regularly at newsstands, although Julian, a nondriver, vowed he'd never own a car. Her thumbs ached, and in order to relieve them, she took to imaginary hitchhiking, the game she'd played as a small child. She hitchhiked curtain-bottoms creeping on windowsills. She hitchhiked the black shadow thrown by the white piano. Cockroaches scurried when the bathroom light went on — she tried to flag them down. This return to girlhood beginnings amused her, kept her calm. Julian was sensitive enough to recognize its value to their relationship, although the peculiarity of it caused nervous coughs to punch the bags of his lungs.

She was a ratty housekeeper. She hadn't the experience or the aptitude. So Julian, on top of his picture-making, his conferences with art dealers, collectors and advertising men, had to attend to domestic chores. When he washed dishes, Sissy, a bit embarrassed, would retire to the bedroom to chat with the birds. The birds and Sissy had real rapport. Was it an interest in "freedom of movement" that they had in commom?

One Sunday, the newlyweds went together to the Museum of the American Indian on One hundred fifty-fifth Street. It was Sissy's idea. There was nothing displayed from the Siwash, not even a bead. On the way home, they quarreled.

At least once a week, Howard and Marie dropped in (Rupert and Carla had separated) to play Botticelli and discuss the international situation, which was desperate, as usual. Occasionally, one or the other of them, Howard or Marie, would catch Sissy alone (she was inclined to wander away from the group) and try to kiss her and prowl in her clothes. It wasn't right, but it made more sense to her than politics or Botticelli.

A certain amount of morbid gossip spread about the couple: the elegant and talented Mohawk, the lovely and deformed Yoni Yum/Dew Girl (revealed at last!). Sissy was immune, but the stories made Julian squirm. When questioned about his wife's background, he would lie that the small amount of hitchhiking she had done had been part of a publicity stunt dreamed up by the Countess. Later, he would feel guilty for denying her, and she took his guilt for discontent.

Nights in bed, and mornings, too, beneath blankets no Indian loomed, the strange tensions of their relationship dissolved in tenderness and passion. They caressed one another until their hides shone.

They embraced until their 206 bones squeaked like mice. Their bed was a boat in a weird sea.

If space is love, Professor, then is love space? Or is love something we use to *fill* space? If time eats the doughnut, does love eat the hole?

31.

THERE WAS SOMEONE at the door. The buzzer was carrying on like a maraca with a crush on a June bug. It must be the Countess.

As if the Gitches weren't subjected to pressures enough, there was the bitching of the Countess.

No one recognized more lucidly than the Countess the heroism of Sissy's attempt at normal womanhood; no one could list more completely than he the sacrifices Julian made for his marriage (The painter had gone so far as to get rid of his poodle). Still, the Countess couldn't resist digging at them, mocking their motives. Perhaps he suffered the secret shame of those men who dam rivers and break horses. The Countess, after all, had initiated the marriage that had "tamed" Sissy Hankshaw — and all he had to show for his meddling with freedom was the hollow prize of the marriage itself, and another successful advertising campaign: Julian's watercolors were at least the rage that Sissy's poses once had been.

It was the middle of September. The marriage was nine months old. The evening before, they had had such a spat that it took most of the night to patch things. On this morning they were enjoying a fragile, vulnerable happiness. They surely didn't need the Countess's cynical stick stirring things up.

The instant he crossed their threshold, however, it was apparent that the Countess hadn't called merely to indulge himself. He was waving his cigarette holder like a brakeman's lantern; his dentures were chasing his words the way Tom chased Jerry.

"Sissy, Sissy, blushing bride, you can desist from wearing paths in these oaken floors. The Countess has arrived with a job for you, and what a job . . ."

"A job for *me?*"

"Don't interrupt your elders, particularly if they're royal. A job for you, yes. I am once more about to make advertising history. And only you, the original Yoni Yum/Dew Girl, could possibly assist me. Julian, knock it off! Wipe that wounded rabbit look off your face. And if you emit so much as one wheeze, I'll chop you right out of my totem pole. This assignment will in no way interfere with our water-color campaign. It has eighteen months to run, as you know, and if you're a good little Injun I may renew your contract. No, this project isn't for magazines at all. I'm going to film a commercial such as television has never seen."

"But you haven't used a TV spot in years," protested Julian. "I thought you were through with the tube."

"A countess is entitled to change her mind. Shit O dear, I've *got* to go back to TV. I've no choice anymore. Didn't you read about it in the papers? Those bleeding-heart do-gooders in the government are out to ruin me! Listen to this."

From one of the many folds in his crumpled linen suit, the Countess removed a newspaper clipping and commenced to read:

> WASHINGTON (UPI) — The Food and Drug Administration (FDA) said Wednesday female deodorant sprays are medically and hygienically worthless, and may cause such harmful reactions as blisters, burns and rashes.
>
> It proposed a warning label on each can of spray to tell the consumer:
>
> "Caution: For external use only. Spray at least eight inches from skin. Use sparingly and not more than once daily to avoid irritation. Do not use this product with a sanitary napkin. Do not apply to broken, irritated or itching skin. Persistent or unusual odor may indicate the presence of a condition for which a physician should be consulted. If a rash, irritation, unusual vaginal discharge or discomfort develops, discontinue use immediately and consult a physician."
>
> In addition to the warning label, the products would not be allowed to make claims on the label for medical or hygienic value.
>
> The agency said it acted because it has been receiving complaints from consumers, some of whom suffered more serious problems after the initial irritation or rash.
>
> "Although FDA judges that the reported reactions are not sufficient to justify removal of these products from the market, they are considered sufficient to warrant the proposed mandatory label warnings," it added.

"Shit O dear, that's enough to make *me* asthmatic. The nerve of those twits. What do they know about female odor? None of those politicos sleeps with his wife. They all go to whores and whores know how to take care of themselves. They're my best customers. I'll bet Ralph Nader is behind this. Why he's probably got his kiddie corps of Ivy League law students out inspecting vaginas from coast to coast, looking for fresh blisters and unusual discharges. It's an affront to a Christian nation. I'm the one who's trying to clean things up, rid the human race of its most pagan stench. But do you think those dupes understand that? And after my sizable contribution to the President's campaign fund! I'm going to bend ears in the White House about this. I'll get action, too; you wait and see. They accepted my donation, so they're aware they'd better serve my interests or I'll buy some leadership that will. These swine are not the pearls I've dreamed of.

"But it'll take time, precious time, to head off this FDA plot. The government moves slower than a candied turd. So, meanwhile, to offset their monkey business, I plan to hit TV with a commercial that'll spin eyeballs and win hearts by the millions. Don't interrupt!

"Here's my concept. You know about my ranch out West? It's a beauty ranch. Oh, it's got a few head of cattle for atmosphere and tax purposes. But it's a beauty ranch, a place where unhappy women — divorcées and widows, mainly — can go to lose weight, remove wrinkles, change their hair styles and pretty themselves up for the next disappointment. You've heard of such places, surely. Only my ranch is different. It does some real good. My staff teaches its clients how to take care of their more intimate beauty problems, the problems swish salons don't dare tackle, the problems other health spas ignore. You know the ones I mean. Why, my ranch is named the Rubber Rose, after the Rubber Rose douche bag, my own invention, and bless its little red bladder, the most popular douche bag in the world.

"So get this. There's a worthless marshy lake at one end of the ranch. It's on the migratory flight path of the whooping cranes. The last flock of wild whooping cranes left in existence. Well, these cranes stop off at my little pond — Siwash Lake, it's called — twice a year, autumn and spring, and spend a few days each time, resting up, eating, doing whatever whooping cranes do. I've never seen them, understand, but I hear they're magnificent. Very big specimens — I mean, *huge* mothers — and white as snow, to coin a phrase, except for black tips on their wings and tail feathers, and bright red heads. Now, whooping cranes, in case you didn't know it, are noted for their mating dance. It's just the wildest show in nature. It's probably the reason why birdwatching used to be so popular with old maids and deacons. Picture these rare, beautiful, gigantic birds in full dance — leaping six feet off the mud, arching their backs, flapping their wings, strutting low to the ground. Dears, it's overwhelming. And now picture those birds doing their sex dance on TV. Right there on the home screen, creation's most elaborate sex ritual — yet clean and pure enough to suit the Pope. With lovely Sissy Hankshaw — pardon me, Sissy Gitche — in the foreground. In a white gown, red hood attached, and big feathery sleeves trimmed in black. In a very subdued imitation of the female whooping crane, she dance/walks over to a large nest in which there sits a can of Yoni Yum. And a can of Dew. Off-camera, a string quartet is playing Debussy. A sensuous voice is reading a few poetic lines about courtship and love. Are you starting to get it? Doesn't it make the hair on your neck stand up and applaud? My very goodness gracious!"

Julian was impressed, and Sissy, although she sensed that the big sleeves on her costume would be designed to conceal her hands, was pleased. Scratching his jaw-stubble with his cigarette holder, the Countess went on.

"Grandiose, lyrical, erotic and Girl Scout-oriented; you can't top it. Needless to say, however, it isn't going to be easy. Say, do you happen to have any Ripple on ice? I've hired a crew of experts from Walt Disney Studios, the best wildlife cinematographers around. No Ripple; a pity. Forget it; Scotch won't do. Ugh! Didn't know I spoke Indian, did you, Julian?

"Now, I realize that you two are wallowing in a quagmire of marital bliss, and I hate to pry you apart even for a few weeks. But the deal is, the Disney boys will be heading for Dakota any day now to start setting up; these whooping cranes don't like human beings even a tiny bit — probably have a keen sense of smell, poor birds — and the camera crew has to build blinds and disguise its equipment; this is very tricky business. Well, I want Sissy out there within a week. She must meet the crew and familiarize herself with the unusual requirements of the job. The cranes show up at the lake anywhere from late September to late October. You never know from one year to the next, and we've got to be ready, have everything down pat when they do arrive. Got it?

"Also, Sissy sugar, you can do me a personal favor out there. As if I weren't already as busy as a fiddler's bitch, I've got to go down to Washington, D.C., and sic my boys in the White House on those FDA yokels. I won't get out to Dakota until the last minute. So I'd like you to look the Rubber Rose over real carefully, if you would, and report on what's happening there. I've been having some trouble on that ranch and I could use inside information."

Julian's eyes narrowed. "What kind of trouble?" he asked.

"It's a long story," said the Countess, his dentures thrashing in his oral cavity like two hard-shelled marine animals attempting to mate in a pocket of pink coral. "It's a long story and no decent drink to wet it with. Well, I'll try to make it snappy. Sometime ago a cute little hellion, a teen-ager from Kansas City who was dying to be a cowgirl, found out about the Rubber Rose and soft-talked me into giving her a job there. She called herself Bonanza Jellybean, and that should have tipped me off. But like a fool, I hired her anyway and put her to doing odd jobs around the house and stables, sort of a flunky for Miss Adrian. Miss Adrian is my ranch manager; she used to run the Minnie Mouse Beauty Village at Opa Locka, Florida, and really knows the business. Well, it wasn't long before this teenybopper was spending more time in the saddle than she was in the kitchen; she was out riding with the cowhands, going on all the pack trips and taking on more and more responsibility for herself. Julian, it's certainly more pleasant visiting you without that poodle mistaking my left leg for Lassie. Do you hear from old Butty regularly? Good old dog!

"So. Early spring, just before the season opened, Jellybean and a couple of the younger beauticians — Christ knows how she won them over — barricaded themselves in the ranch house, holding Miss Adrian hostage, and started telephoning demands to me in New York. They demanded that I fire all the male ranch hands and replace them with females. Shit O dear! Jelly claimed that my company had been exploiting women for years. She charged that I've made a fortune off women and said it was time I started doing something for them in return — as if my whole adult life hasn't been devoted to improving the female sex. Talk about ingratitude! Gracious! She said if the Rubber Rose was a ranch for women, then it should be operated exclusively by women; women shouldn't be relegated to menial and effete cosmetic tasks while men got to perform all the exciting outdoor work. These were her actual words: 'I'm not a hairdresser or a fucking scullery maid; I'm a cowgirl. And there's gonna be cowgirls riding this range or there ain't gonna be any range to ride.' Now where does a young woman from our God-fearing Midwest learn talk like that? Dr. Spock, I ask you."

Julian pounded his coffeetable edition of Sir Kenneth Clark's *Civilisation* with a soft brown fist. "You didn't let her get away with it, did you? By golly, I'd've . . ."

"It would have been simple to notify the Dakota state patrol and have them evict the little snots from the spread. Actually, however, Jelly's idea, although selfishly motivated, was rather sound. You see, most of the guests at the Rubber Rose are pretty well fixed, from insurance settlements, alimony and so forth. A shocking lot of my cowpokes proved to be fortune hunters, out to marry those dumb old broads for their money. And even the ranch hands who were honest family men created a problem because during the moonlight trail rides, chuck wagon campouts and other organized recreation the guests were always falling in love with them, mooning over them, following them around, even fighting over them. Dears, the turnover on that ranch was tremendous. It was a mess. But an all-girl staff would eliminate those hassles. And it would eliminate rude cowboys hanging around sniggering outside the building where guests were receiving super-douche, love oil and nipple-wax training; guests and staff alike found that embarrassing. What's more, it would get the dykes of America off my delicate back once and forever. That wasn't the first time I'd been maligned by them. There're a lot of malcontents in this society of ours, if you hadn't noticed. Yes, the more I considered the idea, the better I liked it. In the end, I told Jelly to go ahead and hire me a gang of cowgirls, if she could find any, and that if they handled the work okay I would pay them men's wages and back them all the way. And that's how I've come to be proprietor of the largest all-girl ranch in the West. Come a cow cow hickey, come a yippee ki yea."

"How has it worked out?" asked Julian.

"In all truthfulness, I don't know. Communications from the ranch have been few and far between. I've called Miss Adrian several times, but the phone's out of order more often than not — it's a rather remote region — and when I've reached her she's been evasive. I think the cowgirls have her intimidated. On top of that, there's that crazed hermit sitting up on his perch watching the place all the time. The old coot is probably working a Chinese hoodoo voodoo on the whole operation. Gives me the shivers. You can understand why I'm curious. And why I'd like Sissy to check out the scene. What do you say?"

Julian answered for them. "Let us have tonight to talk it over," he said. "We'll let you know in the morning."

The Countess wasn't used to being put off, but he agreed. With his monocle casting a harsh glint on the wallpaper, and his good-by mangled by the emery of animated teeth, he departed.

Discussion between the newlyweds erupted almost at once — and for a while it went smoothly enough. They were quick to agree that the offer had merit. They'd been breathing the same air for nine months, night and day, and a short vacation would refresh them both. Sissy's boredom with her new, inactive life was the principal source of their friction. A modeling assignment, especially one as interesting and lucrative as this one, could be a tonic for her. And while she was away, Julian could have some people over for *poulet sauté aux herbes de Provence* (his speciality), and perhaps join a group at Elaine's. By all means, a short separation could have salubrious effects.

It was when Sissy announced her intentions to *hitchhike* to Dakota that conversation took on a tin edge, and Julian foamed and wheezed. He couldn't understand it; he couldn't comprehend it; he couldn't fathom it; he couldn't (choose your synonym). It frightened him, saddened him, drove him to the Scotch bottle and even to the medicine cabinet to fondle his nail scissors theatrically (Having no facial hair, Indians seldom own razors). He unleashed barrage after barrage of his heaviest asthmatic artillery. But Sissy stood her ground, and next morning when the Countess phoned, Julian told him:

"She's delighted to be of service. She'll leave on Sunday. She's starting early because (sob) she insists on hitchhiking. God, just when I thought she was getting over it. Those thumbs of hers, those unfortunate redundancies; they are of no significance, yet how they complicate our lives."

In the bedroom, sorting out her old jumpsuits, Sissy overheard the complaint. Slowly, she turned her hands in the mirror, like stems, like daggers, like bottles missing labels.

They seemed the best part of her body, her thumbs. The substantial, uncomplicated part. No orifices riddled them; no hair hung from them; they secreted nothing and harbored no senses to satisfy. They contained no slimy entrails; ganglia did not adorn them; they produced nothing that might be compared with earwax, tooth decay or toe jam. They were but the sweet, the unadulterated, the thick pulp of her own life, there in smooth volume and closed form, complete.

Trembling while she did so, and blushing afterward, she kissed them. She blessed her life.

These thumbs. They had created a reality for her when only somebody else's crippled notion of reality, some socially sanctioned parody of reality, was to be her lot. And now they were about to transport her to the Rubber Rose Ranch.

Out where tall birds waded in a lake named for her Siwash kin.

Out where Smokey the Bear lay down his shovel to romp with more playful beasts.

Out where starlight had no enemies and the badland wind no friends.

Out where the boogie stopped and the woogie began.

Part III

Though from time immemorial there were girls upon the ranches who could ride wild horses, they did it under protest and did not pride themselves upon it. Even today, in the great cattle countries of the south, no woman rides except upon a journey, and I do not think that even in the United States that many women take part in steer-roping or rounding up the stock.

— Sir Charles Walter Simpson

32.

THE BROWN PAPER BAG is the only thing civilized man has produced that does not seem out of place in nature.

Crumpled into a wad of wrinkles, like the fossilized brain of a dryad; looking weathered; seeming slow and rough enough to be a product of natural evolution; its brownness the low-key brown of potato skin and peanut shell — dirty but pure; its kinship to tree (to knot and nest) unobscured by the cruel crush of industry; absorbing the elements like any other organic entity; blending with rock and vegetation as if it were a burrowing owl's doormat or a jack rabbit's underwear, a No. 8 Kraft paper bag lay discarded in the hills of Dakota — and appeared to live where it lay.

Now empty and leathery-wrinkled, the bag had been twice full. Once, long ago, it had borne a package of buns and a jar of mustard to a kitchenette rendezvous with fried hamburger. More recently, the bag had held love letters.

As a hole in an oak hides a squirrel's family jewels, the bag had hidden love letters in the bottom of a bunkhouse trunk. Then, one day after work, the button-nosed little cowgirl to whom the letters were addressed gathered bag and contents under her arm, slipped out to the corral, past ranch hands pitching horseshoes and ranch hands flying Tibetan kites, saddled up and trotted into the hills. A mile or more from the bunkhouse, she dismounted and built a small fire. She fed the fire letters, one by one, the way her boy friend had once fed her french fries.

As words such as *sweetheart* and *honey britches* and *forever* and *always* burned away, the cowgirl squirted a few tears. Her eyes were so misty she forgot to burn the bag.

Back at the bunkhouse, in the twilight, her companions pretended they didn't know where she had gone or why. Big Red offered her a piece of homemade fudge and showed no surprise when she refused it. Kym, before retiring, smeared a fast kiss across her lips — very casual, as if she were brushing off a piece of lint. And Jelly, who'd been trying to plunk a carefree song on a hard-timed old Gibson, looked up at her and said, "You know, podner, you can tune a guitar but you can't tuna fish."

She was one of them now. God but it's good to be a cowgirl!

33.

THE OUTHOUSE RADIO was playing "The Starving Armenians Polka." Rain, a sudden downpour, a regular Dakota summer cloudburst, had trapped Bonanza Jellybean and Delores del Ruby in the privy. First Delores and then Jelly finished her business and pantsed up, but still they sat there.

"Well, I'm not scared of a little rain," announced Jelly.

"Me neither," said Delores, who would never admit to being afraid of *anything*.

But neither made a move to leave. Instead, they stared out the door at the staircase of water that so resembled the one on which mermaids greet drowned sailors ("Would you like to come up to my room?" asks a mermaid, not much older than a cowgirl. "You bet, you bet," glubs the excited sailor, silently thanking his hometown recruiting officer that he hadn't had the misfortune to die on dry land). The stairs of water hung there, in what used to be air, as if waiting for a midget submarine to slide down its banister.

"Might as well brave it," said Jelly, moving to the door. She was the ranch boss and had to set an example.

"Right," agreed Delores, the forewoman. "I don't know about you but I'm sure not sweet enough to melt." She flicked her whip at a sweat bee that had also taken refuge in the privy. (Actually, she had been trying to wound not the bee but the photograph of Dale Evans upon which it had lit.)

A meeting had been called in the bunkhouse that Saturday morning, a meeting that all cowgirls except those watching the birds were expected to attend, and over which Jelly and Delores had to preside. If the chief cowgirls hadn't stopped off, independently, to unburden their bowels (a habit that should be practiced by all presiding officers *before* they take the floor) and gotten trapped by a cloudburst, the meeting would now be underway. As Rubber Rose meetings went, this one was not likely to be unusual. Mary would complain that some of the cowgirls had been sleeping two to a bunk again, in violation of the agreement that "crimes against nature" were to be confined to the hayloft. Debbie would say that she didn't care who lay with whom or where or how, but that the moaners, groaners and screamers ought to turn down their volume when others were trying to sleep or meditate (here and there a blush). Big Red would proffer an unsolicited testimonial as to the quality and quantity of Rubber Rose cuisine, a testimony in which each boiled potato, every dab of gravy, was described as smaller and less appetizing than the one before. And several of the cowgirls would voice their anxieties about the possible consequences of riding herd on the birds. But Jelly would pacify everyone, as usual, and by meeting's end there would be general smiling, hugging and expressions of solidarity. It promised to be a meeting with a familiar ring, but it had been called and therefore must be held. Jelly and Delores hadn't the right to delay it further just because it was raining Coke bottles and bananas. Let them take their soaking.

Bracing themselves for a tall drink of water, straight, no chaser, they were poised in the shithouse doorway when all at once they saw a barefoot cowgirl — Debbie it was — run across the yard in her karate robe, jump on the Exercycle that was rusting in the weeds and begin pumping the pedals furiously in the yammering rain. "My sacred crocodile!" exclaimed Delores. "She's flipped."

But, ho, in a minute others followed Debbie, everyone of them, in fact; the entire bunkhouse load of them, some thirty young cowgirls, squealing, giggling, naked or near naked, all full of dimples and hormones. They slid and rolled on the wet grass, pushed each other into the mud that was forming by the corral fence, chased one another in and out of the thick folds of rain draperies, stamped their cute feet in puddles and did bellyflops into the overflowing horse trough. The downpour became a crystal chandelier, they its flickering candleflames.

Boss rancher and forewoman eyed each other in astonishment. The hands called to them. Jelly felt minnows flash in her bloodstream. She undressed quickly. More reluctantly, Delores stripped down to her viperskin underthings. Together they dashed into the warm rain.

The cowgirls frolicked until, as suddenly as it had come, the rain went away. Play ceased. The sun placed its horns in their dripping curls. They were panting like puppies as they leaned against one another or picked clods of mud from one another's hair.

"I move that the meeting be adjourned," panted Elaine.

Debbie seconded the motion, and tacked on a Zen proverb: "At the end of the endless game, there is friendship."

"What the heck did she mean by that!" asked Heather, who made use of the privy while Jelly gathered up her clothes.

Jelly studied the tired and sopping cowgirls walking arm and arm back to the bunkhouse. "Just that in Heaven all business is conducted this way," she explained.

34.

WHILE BONANZA JELLYBEAN was cross-state in Fargo, closing the goat cheese deal, she stopped at a rummage sale and picked up a gang of old dresses and hats. The cowgirls were trying them on in front of the bunkhouse mirror. Kym mugged in a floppy pink chapeau that looked like a cross between a strawberry chiffon pie and a bloodhound. Using up her mirror time, Jody palpitated in a frilly green kimono. Delores inquired sullenly if there was anything in black. Elaine and Linda . . .

Wait. Wait a moment, please. Even though we agree that time is relative; that most subjective notions of it are inaccurate just as most objective expressions of it are arbitrary; even though we may seek to extirpate ourselves from the terrible flow of it (to the extent of ignoring an author's plea to "wait a moment, please," for a moment, after all, is a little lump of time); even though we pledge allegiance to the "here and now," or view time as an empty box to fill with our genius, or restructure our concepts of it to conform with those wild tickings at the clockworks; even so, we have come to expect, for better or worse, some sort of chronological order in the books we read, for it is the function of literature to provide what life does not. In light of that, then, your author is calling "time out" to inform you that those events described in the opening chapters of Part III, as well as most of those reported in the various Cowgirl Interludes of Parts I and II, occurred *after* Sissy Hankshaw Gitche had come to the Rubber Rose and gone again.

Conditions at the ranch were a bit different when Sissy arrived for her modeling assignment back in September 1973. Ostensibly, Miss Adrian was still in charge then, the Rubber Rose still functioned as a beauty ranch and the number of cowgirls there was no more than fifteen. Drastic changes had been made, to be sure, in the Countess's original plans for the spread, but it was not the same configuration of appetites nor had it the same mood or significance as the place about which the author has been sporadically writing.

If he has confused you, the author apologizes. He swears to keep events in proper historical sequence from now on. He does not, however, disavow the impulses that led to his presentation of cowgirl scenes out of chronological order, not does he, in repentance, embrace the notion that literature should mirror reality (as the bunkhouse looking glass mirrored young cowgirls in old clothing, whatever the continuity). A book no more contains reality than a clock contains time. A book may measure so-called reality as a clock measures so-called time; a book may create an illusion of reality as a clock creates an illusion of time; a book may be real, just as a clock is real (both more real, perhaps, than those ideas to which they allude); but let's not kid ourselves — all a clock contains is wheels and springs and all a book contains is sentences.

Happily, your author is not under contract to any of the muses who supply the reputable writers, and thus he has access to a considerable variety of sentences to spread and stretch from margin to margin as he relates the stories of our Thumbelina, of the ranch a douche bag built and — O my children, cock your ears to this! — of the clockworks and its Chink. For example:

This sentence is made of lead (and a sentence of lead gives a reader an entirely different sensation from one made of magnesium). This sentence is made of yak wool. This sentence is made of sunlight and plums. This sentence is made of ice. This sentence is made from the blood of the poet. This sentence was made in Japan. This sentence glows in the dark. This sentence was born with a caul. This sentence has a crush on Norman Mailer. This sentence is a wino and doesn't care who knows it. *Like many italic sentences, this one has Mafia connections.* This sentence is a double Cancer with Pisces rising. This sentence lost its mind searching for the perfect paragraph. This sentence refuses to be diagramed. This sentence ran off with an adverb clause. This sentence is 100 percent organic: it will not retain a facsimile of freshness like those sentences of Homer, Shakespeare, Goethe et al., which are loaded with preservatives. This sentence leaks. This sentence doesn't *look* Jewish . . . This sentence has accepted Jesus Christ as its personal savior. This sentence once spit in a book reviewer's eye. This sentence can do the funky chicken. This sentence has seen too much and forgotten too little. This sentence is called "Speedoo" but its real name is Mr. Earl. This sentence may be pregnant, it missed its period This sentence suffered a split infinitive — and survived. If this sentence had been a snake you'd have bitten it. This sentence went to jail with Clifford Irving. This sentence went to Woodstock. And this little sentence went wee wee wee all the way home. This sentence is proud to be a part of the team here at *Even Cowgirls Get the Blues.* This sentence is rather confounded by the whole damn thing.

35.

THE TROUBLE with seagulls is that they don't know whether they are cats or dogs. Their cry is exactly midway between a bark and a meow.

No such ambivalences exist in the Dakotas. The Dakota sky is all of one piece; the Dakota wind is nothing if not direct; the Dakota dust suffers no identity crisis; the whooping cranes that sojourn twice each year in the Dakotas (where gulls don't dare to fly) know precisely what they are — their inimitable whoops attest to that.

As one might expect of such singular, straightforward, no-nonsense territory, the topography of the Dakotas is almost uniformly flat. Vast vistas of arid grasslands, open and unmodulated, thirsty and exposed, as level and smooth as a child's back before the first slouches and pimples set in, stretch from horizon to horizon like the most lonesome old chord on God's harmonica. Neither from danger nor boredom is there a place to hide. No Pan ever chased a tittering nymph across these solitary plains.

At the western edge of the Dakotas, however, the monotony of the landscape, now gradually tilting toward the Rockies, is interrupted by a topographical turmoil so harsh and wild that humans, with a sense of morality that must amuse amoral Nature, have seen fit to call it the *Bad*lands. The Ziegfeld Follies of erosion, the badlands flaunt their geological naughtiness in tall, towerlike buttes — heaping layer after layer of tormented rock and soil toward the sky — and sculptured canyons so deep and chaotic they can break a devil's heart.

(In writing about the Dakotas, it is easy to speak of gods and devils, just as in writing about spiritual matters, it is wise to ignore them.)

Between the forlorn prairie pancake and the eerie badlands ruins, there lies a narrow band of humpy hills, green and pastoral. Less than two miles wide in places, this band seems gentle and friendly in comparison to the physiographic excesses on either side of it. Small lakes glimmer in its hollows, and groves of trees are fairly common. To be sure, it collects a full share of summer scorching and winter blizzards; the near-constant Dakota wind extends it no special privileges; thunderstorms as righteously aloof as a B-52 pilot over an orphanage bomb it heavily with raindrops and hail; tornadoes have its number in their little black books and sometimes call. Nevertheless, if it is not quite an oasis, the ribbon of rises is definitely Dakota's sweeter streak. The hills are carpeted with midlength prairie grass. Cows have a tooth for this grass, as the buffalo did before them, and because the soil here is rich in lime, it provides the calcium that grazing animals need in their forage. Thus, the Dakota hills are partitioned into cattle ranches.

Small by local standards, the Rubber Rose takes up 160 acres of the green hill country, and, said a traveling Texan who saw it once, "Ah think A'll wrap this heah place up in a napkin and take it home." It also is one of the more isolated ranches: thirty miles from the closest town, sixteen miles from the house next door. At one time, it was part — nearly all — of the Siwash Indian reservation.

The ranch's buildings are clustered at its extreme western end, the badlands end, at the base of a butte higher, broader and longer than any in its vicinity. In fact, it is one of the most outrageous ridges in the entire badlands, and all the more conspicuous because of its position on the eastern perimeter of the badlands proper, a kind of last fling, as it were. Shaped like an unfrosted wedding cake from which misogamists had taken several cynical bites; no, shaped more like a ship that has been heavily shelled and has broken away from a convoy (its fellow buttes) to flounder against the surf of low green hills, the superbutte mellows into patches of grass and bushes here and there, but for the most part it is a barren monolith too rugged and steep for an ordinary human to climb. This mountain is known as Siwash Ridge. If it is a ship, it carries a cargo of limestone and phantoms. If it is a ship, it flies the flag of the forbidden. If it is a ship, the Chink is its captain, for he lives on its flying bridge in solitude.

Siwash Lake is at the opposite, or eastern, end of the ranch, a hazel eye reading and rereading Page One of the prairie.

And somewhere on that prairie, narrowing the miles between her and the Rubber Rose, her thumbs a match for the vastness surrounding her, Sissy Hankshaw Gitche was riffling traffic. A piece of her, perhaps the biggest piece, was flooded with ecstasy at being free, careening across the continent again, doing this crazy and apparently meaningless thing that, even after a nine-month layoff, she did better than anyone alive; but another piece of her missed Julian, ached for the attentions he lavished on her body and mind. And in her ambivalence, she, who was once as unwavering as the whooping crane, was now more like the gull.

36.

SHE ENTERED MOTTBURG in a Chevy pickup with a loose fender. It rattled worse than the Countess's dentures. In contrast, the cattleman at the wheel made no noise at all. He wore grim lips and a far-away squint, both mute. Dakota men are like that.

Deposited at a feed store, she aimed her long strides immediately for the other end of town. It wasn't far. At the outskirts, she stopped to speak to an elderly woman who sat nodding in a wicker chair in front of a little mom-and-pop gas station and general store. The old woman held Indian summer in her lap like a cat.

"Excuse me, ma'am. Could you direct me to a ranch that's called the Rubber Rose? Mottburg is supposed to be the nearest town."

Her eyes half-closed like a lizard's, the woman raised her chin without raising her lids. "Are they real?" she asked in a voice that was surprisingly perky.

"You mean my thumbs? Yes, they're very, very real."

"Oh, well, excuse me then, honey, I didn't mean to get personal. Since you're asking about that Rubber Rose Ranch I thought maybe you was part of that moving picture show they're making out there. I figured maybe they was *props,* make-up, you know. Are you going to be in that moving picture? What's it about, anyway?"

Sissy started to inform the lady that the cinematographers she obviously had seen heading for the Rubber Rose were there to film the whooping cranes, but something — some protective instinct, perhaps — stopped her short. For some reason, she wasn't sure that she should mention the cranes.

The plainswoman noticed Sissy's hesitation. "Aw, it don't matter," she said. "It'll probably never come to Mottburg, anyway. 'Specially if it's one of them brand X naked pictures. All the show here ever shows anymore are bear-poop-in-the-trail movies put out by the Mormon Church. And then every Christmas they run *The Sound of Music* again. Lord, I've seen that picture four times. If they try to drag me to it this year I'm going to tell 'em my eyes are too weak. I hate to fib, but enough's enough, don't you think? Now, if they was to bring in a Bette Davis picture . . . That's my meat. Do you like Bette Davis?"

Sissy smiled. "I don't recall anything I've seen her in, but I hear she's a marvelous actress." Sissy didn't know if she liked Bette Davis or not, but she liked the old woman.

"Well, I've seen her many a time, and Joan Crawford, too. I had plans to be a sophisticated lady like them once, but I got stuck out here, got stuck and never got away. I managed the Mottburg Grange for thirty years. They retired me a while back. Figured I was senile. They reckon old Granny Schreiber is out of it now, but I know what's going on, every inch of the way."

Sissy set her rucksack down. "Say, Miss Schrieber . . ."

"*Mrs.* Schreiber. How else would a woman get stuck in a place like this if it wasn't for a man? Lord!"

"Mrs. Schrieber, then, I'm wondering if you know anything about the Siwash Indians. Aren't they a tribe in these parts?"

"Yes and no. The Siwash? Yes and no. Honey, I'm sorry if I'm staring. I know it's rude; it's just that you're an uncommon sight."

"That's all right, Mrs. Schreiber. I'm used to being stared at. Why, I bet somebody as sophisticated as Bette Davis would stare at *my* thumbs. Now about the Siwash?"

"Yes, the Siwash. They wasn't from around here originally. The Siwash was a small tribe that got chased off the Pacific Coast by their enemies. They were said to be working a lot of bad medicine and the other tribes hated 'em. Well, they migrated all the way to Dakota and the Dakota Sioux took 'em in and looked after them; gave 'em a parcel of their own land. Later, after the reservations were established, the Sioux talked the Congress into giving the Siwash two hundred acres for their own little reservation. During the war, World War Two I reckon it was, there's been so dang many I can hardly keep 'em straight, what was left of the Siwash moved to the cities to take jobs. They let Congress sell off their reservation land to white ranchers. All but Siwash Ridge, that is. They claimed that that old butte — you can see it from here if the dust ain't up and you look hard enough — they claimed it was holy and they was going to hold on to it forever. So that ridge is still Siwash territory. But there's no Siwash left around here. Unless you count that old coot that lives up on the butte."

"You mean the man they call the Chink? Is he an Indian? I assumed he was Chinese."

The wrinkled woman rocked her body, parrot-style, in the sun. "Maybe he's a Chinaman and maybe he ain't. What I know is, he's got a paper from the Siwash saying he's their number one medicine man, and giving him permission to live on their sacred mountain." She rocked. "Maybe he's a Chinaman. Maybe he's something else. Folks here where he does his trading don't rightly know what he is. They think he's half-animal, some kind of spook." She stopped rocking. "But he's always got a wink and a word of flapdoodle for old Granny Schreiber, and that's more'n any the old geezers in Mottburg have got. Lord, I'd go to the Saturday night dance with him any time. Granny Schreiber can still polka, don't you know."

Sissy laughed and picked up her rucksack. "I'm sure you're a better dancer than I," she said. "It's been really fine talking with you, Mrs. Schreiber. Could you tell me how to get to the Rubber Rose?"

"Follow the main highway on out of town for a good nine or ten mile. You'll see a bitty dirt road turn off to the right. Look sharp. There ain't any sign, but there's a pile of rocks that's been whitewashed. You follow that road until the land starts getting hilly. Then there's another road branches off, not much wider 'n a path. There's a sign on that one. You haven't told me whether you're going to be in that moving picture, or going to look for the Chink like them other young fools, or whether you going to work on the ranch. It's none of my business. But I know you're not going for a beauty treatment; you're too pretty for that. Unless there's something they can do for your thumbs . . ."

Sissy waved as she walked away. "There's nothing I *want* done for my thumbs, Mrs. Schreiber. Thanks a lot for your help. I'll see if there's a part in the movie for you."

"Do that. Do that," said the old woman. She cackled. Then she reached out lazily, as if to scratch Indian summer behind its ears.

37.

SISSY found the dirt road. She made little puffs of dust as she walked. A rattler warmed its chill blood on a rock. There was a feeling of yippee and wahoo in the air. In the distance, Siwash Ridge tipped its hat — but it didn't say howdy.

From the supposed direction of the ranch there approached a VW Microbus. It was painted with mandalas, lamaistic dorjes and symbols representing "the clear light of the void" — quite an adornment for the vehicular flower of German industry.

When the Microbus drew alongside Sissy it stopped. It bore two men and a woman. They were approximately twenty-four years old and had intense expressions. The female, who sat in the middle, spoke. "Are you a pilgrim?" she asked.

"No, I'm more of an Indian," answered Sissy, who had missed a good many Thanksgiving dinners.

The trio didn't smile. "She means are you going to see the Chink?" explained the driver.

"Oh, I may and I may not," said Sissy. "But seeing him is not my main objective out here."

"That's good," said the driver. "Because he won't see you. We came all the way from Minneapolis to see him and the crazy bastard tried to stone us to death."

"Oh, Nick, you're exaggerating," said the female. "He didn't try to kill us. But he did throw rocks at us to chase us away. Wouldn't let us within forty yards of him."

"Just look at Charlie's arm," said the driver to the woman. Then, to Sissy, "The old goat caused Charlie to fall down. He's got a bruise the size of an orange. Lucky he didn't break his neck." On the far side of the bus, Charlie was holding his shoulder, brooding.

With a long skinny finger — all the better for probing the more narrow crannies of the cosmos — the woman pushed her rimless glasses up on her nose. "I told you we should have chanted before we started up the butte. We weren't centered-in enough."

"Balls!" exclaimed the driver. "We're the third group of pilgrims he's chased away this month. A guy from Chicago, a truly mystical person, got as far as the entrance to the cave last spring only to have the Chink crack him over the head with a stick. The Dalai Lama himself couldn't get an audience with that maniac. He's gone bananas up on that ridge."

"Pardon me," said Sissy, "but exactly why do you 'pilgrims' want to see the Chink?"

"Why does any pilgrim journey to see any saint? Why does any novice seek out a guru or a master? For instruction. We wished to be instructed.

"And if he had been receptive, we wanted to invite him to lead a seminar at our community. The Missouri River Buddhist Center."

"Yeah," said the driver, "but I no longer believe that guy's a master. He's just a dirty, uptight old mountainman. Why, he pulled out his pecker and shook it at Barbara. I'd stay away from there if I were you, lady. Say, you aren't going to the butte in hopes of any kind of faith healing, are you?"

Sissy had to smile. "Certainly not," she said crisply. "I'm in perfect health."

She walked on down the road, swinging her thumbs, leaving the pilgrims to argue about whether or not the Chink's rock-shower and pecker-wag actually had been intended as spiritual messages.

38.

If little else, the brain is an educational toy. While it may be a frustrating plaything — one whose finer points recede just when you think you are mastering them — it is nonetheless perpetually fascinating, frequently surprising, occasionally rewarding, and it comes already assembled; you don't have to put it together on Christmas morning.

The problem with possessing such an engaging toy is that other people want to play with it, too. Sometimes they'd rather play with yours than theirs. Or they object if you play with yours in a different manner from the way they play with theirs. The result is, a few games out of a toy department of possibilities are universally and endlessly repeated. If you don't play some people's game, they say that you have "lost your marbles," not recognizing that, while Chinese checkers is indeed a fine pastime, a person may also play dominoes, chess, strip poker, tiddlywinks, drop-the-soap or Russian roulette with his brain.

One brain game that is widely, if poorly, played is a gimmick called "rational thought." Although his ancestors had no knowledge of this game, and probably wouldn't have played it if they had, Julian Gitche was fond of it. He tried to teach it to his wife, whose thumbs-first approach to life he found disturbingly irrational and frivolous (Long live the second phalanx!). Sissy gave it a whirl. She was eager for diversions in the Tenth Street apartment — and having survived nine months of matrimony, how could she feel any terror at "rational thought"? She learned the rudiments of logic and, with Julian's encouragement, decided to apply them to her trip to the Rubber Rose.

Thus, when, nearing her destination, she sat to rest on a hunk of petrified log (all multicolored and looking like a packaged loaf of prehistoric Wonder Bread), instead of letting her mind scat lightly over the pleasures and possibilities of the hitchhike, savoring its unarticulated intonations, rhythms and spatial tensions, she reminded herself of her pragmatic purposes and attempted to outline them, as any golden Greek might have done.

(1) She would pose for the Countess's hired cameras, modeling to the best of her ability.

(2) Mingling with cowgirls, staff and guests, she would attempt to assess the prevailing situation at the ranch.

(3) She would depart from the Rubber Rose as quickly as she might.

There! The primary aims. Now, she would break them down into (1a), (1b) etc. Logic was kind of fun, at that.

Alas, the brain is a toy that plays games of its own. Its very most favorite is the one-thing-leads-to-another game. You know it. It goes like this: when Sissy thought about outline form, that led her to think of being taught outline form by Julian, which led her to think of Julian himself, which led her to think of Julian loving her, which led her to think of love. One thing leads to another. Eyes closed tight inside the pale blue beehive of Dakota sky, waves of grasses whispering her name, meadowlarks squandering their songs on her, she began to squirm on the warm stone. She unzipped her jumpsuit at the crotch, and, as if looking up Eros in the Yellow Pages, let her fingers do the walking.

For you dears who have abused yourselves nowhere but in bed or the john at school, let Sissy tell you it can't be beat in the middle of an empty prairie — an ocean of sunlit grassheads pushing the sky away in every direction, while darting breezes weave the perfumed kisses of the earth. Unbeknownst to Sissy, she was following in the fingersteps of quite a number of little ladies who rode that range. Even cowgirls get the blues.

Unfortunately, Sissy had turned but a few pages when she was interrupted by a Cadillac limousine that popped out of a prairie dog hole.

39.

No. No no no. Of course not. The Cadillac hadn't come out of a prairie dog hole. It had come down the same dirt road that Sissy had been walking. Only it drove up so suddenly — despite the fact that one could see at least twenty miles in every direction — Sissy barely had time to zip up, and she said to herself, "Where did that car come from, out of a prairie dog hole?"

It was the first time in her hitchhiking career that she regretted seeing an automobile approach.

At the wheel of the Cadillac was a teen-aged girl in a Stetson. It was the rear door of the limousine that opened, however, and a refined, matronly voice that called, "By any chance are you Sissy Hankshaw?"

"Yes I am," said Sissy Gitche. Who else could she be?

A chic middle-aged woman leaned out of the car. "My goodness. Why didn't you telephone? Someone would have driven into Mottburg to pick you up. I'm Miss Adrian. From the ranch. The Countess wrote that I should expect you. Get in, won't you? You must be exhausted. It's warm today. Gloria, assist Miss Hankshaw with her luggage."

Gloria nodded amicably at Sissy, but made no move to help her. Sissy swung her rucksack into the roomy vehicle. She started to follow it, but stepped back long enough to flash a thumb (Better to hitch a car that has already stopped than not to hitch at all). Then she entered and sat beside the immaculately groomed Miss Adrian. Something about Miss Adrian reminded Sissy of Julian's white piano. In her mind, Sissy set a vase of roses on top of Miss Adrian. They looked just fine there.

The instant Sissy shut the door, the cowgirl chauffeur floored the Cadillac and it lurched away in a homemovie of out-of-focus dust. The roses fell off the piano. The piano showed its teeth. "Little twit." The tone was low and deep: F sharp below middle C.

Miss Adrian regained her composure. "You really ought to have phoned. I'm dreadfully sorry you had to walk this long distance, out here in the wilds. You didn't try to reach me, did you? We were just now in Mottburg escorting some guests to the afternoon train." Miss Adrian sighed. An angry sigh. "More guests leaving ahead of schedule. Three guests checked out today. They decided to transfer to Elizabeth Arden's Maine Chance spa in Phoenix, Arizona. It costs a thousand dollars a week at Elizabeth Arden's. It costs seven hundred and fifty dollars at the Rubber Rose; less if one stays a month. So why are our guests leaving and going to Elizabeth Arden's?" Miss Adrian paused. She pushed a button, sending a partition of soundproof glass gliding shut between the passenger compartment and the driver's seat. Through the glass, Sissy could see but not hear Gloria laughing. "I'll tell you why," Miss Adrian took up again. "It's that plague of cowgirls.

"Miss Hankshaw, I can hardly wait for the Countess to get here and attend to this mess. You can't imagine how horrid it's become. At first, when they stayed in their place, it was all right. I must admit, they performed the ranch chores virtually as well as the male hands had. But they've gradually infiltrated every sector of our program. The one named Debbie considers herself an expert on exercising and diet. With Bonanza Jellybean's permission, and against my explicit orders, she's been coercing the guests into trying something called kundalini yoga. Do you know what that is? Let me enlighten you.

It's trying to mentally force a serpent of fire to crawl up your spinal column. Miss Hankshaw, our guests can't comprehend kundalini yoga, let alone do it. And Debbie has completely taken over the menu. One month she has us eating nothing but brown rice, the following month it's a so-called nonmucus diet and the next it's something else. Yesterday, in fact, she ordered a new cookbook by a Tibetan Negro, entitled *Third Eye in the Kitchen: Himalayan Soul Food.* God knows what that will be like. Even the other cowgirls are complaining.

"Miss Hankshaw, I am proud of the Rubber Rose. Basically, we offer the same program as Elizabeth Arden's: mat exercises, swimming exercises, sauna, steam bath, paraffin-wax bath, massage, facials, whirlpool bath, scalp treatment, diet training, manicure, pedicure, hair-styling, make-up classes. But it's more fun here. Arden's Maine Chance is elegant and posh. We offer a rustic, informal dude ranch atmosphere with riding and campouts and so forth. What really sets us apart, however, from the Maine Chance and all other spas is our program of intimate conditioning. Miss Hankshaw, we are adult women, you and I; we can speak frankly about such things. When a woman comes to a beauty spa, she does so to make herself sexually attractive to men. That's it in a nutshell. There often are other considerations, of course, but essentially our client is a mateless bird in need of preening." (The ornithological allusion set Sissy to thinking of past parakeets and future whooping cranes.) "Other spas recognize this, but they don't go far enough. What use is it to lure a man to bed, pardon me if I am blunt, if he is to be offended or disappointed there? That is why we at the Rubber Rose stress feminine hygiene, vagina-tightening exercises and so forth. Well, this week the cowgirls invaded the sexual reconditioning room, and the uncouth practices they advocated there my tongue refuses to describe. Shocking beyond belief. The little barbarians are destroying all that I've built, mocking all that the company stands for. When the Countess gets here . . . I've been afraid to complain in the past. Oh, Jellybean is more bark than bite, and most of the girls, for all their bad manners, wouldn't harm a fly. But there's a new one, one they call del Ruby. She has the good will of a scorpion; oh, if you could see the way she looks at me! Anyway, I've considered it prudent to avoid a confrontation that might further upset the guests. But now that the season is practically over — we operate April through September — and the Countess is finally coming . . ."

They were in the hills now. The sun was sinking. Taking its tambourine with it, the wind went home to supper. Grass lost the beat and fell still. An American loneliness, which is like no other loneliness in the world, was spreading on all sides of the Cadillac, creeping out of the cooling soil, out of the air itself; smelling sweet, colored like the pinched feet of tired salesmen, tasting of sweat and beer and fried potatoes, haunted by childhood dreams and the ghosts of Indians — a lonering gloaming coiling like a smoky snake out of the busted suitcase of the continent. The limousine moved through the hush like a dentist's drill.

Inside the vehicle, Miss Adrian continued to talk. Obviously she was distraught. Sissy said nothing. Maybe Sissy was not even listening. Who could tell? Sissy sat as she usually sat, supporting her thumbs affectionately upon crossed legs — and smiling. She grinned the invincible soft grin that some people associate with madness, that others attribute to spiritual depth, but that in reality is simply the grin that comes from the secret heart of very private experience.

40.

BANG! Bang bang bang! Bang squared and bang cubed. Bang conjugated and Bang koked.

They arrived at the ranch to the sound of gunfire.

"O merciful Jesus!" cried Miss Adrian. "They're murdering the guests!"

The main house, the bunkhouse, the stables and outbuildings were deserted. There was no one around the spread at all except for a couple of men in Hollywood sweaters, loitering by the corral. More gunfire.

Miss Adrian was hysterical. She ran up to one of the men and seized him by the shoulders. "Where are the guests?" she shrieked.

The man seemed indignant. "Take it easy, lady," he said. "They went on a short ride with the cowgirls. Rode over the hill yonder. You're Miss Adrian, aren't you? We need to talk to you about the filming."

"Not now, you fool, not now. Those crazed bitches have led innocent women out and are slaughtering them at this moment. We'll all be killed. Oh! Ohhhh!"

The other cameraman spat out a wad of chewing gum, launching it on a trajectory that carried it over the corral fence. "There's a slaughter going on all right, but it's not the fat ladies that are getting it. Your hired hands are killing the cattle." He looked guiltily at the pink cud of gum, lying now among horse droppings and clods. "It'll be okay if a nag steps in that, I guess. Chewing gum is made out of horses' hooves to begin with. Everything has got a homing instinct, even Dentyne."

In the twilight, Miss Adrian's complexion looked like a silver spoon that had been left overnight in a dish of mayonnaise. "The cattle? They're killing the cows? All of them?"

"That's what they said, Miss Adrian. They invited your guests to go along so's to see what ranch life was really like. They invited the staff, too. It's getting dark. They should be back pretty . . . Here they come now."

As the party rode into sight, Miss Adrian counted the guests. All present. She counted her staff. The manicurist and masseuse were having the time of their lives. They had never been allowed on a Rubber Rose outing before. Had Miss Adrian gone on to count the cowgirls, she would have discovered four missing: the three left behind to guard the slain cattle — and Debbie, who, as a vegetarian, would have no part in the slaughter and was even now over at Siwash Lake in the bird blind with a cinematographer, making love not beef.

41.

THE *Even Cowgirls Get the Blues* hearty stew recipe:

Peel onions. Pare potatoes and carrots. Cut meat into bite-size chunks. Drop into boiling water. Add sprinkle of parsley, sage, rosemary, simon and garfunkle. Caution: Under no circumstances use beef from the Rubber Rose Ranch.

To a veterinarian, the Rubber Rose herd was one of the greatest spectacles on Earth.

Threadworms? The Rubber Rose cows had so many threadworms in their bronchial tubes that they coughed from dusk to dawn like an opium den full of Julian Gitches. Hair balls? These cows had hair balls to rival the tumbling tumbleweeds. They had fevers and fissures and gas and gnats. They had hernias of the rumen and hernias of the rennet. The entire herd suffered from variola, displaying its symptomatic pustular eruptions upon their teats and udders. Actinomycosis, known to farmers as "big jaw" or "wooden tongue," rattled the teeth of these bovines. A peek down their throats would disclose evidence of parotitis, not to mention pharyngeal polypi as large as boysenberries. There were random cases of foul foot, inverted eyelid and scurfy ear, and one of the bulls was so afflicted with orchitis that he walked with a straddling gait, lest his geranium red testicles sound a painful gong against his thighs.

According to Bonanza Jellybean, the Rubber Rose herd was indicative of the Countess's values. He had purchased a cheap, weak strain to begin with, to hear Jelly tell it, whereupon improper care by a succession of uninterested ranch hands had taken its toll. After futile attempts at restoring the herd to health, Jelly decided to put it out of its misery. Actually, it had been Delores's idea. Debbie, who would swat no living thing, and who believed that nature must run its course, opposed euthanasia. Miss Adrian, naturally, opposed it also. She was furious at the deed. "How dare you slaughter the Countess's cattle! Just wait until he gets his hands on you! What is a ranch without cows?" And so on.

Jelly's response — "We're going to replace them with goats" — only made her more angry. She was for telephoning the Countess that very evening, except that the cinematographers managed to squeeze a word in and inform her that they'd already tried, unsuccessfully, to phone the Countess — he was a guest of the President at the White House and couldn't be reached.

The cinematographers were a bit upset themselves. They had received a letter of instructions from the Countess that day, and only then did they realize that the douche bag tycoon expected them to film a mating dance. A mating dance? Oh dear. Like most geniuses, the Countess was a very limited person. Sigmund Freud was so ignorant of art that the Surrealist painters had to explain their use of Freudian symbols over and over again, and still he didn't get it. Einstein never could remember to take the biscuits out of the oven. Those same forces that drive a genius to create the things or ideas that entertain or enlighten us often gobble so much of his personality that he has none left for the social graces (Should you invite Van Gogh to your home he might stand on your sofa in his muddy boots and pee where he pleased), and the very act of creation requires such focused concentration that vast areas of knowledge may be completely overlooked. Well, so what? There is no evidence that generalized skills are in any way superior to specialized brilliance, and certainly that sputterless little candleflame of the mediocre mind known as "common sense" has never produced anything worth celebrating. But back to the point. The Countess, in the demands of his genius, had overlooked one small fact of nature — *birds mate in the spring.*

Birds mate in the spring. No amount of coaxing, libidinous stimulation or aphrodisiac birdseed will cause them to punch in early. Even horned owls will couple only in springtime.

The Countess had retained an expert wildlife camera crew to shoot whooping crane footage. He was a trifle tardy in advising it that he expected film of the mating rite. The cinematographers were vexed, but they offered a possible alternative to moving the operation to the Gulf Coast and waiting for spring. It seems, they told Miss Adrian, that a whooping crane will sometimes dance outside the breeding cycle. They have been known to perform their ballet simply as a physical or emotional outlet. Occasionally a crane may execute a short but dazzling dance just for the hell of it. Perhaps one or more cranes might be inspired to perform during the Siwash Lake stopover. If the cameramen were alert, they might get enough dance footage to suit the Countess's purposes. But as for this model who was supposed to be in the film, she would have to be shot separately and superimposed.

Miss Adrian didn't know what to tell them. "You'll just have to discuss it with the Countess," she said. She had a poison headache.

"Come along, Miss Hankshaw," she uttered through the pain. "I'll show you to your room, and see that you get something to eat — if there *is* anything to eat besides brown rice and bean sprouts."

The camermen stared at the pair of thumbs that came swinging around from the opposite side of the Cadillac: pillows of sugar, clouds of meat, filling the lenses of their camera eyes.

One of the men wiped his brow. "Come back, Walt, all is forgiven," he moaned.

The Rubber Rose. Disney's was never like this.

42.

FOR THE NEXT FEW DAYS, the ranch stood on one leg (more in imitation of flamingo anxiety than of what the poet García Lorca called "the ecstasy of cranes"). The ranch wasn't going to set its other foot down until the Countess came.

Meanwhile, the cowgirls dug a lime pit in which to bury the snuffed cattle. After it was dug, they had to fill it up again. That's the way it is with holes; they're insatiable. The hands worked from early morning until sundown. They took their meals from the chuck wagon, and when supper was done, rode to the bunkhouse and bombed directly into bed. From her window, Sissy watched them come and go, heard their weary laughter and observed the dimples in their skintight Levis opening and closing like the mouths of tropical fish.

Taking advantage of the hands' absence, Miss Adrian sought to re-establish her control over the health-and-beauty program. No longer did ladies grunt in carbohydrate confusion, trying to squeeze a "fiery serpent" up their spines.

Sissy was given a tour of the facilities, most of which were in a wing of the main house: the sauna and the buildings that housed steam baths and the mysteries of "sexual reconditioning" were separate, a few yards away. Miss Adrian invited Sissy to use the pool and the sauna whenever she wished, but the manager was busy putting things straight and had little time for the thumby model from New York.

The cinematographers spoke with her the first morning, as they picked up additional provisions for the blinds, which, due to the presumed approach of Crane Hour, they dared not leave again. They offered to show her the pond and the blinds, but repeated what they'd said earlier about having to film her separately. "No whooping crane is gonna let you get that close to it," they said. "Hell, whoopers don't even like other birds around." The cameramen weren't entirely sure there was going to be any filming. Nobody would know anything until the Countess arrived.

So the ranch stood on one leg and waited.

And all the while, this clumsy balancing act was being nonchalantly scrutinized — leisurely leered upon, some might say — by a short man with a long white beard, a sure-footed man whose periodic appearances along the eroded poop decks and wind-carved turrets of Siwash Ridge had such an air of the occult, the supernatural, that he may excite the imaginations of many an eager mind, while others may find him merely disconcerting and shake their heads suspiciously.

But now, as we observe events at the ranch, and observe, further, the old gentleman who observed them, now is not the time for either reckless excitement or cynical scoffing. We must regard this business coolly, objectively, with a philosophy of operative wholeness. We must suspend, temporarily, a critical or analytical approach. Let us, rather, gather facts, all the facts, regardless of aesthetic appeal or theoretical social worth, and spread those facts before us not as the soothsayer spreads the innards of a turkey but as a newspaper spreads its columns. Let us be as journalists, then. And like all good journalists, we shall present our facts in an order that will satisfy the famous five *W*'s: wow, whoopee, wahoo, why-not and whew.

43.

On the fifth morning, as the Indian summer sun popped up from behind the hills like a hyperthyroid Boy Scout, burning to do good deeds, Sissy was awakened by the tinkle of breakfast trays. She yawned and stretched and held her thumbs up in the sunlight to make sure there had been no overnight change. Then she propped herself up on pillows — she felt rested but uneasy — and awaited the knock at her door.

Breakfast in bed was a tradition Miss Adrian had installed at the Rubber Rose. It seemed like a nice idea to Sissy until she lifted the cloth cover from her first tray and encountered decaffeinated coffee with saccharine, fresh grapefruit without sugar and a piece of Melba toast: the guests were on a strict 900-calories-a-day regime. At least they were when Debbie was not running the kitchen. Sissy had had more luxurious breakfasts in jail.

The morning maid, who doubled as a bath therapist, delivered her tray this fifth day and stood by, as if to take sadistic amusement in watching Sissy unveil a meal that would piss off the taste buds of a saint. But when our Sis removed the cover, she discovered (in addition to a vase of prairie asters) a double-meat cheeseburger, a package of Hostess Twinkies, a cold can of Dr. Pepper and a Three Musketeers bar; in short, just the sort of repast she might have procured for herself had she been on the road.

A dragon who'd been served Princess Anne on a platter could not have grinned with more gastronomical satisfaction.

"Compliments of Bonanza Jellybean," said the maid. "She'll be up to see you directly."

Sure enough, about the time Sissy clinked the last droplet of the Doctor's peppy nectar out of the can and dabbed a final trace of chocolate from her lips, there was a fist against her door and in sailed the tresses, teeth and titties of a cowgirl so cute she made Sissy blush just to look at her. She wore a tan Stetson with as aster pinned to it, a green satin shirt embroidered with rearing stallions snorting orange fire from their nostrils, a neckerchief, a leather vest as white as a corpse, of the same cadaverous leather a skirt so short that if her thighs had been a clock the skirt would have been five minutes to midnight, and a pair of handtooled Tony Lama boots, the toes of which you could pick your teeth with. There were silver spurs fastened to her boots, and encircling her trim waist, just above the slightly bulging baby fat of her belly, a wide, turquoise-studded belt, from which dangled a holster and the holster's inhabitant, a genuine six-shooter with a long nose like bad news from the clinic. She flashed honey thighs when she walked, her breasts bounced like dinner rolls that had gotten loaded on helium and, between red-tinged cheeks, where more baby fat was taking its time maturing, she had a little smile that could cause minerals and plastics to remember their ancient animate connections.

She grasped Sissy's elbow (not daring to get too close to the thumb) and sat on the side of the bed. "Welcome, podner," she said. "By God, it's great to have you here. It's an honor. Sorry I took so long getting to you, but we've had a mess of hard work these past few days — and a heap of planning to do." When she pronounced the word "planning," her voice assumed a conspiratorial, almost ominous, tone.

"Er, you seem to know who I am," said Sissy, "and maybe even what I am. Thanks for the breakfast."

"Oh, I know about Sissy Hankshaw, all right," said Jelly. "I've done a little hitchhiking myself. Ah shucks, that's like telling Annie Oakley you're a sharpshooter because you once knocked a tomato can off a stump with a fieldstone. I haven't done a lick of serious hitching. But starting when I was about eleven, I used to run away from home every couple of months and try to find a place where I could be a cowgirl. Somebody always sent me back to Kansas City, though. No ranch ever let me stay and some of 'em had me locked up. Lot of times the law picked me up before I could get outta Kansas. But I got around enough to hear about *you*. First time was in Wyoming. Some deputy says to me, 'Who do you think you are — Sissy Hankshaw?' I says, 'No, you dumb fuck, I'm Margaret Meade,' and he whipped me good, but not before he'd aroused my curiosity about this Sissy Hankshaw person. Later, I'd hear tales about you from people I'd meet in jail cells and truckstops. I heard about your, uh, your, ah, your wonderful thumbs, and I heard how you were Jack Kerouac's girl friend . . ."

Setting her tray on the bedside table, Sissy interrupted. "No, I'm afraid that part isn't true. Jack was in awe of me and tracked me down. We spent a night talking and hugging in a corn field, but he was hardly my lover. He was a sweet man and a more honest writer than his critics, including the Countess's little playmate Truman, who said such bitchy things about him. But he was strictly a primitive as a hitchhiker. Besides, I always traveled alone."

"Well, that doesn't matter; that part never interested me anyway. The beatniks were before my time, and I never got anything outta the hippies but bad dope, clichés and the clap. But you, even though you weren't a cowgirl, you were sort of an inspiration to me. The example of your life helped me in my struggle to be a cowgirl."

New York City keeps its allotment of sunshine in a Swiss bank account and tries to get by on the interest, which is compounded quarterly. In contrast, the Dakota sun is as open as the books of a village church steward, and even in September, after summer's big bucks have all been spent, it is so charitable no one would think of demanding an audit. Sunlight streaked into the credits column of the Rubber Rose, making a series of warm entries upon the bare legs of Bonanza Jellybean and upon the upraised legs of Sissy H. Gitche, bare, too, beneath the quilt. During a sunlit pause in conversation, the puffs and huffs of the guests at their early exercises were heard, and for no good reason, the two women giggled.

"Tell me about it," said Sissy.

"About . . ."

"About being a cowgirl. What's it all about? When you say the word you make it sound like it was painted in radium on the side of a pearl."

Jelly drew her feet up on the bed, not minding that her boots bore testimony to the digestive facility of the equine species. "I saw my first cowgirl in a Sears catalogue. I was three. Up until then I had heard only of cow*boys*. I said, 'Mama, Daddy, that's what I want Santa Claus to bring me.' And I got a cowgirl outfit that Christmas. Next Christmas I got another one because I'd worn that first one to shreds. I asked for a cowgirl suit, as we called 'em, every Christmas until I was ten, and then my folks told me, 'You're too big now; Santa doesn't have any cowgirl suits that'll fit you. How'd you like a Barbie doll with her own fashion wardrobe?' 'Bullshit,' I said. 'Dale Evans wears cowgirl suits and she's way bigger than me. I want new cowgirl clothes and a gun that shoots.' I'd been teased by my classmates for some time because of my particular fantasy, but that year was when my real struggle began."

As if prodded by a hard memory of childhood, Jelly sat up straight, making the bed creak. Sissy realigned her own posture, and another creak was issued. Sissy's creak followed Jelly's creak down the hall of sonar eternity. Sounds travel through space long after their wave patterns have ceased to be detectable by the human ear; some cut right through the ionosphere and barrel on out into the cosmic heartland, while others bounce around, eventually being absorbed into the vibratory fields of earthly barriers, but in neither case does the energy succumb; it goes on forever — which is why we, each of us, should take pains to make sweet notes.

"I just said 'fantasy' and 'struggle' in the same sentence, and on one level, at least, I guess that's what it's about. That's what it's about for cowgirls, and maybe everybody else. A lot of life boils down to the question of whether a person is going to be able to realize his fantasies, or else end up surviving only through compromises he can't face up to. The way I figure it, Heaven and Hell are right here on Earth. Heaven is living in your hopes and Hell is living in your fears. It's up to each individual which one he chooses." Jelly paused. "I told that to the Chink once and he said, 'Every fear is part hope and every hope is part fear — quit dividing things up and taking sides.' Well, that's the Chink for you. What do you think?"

"I'd like to hear more," said Sissy. She was feeling a certain kinship with this duded-up bundle of wild muscle and baby fat. "Can you be more specific?"

"Specific. Okay. I'm talking about our fantasies. You know the difference between fantasy and reality, don't you? Fantasy is when you wake up at four o'clock on Christmas morning and you're so crazy excited you can't possibly go back to sleep. But when you go downstairs and look under the tree — podner, that's reality.

"They teach us to believe in Santa Claus, right? And the Easter Bunny. Wondrous critters, both of 'em. Then one day they tell us, 'Well, there really isn't any Santa Claus or Easter Bunny, it was Mama and Daddy all along.' So we feel a bit cheated, but we accept it because, after all, we got the goodies, no matter where they came from, and the Tooth Fairy never had much credibility to begin with. Okay. So they let you dress up like a cowgirl, and when you say, 'I'm gonna be a cowgirl when I grow up,' they laugh and say, 'Ain't she cute.' Then one day they tell you, 'Look, honey, cowgirls are only play. You can't *really* be one.' And that's when I holler, 'Wait a minute! Hold on! Santa and the Easter Bunny, I understand; they were nice lies and I don't blame you for them. But now you're screwing around with my personal identity, with my plans for the future. What do you mean I can't be a cowgirl?' When I got the answer, I began to realize there was a lot bigger difference between me and my brother than what I could see in the bathtub.

"You dig me, don't you? A little boy, he can play like he's a fireman or a cop — although fewer and fewer are pretending to be cops, thank God — or a deep-sea diver or a quarterback or a spaceman or a rock 'n roll star or a *cowboy,* or anything else glamorous and exciting (Author's note: What about a novelist, Jellybean?), and although chances are by the time he's in high school he'll get channeled into safer, duller ambitions, the great truth is, he can be any of those things, realize any of those fantasies, if he has the strength, nerve and sincere desire. Yep, it's true; any boy anywhere can grow up to be a cowpoke even today if he wants to bad enough. One of the top wranglers on the circuit right now was born and raised in the Bronx. Little boys may be discouraged from adventurous yearnings by parents and teachers, but their dreams are indulged, nevertheless, and the possibilities of fulfilling their childhood expectations do exist. But little girls? Podner, you know that story as well as me. Give 'em doll babies, tea sets and toy stoves. And if they show a hankering for more bodacious playthings, call 'em tomboy, humor 'em for a few years and then slip 'em the bad news. If you've got a girl who persists in fantasizing a more exciting future for herself than housewifery, desk-jobbing or motherhood, better hustle her off to a child psychologist. Force her to face up to reality. And the reality is, we got about as much chance of growing up to be cowgirls as Eskimos have got being vegetarians. I'll tell you."

Sissy's right thumb, which she'd been hesitant to move lest it disturb Jelly's oration, had gone to sleep — and when a Sissy thumb sleeps it SNORES! She massaged it vigorously. "What about in movies or rodeos?" she inquired.

"Ha!" said Jelly with dramatic disdain. "Movies. There hasn't been a cowgirl in Hollywood since the days of the musical Westerns. The last movie cowgirl disappeared when Roy and Gene got fat and fifty. And there's *never* been a movie *about* cowgirls. Delores del Ruby, she's really down on Dale Evans. Says she was just an accessory for the good guy in the white hat, a weakling to be protected, a piece of sex interest who never got laid. I don't know. I thought ol' Dale looked mighty fine up there on that screen. But she did ride second saddle, all right. Well, galloping your pretty ass off trying to escape the hoss thieves was better than nothing. Today, we got nothing."

As Sissy kneaded circulation back into her thumb, it took on a rosy glow, like the Renaissance cherub that sneaked a bite out of a madonna's halo. Jelly was astonished, but she continued talking.

"Let me tell you about rodeos." she said. "In the Rodeo Hall of Fame in Oklahoma City there are just two cowgirls. Two. The Rodeo Cowboys Association has more than three thousand members. How many do you suppose are women? You could count 'em on your fingers, thumbs excluded. And all of 'em are trick-riders. Trick-riding is what cowgirls have almost always done in rodeos. Our society sure likes to see its unconventional women do tricks. That's what prostitutes call it, you know: 'tricking.'

"For nine years, from nineteen twenty-four through nineteen thirty-three, females were allowed to enter events just the same as the cowboys: putting up entrance fees, riding bucking broncs, wrestling bulls, roping calves, doing all the things men did. They did okay, too. Tad Lucas, the greatest cowgirl who ever lived, earned ten thousand dollars a year in prize money, and that was at a time when six or seven thousand was a hell of a good season for a rodeo cowboy. But the RCA cut women off in thirty-three. Said it was too dangerous. Well, it was dangerous. Tad Lucas broke nearly every bone in her body at one time or another. The Brahma bulls damn near made chop suey of her. But the men got hurt, too. They were wired together like birdcages, most of 'em. Ah, but it wasn't so brutal when it happened to a man. Why is it men are allowed to do dangerous things and hurt themselves and women aren't? I don't know. But I do know that they outlawed cowgirls, except for trick-riders and parade queens. A woman has not been permitted to compete for prize money in a rodeo in forty years. Say, podner, that's really something the way your thumb kinda shines when you rub it. How do you *do* that?"

The digit in question was now wide awake. It has been said that consciousness of light *is* light, which would explain the luminous doughnuts that rolled 'round the heads of Buddhas and Christs, but can thumbflesh have consciousness, have speed, have spirit? "I think it's the blood," said Sissy. "There're large veins in there, close to the surface." Although, energized as it was, she would have preferred to stick it in the air by some road where traffic was flying, Sissy stuck the thumb under the quilt. Jelly watched it go with eyes that suggested she would have liked to follow it. "Apparently," ventured Sissy, "there just isn't any demand for cowgirls."

"That's not exactly true," said Jelly, slowly, forcefully. "That's not exactly true. The System has no demand for them; you're right about that. But there is a demand — and that demand comes from the hearts of little girls.

"Cowgirls exist as an image. A fairly common image. The *idea* of cowgirls prevails in our culture. Therefore, it seems to me, the *fact* of cowgirls should prevail. Otherwise, we're being ripped off again. I mean, isn't that the way religions mess people's heads around: beautiful concepts without anything factual to back 'em up? When I was a kid and I was told that this role I'd been allowed to love so much was impossible to attain, wow, did I get mad! And I've been mad ever since. So I decided to try to do something about it — to satisfy my own inner needs and to show society it couldn't get away with making me love something that didn't exist."

Unable to restrain herself, Jelly lay her hand atop the ovoid mound Sissy's thumb made under the cover. It was warm. "How about you, Sissy? Did you want to be a cowgirl when you were small?"

"Can't say as I did. But you have to understand, I was rather a special case." What would Bonanza Jellybean think were Sissy to disclose that she had wanted to grow up to be an *Indian?* Take um heap many scalps beside um sky-blue waters. "It's funny. I once hitched a ride on a camel in Afghanistan, but I've never been on a horse in my life."

"We'll take care of that. You're at the Rubber Rose now. But let me confess something to you before you start thinking I'm another Tad Lucas. Until last year, the only thing I'd ever straddled was the Shetland ponies at the Kansas City Zoo. And a man or two, of course. But I'm a cowgirl. I've always been a cowgirl. Caught a silver bullet when I was only twelve. Now I'm in a position where I can help others become cowgirls, too. If a child wants to grow up to be a cowgirl, she ought to be able to do it, or else this world ain't worth living in. I want every little girl — and every boy, for that matter — to be free to realize their fantasies. Anything less than that is unacceptable to me."

"You're political, then?" Sissy had been learning about politics from Julian.

"No ma'am" said Jelly. "No way. There's girls on the Rubber Rose who *are* political, but I don't share their views. I got no cowgirl ideology to expound. I'm not recruiting and I'm not converting. Whether or not another girl chooses the cowgirl path is immaterial to me. It's a personal matter. I'm willing to help other cowgirls; to make it easier for them than it was for me. But don't get the notion I'm trying to create a movement or contribute to one. Delores del Ruby makes a big fuss about cowgirlism being a force to combat cowboyism, but I'm too happy just being a cowgirl to worry about stuff like that. Politics is for people who have a passion for changing life but lack a passion for living it."

Beneath Jelly's dollbaby grip, the Sissy plasma, like a swarm of red bees, followed its charted currents in the thumb's interior passageways. Jelly pressed lightly upon this hive, in which such quantities of blood were buzzing, and gave its owner a look that even upon the countenance of a cowpoke could only be called sheepish. "Did that last comment sound too profound to be coming outta my mouth? It's not original. It's something I picked up from the Chink."

"Really? The Chink, huh? I've gathered that you sometimes speak with him. What else have you learned from the Chink?"

"Learned from the Chink? Oh my. Ha ha. That's hard to say. We mostly . . . Uh, a lot of his talk is pretty goofy." Jelly paused. "Oh yeah, now that I think of it, the Chink taught me something about cowgirls. Did you realize that cowgirls have been around for many centuries? Long before America. In ancient India the care of the cattle was always left up to young women. The Indian cowgirls were called *gopis.* Being alone with the cows all the time, the *gopis* got awfully horny, just like we do here. Every *gopi* was in love with Krishna, a good-looking young god who played the flute like it was going outta style. When the moon was full, this Krishna would play his flute by a river and call the *gopis* to him. Then he would multiply himself sixteen thousand times — one for each *gopi* — and make love to each one the way she most desired. There they were, sixteen thousand *gopis* balling Krishna on the river bank, and the energy of their merging was so great that it created a huge oneness, a total union of love, and it was God. Wow! Quite a picture, huh? When I repeated this story to Debbie, she got so enthused she wanted us to call ourselves *gopis* from then on. We discussed it at a bunkhouse meeting, though, and decided '*gopis*' sounded too much like 'groupies.' Well, we don't need that. We got enough static, with the folks around Mottburg calling us sluts. And lesbians."

Sissy's thumb twitched. Jelly swallowed hard. They gazed into each other's eyes, Sissy trying to tell how Jelly felt saying the word, Jelly trying to ascertain how Sissy felt hearing it, and as they gazed, soft little shocks danced between them, like drunken oysters strutting along a harp string.

They might have gazed until the cows came home, except that, in addition to the cows' being lately deceased, a whistle pierced the sunlight just outside the window.

"That couldn't be Krishna, could it?" smiled Jelly. "A bit shrill for a flute. Just our rotten luck."

She walked to the window and exchanged hand signals with someone outside. Turning to Sissy, she said, "Gotta run now. Delores says I'm needed. Somebody's here. Maybe it's the Countess." She fast-drew her six-shooter, spinning it expertly in her kewpie fingers. "Sissy, cowgirl history is about to be made. I'm damn glad you're here to witness it." With her gun-spinning pinkies, she tossed a kiss and was gone.

A sneeze travels at a peak velocity of two hundred miles per hour. A burp, more slowly; a fart, slower yet. But a kiss thrown by fingers — its departure is sudden, its arrival ambiguous, and there is no source that can state with authority what speeds are reached in its flight.

44.

WHEN HER SWALLOWS had finished Capistranoing, Sissy hopped out of bed. From the window, she could see cowgirls gathering in a circle. Someone or something was in the center of the circle. Sissy performed an abbreviated toilet, zipped herself into a red jumpsuit and hurried outside. It didn't bother her much that she didn't know what to expect. She never had.

What was in the center of the circle was a goat. Billy West, Mottburg's three-hundred-pound midnight rambler, had dropped it off as a sample. There were plenty more goats where that one came from, said Billy West. For the cowgirls, a discount price of twenty dollars a goat.

Debbie was scratching the animal's ears. She was hugging it. "I'm like Mahatma Gandhi," she said. "I'll never be without a goat again."

"It's cute," said Kym. "Way cuter than a cow."

"Goats are always testing you," said Debbie. "They're like Zen masters. They can tell instantly if you're faking your feelings. So they play games with you to keep you true. People should go to goats instead of psychiatrists."

"It's so loving," said Gloria. She cut in on Debbie, gave the beast a hug.

"Goats are the ultimate male and female," said Debbie. "Watching a pair of goats is understanding what the male-female trip is all about. Every couple ought to be given a pair of goats when they get married. There'd be no more need for marriage counselors."

"Look at those playfully wise eyes," cooed Heather.

"When can we get more?" inquired Elaine.

"Oooo! It licked me!" squealed Gloria.

When she tired of watching the goat, Sissy started back to her room. She thought she might hitchhike the wallpaper or something. But Jelly caught up with her. "Looks like we're gonna become goatgirls," she said.

"Will that make a difference?" asked Sissy. "A difference to your fantasy, I mean."

"Not a speck," said Jelly. "It's like the gourmet the Chink told me about who gave up everything, traveled thousands of miles and spent his last dime to get to the highest lamasery in the Himalayas to taste the dish he'd longed for his whole life, Tibetan peach pie. When he got there, frostbitten, exhausted and ruined, the lamas said they were all out of peach. 'Okay,' said the gourmet, 'make it apple.' Peach, apple; cows, goats. You understand?"

Sissy thought that it must have something to do with the primacy of form over function, thus approximating her own approach to hitchhiking, wherein an emotional and physical structure created by variations and intensifications of the act of hitching was of far more importance than the utilitarian goals commonly supposed to be the sole purpose of the act. She was still thinking it over when Jelly said, "Say, there's a sexual reconditioning class in five minutes. Some of us are gonna crash it. To pass on some helpful information and correct some misconceptions. You like to come along?"

The S. R. building was of rustic exterior. It could have been a blacksmith shop. Inside, there were thick rubber mats and harem cushions all over the floor of a single, dimly lit room. At the rear of the room, partly concealed by a brocade curtain, was a flush toilet, gleaming in porcelain ostentation like one of the Countess's incisors. At the front there stood a long, low table, upon which was displayed a harvest of vials, bottles, boxlets, spray cans and ointment tubes, as well as a pair of dainty pink rubber apparatuses that looked like the twin nieces of an enema bag. Approximately a dozen women sat upon the floor, facing the table. Half of them were noticeably overweight, several were as skinny as light verse and appeared to be as burned-out as old sparkplugs although a few of the women seemed to Sissy to be quite attractive and in no need of the Rubber Rose Ranch's ministrations. Sissy wondered what lemons her destiny would have to suck before she might find herself a client of a place such as this.

Led by Debbie, the cowgirls set right to work. "There's only one excuse for ever douching," Debbie informed her captive audience, "and that's to cure an irritation or infection. In which case, you want to be real careful about what you slosh on the inflamed tissues. There are eleven herbs or natural substances suitable for douching the vagina. These are: fennel, fit root, slippery elm, gum arabic, white pond lily, marsh mallow . . ."

"Marshmallow?" asked one of the more obese ladies, incredulously.

Debbie was earnest. "Marsh mallow or *Althaea officinalis* is a pink-flowering plant that grows in marshy places. It's an excellent medicinal herb, a fact that's often obscured by the sweet white confectionery paste that can be made by boiling down its mucilaginous roots. Now, where were we. Marsh mallow, wild alum root, uva ursi, fenugreek, bayberry bark . . ." Debbie clicked off the herb names, but the fat woman was no longer listening. Her eyes had glazed over as she pondered the pleasures of a marshmallow douche, losing her conscious mind in toffee whipped-cream molasses visions of vaginal delight.

Somewhat later in the lecture, Delores grabbed a can of Dew spray mist from the table and slung it in the air. Jelly drew her six-gun and tried to blast it before it hit the floor. She missed, but the class got the point. The shot brought Miss Adrian running from the main house, where she'd been delayed while attempting once again to phone the Countess in Washington, D.C. She arrived in time to hear:

"There isn't a man alive, unless he's some masochistic chemical fetishist, who'd dip his genitals in benzethonium chloride, and any woman who sprays hers with it is a dupe."

Thinking of the ranch's image, thinking, too, perhaps, of Delores's whip and Jelly's pistol, Miss Adrian struggled to restrain herself. "Girls," she said. "Girls."

"Just a minute, ma'am," urged Jellybean. "We're almost through. We got one more little piece of pertinent info to pass along. A vivacious lady like yourself might find it interesting." She bade Miss Adrian stand aside, then turned to the audience.

"Now as Debbie has already mentioned, not only is a woman's natural essence nothing to be ashamed of, the truth of the matter is it's a positive thing that works in our favor. Here's a little self-celebration I bet you ladies never thought of. What you do is reach down with your fingers and get them wet with your juices. Then you rub it in behind your ears . . ."

"Behind your ears???"

This brought the class to full attention. It even brought the fat lady back from marshmallow land. It brought Miss Adrian to the edge of a dead faint.

"Yeah, behind your ears. And a dab on your throat, if you want. When it dries, there's no whiff of low tide about it at all. It's a wonderful perfume. Very subtle and very mischievous. Men are attracted, I guarantee you. Why, in Europe women have been using it for centuries. That's why Neapolitan girls are so seductive. You don't believe me, do you? Here, I'll prove how nice it is."

Jelly slipped her hand up inside her skirt and began priming the essence. Before she could complete the demonstration, however, Miss Adrian, pale and shaking, began to blubber. She was raving about something, but nobody could understand her. She made a sudden lunge for Jelly's gun, but Jelly, who was getting pretty good at the fast draw, whisked her hand out of her crotch in time to ward off the older woman's gambit. The cowgirls figured it was time to retreat.

Tittering and jabbering, they went to the stables and saddled up. Jelly and Big Red helped Sissy mount a calm mare. They rode eastward for two or three miles, to where the hills began leveling off into prairie. The breeze in the grasses made a sound like a silk-lined opera coat falling to the floor of a carriage. Continuously. Except that the breeze in the grasses was actually the breeze in the asters, for wherever the party trotted or looked, the ground was wiggling with asters, yellow-eyed and purple-petaled, like daisies wine-stained after an orgy of the gods.

More than one cowgirl thought of old high school English Wordsworth, him wandering lonely as a cloud that floats o'er vales and hills, when all at once he saw a crowd, a host, of golden daffodils. But these asters were no crowd, and no host, either: they were a planet, a universe, a goddamned *infinity* of flowers. Who'd have thought that Gary Cooper's prairie; Crazy Horse's prairie; the westward ho the wagons! prairie; the hard, flat belly of America prairie became in September such a garden of gentle blooms? Everywhere, asters waved as if practicing the art of waving. The purity of the movement gave Sissy's thumbs the Big Itch, but the cowpokes were stilled by the solitary sweep of the spectacle, and they, all of them, rode back toward the ranch with a papery noise of peace in their minds, asters of the heart forcing their way to the light.

Upon arrival, they discovered the goat, which they'd tied to the corral fence with a long rope, busily eating the top off the cinematographers' convertible. It had already eaten the front-seat upholstery and part of the steering wheel of Miss Adrian's Cadillac limousine. And, as hors d'oeuvres, perhaps, it had cruised the bunkhouse clothesline, devouring no fewer than fourteen pairs of panties, including Delores's bayou snakeskins, Heather's lace bikinis and Kym's lone pair of Frederick's of Hollywood peekaboos with their valentine-shaped cutout.

That evening, around the fireplace, there were some second thoughts about goats.

45.

"THE COW MILK MOLECULE is one hundred times larger than the molecule of mother's milk. But the goat milk molecule and the human milk molecule are practically the same size. That's why goat milk is easy for us to digest and cow milk is like sand in the gas tank of the gut."

"Did you ever taste 'gator's milk?" asked Delores. Debbie didn't know how to take that question.

"Debbie's right," said Bonanza Jellybean. "More and more people are discovering that cow's milk isn't fit for human consumption. Billy West says if we can produce enough goat's milk on the ranch to make it worth his while, he'll run it into Fargo regularly. He won controlling interest in a cheese factory there in a crap game. They'd make goat cheese from our milk and supply health food stores throughout the plains states. If we can deal in enough volume — and keep the goats from eating the fucking boots right off our feet — the ranch could be self-supporting."

"And we'd be performing a service," added Debbie, ever-mindful of karma. "Goat's milk is so good for babies whose mamas can't nurse."

"Speaking of babies," said Delores, "I hope you itchy-clits who are sneaking down to the lake every night are taking precautions."

Nobody responded vocally, although there was some nervous — and angry — squirming. Delores continued. "I'm aware that Tad Lucas rode broncs until her ninth month, but I don't think pregnant cowgirls are going to be any asset on this ranch. It's bad enough we've got cranes coming; we don't need storks. I feel that those filmmakers should be removed from the Rubber Rose as soon as possible. Men can cause nothing but trouble here. I also feel that our guest" — she nodded her dark curls toward Sissy — "should be excused while we discuss this matter further."

Jelly started to speak in Sissy's behalf, but, assuring everyone that she understood, Sissy arose and left the bunkhouse.

A moon hung over the ranch like the muzzle of a melancholy mule. Preferring moonlight to the electric shine in the main house, where the guests were playing bridge and reading novels by John Updike, Sissy strolled around the grounds. She considered the fact that that same moon that was pouring its mule milk (data on the molecular relation to human milk unavailable at this time) upon hilltops and willow trees and cowgirl intrigues was the same moon that was beaming on the roof of Julian's remodeled tenement. It was a trite consideration, the kind of thought that escapes from the noodles of amateur songwriters and lovesick fraternity boys. But it placed her in touch with toothier sentiments. She and Julian Gitche, united emotionally and legally (whatever *that* meant), were also connected by moonlight. And by forces even more tentative and obscure. Perhaps everything was connected to everything, in a discernible if nebulous way, and if one might only trace the fibers and filaments of those connections, one might . . . One might what? Observe the Grand Design? Untangle all the puppet strings and discover whose hands (or claws) are pulling them? End the ancient search for order and meaning in the universe? "Criminey," sighed Sissy, kicking a horse biscuit (or was it a nylon-flavored cookie from the goat's oven?). "If my brain were only as outsized as my thumbs, I might be able to put the whole picture in focus."

Don't bet on it, Sissy, honey.

Were your brain appreciably larger, large enough to put the strain on your Princess Grace neck that your loppy preaxial digits put upon your wrists, you conceivably would possess a superior intellect. It is also conceivable, however, that, with the nervous system required to fire a brain of that size, you would be so sensitive to the follies of civilization that you would feel compelled to take to the sea the way the big-brained dolphin did. Your death certificate would speak of "suicide" and "drowning," as if your death certificate were jacket notes for the Golden Gate Bridge. No, big brains are for dolphins, who are great swimmers, and for Martians, who, judging by their infrequent visits, don't seem to get much of a bang out of Earth. Our brains are probably too large as they are.

Recent neurological research indicates that the brain is governed by principles it cannot understand. And if the brain is so weak or timid that it is incapable of comprehending its own governing principles, the physical laws it appears bound to obey, then it is not going to be much use to anyone confronting the Ultimate Questions, not even if it were as big as a breadbox (Ugh, what a sickening thought!). This author's advice to his readers is to make the best you can of your brain — it's pretty good storage space and the price is right — and then turn to something else.

The way that Sissy, for example, having tired of pondering invisible connections, turned to her thumbs and began hitchhiking cricket chirps as she walked back to her room.

46.

IT WAS THE SIXTH DAY, the day upon which, in the Judaeo-Christian version of Creation, God said, "Let there be strict potty training and free enterprise." Sissy stepped out of the main house. Immediately, her eyes turned, as they invariably did, toward Siwash Ridge.

Sometimes she could distinguish a human figure up there, silhouetted against the multicolored limestone, or emerging, closer to the base, from a clump of juniper bushes, trailing its beard behind it. On this morning she was rewarded by the blurred sight and muffled noise of a commotion.

A group of cowgirls was watching the butte, also. They were leaning against the vehicle known as the "peyote wagon," a Dodge pickup with a handmade wooden camper on its bed. The eaves of the camper were carved to resemble the open jaws of alligators, and caimans, green-skinned and fearsome of teeth, protruded in bas-relief along both sides of the luridly painted compartment. Images of iguanas and tongue-flickering saurians adorned the rear doors; the hospital white mouths of moccasins yawned from every space that was not already undulating with the killing coils, squamous wiggles and hypnotic eyes of swamp crawlers and other manifestations of the original Totem. There was no mistaking the owner of that vehicle, dressed as she was in darkest black from her Spanish-style riding hat to her mambaskin boots: Delores (with an "e") del Ruby.

It was that same Delores who stomped away upon Sissy's approach, calling back coldly over her shoulder, "The feminine hygiene business takes women for fifty million dollars a year."

Sissy was stunned by the hostile reference to her Yoni Yum/Dew Girl activities. As if it were a baby adder from the peyote wagon's façade, her lower lip was seized by tiny spasms. She was accustomed to having her thumbs, and the use to which she put them, ridiculed, but her modest modeling career had been the single thing about her life that people had deemed worthy.

"Don't pay any attention to Delores," said Kym. "She's got a sharp stick up her ass."

"Yes," agreed Debbie. "I'll sure be glad when she has her Third Vision." Debbie's brow made viperine movements of its own. "On second thought, maybe I won't be glad at all."

The cowgirls half-laughed, half-grumbled. They seemed embarrassed by Delores's rudeness, yet there was plenty of reason, considering the previous day's behavior in the sexual reconditioning class, for Sissy to believe they shared their forewoman's scorn for the industry she represented. Perhaps some re-evaluation was in order. For the moment, however, there was commotion on that ridge that to one sixteenth of her was supposed to be sacred.

"Uh, what's happening up there?" asked Sissy, hoping that her voice did not tremble.

Kym answered. "Oh, it's another bunch of salvation-seekers trying to see the Chink. He's chasing them away, as usual. What a farce."

"Shit," swore Big Red. "It's Debbie's fault. Debbie wrote all her friends and told 'em there was this big boohoo livin' up yonder, and the word just spread like hot butter. So's now they come from as far away as Frisco expectin' that old fart to tell 'em what's what. Only he don't ever tell nobody nothin'."

"He tells Jellybean a lot," corrected Debbie.

"Maybe he does and maybe he don't," countered Big Red. "I 'spect Jelly's just humoring him to keep him from causing us any trouble — and he's doing the same with her. Well, there they go! Look at your pilgrims hightailin' it, Deb. Be gettin' too cold for salvation pretty soon; maybe the old geek will get a few months' peace. Not that he deserves it."

Sissy wondered why Debbie thought the Chink to be some kind of grand boohoo to begin with. She asked about it.

"That's a good question," said Debbie, who was approximately as darling as Bonanza Jellybean, although, as were her companions, more conventionally attired. "That's a good question. You know, Sissy, every sage or holy man or spiritual leader or whatever you choose to call them does not go around preaching, writing books, gathering disciples or holding rallies in the Houston Astrodome. Some remain almost invisible among us. Swami Vivekananda once said that Buddha and Christ were second-rate heroes. He said the greatest men that ever live pass away unknown. They put forth no claims for themselves, establish no schools or systems in their name. They never create any stir but just melt down into love . . ."

"Love!" interrupted Big Red. "Grease is more like it."

Debbie smiled patiently. "Vivekananda warned that the statesmen and generals and tycoons who seem so big to us are really low-level figures. He said, 'The highest men are calm, silent and unknown.' Isn't that beautiful? The true masters seldom reveal themselves, except in the vibrations they leave behind, and upon which the lesser gurus build their doctrines. But there are ways to recognize them. The Chink, as he is called, seems a difficult person — he refuses to even snigger in my direction — but in his silence and mysterious manners he gives signs of . . ."

"Yeah, if you can call shakin' his dick a sign," interjected Big Red.

". . . signs of high wisdom," Debbie continued. "It was wrong of me to write my former sisters and brothers in the League of the Acid Atom Avatar about him, even though many of them are desperate for illumination, I see that now. But I'm not wrong in my estimation of him, of that I'm sure." She paused, rubbing her ringed fingers along the curves of a carved coral snake. "I've been meaning to ask *you,* Sissy: I understand that you've done more traveling than just about anybody. In your constant moving among the peoples, didn't you ever come across a person whose wisdom stood out from the others, who seemed to have knowledge about the living of life that the rest of us lack?"

The question was put seriously, so Sissy gave it thought. Oddly enough, she hadn't really interacted with a great many people, nor even observed many carefully. She had collected rides, not drivers. And as for pedestrians . . . shadows in the memory of a streak. However, there was that time in Mexico, not far south of the border.

Sissy had been hitchhiking down a road so dusty it could have strangled a camel. At one point the road passed the home workshop of a cabinetmaker. Fifteen or twenty pieces of newly carpentered furniture were lined up in the heat alongside the road. A man of indeterminate age was varnishing them. From a two-gallon can, the Mexican was carefully applying varnish with a brush. Whenever a car or truck went by, which was fairly frequently, thick clouds of dust roiled up, settling like Lawrence of Arabia's memories upon the sticky furniture. But the Mexican went on with his work, smiling, singing to himself and paying no more attention to the dust than if it were a radio broadcast in a foreign language. So impressed had been Sissy that she nearly stopped to talk to the man; he let loose elaborate bright balloons in her heart. In the end, though, she had kept on hitching — subsequently thinking of the varnisher only in times of stress, frustration and self-doubt.

To speak of such things was embarrassing to Sissy, but she was about to tell Debbie of the marvelous Mexican when Jelly came trotting up on her horse. Jelly had been observing the Siwash Ridge ruckus from a closer perspective, ascertaining that it would have no repercussions upon the ranch. Now she called to the cowgirls, "Hey, podners, Delores is wanting you in the bunkhouse for drill. Let's be hitting it."

"Drill!" huffed Big Red. "I should have stayed in the goddamned Wacs."

"This is a mistake," said Debbie. "There are higher ways for women to deal with things."

Some eagerly, some reluctantly, the cowgirls walked off toward the bunkhouse. Jellybean dismounted.

"Aren't they a great bunch of podners?" she asked.

Sissy nodded. "Where do they come from?" she inquired.

"Oh, East, West and the cuckoo's nest. Lot of 'em grew up on farms and ranches and kinda liked the life, but when they got outta high school there was nothing for 'em to do but marry some local jerk or else try to get by in a college that wasn't prepared to teach 'em anything they really wanted to know. A couple of 'em, like Kym and Debbie, came buckin' out of middle-class suburbia. Big Red was the only working cowgirl in the lot; she'd ridden in barrel races all over Texas. 'Course Big Red is twenty-seven years old; the rest of us are a heap younger. Except for Delores. Nobody knows how old she is or what she was doing before she showed up here, but, God, she sure can rope and ride. I was after girls who wanted to be cowgirls and I never asked too many questions. Ones I tried to weed out were the ones that were in love with horses. You know, the Freudian thing. Lot of parents, about the time their baby daughters start pushing out their sweaters in front, they buy 'em a horse to divert their attention from boys. What they really buy 'em is a thousand-pound organic vibrator. A horse is great for good clean hands-above-the-sheets masturbation, and some girls never outgrow the thrill of it. Those kind just don't make real cowgirls."

Siwash Ridge had become as quiet and inanimate as the geology book that might describe its formation. Indian summer, the ham, was taking yet another curtain call, and the hills, warmed into an expansive mood, heaped bouquets of asters at its feet. Goldenrod, too. And butterfly weed. Giant sunflowers, like junkie scarecrows on the nod, dozed in one spot with their dry heads drooped upon their breastbones. Their lives extended another day, flies buzzed everything within their range, monotonously eulogizing themselves, like the patriots who persist in praising the glory of a culture long after it is decadent and doomed.

Eventually, Jelly spoke again. "You sure brought some cute weather with you. Looking around today, you'd never believe the snow and howling winds that are gonna slam this place in a month or two."

"New York gets a long case of the won't-quit shivers, too," Sissy said. "I've never spent a whole winter in one place before, not since I was a kid."

"One just has to snuggle up," said Jelly, copping a glance at the bunkhouse. "Miss Adrian, when she first told me you were comin' out here, she said that you'd been recently married."

"About nine months ago."

"Hmm. Yeah. I never figured that you'd be the type to marry and settle down."

"Nobody did," said Sissy, sort of laughing. "Including me. But it's all right."

"I've got this theory," Jelly said. "Men — in general — are turned on by women who are attached. It's an ego challenge to break that attachment and transfer it to themselves. Women — in general — are turned on by men who are unattached. Freedom excites 'em. Unconsciously, they're aching to end it." She scanned Sissy's face. "It would have been the opposite in your case, though. Or was it like that?"

"I don't know. Maybe. I've never thought about it that way. You see, Jelly, I was alone for a long, long time. Few women are alone by choice — maybe that's our major weakness — but upon the advice of nature I chose not to be boxed in or play it straight. Alone, I was able to shake to the big beat, dance the fourth dimension and make transportation talk out of its head. Only nobody cared. Oh, Jack Kerouac and a dozen other desperate souls, maybe, had a whiff that I was something more than world's champion, but nobody else. Well, so what? I did believe that my accomplishments might have lifted human spirits, the way that a comet fills people with joy for no logical or productive reason when it shoots across the sky. If they had paid attention. They didn't, and that's okay, because I was really hitchhiking for myself. Myself and the great windy powers. Then, all of a sudden, there was somebody who needed me. For the first time in my life, I was needed. It was a powerful attraction."

Jelly was scratching her horse's ears. The animal was named Lucas, after Tad. "I guess men need wives, all right," she said. "Just as women *think* that they need husbands."

"Julian needed more than a wife," said Sissy. "By most standards, I'm not even a very good wife. On a conscious level, Julian doesn't appreciate or understand me a drop better than anyone else, but somewhere in him he knows he needs what only someone like me can offer. Julian is a Mohawk Indian who has been deformed by society. He denies being Mohawk, denies any possible physical or psychic benefit from it. He needs to be loved in a way that will put him in touch with his blood. And that's the way I'm trying to love him."

Taking her time, Jelly mounted. "That makes a certain amount of sense," she said. "If love can't re-create lovers, what good is it? But let me give you this caution, Sissy, my podner: Love is dope, not chicken soup."

When Sissy continued to look puzzled, Jelly added, "I mean, love is something to be passed around freely, not spooned down someone's throat for their own good by a Jewish mother who cooked it all by herself."

With that, Jelly swung down along Lucas's side, in imitation of a stunt once performed at high speeds by the horse's namesake, and kissed Sissy, half upon the mouth, half upon the chin. Then she righted herself and galloped away.

That afternoon, in the bunkhouse, when Gloria made a comparison between Sissy's thumbs and the hunchback of Notre Dame, Bonanza Jellybean slapped her chops.

47.

"THE POLISH SAUSAGE POLKA" was interrupted for a news bulletin about the international situation, which, as listeners in the bunkhouse soon learned, was desperate, as usual. Speaking of desperation, there was an expression of mild despair upon Big Red's face as, without knocking, she opened the door of the main exercise room.

Guests and staff alike stiffened when Big Red entered, for all of them were a bit uneasy about cowgirls by then, and Big Red, the flaming tower of freckles, was the roughest-looking cowgirl on the spread. There was no cause for alarm, however. Big Red had overheard Miss Adrian announce that the final weigh-out was to be held this day. At the close of the day's activities, guests were to assemble in the main exercise room for their last ride upon the Rubber Rose scales. The following day, at the low-cal barbecue that would mark the official end of the ranch's season, prizes would be awarded those women who had squirted off the most poundage into the dry Dakota air. Big Red coveted no award, was not eligible for one and, frankly, deserved none, but she did wish to consult the scales. Wearing her one-piece forest green swimsuit, she took a place in line before the oracle. After easily obtaining the guests' permission, Miss Adrian ushered Big Red to the head of the line.

The hugest cowgirl weighed, winced, grunted and, to everyone's relief, left as she had come. On the way back to the bunkhouse, Indian summer paying its respects to the flesh that bubbled out around the edges of her swimsuit, Big Red had a flash, a mental visitation perhaps no less intense than Delores del Ruby's First and Second Visions. Seized by inspiration, Big Red thought, "Wouldn't it be dadburned wonderful if there was a machine that you could hook up to your plate of food that would extract the flavors from it. After you'd ate all your belly could comfortably hold, you could stick a plastic tube in your mouth, switch on the little machine, and the flavors would continue to run into your mouth for as long as you pleased, without nothin' goin' into your belly to make it fuller and fatter. Mmm, Lord, Lord; ham gravy, cheese 'n onion pie, chili, rice puddin', Lord."

In the main exercise room of the Rubber Rose, there was an immediate market for such an apparatus, and, no doubt, sales around the world could be counted in tens of millions, the international situation notwithstanding. It would, moreover, constitute an unprecedented boon for mankind, keeping as many people off the streets as television and saving move lives than a cancer cure.

Therefore, in the public interest, *Even Cowgirls Get the Blues* offers the Big Red flavor device idea free of charge to any inventor who can make it a reality.

48.

"JULIAN, I have a friend."

"A friend you say, dear?" It was a barely tolerable connection. "That's good. New friends are fun."

"You don't understand. I have a girl friend. I've never had a girl friend before."

"Oh, now, honey, you exaggerate. Isn't Marie your friend?"

"Marie is *your* friend. She's only interested in me as an exotic cunt."

"Sissy! We're on the telephone!"

"Sorry. I just wanted to tell you about Jelly, but never mind."

"Jelly is that troublemaker you're supposed to be keeping an eye on for the Countess, isn't she? How's it going with those cowgirls? I hope everything is smooth out there. I worry about you constantly."

"No need to worry about me, ever. I carry my guardian angels around on my hands."

"Sissy, you mustn't mock yourself like that; it isn't healthy. Well, now, dear, my concern for you hasn't totally prevented me from enjoying myself. Numerous eat-abouts. Elaine's, La Grenouille, La Caravelle. Dancing Friday night at Kenny's Castaways with the Wrights and the Sabols. Howard was working late so Marie came with what's-his-name, Colacello. Cheek-to-cheek dancing is the *rage* in New York these days. I hadn't realized. I hope you'll go with me after you return. You'd love it if you'd give it a chance. A few people are coming here for a kitchen supper this evening. Cozy. I'm setting up a backgammon table. Wish you were here. Oh, I bought an enchanting doll at the Brooklyn Museum gift shop today — folk art. Wait until you see it. I'm almost finished with the painting I started the day before you left, the big one you thought was going to be a wigwam. It's nothing of the sort of course; it's . . ."

"Julian, what's that noise?"

"Noise? Oh, that. That's a surprise, dear. That's . . . Can't you guess? That's *Butty*. Carla and Rupert are together again. God, yes, I meant to tell you. Carla moved back into town and she can't keep Butty in their flat. So the old boy is here again. If you mind, I can always sell him. Dogs such as Butty are the *rage* in New York now; all the trend-benders own at least two. Andy Warhol brought his miniature dachshund, Archie, to Kenny's Castaways the other night. Imagine. Now, Sissy, about those cowgirls you're running with, watch your step, will you?"

The long-distance wires made those sounds that are part gurgle, part bleep; the sounds a baby robot might make in its crib. Endearments were exchanged and Julian hung up — without a clue that the call he had terminated had been made possible by Bonanza Jellybean, who, as an act of friendship, had postponed snipping the Rubber Rose telephone lines.

49.

If we may say that the civilized man is clever but not wise, we may say, also, that the prairie is dry but not without water. Upon the prairie there are occasional rivers, streams, lakes, ponds and flooded buffalo wallows. Like the American System itself, most of the prairie ponds and lakes are fly-by-night operations. Although they may thrive temporarily, supporting a teeming food chain that can run from aquatic plants to muskrats to owls; from nymphal insects to sunfish to snapping turtles; or from salamanders to magpies to weasels, in time the ponds and lakes are invaded by vegetation, filled with silt and reduced during summer droughts until they gasp (!) and die, changing into marsh and then prairie again. Often a prairie pond is not around long enough to earn a name.

Siwash Lake, since it found a home in a relatively deep depression between the hills of the terminal moraines left by the continental ice sheet, has enjoyed a certain permanence, although as evidenced by its imploding margins of arrowhead, cattail and reed, it, too, is entering the swamp phase of its existence and eventually will be unable to provide enough moisture to freshen a tadpole's highball.

There are a few good years left on the little lake yet, however, and it was shimmering like a blob of invisible ink when Sissy and Jelly caught sight of it from the hill behind the cinematographer's blind. Sissy and Jelly walked over the crest of the hill, having tied their horses at the cherry tree, and there was the lake, laking. Knee-deep in wheatgrass and asters, Sissy and Jelly walked over the crest of the hill naked, having left their clothing at the cherry tree, and the lake was below them, shimmering. Sissy and Jelly walked over the crest of the hill naked, for the sunning that was in it, and it was truly difficult to believe, as they gazed at Siwash Lake, that they, too, Sissy and Jelly, were mostly water. (The brain, with its fragmentary and elusive qualities, yes, water; but body meat?)

Since the hidden cameras were trained on the lakeshore, they could not record the images that moved at the crest of the hill, nor could the concealed microphones steal conversation. Sissy and Jelly were talking when they walked over the crest, and after they had studied the lake for a while, they sat and talked again.

"She was living in Louisiana, in a shack town built by runaway slaves deep in the bayous. That's one story, anyway. I've also heard that she was traveling through Yucatán with a circus, popping false eyelashes off a trained monkey with a bullwhip. It doesn't matter. Wherever it was that she was, she ate peyote one night and had a vision. Niwetúkame, the Mother Goddess, came to her on the back of a doe, hummingbirds sipping the tears she was shedding, crying 'Delores, you must lead my daughters against their natural enemy.' Delores thought about it for a long time — it was one hell of a vivid vision — until she determined that the natural enemy of the daughters were the fathers and the sons. That night she whipped the shit out of her black lover, or the circus owner — it doesn't matter which — and ran away. For a while she drove around, making a living selling peyote buttons to hippies. Then, Niwetúkame came to her again, saying that she must go to a certain place and prepare for her mission, the details of which would be revealed to her in another vision. The place the Peyote Mother directed her to come was the Rubber Rose Ranch. Isn't that incredible? She zonks out on peyote at least once a week, but so far her Third Vision hasn't happened. Meanwhile, she and Debbie are rivaling each other like a couple of crosstown high schools. Tension. Cowgirl tension! What a drag."

"What is Debbie's position?" Sissy asked. A breeze swatted her ribcage with grassheads.

"Well, as I understand it, Debbie feels that people have a tendency to become what they hate. She says that women who hate men turn into men. Eee! That grass tickles, doesn't it?" Jelly was being swatted, too. "Debbie says that women are different from men and that that difference is the source of their strength. Way back before Judaism and Christianity, women were in charge of everything, government, economics, family, agriculture and especially religion; both Debbie and Delores agree on that. But Debbie says that if women are to take charge again, they must do it in the feminine way; they mustn't resort to aggressive and violent masculine methods. She says it is up to women to show themselves *better* than men, to love men, set good examples for them and guide them tenderly toward the New Age. She's a real dreamer, that Debbie-dear."

"You don't agree with Debbie, then?"

"I wouldn't say that. I expect she's right, ultimately. But I'm with Delores when it comes to fighting for what's mine. I can't understand why Delores is so uptight about the Chink; he could probably teach her a thing or two. Or how can anybody dislike Billy West, that good ol' rascal? God knows I love women, but nothing can take the place of a man that fits. Still, this here is cowgirl territory and I'll stand with Delores and fight any bastards who might deny it. I guess I've always been a scrapper. Look. This scar. Only twelve years old and I was felled by a silver bullet."

Jelly took Sissy's hand, carefully avoiding its first or most preaxial digit, and helped her to feel the depression in her belly. It was as if she had bought her navel at a two-for-one sale.

Ignoring the possibilities that she had piqued Sissy's curiosity or lit up her limbic switchboard, Jelly continued to speak. "God, I dig it out here. This raw space. Nobody has ever nailed it down. It's too big and too tough. Men saw it as a challenge; they wanted to compete against it, to conquer it. For the most part they failed, and now they hate it. But women can regard it in a different way. We can flow with it, merge with it and love it. The Chink says that these plains exist on the edge of meaning, at a zone between meaning and something so great it's got no meaning. I think I understand. Why any cowgirl wouldn't be content with this I don't know, but I reckon some people just can't have fun unless everyone else is having fun, too."

Sissy kept her hand on Jelly's tummy, for as soon as the cowgirl quit talking she wished to inquire how she happened to catch a *silver* bullet in such a tender spot at such a tender age. Before she had a second to ask, however, Jelly lobbed a question of her own. "Say, Sissy, you working for the Countess and all, I wonder if you've had a chance to try the perfume trick we told the guests about the other day?"

"Er, well, no, I haven't. It actually works, does it?"

"Sure it works. Why don't you try it?"

"You mean now?"

She meant now, Sissy. *N* for narcissus, *N* for nasty, *N* for *nigi* (*Nigi* is Japanese for "rainbow." It also means "two o'clock." Thus, in Japan there are at least two rainbows daily); *O* for orchid, *O* for odoriferous, *O* for om (The meditation mat is the yogi's horse; git along little yogi, gotta reach El Snuffing Out Candle before sundownownownownownownownownownownownowown . . . Only mantra west of the Pecos); *W* for wisteria, *W* for wet, *W* for Walla Walla (a city in eastern Washington), Wagga Wagga (a city in southeastern Australia) and Wooga Wooga (a café in the astral dimension where Charlie Parker jams every Saturday night): *N*O*W*, Now. She wanted to watch you spread it, Sissy, opening like a ballet slipper, a gaping shellfish. She wanted to spread it, Sissy, her petite fingers wading in the swamp of it, raising its temperature, widening its smile. Oh why is it so difficult between women? Between a man and a woman it's yes or no. Between women it's always maybe. One mistake and the other runs away. Even when women embrace they must keep their hearts still, eyes blank. Words are out of the question. But it's worth it, Sissy, worth the pretensions, interruptions and caution. When a man is in you, you cannot imagine what it is his body is feeling, nor can he know your pleasures accurately. Between women, each is precisely aware: when she does *that* she is certain that the other is feeling *this*. And it's so soft, Sissy. So soft.

Krishna, or as he is called in the West, Pan, the god Jesus Christ drove into hiding, was the only god who understood women. Krishna/Pan lured maidens into the woods, but he never raped, nor did he seduce with false promises or insincere declarations of love. He awakened them with special ancient vaudeville; he turned them on. It is that way that women visit each other: as music, as clowns.

Woman has not suffered civilization gladly. It has been suggested, in fact, that all of civilization was merely a dike thrown up by men, fearful of sexual competition, in order "to hold back wild and unruly feminine waters." Now, however, She may be commandeering the shining inventions of civilized man and turning them to Her own dark uses. For example, kissing.

Kissing is man's greatest invention.

All animals copulate, but only humans kiss.

Kissing is the supreme achievement of the Western world.

Orientals, including those who tended the North American continent before the ravagement, rubbed noses, and thousands still do. Yet despite the golden fruit of their millennia — they gave us yoga and gunpowder, Buddha and corn on the cob — they, their multitudes, their saints and sages, never produced a kiss.

The greatest discovery of civilized man is kissing.

Primitives, pygmies, cannibals and savages have shown tenderness to one another in many tactile ways, but pucker against pucker has not been their style.

Parakeets rub beaks. Yes, it's true, they do. However, only devotees of premature ejaculation, or those little old ladies who murder children with knitting needles to steal their lunch money to buy fresh kidneys for kittycats could place bird-billing in the realm of the kiss.

Black Africans touch lips. Quite right; some of them do, as do certain aboriginal tribesmen in other parts of the world — but though their lips may touch, they do not linger. The peck is a square wheel, awkward and slightly ominous. What else did Judas betray Our Savior with but a peck: terse, spit-free and tongueless?

Tradition informs us that kissing, as we know it, was invented by medieval knights for the utilitarian purpose of determining whether their wives had been into the mead barrel while the knights were away on duty. If history is correct, for once, then the kiss began as an osculatory wiretap, an oral snoop, a kind of alcoholic chastity belt, after the fact. Form does not always follow function, however, and eventually kissing for kissing's sake became popular in the courts, spreading to the tradesmen, peasants and serfs. And why not? For kissing is *sweet.* It was as if all the atavistic sweetness still remaining in Western man was funneled into kissing and that alone. No other flesh like lip flesh! No meat like mouth meat! The musical clink of tooth against tooth, the wonderful curiosity of tongues.

If women took short delight in lesser inventions, such as the wheel, the lever and the blade of steel, they applauded kissing, practicing it upon their men, for fun and profit, and upon each other — within limits. Because they were designed to suckle both male and female child at their breasts, women are not as sexually restrictive as men. They have always been prone to kiss other women, a practice that has made our Faith uneasy and our smut-sniffers pale. In 1899, even so relatively liberal a Victorian as Dr. Mary Wood-Allen felt compelled to write, in *What a Young Woman Ought to Know,* "I wish the friendships of girls were more manly. Two young men who are friends do not lop on each other, and kiss and gush. Girlish friendships that include fondling and kissing are not only silly, they are even dangerous."

WHO WILL SING THE PRAISES OF SILLY AND DANGEROUS KISSING? She feared to fondle your secret parts, Sissy, and you feared to fondle them in front of her. But your mouths were bold — and silly and dangerous — and you leaned toward one another slowly, sliding cheeks, and kissed. Meeting with a passing bee's pulsation, you mashed your mouths flat until soon your tongues were entangled in bubbles and breaths. Long, thick tongues painted each other with tongue stuff; painting away gradually the feminine fears so that you could extract your fingers from her sterling scar and slide them down her belly. When the hair and juice whispered against your fingertips — whispered dirty words such as "pussy," "cunt," and "snatch" — you thought of Marie, always grabbing you there, and you almost pulled away. But Jelly moaned in your mouth, flooding it with sweetness, and in a moment her own hand was exploring the hot folds of your vulva.

Embraced, you toppled over in the wheatgrass. Her Stetson fell off and rolled away in the direction of Oklahoma City. Maybe it wanted to say howdy to Tad Lucas. Your eyes sent an archeological expedition to Jelly's face, and hers to yours; both unearthed inscriptions and pondered their meaning. She whispered that you were beautiful and brave. She called you a "hero," meaning heroine, but her fingers were not fooled for an instant. You tried to tell her how much her friendship meant to you. Did you get the words out or didn't you? Teeth of foam, lips of pie.

After a hungry stillness, like intermission at a wolf dance, rhythms were established. You were socked into one another now, it had been acknowledged and approved, and so you arched and pushed and corkscrewed and jackknifed, softly but with pronounced cadence. Finger-fucking is an art. Men indulge in it; women excel at it. Ohh. Fireman save my child!

You felt as if your hand were up a jukebox, a flesh Wurlitzer spewing colored electrical sparks as it played itself to pieces on the Dime of the Century. Your clitoris was a switch without an "off." She snapped it on on on and further on. You crooked your tongue around an erect nipple. She smiled at your quiverings when she parted your asshole.

Everything became scrambled. You rocked each other in cradles of sweat and saliva, until you could see nothing. You imagined her in a bride's trousseau, pictured her a mare. Did you ferment, the two of you? You smelled like it. Fans of funk and fever opened and closed, chins were aglisten with the juice of kissing. You rocked and rocked, your thumb swacking her belly in rhythm, adding to the excitement — hers and yours.

Eyes closed, or maybe only glazed, you pictured her tight young whatdoyoucallit in your mind. Hair by dripping hair, it gaped before you. Your own clitoris felt as swollen pink as a bubblegum cigar. Oh these things were made to be loved!

Suddenly, you were weeping. Noisy breaths bucked out of you. You called "Jelly Jelly" when you intended only to murmur "mmmm." It didn't matter. Jellybean couldn't hear you. She was screaming. Hysterical from the scalding hot softness of girl-love.

Criminey, how that filly can come, you thought, after your own spasms had subsided. At the same moment, Jelly was wondering how a city apartment house could possibly contain your sex cries. For Jelly, too, was at rest. Only gradually did you both realize that a third auditory ingredient had mixed with Jelly screams and Sissy groans — a brasher, wilder sound, though obviously the work of the same composer.

Sticky fingers were pulled from melons. Soaked inside and out, the two of you sat up. There came that noise again, only louder, more eerie. Had your hairs, short and long, not been so damp they might have stood. It was a mighty trumpeting, a whoop such as the World might have made on the day it was born.

It was then that you ladies, your rosy bodies imprinted with patterns of crushed leaves and stems, looked to see a squadron of white satin airliners circling Siwash Lake, a flock of birds so grand and giant and elegant that your hearts squeezed out eternity's toothpaste.

50.

DESCRIBE THE WHOOPING CRANE (*Grus americana*) in twenty-five words or less.

The whooping crane is a very large and very regal white bird with long black legs, a sinuous neck and a thrilling trumpetlike voice.

Okay. I'll grade that a C.

Only a C? May I try again?

Go ahead.

The most spectacular of our native wading birds, the whooping crane stands about five feet tall and has a wingspread of nearly eight.

No improvement, I'm afraid. Still a C.

One more try?

Be my guest.

Imagine Wilt Chamberlain in red yarmulke and snowy feathers . . .

Hold it. You're assuming that the reader knows who Wilt Chamberlain is. Many people don't follow basketball and wouldn't understand that Wilt signifies size and strength and arrogance made palatable by grace.

I give up. The whooper enters one's spirit the instant it enters one's senses. It is perfect radiant sky monster and I cannot describe it.

Better. Make that a B.

51.

"PAIUTE INDIANS called the crane *kodudududududu,*" said Sissy. "Isn't that a funny name?"

Jellybean was delighted. "Say it again," she urged.

"*Kodudududududu.* Six *dus.* *Kodudududududu.*"

They both laughed.

"You know a lot about Indians, don't you?" asked Jelly. She brushed dead cherry leaves from her panties before stepping in.

"A little," said Sissy. She was slower getting into her undies because of her thumbs.

"And birds, too. I can't get over the way they let you walk up so close to 'em. Whoopers are supposed to be really skittish. 'Specially when they're migrating."

"Maybe they've never seen a human being nude before. We're different when we're naked. But I do have a way with birds, I guess. I told you about Boy, only parakeet to ever flag down a Diesel rig."

Sissy looked at Jelly's popover tits as they disappeared into glossy shirt of cactus sunset design. In the looking, her blue gaze grew solemn. "I understand a tad about Indians and birds," she said softly, "but I don't know if I understand what happened up there."

Jelly's eyes snagged Sissy's, elevated them. "Something *nice* happened up there."

"Yes," admitted Sissy. "It was nice."

"Do you feel bad about it?"

"No, oh no. I don't feel bad. I feel . . . different. Or maybe I don't feel different; maybe I feel like I *should* feel different." She was thoughtful. She zipped up. "Have you had sex with girls much before?"

"Only since I've been at the Rubber Rose. Between Miss Adrian and Delores, every eligible male's been scared away from here, and there's usually trouble of one kind or another if we fool around with the hicks in Mottburg. That leaves your fingers or other women, and at least half the cowgirls on the ranch have been in each other's pants by now. There's not a queer among 'em, either. It's just a nice, natural thing to do. Girls are so close and soft. Why did it take me all these years to learn that it's okay to roll around with 'em? It's 'specially good when it's somebody you really like a lot." She hugged Sissy and sugar-doodled a few kisses around her neck and ears.

A pair of smiles rode across the Dakota hills.

Perhaps a person gains by accumulating obstacles. The more obstacles set up to prevent happiness from appearing, the greater the shock when it does appear, just as the rebound of a spring will be all the more powerful the greater the pressure that has been exerted to compress it. Care must be taken, however, to select large obstacles, for only those of sufficient scope and scale have the capacity to lift us out of context and force life to appear in an entirely new and unexpected light. For example, should you litter the floor and tabletops of your room with small objects, they constitute little more than a nuisance, an inconvenient clutter that frustrates you and leaves you irritable: the petty is mean. Cursing, you step around the objects, pick them up, knock them aside. Should you, on the other hand, encounter in your room a nine-thousand-pound granite boulder, the surprise it evokes, the extreme steps that must be taken to deal with it, compel you to see with new eyes. And if the boulder is more special, if it has been painted or carved in some mysterious way, you may find that it possesses an extraordinary and supernatural presence that enchants you, and in coping with it — as it blocks your path to the bathroom — leaves *you* feeling extraordinary and supernatural, too. Difficulties illuminate existence, but they must be fresh and of high quality.

To the obstacles that had conspired to prevent Sissy Hankshaw Gitche, white female Protestant of South Richmond, Virginia, from attaining normality, from filling a responsible and orderly role, from operating as a productive, well-adjusted contributor to the human community, now must be added friendship with Bonanza Jellybean. Whether this latest obstacle was to elevate Sissy or nudge her toward the breaking place, as a certain straw is reported to have done to a certain burdened camel, was impossible to judge from her smile, for it was simultaneously gladdened and apprehensive. It is of little or no value to analyze mental states such as this. The kingdom of formal ideas will always be a weak neighbor to the kingdom of thrills, and Sissy was a princess of thrill. Blood bunched in her head like grapes in a wig. It sang there like a popular ballad — even though the only radio station in the area played nothing but polkas. Jelly had promised to come to her room that night, with marijuana and new positions. If those prospects excited her, she was also excited by the memory of the whooping cranes, a sight all the more breathtaking because of the knowledge that those huge, elegant fugitives were so few in number and perched so precariously on the brink of total extinction. No heat, no agony, no bloody struggle, but a band of exquisite creatures (for which the world has no replacement) poised coolly — defiantly! — on the winking eyelid of doom.

Perhaps crane and cowgirl merged in her mind into a single bright-eyed beaky goblin of love. If so, it took flight when she and Jelly rode up to the corral. Delores and Big Red hurried to meet them. "He's here," announced Delores, pointing with her whip.

Sure enough, across the yard, in the midst of the low-cal barbecue then in progress, monocle reflecting sunlight, cigarette holder stabbing air, stood the Countess. Except for stains of White House ketchup on his ascot, he looked the same as ever, and why shouldn't he, for only a couple of weeks had passed since Sissy last saw him, although it seemed like years.

"Look at him," hissed Delores. "Perverse as a pink pickle."

"Sick as a vice squad," elaborated Big Red.

"He's in a snit," Delores said. "He wants to see you right after the barbecue."

Jellybean chuckled sardonically. She dismounted. "Get the girls," she said. "He's gonna see me right now."

Left abruptly in the corral with a horse she could not unsaddle, Sissy was alarmed. Obviously, a confrontation was brewing, and she wished no part of it. How many years had the Countess been her benefactor? Many. If not for him, she probably could not have survived. When she caught sight of him, her impulse had been to rush up in fond greeting. Yet she didn't dare. Confused and double-confused, loyalties torn, guilt rising, she abandoned the horse and made her way as stealthily as she could to the rear of the main house, stumbling only momentarily over the chain of the goat.

She slipped inside through the kitchen, where sacks of Debbie-ordered brown rice sat with Oriental asceticism, stoically ignoring the smells of roasting veal that wafted in from the party. She loped down the hall, entered her room, locked herself in. As the latch was turning, she overheard Jelly say something like, "Any of you ladies who would like to join us, you're welcome to stay on as a full working podner at the Rubber Rose. Rest of you get packed — and I mean now. You've got fifteen minutes to move your lard asses off this ranch."

There were loud gasps, panicky murmurings and barbecued blubberings. The screen door screeched open and Sissy heard a chaos of footsteps in the hall.

From her window, Sissy could see and hear Miss Adrian screaming threats of prison and other punishments at the cowgirls. The Countess, on the other hand, appeared to be taking the incident in his snide. He stood calmly, reducing the material existence of a French cigarette, and observed Jellybean and sisters with an expression of sarcastic amusement. "You pathetic little cutesy-poos," he seemed to say. "Do you actually suppose this exhibition of childish melodrama is advancing the cause of freedom?"

"You owe us this here ranch, as token payment for your disgusting exploitations," said Jelly.

"Then take it," the Countess said tranquilly.

Perhaps he meant it as compliance, but the cowgirls regarded his statement a challenge.

Jelly shouted a command. The hands, who carried axes, picks, pitchforks and shovels, retreated. The Countess, still grinning, reached for an hors d'oeuvre and subjected his cigarette to a measured, self-assured puff. Miss Adrian shook her fist and yelled, "Go to your bunkhouse and remain there!" as if she had just led a rout. The guests were in their rooms packing, save for one lady who had tossed her cup of punch at Miss Adrian and joined the revolution. The masseuse had joined, too, and she egged on the rest of the staff members, who stood off to one side of the barbecue pit, hoping to appear neutral.

When they had retreated about thirty yards, the cowgirls stopped. With astonishing rapidity, they unbuckled, unbuttoned and unzipped — and stepped out of their jeans and underpants. Then, nude from the waist down, thatched pubises thrust forward, up front and leading the way, they began to advance. The Countess's grin went down his throat like bathwater down a drain.

"Better reach for your spray cans!" taunted Gloria.

"Not one of these pussies has been washed in a week!" yelled Jellybean.

Rather pale now, his nose twitching, the Countess dropped the caviar canapé he'd been holding. A prairie ant helped itself to the spoils, the first ant in the history of the Dakotas to make off with a gobule of Iranian caviar. He or she'll go down in the Ant Hall of Fame.

On came the cowpokes, while behind them, in rows, fifteen separate little piles of jeans and panties bowed low to the ground, like a pilgrimage of rag Muslims prostrating themselves to the Mecca of duds. On came the cowpokes, pelvises pumping, laying down what the trembling Countess believed to be a devastating barrage of musk.

Lost in her own hysteria, Miss Adrian charged. A barbecue fork she hurled drew blood from Heather's eyebrow. Quick as a frog's tongue, Delores's whip cracked. Its lash curled around the ranch manager's ankles, pulling her feet from under her. She hit the sod in a jangle of jewelry and an explusion of breath. Then the rampage began.

A Molotov cocktail said good-by to Big Red, hello to the sexual reconditioning building. Within minutes, the structure was blazing. Other cowgirls, bare asses flashing, stormed the wing of the main house where the beauty parlor and exercise rooms were located. Sounds of glass breaking and wood splintering echoed through the house. The air was singed with cries of "Wahoo," "Yippee," "Let 'er buck" and "The vagina is a self-cleaning organ."

Sissy hadn't a clue what to do. Her darling Jellybean had obviously forgotten her. The Countess would be furious with her for failing to warn him of the impending revolt. Julian would not be pleased, either. And for all she knew, she might be in physical peril. Delores and her pals did identify her with the Countess's business. The sauna was burning now and the ranch was swirled in smoke.

Acting on orders from that very large portion of the brain that is completely uninterested in anything but survival, Sissy fled the house by the way she had entered. Crossing the croquet court, passing the pool, she ran to the base of Siwash Ridge and then southward along the mountain's foot. Eventually she came to a place where the juniper bushes were broken to reveal a crude path beginning a steep ascent. Because the butte promised both protection and a view of the proceedings, Sissy elected to climb.

She shouldered her way through low, silvery boughs. The trail was acting funny. It would switch back where there was no reason for it to switch or it would head straight for the edge of the cliff, only to turn aside at the last possible inch and bob up and down as if it were laughing. It seemed to have a mind of its own. A deranged mind, at that.

Sissy walked lightly but firmly, as if she were trying to calm the trail down, as if she were giving it therapy. It did not respond.

Sweating, panting, startled by rabbits and magpies, she accepted the first opportunity — approximately halfway up the ridge and twenty minutes' climb — to rest on a flat rock, from which she might look down upon the Rubber Rose. The ranch was farther away than even the deceptions of the trail had led her to imagine.

The whoopjamboreehoo was still raging. Noise and smoke. The main house had been spared the torch, but several of the outbuildings were in ashes. She thought she could detect cowgirls attempting to quiet horses that had panicked in the corrals. She did see Miss Adrian's Cadillac roar out of the drive, but she had no way of telling what passengers it bore. Somewhat later, the cinematographers' rented convertible and their equipment van also drove away. Had the filmmakers been evicted or had others commandeered their vehicles? Sissy sat and wondered. She also wondered if and when she should return to the ranch. The sun was already kneeling on the doorsill of the West, and as night approached she could feel cold scratchings on her flesh.

After a while she felt something else. Eyes, she felt. Eyes watching her. Not little pink rabbit eyes or jumpy bright bird eyes. Big carnivorous eyes. A wildcat or wolf, for sure. Again, that vast battery of efficient brainpower, insensitive to beauty, romance, fun or freedom; suspicious and careful, as conventional as eggs-for-breakfast, as cheerless as a banker's socks; that stiff-collared DNA fogy who happens to be the major stockholder in human consciousness, issued orders. Obeying, for no commands are as difficult as these to disobey, Sissy picked up a stone and turned around slowly.

"Ha ha ho ho and hee hee," snickered the thing that was watching her. It stood ten yards away. It was, of course, the Chink.

The Chink's problem was that he looked like the Little Man who had the Big Answers. Flowing white hair and a dirty bathrobe, weathered face and handmade sandals, teeth that would make an accordion jealous, eyes that twinkled like bicycle lights in a mist. He was short but muscular, aged but handsome and O the smoky aroma of his immortal beard! He looked as if he had stolen down from the ceiling of the Sistine Chapel, by way of a Yokohama opium parlor. He looked as if he could talk with animals, discussing with them subjects Dr. Dolittle wouldn't comprehend. He looked as if he had rolled out of a Zen scroll, as if he said "presto" a lot, knew the meaning of lightning and the origin of dreams. He looked as if he drank dew and fucked snakes. He looked like the cape that rustles on the backstairs of Paradise.

They scrutinized one another with mutual fascination. Sissy held her breath and the Chink said, "Ha ha ho ho and hee hee."

At last she thought of something to say, but, as if he sensed that she was about to speak and did not want her words in his strangely pointed ears, he whirled, and scampered up the mountainside whence he had come.

"Wait!" she cried.

Warily, he stopped and turned, poised to flee again.

Sissy smiled.

She raised her ripe right thumb.

And jerking it and swooshing it and wringing every flicker from it, as though this were its farewell performance and it must please the gods, she hitchhiked the hermit and his mountain.

And got a ride to the clockworks.

Part IV

I am not of your race. I belong to the Mongol clan which brought to the world a monstrous truth: the authenticity of life and the knowledge of rhythm . . . You do well to hem me in with the hundred thousand bayonets of Western enlightenment, for woe unto you if I leave the dark of my cave and set about in earnest to chase off your clamorings.

— Blaise Cendrars

52.

For Christmas that year, Julian gave Sissy a miniature Tyrolean village. The craftsmanship was remarkable.

There was a tiny cathedral whose stained-glass windows made fruit salad of sunlight. There was a plaza and *ein Biergarten.* The *Biergarten* got quite noisy on Saturday nights. There was a bakery that smelled always of hot bread and strudel. There was a town hall and a police station, with cutaway sections that revealed standard amounts of red tape and corruption. There were little Tyroleans in leather britches, intricately stitched, and, beneath the britches, genitalia of equally fine workmanship. There were ski shops and many other interesting things, including an orphanage. The orphanage was designed to catch fire and burn down every Christmas Eve. Orphans would dash into the snow with their nightgowns blazing. Terrible. Around the second week of January, a fire inspector would come and poke through the ruins, muttering, "If they had only listened to me, those children would be alive today."

It was a fascinating gift and not inexpensive, but Sissy might have known there was a catch to it.

Julian couldn't keep to himself very long the information that the village had been made by a young man who had had both arms amputated after a tricycle accident at age three. He had made the village with his toes. Moreover, the fellow was in trade school, studying to be a pastry cook. In another year, he would be decorating cakes.

Naturally, this was supposed to be inspirational to Sissy.

Julian even arranged for Sissy to meet the student chef, whose name was Norman. He left the disabled pair alone in a coffee shop, where they might speak heart to heart for half an hour. When Julian returned, he found that Sissy had talked Norman into carving a Tyrolean with enlarged thumbs to hitchhike up and down the streets of her village.

53.

The christmas holidays were mellow and cozy for the Gitches, after a rather tempestuous autumn.

Sissy had returned to New York on October 8, to face an angry, anxious husband and an incredulous Countess. Where had she been; why hadn't she telephoned; had she aided and abetted the Rubber Rose coup d'état and so forth. She was Perry Masoned from pillar to post, and Franz Krafkaed, too. Only when she threatened to leave again did the interviews finally cease.

For the Countess's part, his attitude toward the revolt on his ranch was ambivalent. One day he would curse the cowgirls as the most disgusting cat pack of female filth to ever gag a decent nostril, and the next day he would reiterate how much he admired women who could make their way without men and would wish them luck. He'd lost interest in the ranch, he said. Now that he had friends in the White House, the taxes the Rubber Rose saved him were a drop in the bucket; he could save more with a single phone call.

"That ranch is anal excruciation," the Countess complained, his dentures working over his ivory cigarette holder like a chiropractor realigning the spine of a Chihuahua. "When the market improves, I'm going to sell it. Then we'll watch how the new owners handle those little primitives. Say, are you certain the old fleabag who lives on the butte had nothing to do with all this?"

The Countess was never quite satisfied with Sissy's explanations, but he grew quickly bored with making an issue of it. He scrapped his plans for a whooping crane TV commercial and threw himself into new projects.

Julian, on the other hand, had to be forced to muzzle his interrogations and even then his soft brown eyes narrowed harshly at the most innocent and irrelevant references to Sissy's Rubber Rose assignment. He turned off the radio once when the deejay announced a song by Dakota Staton.

Actually, Sissy would have appreciated someone with whom to talk about Jellybean and the Chink — but there was no one she felt she could turn to. Julian, certainly, would not have been a good listener. As it was, he spent a great deal of time, even at his easel, wondering about the changes that had come over his wife, wondering about their origin, whether they were for better or worse. Before her trip West, Sissy had been an ardent lover but a reluctant student. Upon her return, however, she exhibited wolfish intellectual appetites for Julian's discourses upon history, philosophy, politics and the arts, but her responses between the sheets seemed no more than perfunctory. Had the Yale man gained a brain and lost a vagina? And was the Indian happy about it?

As mentioned, the cheer of Christmas brought an end to their discord. One day, while shopping in East Village boutiques, Sissy snapped out of the stupor she'd been in for weeks. Between second and third fingers, she held a sprig of mistletoe over Julian's head and kissed him right on the street. She hummed a carol on the way home. Through the holidays, she was gay and bright, with only an occasional far-away look in her eyes.

Then, on December 31, a few hours before the Gitches were to join the Barths for New Year's Eve at Kenny's Castaways, the news broke that several hospitals in both America and Denmark had been privately following a policy of letting deformed babies die. On the CBS Evening News, one doctor was heard to say, "If a baby is too deformed to be loved, then its life is going to be hell. Death is mercy for the unlovable." The disclosure slammed Sissy into a dungeon of depression, from which she did not begin to emerge until sometime in February, when she came across by chance an item in the *Times*.

> MANILA, Philippines (AP) — A Manila newspaper reported yesterday the birth of a boy with six fingers on each hand and six toes on each foot.
>
> "This will bring good luck to the family," said the infant's elated mother.

54.

ALTERNATELY skipping and staggering, an overwhelmed Sissy had come down the Siwash Trail after three days at the clockworks. She found a work party of cowgirls, headed by Delores, removing hair dryers and Exercycles from the damaged wing of the main house while a second party, led by Big Red, was busily renovating the old ranch privy. Bonanza Jellybean was nowhere to be seen. Kym disclosed that Jelly and Debbie had hauled a couple of sacks of brown rice out to Siwash Lake in the chuck wagon. They were going to feed the whoopers, who were there now in full strength, and see if the birds couldn't be enticed to extend their usual stay on the ranch.

The cinematographers were no longer at the pond. They had gone off to the Pacific Northwest to shoot a new Walt Disney family feature, *The Living Mud Puddle.* They would be spending a lot of time poking their wide-angle lenses under wet rocks.

Sissy debated waiting for the boss cowgirl's return. She packed slowly, but when the rucksack had been snapped shut there was still no Jellybean. Kym suggested that maybe Jelly and Debbie had stopped to "roll around." That settled it. Sissy shouldered her rucksack and trudged away. She had walked no more than three miles when the goat-chawed Cadillac limousine — which, as it turned out, was registered to the Rubber Rose — pulled up alongside her. Kym leaned out the driver's window. "Well," she called. "Aren't you gonna hitchhike me?"

Kym, who had defied Delores in order to give Sissy a ride, dropped her off at the main highway. She hugged her. "You're always welcome," she said. Over the cowgirl's shoulder miles of wheatgrass shimmered like the brushed hairs of a *gopi.* Violet hills and burnt umber buttes rested in their still American places like novels on Zane Grey's bookshelf. The sun, which in those parts appears as a half-breed — its father a prairie fire and its mother a wolf bite — shampooed Siwash Ridge in blood, so that it resembled the freshly scalped head of a trapper. This was the West. Dakota.

Back in Manhattan . . . Sissy gazing over the primordial rim . . . of mixing bowls . . . dishpans . . . brandy snifters. Sissy listening to the lope of Tenth Street traffic. Sissy staring down the poodle. Sissy, the next time Marie made a pass at her, surprising them both by taking the offensive, and afterward, while getting dressed, feeling that it had been a mistake and swearing off women forever. Sissy pumping Julian for ideas, facts, opinions — then sometimes interrupting his lectures to snigger "Ha ha ho ho and hee hee." Sissy painting her nails so that they were a blizzard of cherry coughdrops when she hitched from room to room. Sissy introspective, Sissy brooding, Sissy calm as ever except that now her lifelong serenity seemed thin and brittle and she gave people the disquieting impression that at any moment she might lunge away in an unexpected direction.

Julian refused to give up on her. "She is immature and self-indulgent," he explained. "Those traits can be overcome." It was the Mohawk's belief that his wife had been born into an ordinary family in the ordinary way, and had not some gene broken down under pressure, some chromosome slipped and fallen on its ass, she might have become a woman like any other. "She's lovely and intelligent. She needs only to be taught to overcome her affliction instead of reveling in it."

"Quite probably you are correct," agreed Dr. Goldman. "As you know, some social and behavioral deviants develop subcultures that, like the ethnic and racial ghettos, constitute havens where the individuals can live openly and with mutual support and insist that they are just as good as anyone else. Social deviates such as homosexuals and drug addicts may congregate in enclaves or live in small communities and take the line that they are not only as good as, but actually better than, 'straights,' and that the lives they lead are superior to those led by the majority. The socially stigmatized individual, by entering a subculture, accepts his alienation from the larger society, and by identifying himself with like souls claims that he is a full-fledged 'normal' or even a superior human being and that it is the others who are lacking. This type of adjustment is much more available to ethnic minorities, such as Jews, Amish or Black Panthers, and to stigmatized social deviants, such as hippies, drug addicts and homosexuals, than it is to the blind, the deaf and the orthopedically handicapped. So your wife may have chosen to become a subculture of one, so to speak.

"You say that she frequently makes a sincere effort to function as a normal woman in a normal household; well, every nonconformist secretly believes that he or she could live a straight life if only they so chose, and no doubt your wife yearns to prove that, within her dextrous limitations, she can adapt at will. Yet, as you say, so long as she indulges her handicap and the fantasy life she has constructed around it, she is not likely to succeed.

"At this juncture, however, I see no need in forcing her to visit the clinic against her will."

"No, no, I wouldn't wish that," said Julian.

But that evening when he returned home and saw what Sissy had done, he telephoned Dr. Goldman:

"I'm bringing her in," he wheezed.

55.

"THERE ARE two kinds of crazy people," Dr. Goldman said. He said this privately, to close friends, and with no intention of being quoted. "There are those whose primitive instincts, sexual and aggressive, have been misdirected, blunted, confused or shattered at an early age by environmental and/or biological factors beyond their control. Not many of these people can completely and permanently regain that balance we call 'sanity,' but they can be made to confront the source of their damage, to compensate for it, to reduce their disadvantageous substitutions and to adjust to the degree that they can meet most social requirements without painful difficulty. My satisfaction in life is in assisting these people in their adjustments.

"But there are other people, people who *choose* to be crazy in order to cope with what they regard as a crazy world. They have *adopted* craziness as a lifestyle. I've found that there is nothing I can do for these people because the only way you can get them to give up their craziness is to convince them that the world is actually sane. I must confess that I have found such a conviction almost impossible to support."

By Dr. Goldman's unofficial classifications (and he would have been the first to term them personal and oversimplified), the mental "problems" of Sissy Hankshaw Gitche should have fit squarely into the first category, for she had certainly been attended by sufficient traumas in her formative years. Yet, after two sessions with her, one in which she was administered the talk serum to penetrate her reticence, Dr. Goldman was left with the uneasy notion that Sissy belonged partly, if not wholly, in the category of the voluntarily crazed.

Since he was frustrated, annoyed, even a little scared by the second category, Dr. Goldman decided to turn over Sissy's case to one of his assistants. In particular, he decided to dump Sissy's case on Dr. Robbins, the young intern who had only recently assumed duties at the upper East Side clinic.

Dr. Robbins spent much of his time in the garden, a dreamy expression on his face. He looked like Doris Day with a mustache. He had been overheard yelling at a patient who complained of a lack of purpose in life: "Purpose! Purposes are for animals with a hell of a lot more dignity than the human race! Just hop on that strange torpedo and ride it to wherever its going."

To a patient who had expressed a wish to overcome his alleged irresponsibility, Dr. Robbins had said, "The man who considers himself 'responsible' has not honestly examined his motives."

To a patient expressing outrage, Dr. Robbins had shouted, "Don't be outraged, be outrageous!"

At least two patients had received from Dr. Robbins the following advice: "So you think that you're a failure, do you? Well, you probably are. What's wrong with that? In the first place, if you've any sense at all you must have learned by now that we pay just as dearly for our triumphs as we do for our defeats. Go ahead and fail. But fail with wit, fail with grace, fail with style. A mediocre failure is as insufferable as a mediocre success. Embrace failure! Seek it out. Learn to love it. That may be the only way any of us will ever be free."

It should come as no surprise that some of the clinic staff looked upon the new intern with less than favor. Dr. Goldman, however, resisted pressure to dismiss Dr. Robbins. "These young guys come out of school nowadays with their heads dripping Erik Erikson and R. D. Laing. Robbins is bright and those radical ideas are temporarily attractive. After he's been in the field for six months he'll recognize what idealistic hogwash they are and gradually reject them."

Dr. Goldman summoned Dr. Robbins from the garden, where he'd been fingering a crocus. He gave him Sissy's file. "When you interview Mrs. Gitche, you should consider the following variables: Depression — tensions combined with guilt derived from feelings that deformity is a punishment, tending to immobilize the deformed with consequent sadness, helplessness and inadequacy; Pessimism — a defense against the environment reflected by verbalization of a limited level of aspiration; Inadequate feminine role identification — poor identification with that which in our society constitutes womanhood, with resultant passivity and lethargy; Sociopathic impulsivity — emotions translated into aggressive action regardless of consequences to others; Inadequate compensatory ambition — the inability to mobilize additional effort to overcome the physical limitations of deformity; and, especially in this case, Inverted compensation — denial of the deformity or an irrational capitalization upon the deformity, exaggerated to the point of delusions of grandeur. A well-prepared line of questioning should narrow these variables down fairly quickly to one or two of primary interest and I rather suspect it will be the last that you will find yourself acting upon."

When he met with Sissy the next morning, however, Dr. Robbins ignored Dr. Goldman's suggested line of inquiry, asking Sissy directly and simply, "Okay, why did you turn your husband's birds loose?"

"I couldn't bear to see them caged any longer," answered Sissy. "They deserved to be free."

"Yeah, I understand. But don't you see, those birds had been in a cage their whole lives with somebody to provide for them. Now they're having to fend for themselves in a huge alien city where they don't know the rules and where they're probably frightened and confused. They won't be happy being free."

Sissy didn't hesitate. "There's just one thing in this life that's better than happiness and that's freedom. It's more important to be free than to be happy."

Dr. Robbins did hesitate. "How did you arrive at that opinion?" he inquired.

"I may have always felt it," Sissy said. "But it was the Chink who put it into words for me."

This time Dr. Robbins hesitated longer. As if he could bow it like a violin, he ran a finger back and forth through his shaggy mustache. The music that resulted was soft and dry, the sort that might make one flake of dandruff say to another, "Darling, they're playing our song." Then, the intern buzzed the office intercom. "Miss Waterworth," he said, "cancel my appointments for the remainder of the day."

Dr. Robbins arose, his mustache rising with him. "Sissy," he said with a smile, "let's get a bottle of wine and go out in the garden."

56.

THE GARDEN was an anatomy lesson of calyxes and pistils. With no more embarrassment than an old professor, spring was turning the pages. On leather couches throughout the clinic, throughout the upper East Side, in fact, people were confessing the most bizarre and boring details to analyst after analyst, but out in Dr. Goldman's walled garden the flowers didn't care. The flowers stood around with their petals hanging out, lasciviously awaiting whatever bees might make it through the smog. And for the adjustments of neither the first nor second category of psychosis did the flowers care.

Sissy didn't much care, either. Julian had promised that if she was a "good girl" and stayed at the clinic for a minimum of thirty days, he would take her upstate to meet her in-laws. Julian's father and his father's father were deceased, and his mother and paternal grandmother had moved back near Mohawk, New York, where, to Julian's discomfort, they had reassumed some of the old ways. For the length of her marriage, Sissy had yearned to probe the Indianness in her husband's background. Yet it wasn't merely the prospect of finally meeting the squaws in his closet that had her rosebudding that May morn. Sissy was being affable to Dr. Robbins, Sissy was glowing in each of her sockets, primarily because of the letter she'd just received.

The letter had been delivered earlier that morning by a flunky of the Countess's. It was, in fact, addressed to her in care of the Countess, with a notation on the envelope: "Please forward — or it'll be your ass." The postmark wore the word DAKOTA as the queen of ink would wear a necklace.

Dearest Sissy,

Gee, it's been quite a spell hasn't it? It's not like I haven't had time to write. We were snowed in all blessed winter as usual, with nothing much to do. But although I thought of you a thousand million times, I just couldn't get it together to compose a letter. Today, though, the first whoopers came back — on their way north to hatch their chicks — and seeing them out there at the lake again was such a flashback, and made me miss you so much, that I just had to take pen in hand, as they say.

Let's see now, what's the news? Well, we traded our Cadillac to Billy West for forty goats. Delores says we were robbed, but how else were we going to get a herd of goats? I ask you. We got no money to speak of and these are all prime animals, rustled out of Minnesota, but no sense spreading that around.

So we've got our goats out to pasture and we've been busy putting in the garden and making repairs. The ranch got sort of messed up in our takeover, but I guess you noticed that. Sorry if I didn't pay attention to you at that time, but I was under a heap of pressure to pull the whole caper off. I'm just glad you got out of the way, and hope the Countess, as he calls himself, hasn't given you any trouble about it.

We got a bunch of new cowgirls, almost twice as many as before. They're from all over. Some were involved in radical politics, some worked in the peace movement and some were pretty heavy into drugs. We even got a Gospel-quoting Jesus lady, her name's Mary. Linda is a professor's daughter from Berkeley, California — she and Kym are really hitting it off. Then there's Jody, she's a regular simple ranch girl out of Nebraska somewhere. But they're all cowgirls now.

Lost a couple, too. That rich woman from Detroit, the guest that joined up with us, she got such a case of cabin fever along about February that she hired a helicopter to come in and fly her out. She actually was talking out of her head. Then Gloria, she managed to get herself knocked up in Mottburg. I hated to see Gloria go, she was one of the original beauticians that helped me get cowgirls on the Rubber Rose in the first place. But Delores insisted that Gloria couldn't have a baby on the ranch, and of course there's nowhere in the Dakotas where a woman can get an abortion. So she had to split. That was weird, too, because Delores and Gloria were close friends. Delores and Debbie went round and round about it. Delores said that if women have any hopes of getting out from under men's thumbs — oops! pardon me, Sissy, I better say that a different way. Delores said that if women have any hopes of ceasing to be enslaved by men, then they've got to control and escape their biological roles, they've got to free themselves from motherhood. It's motherhood, both the fact and the threat of it, that makes us — wait a minute, got to look up this word in Kym's dictionary — *vulnerable* (according to Delores). She's all for testtube babies, made in laboratories and cared for by professional nurseries. Well, Debbie, she says such ideas are dumb. Debbie says sexual reproduction is the basic and primary difference between men and women, and we'd better not forget it. She says the ability to bring life into the world puts a woman closer to the Divine Mystery of the universe than males are, and that her motherly feelings are what gives her her protective and peaceful qualities, thus accounting for what is best in her — and best in the human race. She says the capacity for motherhood is the source of women's strength. Only women stand between technology and the destruction of nature, Deb says. If we're ever going to get the world back on a natural footing, back in tune with natural rhythms, if we're going to nurture the Earth and protect it and have fun with it and learn from it — which is what mothers do with their children — then we've got to put technology (an aggressive masculine system) in its proper place, which is that of a tool to be used sparingly, joyfully, gently and only in fullest cooperation with nature. Nature must govern technology, not the other way around. Only then can *all* oppression end. Nothing is more vital to the human species than the reproduction of life. That is woman's trump card. But if we allow babies to be created in plastic wombs or by any other than natural means, we are letting the sacred life process fall into the hands of men. The final and greatest power on Earth will be in the hands of logic-mad reason-crazed juiceless technocrats. They already own death, and use it to repress life. If women let them, they may also own life.

What do you think of all that? Me, I guess I have to take Debbie's side this time. I might not be objective, however, because it's impossible for me to get pregnant. Result of being shot with a silver bullet.

Oh, Sissy, now I'm remembering your sweet hands on my scar!

In a few minutes, I'm going to return to the scene of our love. Last fall, Debbie and I left mountains of brown rice for the cranes to munch, and they stayed at the pond longer than they ever had in the past. This time we're going to try a different diet on them to see if they won't stay even longer.

By the way, you might be interested in knowing that the Chink survived the winter in fine shape. I'm visiting him once a week again. Now you know my little secret, huh? Well, I hear tell that you didn't exactly sit at his feet listening to Bible stories. Ha ha. He's really something, isn't he? The billy goat!

Let's see. Delores still hasn't had her Third Vision. Peyote is making her look green around the jaws. Billy West is going to try to snatch us a stereo because that goddamn radio plays nothing but polkas. Heather's eyebrow healed up fine. Big Red led a revolt against Debbie's cooking, so we're taking turns on the chuck wagon these days. Kym may have a poem published in *Rolling Stone*. Elaine has a bladder infection. I guess that's all the news for now.

Sissy you are such a special person. I can't tell you how much you mean to me. I hope you're happy. Oh, I know that you are. You're so on top of it you could never be unhappy. You're an example to us here.

I'm pretty happy myself. Riding the range in the spring sunshine I see my shadow against the grass and I swear that shadow extends far beyond this place. This prairie. This world. It's like my life is sparkling in every direction, through all of space and all of time. You of all people understand.

I love you,
Bonanza Jellybean

As if it were a gift neither expected nor deserved, the letter caused new life to begin in Sissy. Observing her, Dr. Robbins sensed this stirring. He knew that whatever it was would be hard to name and hard to trace — it always is. And he recognized that no doctor, not even in the name of healing, has a right to set his shoes among the bloomings of the human soul. He poured wine. He inhaled the garden (although not deeply, for East Eighty-sixth Street was but a wall away). He observed her. Sunlight enhanced her yellow hair, her fruit-taste complexion, her pouty lips. Sunlight even did something for the inflated rubber turkey legs that were her thumbs — although Dr. Robbins was not sure what.

"Tell me about this Chink," said Dr. Robbins.

Sissy was ready. She let out a sigh that could have inflated the whole turkey. And then she told him everything.

57.

To NEITHER the Siwash nor the Chinese does the Chink belong.

As are many of the best and worse contributions to the human race, the Chink is Japanese. With their flair for inventive imitation, the Japanese made the Chink.

He was born on an island in the Ryukyu chain. It was called an island, but in actuality it was a volcano, a half-submerged dunce cap that Nature had once placed on the noggin of the sea for forgetting which had come first, land or water. For centuries this volcano had sent shock after shock of purple smoke into the sky. It was a chain smoker. A Ryukyu chain smoker.

Upon the sides of this smoking volcanic cone the Chink's parents had raised yams and upon the sides of this smoking volcanic cone the little Chink had played. Once, when he was six, he climbed to the top of the volcano. His sister found him there, on the edge of the crater, unconscious from the fumes, his hair and lashes singed. He had been looking in.

When he was eight, he emigrated to the United States of America, where his uncle tended gardens in San Francisco. Dr. Goldman's garden was okay for a clinic in New York City, but the Chink's uncle would not have wanted one of his gardens to marry it.

The Chink picked up English and other bad habits. He went to high school and other dangerous places. He earned American citizenship and other dubious distinctions.

When asked what he wished to do with his life, he answered (although he had learned to appreciate movies, jukebox music and cheerleaders) that he wanted to grow yams on the side of a volcano — but as that was impracticable in the city of San Francisco, he became, like uncle, a gardener. For more than a dozen years he made the grass greener and the flowers flowerier on the campus of the University of California at Berkeley. Dr. Robbins would have admired his work.

By special arrangement with his employers, the Chink attended one class a day at the university. Over a twelve-year span he completed a good many courses. He never graduated, but it would be a mistake to assume he did not receive an education.

He was astute enough to warn his relatives, on December 8, 1941, the day after Pearl Harbor, "The shinto is gonna hit the fan. We'd better get our yellow asses back to some safe volcano and eat yams till this blows over." They didn't listen. After all, they were patriotic, property-owning, tax-paying American citizens.

The Chink wasn't anxious to flee, either. He was in love again. Camping on the rim of a different volcano. So to speak.

On February 20, 1942, came the order. Two weeks later, the Army took steps. In March, evacuation was in full swing. Some 110,000 people of Japanese ancestry were moved out of their homes in "strategic" areas of the West Coast and settled in ten "relocation" camps further inland. They could bring to camp only what they could carry. Left behind were houses, businesses, farms, home furnishings, personal treasures, liberty. Americans of non-Nip ancestry bought up their farmland at ten cents on the dollar (The crops failed). Seventy percent of the relocated people had been born and reared in the U.S.

"Loyal" Japanese were separated from "disloyal." If one would swear allegiance to the American war effort — and could pass an FBI investigation — one had the choice of remaining in a relocation camp or finding employment in some nonstrategic area. The camps were militaristic formations of tarpaper barracks, supplied with canvas cots and potbellied stoves. Six to nine families lived in a barracks. Partitions between "apartments" were as thin as crackers and did not reach the ceiling (Even so, there were an average of twenty-five births per month in most camps). There was no great rush to leave the camps: a loyal family that had been relocated on an Arkansas farm had been killed by an irate anti-Jap mob.

Disloyal Japanese-Americans — those who expressed excessive bitterness over the loss of their property and the disruption of their lives, or who, for various other reasons, were suspected of being dangerous to national security — were given the pleasure of one another's company at a special camp, the Tule Lake Segregation Center in Siskiyou County, California. The Chink had been asked if he supported the American war effort. "Hell no!" he replied. "Ha ha ho ho and hee hee." He waited for the logical next question, did he support the Japanese war effort, to which he would have given the same negative response. He was still waiting when the military police shoved him on the train to Tule Lake.

Tule was even less of a lake than Siwash. It had been drained so that land could be "reclaimed" for farming. *Reclaimed!* Which came first, land or water? Give the wrong answer, you have to sit in a corner with a volcano on your head.

The detention camp had been built on that part of the dry lake bottom that was unsuitable for cultivation. However, the inmates (or "segregees," as the War Relocation Authority preferred to label them) were put to work on surrounding farmland, building dikes, digging irrigation ditches and producing crops that proved once again that the greenest thumbs are often yellow.

(Perhaps the author is telling you more about Tule Lake than you want to know. But the camp, in Northern California near the Oregon border, still exists, and while time, that ultimate diet pill, has reduced its 1032 buildings to their concrete foundations, the government yet may have plans for them which may someday be your concern.)

Baked in summer, dust-blinded in fall, frozen in winter and mud-up-to-elbows in spring, the Tule Lake camp was surrounded by a high barbed-wire fence. Soldiers in lookout towers kept constant watch — on kids swimming in ditches, adolescents hunting rattlesnakes, old men playing Go and women shopping for notions in a commissary where the latest issues of *True Confessions* were always on the racks. It was reported that, even if the guards were removed, the segregees would not try to escape. They were afraid of Tule Lake farmers.

The Chink petitioned to be allowed to join his family in a less restrictive camp. But his FBI check disclosed that he had, over a period of years, pursued such heathen practices as jujitsu, ikebana, Sanskrit mushroom magic and Zen archery; that at UC he had written academic papers that suggested anarchist leanings; and that he had had repeated intimate relations with Caucasian women, including the niece of an admiral in the U.S. Navy. Please to remain at Tule Lake.

In early November of 1943, there was trouble at Tule Lake. A careless GI truck driver accidentally killed a Japanese farmworker. Angered, the segregees refused to complete the harvest. There followed a confrontation that Army spokesmen identified as a "riot." Among the 155 ringleaders who were beaten and imprisoned in the stockade was the man we now call the Chink. The Chink had not participated in the "riot," had, in fact, been looking forward to the rhythm of harvest, but camp authorities claimed that his notoriously insubordinate attitude (not to mention the crazed way he had of venerating plants, vegetables and other men's wives) contributed to unrest at the camp.

If he liked the segregation center little, he liked the stockade less. For several days and nights he meditated upon the yam, that tuber that, while remaining sweet to the taste and soft to the touch, is so tough it will thrive on the sides of live volcanos. "Yam" became his mantra. *Om mani padme yam. Hare yam-a. Wham, bam, thank you yam. Hellfire and yam nation.* Then, like the yam, he went underground. He tunneled out of the stockade, out of the camp.

In wartime America, where even toddlers and lobotomy patients remembered Pearl Harbor, the sneaky little slant-eyed yellow-bellied infidel was on the yam. So to speak.

58.

THERE IS an Elizabethan maxim, "To tend a garden is to be civilized."

Sir Kenneth Clark's boundless love for Western civilization seems to purr most contentedly when he is displayed, tweed-suited, in a landscaped garden.

The formal garden is an outdoor room where Nature is purged of its wildness, or, at least, is held in limbo.

It was in a high-quality garden that the fall of man began. The question is, fall from *where* into *what?* Innocence into sin? Substance into form? Primitivism into civilization?

Granting that primitive, unfallen man had access to nourishing psychic processes, which the clipped hedges of civilization have obscured, would it be unfair to conclude that the ecstatic mind degenerates as it begins to contemplate gardening?

Japanese gardening, with its emphasis upon irregular interval, as opposed to European gardening, with its emphasis upon ordered form, generates points of departure rather than sets of conditions . . .

Dr. Robbins, already vicariously affected by the Chink, was eyeballing the clinic garden from new perspectives while Sissy went inside to use the facilities. Suddenly, Miss Waterworth's red Bibanas wedgies appeared among the tulips.

"Excuse me, Dr. Robbins," Miss Waterworth said, "but Dr. Goldman has asked that you reconsider your request to cancel the rest of your day's appointments."

From where he lay in the barbered grass, cradling the one-third-empty bottle of Chablis, Dr. Robbins did not look up, but continued to focus upon the red shoes. He was reminded of the skinned knees of our betrayed Savior kneeling in Gethsemane's dew, of the speedy flick-flick of the Serpent's tongue, of the blood that oozed in pain and pleasure in King Louis's Deer Park, of cleverly disguised microphones blossoming among the roses on the White House lawn — and other ominous scenes from past issues of *Better Homes and Gardens.* "One moment, Miss Waterworth," said Dr. Robbins.

Sissy was returning.

"Sissy, you do have more to relate about the Chink, do you not?"

"Oh my yes," she said. "I haven't even told you how he came to live with the Clock People. Or anything. But if my time is up . . ."

"Never mind. Miss Waterworth, you are interrupting the only interesting sentences I have ever heard uttered by a patient — or, I might add, a staff member — in the three months that I've been an asset to this institution. Convey to Dr. Goldman my regrets. Now, Sissy. Another thimble of wine? Do go on."

"Let's see. Where was I?"

"The Chink was so unhappy at the Tule Lake Segregation Center that he dared to escape."

"No," said Sissy. "I've given the wrong impression. The Chink wasn't charmed with the camp, but he was not unhappy there. The soil around Tule Lake grows the finest horseradishes in the world. It grew big white onions and tons of lettuce. He planted, cultivated, harvested and venerated. He wasn't really unhappy."

"Okay," said Dr. Robbins. "I get it. He wasn't unhappy but neither was he free. And freedom is more important than happiness. Right?"

Sipping her wine, Sissy thought it much too dry. The Countess had cursed her with a taste for the Ripple. "No, that's not exactly right, either," she said. "Even though the Chink was still in the early stages of his development, he was advanced enough to know that freedom — for humans — is largely an internal condition. He was free enough in his own head, even then, to endure Tule Lake without undue frustration."

"What made him split, then?" With the top of the bottle, Dr. Robbins prodded his caterpillar mustache. As if trained for just such a function, it undulated until it formed a shaggy question mark.

"You're not yet aware of the Chink's peculiar fascination with the science of the particular, with laws governing exceptions."

The caterpillar repeated its question mark routine.

"You see," explained Sissy, "there were three categories of Japanese-Americans in the country during the war. There were those in detention camps, including Tule Lake; there were those who had been released to perform menial labor in remote, rural areas of the interior; and there were those serving in the U.S. Army. Each member or each category was carefully watched over and supervised by the government. The Chink busted out of Tule Lake because he believed there ought to be an exception. After enough provocation, he took it upon himself to enact the singular as opposed to the general, to embody the exception rather than the rule."

59.

He headed for the proverbial hills. The Cascade Mountains lay to the west, across twenty or more miles of lava beds. The lava felt sharply familiar. Each rip in his shoes brought him closer to his childhood. All night, he jogged, walked, rested, jogged. At sunrise, Mt. Shasta, a cone of diamond ice cream, a volcano on a sabbatical, adorned (like the whooping cranes) with the power of white, was waiting. Encouraging him. An hour after dawn he was in tree-cover.

His plan was to follow the crest trail through the Cascades, down the full length of the Sierra Nevada and into Mexico. In the spring, perhaps, he would wetback into the U.S. again and work the crops. There weren't many farmers who could distinguish a Nip from a Spic, not under a straw hat, not with spine bent to the rutabagas. Alas, Mexico was a thousand miles away, the month was November, there was already snow at the higher altitudes, flop flap was the song of his shoes.

Fortunately, the Chink knew which plants to chomp, which nuts and mushrooms to toast over tiny minimum-smoke fires. As best he could he patched his shoes with bark. His journey went well for a week or more. Then, out of the mysterious dwelling place of weather, there rode an abrupt and burly storm. For a while it toyed with him, blowing in his ears, aging his normally black hair, hanging flakes artfully from the tip of his nose. But the storm was on serious business, and soon the Chink, crouched though he was in the lee of a cliff, realized that, by comparison, the passion of this storm to storm made puny his own desire to reach Mexico. Snow snow snow snow snow snow. The last thing a person sees before he dies he will be obliged to carry with him through all the baggage rooms of lasting death. The Chink strained to squint a sequoia or at least a huckleberry bush, but all his freezing eyes saw was snow. And the snow wanted to lie atop him as badly as any male ever wanted to lie on female.

The storm had its way with him. He lost consciousness trying to think of God, but thinking instead of a radiant woman cooking yams.

Of course, he was rescued. He was rescued by the only people who possibly could have rescued him. He was discovered, hauled in, bedded down and thawed out by members of an American Indian culture that, for several reasons, cannot be identified beyond this fanciful description: the Clock People.

It is not easy, perhaps, to accept the fact of the Clock People's existence. You might read through every issue of *National Geographic* since the Year One and not find an exact parallel to the Clock People's particular distinctions. However, if you think about it for a while — the way Sissy did, the way the author has — it becomes obvious that the civilizing process has left pockets of vacuum that only Clock People could have filled.

60.

THE ROOM in which the fugitive regained consciousness was large and well heated, draped with crude blankets and the skins of animals. Whether it was a cave, a camouflaged cabin or an elaborate tipi/hogan-type dwelling the Chink would not say. He was careful not to disclose any details that might aid in pinpointing the location of his hosts. Sissy, moreover, would never have mentioned the Clock People to Dr. Robbins had she not been assured that conversation between psychiatrist and patient is privileged and confidential, immune, even, from governmental subpoena. That Dr. Robbins was someday to violate that privilege . . . well, let's pass over that for now.

As had been written, the Clock People are of an American Indian culture. Ethnically speaking, however, they are not a tribe. Rather, they are a gathering of Indians from various tribes. They have lived together since 1906.

At the dawning of April 18, 1906, the city of San Francisco awakened to a terrible roar, mounting in intensity. For sixty-five seconds the city shook like a rubber meatball in the jaws of Teddy Roosevelt. There followed a silence almost as terrible as the roar. The heart of San Francisco lay in ruins. Buildings had tumbled into creviced streets; twisted bodies of humans and horses colored the rubble; gas hissed like the Snake of All Bad Dreams from dozens of broken mains. During the next three days, flames enveloped 490 blocks, unquenched by the teardrops of the homeless and lame.

History knows the catastrophe as the Great San Francisco Earthquake. That is not how the Clock People know it, but, then, the Clock People don't believe in earthquakes.

Among the crowds who watched the blazing devastation from surrounding hills was a scattering of American Indians. Largely from California tribes, though including folk from Nevada and Oregon, and in whose midst there moved representatives of the few but notorious Siwash, they were the first of the urbanized Indians. Poor, generally, they held jobs of menial or disreputable stature along the Barbary Coast (It should be emphasized, however, that they had been drawn into the city, each and every of them, not by desire for money — they needed no money where they came from — but by *curiosity* alone). The white San Franciscans camping on the smoky hilltops surveyed the ruins in a state of shock. Perhaps the Indians, too, were overwhelmed by the spectacle, but they, as always, appeared as inscrutable as the other side of a nickel. Yet the Indians were to display shock aplenty. It was when the fires were at last controlled and the citizens began to rush back into the still-warm ashes, singing, praising the Lord, and shouting to one another their plans for rebuilding their metropolis, that Indian eyes widened in disbelief. They simply could not comprehend what they were witnessing. They realized that the white man lacked wisdom, but was he completely goofy? Couldn't he read the largest and most lurid of signs? Even those Indians who had grown to trust the white man were grievously disappointed. Rebuild the city? They shook their heads and muttered.

For several weeks they remained on the hill, strangers united by shock and disappointment as well as by a common cultural comprehension of what had happened below. Then, through communications the nature of which is known best to them, several of the Indians led a migration of a small band of souls into the Sierras, where, in a period of thirteen full moons, they generated the stalk of a new culture. (Or, should we say, under their impetus, the ancient stalk of Life Religion put forth unexpected and portentous shoots.)

61.

On behalf of the Susquehanna, the Winnebago, the Kickapoo, the Chickasaw, the Kwakiutl, the Potawatomi and all the other splendidly appellated aborigines who came to be labeled "Indians" through the ignorance of an Italian sailor with a taste for oranges, it is only fitting that "Indians" misnamed our Japanese-American hero "Chink."

There were very few Japanese in San Francisco in 1906, but Chinese were plentiful. Already there was a Chinatown, and its exotic trappings were a lure to tourists. Drugs, gambling and prostitution abounded in the Chinese quarter, just as they did on the Barbary Coast, and the Indians often had overheard their employers speaking of the competition from the "Chinks."

In the years between 1906 and 1943, the Clock People had, naturally, discussed on many occasions the circumstances of their Sierra migration. More than once, they had wondered aloud why the yellow people had been so unenlightened as to join the whites in resurrecting San Francisco. It had been astonishing enough to watch the white man set about to repeat his mistake, but to watch the Orientals follow him . . . !

Their curiosity about yellow men probably had influenced their decision to rescue this near-frozen outsider. During his days of recuperation, the storm victim had heard several of his hosts inquire about the condition of the "the Chink." His sense of irony was not so frostbitten that he could refrain from perpetuating, once he had recovered, the misnomer.

Eventually, perhaps, he confessed to his Japanese ancestry. Certainly and soon, he confessed to being a fugitive. The Clock People elected to harbor him, and were never to regret it. In the years that followed, the Chink performed many services for them. In return, he was accepted as one of them, and gained privity to all of the secrets of the clockworks.

The pivotal function of the Clock People is the keeping and observing of the clockworks. The clockworks is a real thing. It is kept at the center, at the soul, of the Great Burrow.

The Great Burrow is a maze or labyrinthine sequence of tunnels, partly manmade, partly of geological origin. To be more specific: a natural network of narrow caves, lying beneath a large knoll in the Sierra wilderness, was lengthened and elaborated upon by the Indians who exiled themselves from San Francisco in 1906. Many, if not most, of the tunnels are deadends.

The Clock People, as we now know them, divided themselves into thirteen families, not necessarily along tribal lines. (What is the numerical significance of the Clock People's taking thirteen months to structure their ritual, then separating into thirteen families? Well, briefly, they consider thirteen a more natural number than twelve. To the Babylonians, thirteen was unlucky. That is why, when they invented astrology, they willfully overlooked a major constellation, erroneously assigning to the zodiac only twelve houses. The Clock People knew nothing of Babylonian superstition, but they knew the stars, and it was partly in an effort to override the unnatural twelve-mindedness of Western culture that they chose to give thirteen its due.) To each family was assigned the responsibility for one section of the Great Burrow. Each family knows one section inch by inch, but is completely ignorant of the other twelve sections. So no one family nor individual knows the Way. The Way, of course, being the true path that takes one through the Great Burrow maze to the clockworks.

Moreover, it is not possible for the families to compile a map of the Way, for each family holds as a sacred secret its knowledge of its burrow or section of the Way.

(In naming these tunnel sections "burrows," the Clock People were not particularly identifying with animals — no more so than were the Indians in whose culture totems played such a large and vivid role. Totemically oriented Indians utilized the characteristics of certain animals *metaphorically.* It was simply a form of poetic symbolism. They used animals to think with.)

Okay. Who gets to the clockworks, how and when? Each morning at sunrise that day's designated guides — one from each of the thirteen families — gather at the portal of the Great Burrow. Then they are all blindfolded, except for the guide representing the Family of the First Burrow. The blindfolded twelve link hands and are led by the first guide through any of several routes he or she may take to reach the beginning of the Second Burrow. A guide will purposefully attempt never to use the same route twice. Often a guide will backtrack, and sometimes he or she will instruct the others in the party to let go of each other's hands and spin. Since, by this date, there are around twenty members in each family, an individual acts as guide only about thirteen times a year.

Now, when the first guide reaches the terminus of his burrow and the beginning of the next, he instructs the guide for the Second Burrow to remove his blindfold, and then binds his own eyes. And so it goes until the group is at the large central chamber that contains the clockworks. There, they go about "keeping the time" until the hour for the return trip. Theoretically, the thirteen daily guides emerge from the Great Burrow at sunset, although this occurs in actuality only on those days when there are thirteen hours of daylight.

Occasionally other people accompany the guides on their mission. An aged or sickly person who is about to die or a pregnant woman commencing labor is led, blindfolded, to the central burrow, for insofar as it is possible, all Clock People deaths and births occur in the presence of the clockworks. Aside from birthing or dying, the reason for the daily visits to the clockworks is to check the time.

Maybe we should say "check the *times,*" for the clockworks is really two clocks and the sort of time each one measures is quite distinct.

(Maybe we should also establish that it is the *original* clockworks that is being described here: there was later to be another, and the second figures even more prominently in our story.)

First, there is a huge hourglass, at least seven feet in diameter and thirteen feet tall, made from the finely stitched and tightly stretched internal membranes of large beasts (elk, bears, mountain lions). The hourglass is filled with acorns, enough so that it takes them approximately thirteen hours to pour or funnel, one by one, through the slender passage in the waist of the transparent device. When the daily guides enter the soul burrow, the hourglass is turned on its opposite end. When they depart — in approximately thirteen hours — they flip it again. So "checking the time," or "keeping the time" is, in the twenty-six-hour day of the Clock People, the same as "making time," or, more generally, "making history." The Clock People believe that they are making history and that the end of history will come with the destruction of the clockworks.

Please do not construe the "end of history" or the "end of time" to mean "the end of life" or what is normally meant by the apocalyptically minded when they speak (almost wishfully, it seems) of the "end of the world." That is paranoiac rubbish, and however one may finally evaluate the Clock People, their philosophy must be appreciated on a higher plane than doomsday drivel.

Well, then, what do the Clock People mean by the end of history and how will the clockworks be destroyed?

Zoom in on this: These people, these clandestinely exiled Indians, have no other ritual than this one: THE CHECKING OF THE CLOCKWORKS — the keeping/making of history. Likewise, they have but one legend or cultural myth: that of a continuum they call the Eternity of Joy. It is into the Eternity of Joy that they believe all men will pass once the clockworks is destroyed. They look forward to a state of timelessness, when bored, frustrated and unfulfilled people will no longer have to "kill time," for time will finally be dead.

They are preparing for timelessness by eliminating from their culture all rules, schedules and moral standards other than those that are directly involved with the keeping of the clockworks. The Clock People may be the most completely anarchistic community that has ever existed. Rather, they may be the first community so far in which anarchy has come close to working. That is impressive in itself and should fan with peacock tails of optimism all those who dream of the ideal social condition.

The Clock People manage their anarchism (if that is not a contradiction) simply because they have channeled all of their authoritarian compulsions and control mania into a single ritual. It is clearly understood by all members of the community that there is no other ritual, no other required belief than this ONE — and, furthermore, that they themselves created the ritual: they have no silly superstitions about gods or ancestor spirits who hold this ritual over their heads in return for homage and/or "good" conduct.

Ritual, usually, is an action or ceremony employed to create a unity of mind among a congregation or community. The Clock People see the keeping of the clockworks as the *last* of the *communal* rituals. With the destruction of the clockworks, that is, at the end of time, all rituals will be personal and idiosyncratic, serving not to unify a community/cult in a common cause but to link each single individual with the universe in whatever manner suits him or her best. Unity will give way to plurality in the Eternity of Joy, although, since the universe is simultaneously many and One, whatever links the individual to the universe will automatically link him or her to all others, even while it enhances his or her completely separate identity in an eternal milkshake unclabbered by time. Thus, paradoxically, the replacement of societal with individual rituals will bring about an ultimate unity vastly more universal than the plexus of communal rites that presently divides peoples into unwieldy, agitating and competing groups.

Now, the Clock People, being visionaries, are not content with their time-checking ritual. After all, it is the lone authoritarian, compulsive action that binds them. They chafe to dispense with it. If it could be eliminated, they could pass out of history and into the Eternity of Joy. Timeless, they could bear their children and bury their dead wherever they chose. However, they understand that at this evolutionary stage they still require the ritual, even as they realize that destroying the clockworks is entirely within their power.

They will not destroy it. They have agreed — and this is central to their mythos — that the destruction must come from the outside, must come by natural means, must come at the will (whim is more like it) of that gesticulating planet whose more acute stirrings thoughtless people call "earthquakes."

Here, we can understand a bit more about the origins of their culture. The great rumble of 1906, which destroyed practically the whole of San Francisco, was taken by the Indians as a sign. They had left the land and gone to the city. That the city could be destroyed by the land in sixty-five seconds gave them a clue as to where the real power lay.

Within a natural context the phenomenon would never have appeared as a holocaust. Away from the herding centers we prize as cities, an "earthquake" would manifest itself only as a surface quickening of the globe's protoplastic movements, which, at various depths and various intensities, are occurring all of the time, and so not in time but all over time. Being "all over time" is the same as being out of time, because the notion of time is welded inseparably to the notion of progression, but what is already everywhere cannot possibly progress.

From there, it is a short leap to the ledge of the dream: the Eternity of Joy (a continuous present in which everything, including the dance of aging, which we mistake as a chronological unfolding rather than a fixed posture of deepening cellular awareness, is taken together and always).

When the citizens of San Francisco began immediately to rebuild their city, the Indians were understandably very disappointed. The white (and yellow) San Franciscans hadn't learned a thing. They had been given a sign — a powerful, lucid sign — that urban herding and its concomitant technologies are not the proper way to partake of this planet's hospitality. (Actually, there are countless ways to live upon this tremorous sphere in mirth and good health, and probably only one way — the industrialized, urbanized, herding way — to live here stupidly, and man has hit upon that one wrong way.) The people of San Francisco failed to heed the sign. They capitulated, opting to stay in time and so out of eternity.

Readers may wonder why the Indians, who recognized the earthquake for what it really was, did not simply usher in the Eternity of Joy then and there. Well, they had both a realistic view and a sense of humor regarding their situation. They understood that it would take at least three or four generations to cleanse them of previous cultural deposits. The patriarchs — only two or three of whom are still alive — reasoned that if they could channel all of their fellows' frustrations and self-destructive compulsions into a single, simple ritual, then two things would follow. One, outside that ritual, the community could experiment freely with styles of life instead of the attractions of death. Two, sooner or later, the Earth would issue another potent sign, one powerful enough to destroy their last icon of time-bound culture, the clockworks, ending the ritual even while it was reshaping much of American civilization.

Which brings us, ticking, to the matter of the second clock. The first clock in the original clockworks, the membrane hourglass, sits in a pool of water. The Great Burrow is situated upon a deep fracture, a major branch of the San Andreas Fault. The Sierra fault is clearly shown on geological maps of Northern California (which does hint at the location of the original clockworks, doesn't it? even though the fracture is very long). In addition, the underground stream that feeds the Great Burrow pool flows directly into the San Andreas Fault. That pool of water is the second clock in the clockworks system. Consider its components.

Moments prior to an earthquake, certain sensitive persons experience nausea. Animals, such as cattle, are even more sensitive to prequake vibrations, feeling them earlier and more strongly. By far the most quake-sensitive creatures in existence are catfish. Readers, this is scientific fact; the doubtful among you should not hesitate to check it out. Catfish.

Now, there is a species of catfish, hereditarily sightless, that dwells exclusively in subterranean streams. Its Latin name is *Satan eurystomus,* again for the skeptical, but spelunkers know these fish as blindcats. Relatively rare in California, blindcats are quite common in the caverns and caves of the Ozark states and Texas.

The clockworks pool is inhabited by such catfish. Their innate catfish earthquake sensitivity is compounded by the fact that they are tuned in, fin and whisker, to the vibrations of one of the globe's largest and most frenetic fault systems. When a tremor of any Richterian passion is building, the catfish go into a state of shock. They cease feeding, and when they move at all, it is erratically. By constantly monitoring changes in the Earth's magnetic field or the tilt of the Earth's surface or the rate of movement and intensity of stress where faults are slowly creeping, seismologists have correctly predicted a handful of minor tremors, though with no great exactitude.

The clockworks catfish, on the other hand, have registered upcoming quakes as far away as Los Angeles (in 1971) and as early as four weeks in advance.

On the earthen walls of the Central Burrow, the Clock People have marked in sequence the dates and intensities of all tremors, mad or mild, that have occurred along the two thousand miles of West Coast faults since 1908. The whole pattern, transcribed from the catfish clock, reveals a rhythmic structure that indicates to the rhythmic minds of the Indians that something emphatic is going to be coming along any week now.

This peek on destruction is Pythagorean only in the sense that with the cataclysmic konking of the last vestige of cultural ritual will come the kind of complete social and psychic freedom that only natural timeless anarchy can offer, the birth of a new people into the Eternity of Joy.

The Clock People regard civilization as an insanely complex set of symbols that obscures natural processes and encumbers free movement. The Earth is alive. She burns inside with the heat of cosmic longing. She longs to be with her husband again. She moans. She turns softly in her sleep. When the symbologies of civilization are destroyed, there will be no more "earthquakes." Earthquakes are a manifestation of man's consciousness. Without manmade follies, there could not be earthquakes. In the Eternity of Joy, pluralized, deurbanized man, at ease with his gentle technologies, will smile and sigh when the Earth begins to shake. "She is restless tonight," they will say.

"She dreams of loving."

"She has the blues."

62.

IN THE flippers of dolphins there are five skeletal fingers.

Once upon a time, dolphins had hands.

Observing the residual fingers that remain in their flippers, it is *possible* to conclude that dolphins had opposable thumbs.

Picture a dolphin holding an ace. Picture a dolphin plucking petals from a daisy: loves me, loves me not. Picture a dolphin, way back when, drawing an astrological chart and discovering that all of its planets were in Pisces. Can you see a dolphin fingering its blowhole? A dolphin at a typewriter writing this book?

Imagine the dolphin, a land animal then (although the Pisces Express stops only at the bottom of the sea), wagging a slick thumb in the lizard-filtered air of prehistory, hitchhiking to Atlantis or Gondwanaland. Would you pick up a hitchhiking dolphin? What if you were driving a Barracuda?

Look, look, look, the author wants to say (to the shortsighted and temporal-minded), the dolphin used to have thumbs! Ponder that when you have a moment. Right now, however, dolphin thumb is eclipsed by Sissy thumb. Flexing in a sooty city garden.

Dr. Robbins, bottoming out the wine, wished to know if the Chink swallowed the Clock People's ideas.

The answer was, and is, no, he never was in total agreement with the Clock People's viewpoints and suppositions, and as the years passed, he agreed with them less instead of more. However, he fell into the hands of the Clock People at a time when most of the world was banging heads together bloodily over vague, meaningless manias such as economic expansion and ethnocentric geopolitics, and his own peoples, the Japanese and the Americans, were among the most fanatical about victory as they prayed to the gods of bullets and taught their babies to walk on the edge of the knife. So, when he met the thirteen families of the Great Burrow and learned the rhymes and reasons of the clockworks, the Chink emitted a long overdue "Ha ha ho ho and hee hee." Said he, "It is reassuring to see on the planet signs of intelligent life."

"My sentiments exactly," mused Dr. Robbins, as he watched the shadows of Sissy's thumbs leaping like dolphins against the garden wall.

63.

AMONG THE Clock People, who never had tasted a yam nor seen a whooper, who were unfamiliar with the practice of hitchhiking, who would have been flabbergasted by a can of Yoni Yum and who knew better than to believe in such Fig Newtons of the American imagination as cowgirls, the Chink dwelt for twenty-six years.

For the first eight of those years, he lived virtually as a Clock Person himself, an honorary member of the Family of the Thirteenth Burrow, sharing its food, lodging and women. (Being an anarchistic, or, more precisely, a pluralistic society, some of the Clock People were monogamous, some, perhaps most, practitioners of free love. In a pluralistic society, love quickly shows all of its many smeared and smiling faces, and it should be noted that the term *family* was relevant only to the clockworks ritual, outside which there was uninhibited intermingling. For example, a man from the Family of the Fifth Burrow might impregnate an Eleventh Burrow lady, and the resulting child, once of age, might be assigned to the Family of the Ninth Burrow.)

In 1951, the war now only a glint in the American Legion's shell-popped eye, the Chink moved into a shack that he built some nine or ten miles west of the Great Burrow. The shack was strategically erected at the narrow entrance to the valley, which, with a creek as its racing stripe, totaled out against the base of the tunnel-filled knoll. In the other direction, a couple of miles beyond the shack, was a trail that led to a dirt road that led to a paved highway that led past, eventually, a combination gas station, café and general store. The Chink began to take fortnightly hikes to that store, where he picked up newspapers and magazines, along with other supplies. These he read to those Clock People (all spoke English but few could read it) who were interested; these were mainly the younger ones, the old Indians regarding that "news" that did not have to do with quakes, hurricanes, floods and other geophysical shenanigans as trivia. The belch of civilization, they called it. Maybe the older Indians were right. It was the Eisenhower Years, remember, and the news read as if it had been washed out of a Pentagon desk commander's golf socks.

The Chink also linked the older Indians with the rest of the world, but in a different manner. Throughout the decades, the Clock People had mysteriously maintained periodic contact with certain Indians on the outside. These outside contacts were medicine men or shamans, although exactly what was their relationship to the clockworks ritual and Eternity of Joy legend the Chink was never to ascertain. However, in the mid-fifties, one or more of these outsiders took to showing up at the Sierra store at the precise hours of the Chink's unannounced visits. They'd drink a beer with him and give him a piece or two of seemingly insignificant gossip, which he would feel compelled to pass along once he was back at the Great Burrow. Thus, he functioned as a medium, as the air is the medium for drumbeats, connecting Clock People, young and old, with distant drummers.

He also functioned as an agent of diversion. When hunters, hikers or prospectors entered the area, the Chink used his wiles to guide them away from the vicinity of the Great Burrow. Conversation studded with tips about game, scenic waterfalls or ore deposits was usually enough to divert the intruders, but occasionally a small rock slide or other mishap would have to be arranged. Even so, a few interlopers, especially rangers of the U.S. Forest Service, slipped through the Chink's net. Those who got too close were slain by the Clock People. From 1965 to 1969, seven outsiders took arrows through their breasts and were buried inside the Great Burrow.

These slayings were a source of contention between the Chink and the Clock People, the latter regarding them as the regrettable but necessary price of protection, the former declaring, "There are many things worth living for, there are a few things worth dying for, but there is nothing worth killing for."

The Chink tried to impress upon the Clock People that, with the increase in air traffic over the mountains, as well as in the number of outdoorsmen whom civilization was driving into the wilderness, it was only a matter of "time" before their culture was exposed. What would they do then? Obviously, the System would not be gracious enough to leave them alone. "We will hide in the tunnels," answered some of the middle-aged. "We will defend ourselves to the death," answered some of the youths. "The movements of the Earth will take care of all that," answered the elders, smiling enigmatically.

If the killings upset him, the Chink accepted with ease other contradictions in the Clock People's philosophy. When faced with a contradiction, as he was — as we all are — daily if not hourly, it seemed only fair to him to take both sides.

Yet he grew increasingly impatient with the Clock People's notions, and toward the end of his Sierra stay his hickory dickory mouse of mockery ran frequently up their clock.

Now, a number of the young men of the Great Burrow had lost patience, too. Through the Chink's news broadcasts they had learned of mushrooming militancy among American Indians. They learned of Red Power and of reservations whose proud residents were freshly painted — and armed to the teeth. In early spring of 1969 a quartet of bucks slipped away from the Great Burrow, venturing into the strange world beyond the still snowy mountains, to see for themselves. A couple of months later they returned, excited, feathered, beaded, buzzing of revolution. Two comrades threw in with them and they deserted the Clock People to go face the white man on his own terms — and in his own time. The bucks called at the Chink's shack on their way down the mountains. "You're as tired as we are of sitting around waiting for a motherfucking earthquake," they said in the idiom they had recently adopted. "You're strong and smart and have taught us much. Come with us and join the movement."

"This movement of yours, does it have slogans?" inquired the Chink.

"Right on!" they cried. And they quoted him some.

"Your movement, does it have a flag?" asked the Chink.

"You bet!" And they described their emblem.

"And does your movement have leaders?"

"Great leaders."

"Then shove it up your butts," said the Chink. "I have taught you nothing." He skipped down to the creek to gather watercress.

A few weeks later he accepted the invitation of an aged Siwash chief who was the principal outside confederate of the Clock People, a degenerated warlock who could turn urine into beer, to be initiated as a shaman, an honor that gave him rights of occupancy in the sacred cave on far-away Siwash Ridge. At once he left for the Dakota hills to construct a clockworks whose ticks might more accurately echo the ticks of the universe, which, as he listened, sounded more and more like "ha ha ho ho and hee hee."

64.

WHEN YOU'RE in the saddle all day, you need something to do with your mouth besides sing "Yippee eye oh ki yea." Usually it's too hot and dry for singing, anyhow. You just end up with a throat full of dust.

However, when you're stuck in the saddle from dawn to dusk, you need something of an oral nature to keep you occupied and calm. That's why so many cowboys chew tobacco or puff roll-yer-owns. That's why it really *is* Marlboro Country.

But cowgirls of the New Age, they aren't much into the tobacco habit. Gloria was mighty attached to the Pall Malls that dit-ditted to her in an endless dotted line from South Richmond, Virginia, and Big Red was prone to accept a chaw. On the whole, though, the gals had a nonpreference for tobacco that was close to contempt, even if they did not agree with Debbie, who predicted, "When things really get too bad on the planet Earth and it starts to fall apart from wars and pollution and earthquakes and so forth, then Higher Beings are going to come in flying saucers and rescue the more evolved souls among us; but they can't take smokers aboard their spaceships because people with nicotine in their systems explode when they enter the seventh dimension."

At any rate, cowgirls need something to do with their mouths while riding herd, and this is what they do: they stick a butterscotch Life Saver in one cheek and a clove in the other. They seldom suck and never chew, but just concentrate on the mixture of juices that drips onto their tonsils from the Life Saver and the clove, in a steady drip like rainwater running off the candied rooftops of Fairyland.

Now, aside from being calming and occupying, requiring no spitting and no assistance from the hands, a butterscotch Life Saver and a clove give a person the most interesting breath in the world.

It's no wonder the Rubber Rose ladies were always kissing on each other, although what a cowgirl does with her mouth once she's back at the bunkhouse shouldn't really concern us students of Western lore.

When there were thirty or more cowgirls riding for the Rubber Rose, sometimes the wheatgrass and the hills and the whole wide sky itself would start to smell like butterscotch and clove.

Sometimes the Chink would smell it way up on his ridge. Not when he first came to Dakota, of course. Then he could smell only pollen and sagebrush and woodsmoke and his own hairy self. Who was it once said, "A hermit is mysterious to everyone but the hermit."

65.

WHEN HE FIRST lit on Siwash Ridge, the Chink couldn't catch a whiff of butterscotch/clove cowgirl breath or of Countess-gagging cowgirl snatch. Which is just as well, for had there been cowgirls then on the Rubber Rose range, they might have drawn his nose out of his own business. And he had business aplenty. The cave proved to be as wondrous as advertised, but enormous amounts of labor and ingenuity were required to adapt it to his lifestyle and make it comfortable for year-round residency. Moreover, he had a clockworks to assemble and that is not a simple task. In the process of readying the cave and planning his clockworks, he had also to extricate himself from Clock People consciousness, because twenty-six years among the Indians of the Great Burrow had molded him more than he had realized when he set out again on his own.

The mass of humanity has minds like soft wax. Once an impression is made upon them, it won't change until you change it for them. They are malleable but not self-malleable (a condition politicians and PR men use to sinister advantage). The Chink, however, was perfectly capable of reshaping his ball of tallow: it just took longer than he had anticipated.

When, four years later, he spoke of the Clock People to Sissy, it was with admiration, appreciation and amusement.

In times of widespread chaos and confusion, it has been the duty of more advanced human beings — artists, scientists, clowns and philosophers — to create order. In times such as ours, however, when there is too much order, too much management, too much programming and control, it becomes the duty of superior men and women to fling their favorite monkey wrenches into the machinery. To relieve the repression of the human spirit, they must sow doubt and disruption. The Chink snickered his hell-crazed snicker when he imagined the doubt and confusion that would follow society's eventual discovery of the Clock People. He snickered even though he suspected that the encounter would destroy the Clock People, and even though he scorned the sickening democratic more-is-better fallacy inherent in the notion that the part must be sacrificed for the whole.

"I loved those loony redskins," the Chink said to Sissy. "But I couldn't be a party to their utopian dreaming. After a while it occurred to me that the Clock People waiting for the Eternity of Joy was virtually identical to the Christians waiting for the Second Coming. Or the Communists waiting for the worldwide revolution. Or the Debbies waiting for the flying saucers. All the same. Just more suckers betting their share of the present on the future, banking every misery on a happy ending to history. Well, history isn't ever going to end, happily or unhappily. And history is ending every second — happily for some of us, unhappily for others, happily one second, unhappily the next. History is always ending and always not ending, and both ways there is nothing to wait for. Ha ha ho ho and hee hee."

The shaggy old fart slid his arms around Sissy and . . . no, wait, she wasn't telling Dr. Robbins that part. Yet.

Sometime in the course of things, the Chink had made it clear to Sissy that, while he might not buy the Clock People's dreaming, he did respect the quality of their dream. The vision of an era, however lasting, during which all ritual would be personal and idiosyncratic, made the Chink's heart want to stand up and dance. Furthermore, while a return engagement by Jesus appears as impossible as worldwide Marxist revolution is improbable, a general disruption of the planet by natural forces is inevitable. The Clock People had narrowed the apocalyptic credibility gap.

"In the end, though," observed the Chink, "for all their insight, the Clock People were a collection of human animals banded together to prepare for better days. In short, just more victims of the disease of time."

Ah, time! Back to time. Dr. Robbins struggled to sit upright. The wine had said its good-bys. He was a trifle drunk. His mustache could not deny it. Every so often, Dr. Goldman would appear at the French doors. This didn't bother Dr. Robbins. Dr. Goldman would never have the courage to interrupt, not so long as Sissy continued her exercises. Great digits wallowed in the garden air.

(Dr. Goldman's face, as red and swollen as a smallpox vaccination, pressed to the pane. He saw the thumbs promenade stiffly in their suits of blushes. Then they began to quiver. They made wild and ultrarapid swoops, like water spiders on the surface of a pond. As he watched, a kind of radiant ectoplasm formed all around them. Sissy was smiling absently. Dr. Robbins lay, as if in adoration, at her feet. Dr. Goldman whirled abruptly and strode away.)

In truth, Dr. Robbins was a bit more anxious than he might have appeared. His patient's testimony had gradually become secondary to her hitch practice, her running of the scales. What had begun as casual muscle flex had escalated, as she lost self-consciousness, into a thorough inventory of the extravagant moves and motions stored in her gross appendages. Now she had fallen silent, absorbed in the piloting of her blimps. Dr. Robbins was agog at the display, but he wished, like old-fashioned novelists, to stay to the point, to keep the story flowing. You see, Dr. Robbins had a theory that was apropos the clockworks and the Chink. It had long been Dr. Robbin's belief that the central problem facing the human race was time.

As for defining time, or speculating upon its nature, forget it. Neither tipsy nor sober was he about to dance with the angels on the head of *that* pin. Since embarking upon a career in behavioral science, however, Dr. Robbins had searched to find at least one fundamental truth about the psyche, and the closest he had come to a fundamental was the discovery that most psychological — and, therefore, social, political and spiritual — problems can be linked to pressures exerted by time. Or, more precisely, civilized man's idea of time.

Of course, he wasn't absolutely sure that there *were* any problems. It was entirely possible that everything in the universe was perfect; that all that happened, from global warfare to a single case of athlete's foot, happened because it ought to happen; and while from our perspective it would seem that something horrendous had gone wrong in the development of the human species, vis-à-vis its happy potentialities on the blue green sphere, that that was an illusion attributable to myopia, and that, in fact, development was proceeding beautifully, running right as a Tokyo train, and needing only a more cosmic overview in order for its grand perfection to obscure its momentary fits and faults.

That was a possibility, all right, one that Dr. Robbins had by no means ruled out. On the other hand, if such an approach was, like religion, merely a camouflage system created to modify experience in order to make life more tolerable — another exercise in escapism festooned with mystic crêpe — then one had no choice but to conclude that mankind was a royal fuck-up. Despite our awesome potential; despite the presence among us of the most extraordinary enlightened individuals, operating with intelligence, gentleness and style; despite a plethora of achievements that no other living creatures have come within a billion light-years of equaling, we were on the verge of destroying ourselves, internally and externally, and of taking the entire planet with us, crumpled in our tight little fists, as we shoot down the shit-chute to oblivion.

Now, if that be the case, one is compelled to ask what went wrong; how and when did it go wrong. The answer to that question of questions breathes on so many buds that the wimpy brain gets hay fever, its eyes puff shut, it sneezes away whole bouquets of hidden and half-guessed truths, and it probably doesn't want to know anyway. From his psychiatrist's stance, however, a stance only slightly less allergic than any other, Dr. Robbins was able to venture this far:

Most of the harm inflicted by man upon his environment, his fellows and himself is due to greed.

Most of the greed (whether it be for power, property, attention or affection) is due to insecurity.

Most of the insecurity is due to fear.

And most of the fear is, at bottom, a fear of death.

Given time, all things are possible. But time may have a stop.

Why do people fear death so? Because they realize, unconsciously at least, that their lives are mere parodies of what living should be.

They ache to quit playing at living and to really live, but, alas, it takes time and trouble to piece the loose ends of their lives together and they are dogged by the notion that time is running out.

Was that it, or was the pebble in the dancing slipper the phobia that time does *not* have a stop? If we could live our average 70.4 years and know for certain that that was that, we could readily manage. We might complain that it was far too short, but what there was of life we could live freely, doing exactly what we pleased insofar as our conscience and capabilities allowed, accepting that when it was over it was over: easy come, easy go. Ah, but we aren't allowed the luxury of finality. We dilute and hobble our most genuinely felt impulses with the idea, whether fervently held or naggingly suspected, that after death there is something else, and that that something may be endless, and that the correctness of our behavior in "this" life may determine how we fare in the "next" one (and for those poor souls who believe in reincarnation, the ones after that).

Thus, whether it is in danger of stopping and catching us with our pants down, or whether it runs on forever and demands that we busy ourselves preparing for the next station on the long ride, either way, time prevents us from living authentically.

Perhaps the fault is that we are Dr. Frankensteins who have created time as a monster with three heads: past, present and future. In which case, back to the drawing board! The present is okay, the present is sharp and clean; leave it where it is, on top of and directing the body. But relegate the past to some other anatomical function. The past, for example, would make a perfect asshole. As for the future, let's see, the future could be time's . . .

Thumbs.

Like papier-mâché spaceships in an old Buck Rogers movie, they whooshed in a wobbly fashion toward imaginary worlds. She fueled them with rocket powder mined in her heart. She juggled them without ever letting go, tossing and catching them simultaneously, so that the shower of thumbs — that aerial ballet of warm pineapples — struck over and over again the same rods in the observer's eye. The hammered eye blinked beneath this banging of bubbles. Thumbs tumbled end over end in the field of vision. Thumbs wheeled and thumbs floated. Thumbs squirmed like the tickled bellies of babies. Thumbs spanked the bottom of the sky.

It was all Dr. Robbins could do not to surrender to the spectacle, to let thumbs carry him to wherever thumbs desired he go. After all, this was not a sight many had seen. but he was a stubborn man with time on his hands. So, at last, he exclaimed, loudly enough to pierce his patient's reverie, "Sissy, don't keep me in suspense! What were the Chink's thoughts about time? And how did he apply them to building his own clockworks?"

"Oh," said Sissy, a trifle startled. "Oh yes." She let her thumbs fall into her lap and bounce gently there. "Oh yes. Well, you see, you must understand that the Chink doesn't do a whole lot of talking. He says what he has to say very quickly and seldom repeats or explains himself. He's more apt to be laughing and scratching than expounding ideas. But if I humored him — and let him do what he wanted with me" (Sissy lowered her lashes) — "he *would* share a few of his thoughts. Now, I'm not sure what this has to do with time itself, but the Chink sees life as a dynamic network of interchanges and exchanges, spreading in all directions at once. And it's all held together by the tension between opposites. He says there is order in Nature, but there is also disorder. And it is the balance of tensions between the order and the disorder, the natural laws and the natural randomness, that keeps it from completely collapsing. It's a beautiful paradox, as he describes it. Personally, I don't know. When I mentioned the concept to Julian, he just scoffed. Julian says that *everything* in Nature is ordered and there *is* no randomness. The more we learn about the way Nature works, the more laws we discover. Julian says there isn't any paradox, that the only reason certain aspects of Nature seem disorderly to us is because we haven't understood them yet. Julian says . . ."

"Julian doesn't know his scrotum from Kentucky fried chicken," grumbled Dr. Robbins. "I recognize that paradox the Chink was speaking of; it's inside us as well as all around us. I went into psychiatry with the desire to help set people free. But I soon learned that man is stuck with a lot of conflicting behavioral and emotional traits that have a genetic basis. We have built-in contradictions; they're standard equipment on all models. No matter how much people long to be free — even to the point of valuing freedom over happiness — an aversion to liberty is right there in their DNA. For eons of evolutionary time, our DNA has been whispering into the ears of our cells that we are, each one of us, the most precious things in the universe and that any action that entails the slightest risk to us may have consequences of universal importance. 'Be careful, get comfortable, don't make any waves,' whispers the DNA. Conversely, the yearning for freedom, the risky belief that there is nothing to lose and nothing to gain, is also in our DNA. But it's of much more recent evolutionary origin, according to me. It has arisen during the past couple of million years, during the rapid increase in brain size and intellectual capacity associated with our becoming human. But the desire for security, the will to survive, is of much greater antiquity. For the present, the conflicting yearnings in the DNA generate a basic paradox that in turn generates the character — nothing if not contradictory — of man. To live fully, one must be free, but to be free one must give up security. Therefore, to live one must be ready to die. How's that for a paradox? But, since the genetic bent for freedom is comparatively recent, it may represent an evolutionary trend. We may yet outgrow our overriding obsession to survive. That's why I encourage everyone to take chances, to court danger, to welcome anxiety, to flaunt insecurity, to rock every boat and always cut against the grain. By pushing it, goosing it along whenever possible, we may speed up the process, the process by which the need for playfulness and liberty becomes stronger than the need for comfort and security. Then that paradox that the, er, Chink sees holding the show together may lose its equilibrium. What then, Mr. Chink, what then?" Dr. Robbins scratched his mustache with the stem of his Bulova, thereby simultaneously satisfying itch and winding watch. With time the central problem facing mankind, such efficiency had to be admired.

Sissy, soothing her thumbs, smiled. She liked that baby-faced junior shrink. In some ways, he even reminded her a little of the Chink. In other ways — dress and demeanor — he reminded her of Julian. She supposed that he would be pleased by the former comparison, vexed by the latter. So she said:

"That's fascinating. Not the kind of talk I expected to run into at the Goldman Clinic, I'll tell you. You think a bit like the Chink yourself."

"Is that so?"

"Yes, you do. Although I wouldn't dare to presume to speak for the Chink, it sounds to me like you're talking about the same paradox.

Or, at least, a similar one. Well, to try to get back to your question . . . The Chink sees in the natural world a paradoxical balance of supreme order and supreme disorder. But man has a pronounced bias for order. He not only refuses to respect or even accept the disorder in Nature, in life; he shuns it, rages against it, attacks it with orderly programs. And in so doing, he perpetuates instability."

"Hold on a minute," called Dr. Robbins. He propped his Oxford cloth-shirted back against the stone bench upon which Sissy was sitting. "Let me make sure I'm with you. Wine made me fuzzy. You say — the Chink says — the bias for order leads to instability?"

"Right," said Sissy. "For several reasons. First, worshiping order and hating disorder automatically shoves great portions of Nature and life into a hateful category. Did you know that the center of the Earth is red-hot liquid covered with a hard crust, and that that crust is not a single unified layer but a whole jumbled series of shifting plates? These plates are about sixty miles thick and very plastic. They appear and disappear. They move around and buckle and bump into each other like epileptic dominoes. New mountains and new islands — once in a long while, new continents — are being created and old ones destroyed. New climates are being formed and old ones altered. The whole thing is in flux. Existing arrangements are temporary and constantly in threat of disruption. This whole big city of New York could be sucked into the Earth or quick-frozen or flattened or inundated — at any second. The Chink says the man who feels smug in an orderly world has never looked down a volcano."

Dr. Robbins appeared a tad disappointed. Maybe it was the sun heating the wine in his eyes. "Yeah, I had a geology course in college," he mumbled. "Geophysical turmoil is a reality, all right, but hardly a defense of disorder. I mean, cancer — cellular turmoil — is a reality, too, but that doesn't make it lovable or even acceptable."

"True," agreed Sissy. Her big digits had quieted down. They lolled upon her thighs like exhausted sea cows run ragged by some cowgirls of the deeps. "True. That wasn't the Chink's point. He was saying simply that the vagrancies and violence of nature must be brought back into the foreground of social and political consciousness, that they have got to be embraced in any meaningful psychic renewal."

"Yeah, yeah, okay."

"But as for stability . . . In general, primitive man enjoyed great stability. It blew my mind to hear the Chink say that, but now I can see that it was true. Primitive culture was diverse, flexible and completely integrated with Nature at the level of the particular environment. Primitive man took from the land only what he needed, thus avoiding the hassles that result in modern economics from imbalances of scarcity and surplus. Hunting and gathering tribes worked only a few hours a week. To work more than that would have put a strain on the environment, with which they related symbiotically. It was only among mobile cultures — after the unfortunate domestication of animals — that surplus, a result of overachievement, led to potlatches and competitive feasts — orgies of conspicuous consumption and conspicuous waste — which attached to simple, healthy, effective economies the destructive elements of power and prestige. When that happened, stability was shattered. Civilization is a mutant beast that emerged from the shattered egg of primitive stability. Another thing about primitives; they deified forces of disorder as well as of order. In fact, the gods of wind and lava and lightning were often honored above the deities of more placid things — and not always out of fear."

Still not satisfied, Dr. Robbins dragged his nails through the label on the empty wine bottle. "Interesting," he said. "Pretty interesting. But here you've got the Chink praising disorder on the one hand and stability on the other . . ."

"Exactly," answered Sissy. "Disorder is inherent in stability. Civilized man doesn't understand stability. He's confused it with rigidity. Our political and economic and social leaders drool about stability constantly. It's their favorite word, next to 'power.' 'Gotta stabilize the political situation in Southeast Asia, gotta stabilize oil production and consumption, gotta stabilize student opposition to the government' and so forth. Stabilization to them means order, uniformity, control. And that's a half-witted and potentially genocidal misconception. No matter how thoroughly they control a system, disorder invariably leaks into it. Then the managers panic, rush to plug the leak and endeavor to tighten the controls. Therefore, totalitarianism grows in viciousness and scope. And the blind pity is, rigidity isn't the same as stability at all. True stability results when presumed order and presumed disorder are balanced. A truly stable system expects the unexpected, is prepared to be disrupted, waits to be transformed.

As a psychiatrist, wouldn't you say that a stable individual accepts the inevitability of his death? Likewise, a stable culture, government or institution has built into it its own demise. It is open to change, open even to being overthrown. It is open, period. Gracefully open. That's stability. That's alive."

"Makes sense, makes good sense," agreed Dr. Robbins, upon whose girl-next-door face a wine-stained mustache made little sense at all. Dr. Robbins's mustache was the ruins of a lost city of hair discovered by archeologists in the Bald Mountains, or Dr. Robbins's mustache was a fur coat worn by an eccentric widow to a picnic in Phoenix, Arizona, on the Fourth of July, or Dr. Robbins's mustache was an obscene phone call to a deaf nun. "Yeah," agreed Dr. Robbins, tugging at his mustache as if even he didn't believe it. "I can fit that into my jigsaw puzzle. But *time,* Sissy; where do time and clockworks connect to this?"

"The Chink didn't exactly *say* how they connected, but I think I've got it figured out." Sissy pulled a scrap of paper from a jumpsuit pocket. "A physicist named Edgar Lipworth wrote this," she explained. "He writes, 'The time of physics is defined and measured by a pendulum whether it is the pendulum of a grandfather's clock, the pendulum of the Earth's rotation around the sun, or the pendulum of the precessing electron in the nuclear magnetic field of the hydrogen maser. Time, therefore, is defined by periodic motion — that is, by motion related to a point moving uniformly around a circle.' Got that?"

"Sure," said Dr. Robbins. "And there's the pendulum of the heart beating, the pendulum of the lungs breathing, the pendulum of music finding its beat . . ."

"Those too. Right. Okay, then, civilized man is infatuated with the laws he finds in Nature, clings almost frantically to the order he sees in the universe. So he has based the symbologies, the psychological models with which he hopes to understand his life, upon his observations of natural law and order. Pendulum time is orderly time, the time of a lawfully uniform universe, the time of cyclic synthesis. That's okay as far as it goes. But pendulum time is not the whole time. Pendulum time doesn't relate to trillions of the moves and acts of existence. Life is both cyclic and arbitrary, but pendulum time relates only to the part that's cyclic."

"Although the manner in which we relate to pendulum time is often arbitrary, too," threw in Dr. Robbins. He thought of the arbitrary dial of a clock and how certain arbitrary numbers on that dial, such as nine and five and noon and midnight have been left dog-eared by undue emphasis.

"Yes, I reckon so," said Sissy. "But the point is, although a lot of our experience occurs outside of, or relates only artificially and tenuously to, pendulum time, we still envision time only in pendulum terms, in terms of continuous compulsory rotation. Even the Clock People's hourglass; it wasn't designed for perfect accuracy or anything, but it was modeled upon an orderly flow. It clung to the frayed edges of a time its builders wanted to transcend. The catfish pool came closer to measuring the 'other' time of life, but its limitations . . ."

"Sissy."

"Yes."

Dr. Robbins had spotted Dr. Goldman at the French doors again. "What is the Chink's clockworks like?" he asked.

"Ha ha," laughed Sissy. "Criminey. You wouldn't believe it. It's just a bunch of junk. Garbage can lids and old saucepans and lard tins and car fenders, all wired together way down in the middle of the Siwash cave. Every now and then, this contraption moves — a bat will fly into it, a rock will fall on it, an updraft will catch it, a wire will rust through, or it'll just move for no apparently logical reason — and one part of it will hit against another part. And it'll go *bonk* or *poing* and that *bonk* or that *poing* will echo throughout the caverns. It might go *bonk* or *poing* five times in a row. Then a pause; then one more time. After that, it might be silent for a day or two, maybe a month. Then the clock'll strike again, say twice. Following that there could be silence for an entire year — or just a minute or so. Then, *POING!* so loud you nearly jump out of your skin. And that's the way it goes. Striking freely, crazily, at odd intervals."

Sissy closed her eyes, as if listening for the distant *bonk* or *poing,* and Dr. Robbins, ignoring Dr. Goldman's gestures from the French doors, seemed to be listening, too.

They listened. They heard.

They were assured then, together, the psychiatric intern and his patient, that there was a rhythm, a strange unnoted rhythm, that might or might not be beating out their lives for them. For each of us.

Because to measure time by the clockworks is to know that you are moving toward some end . . . but at a pace far different from the one you might think!

66.

Dr. Robbins had had all the food for thought he could stomach at one sitting. He wished to be home alone with another bottle of wine. He dismissed his patient politely. Then, in order to avoid Dr. Goldman, left the clinic by scrambling over the garden wall, tearing, in the process, a knee out of his thirty-dollar slacks.

Sissy Hankshaw Gitche, who never had talked so extensively before in her life, was weary and glad to be excused. Men of ideas, men such as Julian, the Chink and now Dr. Robbins, intrigued her. But she welcomed the chance to go to her room and dream of cowgirls, while, with a cube of unsalted kosher butter from the clinic dining room, she greased the creases in her thumbs.

Julian Gitche failed to visit or phone his wife upon that day in May. Julian had just contracted to paint a series of watercolors for a West German pharmaceutical house, the firm that once manufactured thalidomide. He was entertaining a representative of the firm and he feared that any whisper of his spouse's physical peculiarities might evoke for the former thalidomide salesman embarrassing memories.

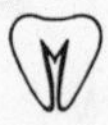

The Chink hoofed into Mottburg that morning to purchase yams and a can of Chun King water chestnuts. His devotion to yams was unflagging, but he increasingly looked to the water chestnut as an example of endurance, of will and of fidelity to the particular. The water chestnut, after all, is the only vegetable whose texture doesn't change after freezing, changeth not after being cooked.

The Countess spent the day in his laboratory, laboring feverishly to develop an antipheromone. A pheromone is an air-borne hormone given off by the female animal, bird or insect to attract a male of her species. The human pheromone had only recently been isolated. The Countess hoped to produce and market a pill that, ingested periodically, would counteract human pheromone activity, eliminating all prurient odors from that part of the female anatomy the writer Richard Condon has so beautifully described as "the vertical smile." (To Richard Condon, a dozen purple asters and a pound of goat cheese from *Even Cowgirls Get the Blues.)*

Bonanza Jellybean rode Lucas out to Siwash Lake to see if the whoopers were still there. They were! She celebrated by sticking a feather in her hat, though she'd be damned if she'd call it macaroni.

The author (who is also one of the above — which one doesn't matter) would like to take this opportunity, here at the conclusion of Sissy's remarkable account of Clock People and clockworks, to advance an earthquake theory of his own. As the author sees it, the Earth is God's pinball machine and each quake, tidal wave, flash flood and volcanic eruption is the result of a TILT that occurs when God, cheating, tries to win free games.

67.

THE FOLLOWING MORNING, Dr. Robbins sent for Sissy early, before Dr. Goldman had a chance to get at her. Again he escorted her into the little walled garden, although this time without a bottle of wine. As a matter of fact, Dr. Robbins's blue eyes were being squashed by about a hundred pounds of hangover.

"Okay," he said softly, wishing not to agitate the punitive and vindictive deities of fermentation, "tell me how you met the Chink."

"I met him at the can-dee sto-ore," sang Sissy. "No, seriously. I'm thankful to have an opportunity to talk to someone safe — trustworthy, you know — about the Chink, but aren't you supposed to be asking me about . . . about the reasons I'm in this institution?"

"I haven't the slightest interest in your personal problems," snapped Dr. Robbins, inwardly cursing the chemical Calvinism that causes alcohol to make us suffer for the good times it gives us.

"Oh? Well, my husband is spending quite a sum of money to have my personal problems aired at this clinic."

"Your husband is a fool. As for you, if you let yourself be subjected to the indignities of psychoanalysis, you're a fool as well. And Goldman is certainly a fool for sending you to me. *I*, however, am no fool. You've told me some of the most fascinating stories I've heard in a long while. I'm sure as hell not going to waste these sunny hours among the flowers listening to your dreary personal problems when I could be hearing more about your adventures with the Chink. Now. Tell me how you met him. And don't hesitate to, uh, to perform the, er, the antics you do with your thumbs. If you'd like."

"But won't that attract attention?" Without the wine to encourage her, Sissy was hesitant to repeat the digital abandon of the day before.

"Sometimes," said Dr. Robbins, glancing with bloodshot peepers at the French doors, "sometimes those things that attract the most attention to us are the things that afford us the greatest privacy." He flopped in the grass.

"Doctor," said Sissy with a smile, "forgive me but I get the impression that you're a bit of a mental case yourself."

"It takes one to know one," replied Robbins. "That's probably why all the penguins ended up at the South Pole."

68.

PART BADLANDS BUTTE, part grasslands hill, part high chaparral, Siwash Ridge is a geological mutant, a schizophrenic formation embodying in one relatively small mountain several of the most prominent features of the American West. A wildly twisting and unpredictable trail zigs and zags up its eastern side, through thickets of scrub oak and juniper, upward over grassy bumps, finally clinging by its shoelaces to limestone walls. The top of Siwash, though disposed in a few places to jut and peak, is very nearly flat: a calcium carbonate aircraft carrier, a ship that water built from land.

Toward the center of the butte top is a horse-deep, circular depression that in fair weather serves the Chink as a sunken living room. From the northern wall of the depression gapes the mouth of a cave.

A person of Sissy's height has to crawl into the cave on her hands and knees, and almost nowhere in the entrance chamber — covered with Japanese straw matting — is there room for a leggy model to stand up straight. The entrance chamber, however, is merely the top level of three levels of caverns. The bottom level, deep inside the butte, consists of two freight car-sized rooms, heated by thermal updrafts and remarkably dry. On the middle level, there are five or six enormous chambers, connected by narrow passageways. In one of these chambers is the clockworks.

From the walls of the middle-level room, fresh pure water drips constantly. It is as if the walls are weeping. It is as if the soul of the continent is weeping.

Why does it weep? It weeps for the bones of the buffalo. It weeps for magic that has been forgotten. It weeps for the decline of poets.

It weeps
for the black people who think like white people.
It weeps

for the Indians who think like settlers.
It weeps
for the children who think like adults.
It weeps
for the free who think like prisoners.
Most of all, it weeps
for the cowgirls who think like cowboys.

69.

HER THUMBS had stopped him. Her thumbs were good at that. If the man who cried "Stop the world, I want to get off!" had only had Sissy's thumbs . . .

She had stopped him cold on the side of Siwash Ridge. So, what next? He wore the wary look of a wild animal. He wouldn't stay stopped long. It was her move. What could she say? His gaze went through her like beavers through a paper palm tree. His was the look of the strong who will not tolerate weaklings. She must speak and she must speak with prehensility, for not even her thumbs would stop him a second time. It was imperative that she say the right thing. He was turning as if to scamper off again.

"Well," said Sissy, with what passed for nonchalance. "Aren't you going to shake your whanger at me?"

It broke him up. He slapped his thighs and giggled hysterically. Ha has, ho hos and hee hees squirted out of his nose and through the gaps in his teeth. When the laughter finally died a nervous chipmunk death, he spoke. "Follow me," he said, in a voice unaccustomed to invitation. "I'll fix you supper."

Follow him she did, although he set a powerful pace up the tricky twilit trail.

"I'm a friend of Bonanza Jellybean's," she said between puffs.

"I know who you are," he said without looking back.

"Oh? Well, there's been some trouble on the ranch. I came up here to get out of the way. It's so dark now I doubt if I could find my way back down. If you could help . . ."

"Save your breath for the climb," he said. His voice wore no pants.

From the top of the butte there could still be seen light in the west. The haunted shapes of the badlands were silhouetted navy blue against a pumpkin-colored horizon. To the east, across shadowed hills, the prairie lay on its back in the dark, hidden, yet making felt its awesome flatness, a flatness that flavors so much of America, beginning with her emotions and her taste; a flatness that makes a perfect surface for those wheels of Detroit whose rotations are for millions the only escape from the chronically flat. Sissy turned from east to west and back again. The faintly lit badlands were so tortured and melodramatic they seemed, like the prose in a Dostoyevsky novel, almost a corny joke. The blacked-out prairie, on the other hand, had a style identical to that of rural weekly newspapers throughout the middle of the nation: blandness in such high concentration as to become finally poisonous. An owl flew over the ridge from *Crime and Punishment* to the Mottburg *Gazette,* scanning the pages for a literate rodent, asking the librarian for a whooo-done-it.

Directly below them, lights twinkled at the Rubber Rose. The ranch was quiet. Sissy could imagine showers running full blast in the bunkhouse as glossy pubes, folded labia and hooded clitorises were lathered and scrubbed clean of the perfume that had been allowed to accumulate to plague the Countess. Sissy imagined she heard popping washcloths, girlish laughter.

When she had caught her breath, Sissy was led to the depression and down a ladder of sticks. The Chink built a fire, an open fire, the depression itself being adequate protection from winds. He roasted yams. He heated meadowlark stew. The stew contained Chun King water chestnuts. Their texture did not change in the cooking. A lesson.

After supper, eaten in silence upon a rough wooden bench, the Chink went into the cave and returned with a tiny peppermint-striped plastic transistor radio. He switched it on. Their auditory nerves were immediately jangled by "The Happy Hour Polka." Still clutching the radio in one hand, the Chink hopped into the wheel of firelight and began to dance.

Sissy in her travels had never seen anything quite like it. The old geezer heeled and toed, skipped and hopped. He flung his bones; he flung his beard. "Yip! Yip!" he yodeled. "Ha ha ho ho and hee hee."

Arms swimming, feet firecrackering, he danced through two more polka records and might have had a fourth except that the music was suspended for a news report. The international situation was desperate, as usual.

"Personally, I prefer Stevie Wonder," confessed the Chink, "but what the hell. Those cowgirls are always bitching because the only radio station in the area plays nothing but polkas, but I say you can dance to *anything* if you really feel like dancing." To prove it, he got up and danced to the news.

When the music commenced again with "The Lawrence Welk is a Hero of the Republic Polka," the Chink lifted Sissy by her shoulders and guided her onto his pock-marked dance floor. "But I don't know how to polka," she protested.

"Neither do I," said the Chink. "Ha ha ho ho and hee hee." In a second they were traipsing over the limestone, arm in arm. Their shadows reeled against the curves of the depression. Night birds flew past with trembling feathers. A bat fluttered out of the cave, took one radar reading and headed for Kenny's Castaways.

When they had danced their fill, the Chink escorted Sissy to the opposite, and darkest, side of the depression and sat her down upon a pile of soft stuff: dried wheatgrass, faded Indian blankets and old down pillows without cases. The stuff reeked. It was that unmistakable sex blend of mushrooms, chlorine and tide pool. And cutting through that odor, the equally unmistakable smell of Bonanza Jellybean: clove, butterscotch Life Savers and a lotion made from cactus juices, which she rubbed daily upon the spot where she had been shot, so she said, by a silver bullet.

"So this is how Jelly spends her visits to the Chink," thought Sissy. She started to wonder whether the other cowgirls, manless as they were, suspected — but halfway through that wonder she interrupted it to wonder if the Chink thought he was going to help himself to *her*. She had always been passive when it came to being pawed, pinched and the like, but no man had ever taken her against her will. In fact, no man had ever taken her but Julian.

Just then the Chink did an astonishing thing. Without preamble, without hesitation, the white-maned Jap reached out and grasped her thumbs! He squeezed them, caressed them, covered them with wet kisses. All the while, he cooed to them, telling them how beautiful and exceptional and incomparable they were. Not even Julian had ever done that, you bet. Even Jack Kerouac hadn't dared touch her thumbs, although he had been fascinated by them and had written to them a poem on a cornhusk, an ode that might have been widely published had not it been eaten by a hungry hobo as Kerouac and the boys boxcared into Denver to search for Neal Cassady's daddy, the most missing man in the history of American letters, leaving it up to this author to tell the story of those awesome appendages.

Even Bonanza Jellybean hadn't loved Sissy's thumbs.

As we might imagine, Sissy was bowled over. She was frightened, stunned, elated, moved almost to tears. Apparently sincere, the Chink extended his adoration of the digits far into the night. When at last he got around to adoring the rest of her, her heart, like her thumbs, was aglow.

"If this be adultery, make the most of it," she cried. As he plunged into her, she arched her spread bottom against the blankets and reared up to meet him halfway.

70.

"So, YOU HAD sexual intercourse with the old man?" asked Dr. Robbins.

"Repeatedly," blushed Sissy.

"And how was it? I mean, how do you feel about it now?"

"Er, I'm not really sure. You see, sex with Julian is like hitching a ride around the block on a fire engine. With the Chink, it was like hitching from Chicago to Salt Lake City in a big old nineteen fifty-nine Buick Roadmaster." She paused to ascertain if her similes had been understood. Dr. Robbins was pulling and releasing his mustache, pulling and releasing, as if his mustache were a window shade in a cheap hotel. The window shade wouldn't hang the way Dr. Robbins wanted it to.

Sissy decided to elucidate.

"With Julian, it's fast and furious. It's always been sort of desperate. There's such *need.* We *cling* to each other, like we were holding on with our genitals to keep from falling into emptiness, a kind of lonely void. I have a feeling that it's like that with a lot of lovers. But with the Chink, it was completely relaxed and smooth and slow and, well, nasty. He giggled and grinned and scratched all the time, and could go for ages without orgasm. A real Roadmaster. Once, he ate yam pudding while he was balling me. Fed it to me, too — with his fingers. He licked it off my nipples; I licked it off his balls. I felt like we were a couple of baboons or something. I liked it. I guess I miss it. But no more than I miss it with Jellybean."

"You mean . . .?"

"Yes."

"I see. Umm. Well, let's stick to the Chink. During those three days of . . . of, er, lovemaking . . ."

"It *was* lovemaking, Doctor. Even though it was nasty. Maybe especially because it was nasty. Love is smutty business, you know."

Dr. Robbins pulled hard on the mustache window shade. It came down with such force it nearly tore loose from its roller. "The old geezer really made you feel something, didn't he?"

"How could I help feeling something? He adored my thumbs."

Dr. Robbins looked hard at Sissy's preaxial digits, then at his own. Magnitude was the only appreciable difference. In both sets of thumbs, Sissy's and his own, Dr. Robbins could see shafts, flat on the volar surface, smooth and rounded on the dorsal surface, that is, semicylindrical in shape. He knew that these bones were bound together with ligaments and cartilages. He remembered that the thumb joint is officially called the carpometacarpal joint, although it is informally referred to as the "saddle joint." Saddle joint. That's nice. Cowgirls could relate to that.

He knew that when Sissy bent a phalanx, revolving took place around an axis passing transversely, determining the movement in a sagittal plane, just as it did when he bent a phalanx. It was just more of a production number with Sissy, that was all.

With effort he could harken back to med school and recall the musculature of the thumb, thinking that a *flexor pollicis brevis* is a *flexor pollicis brevis*, regardless of its size.

But then Dr. Robbins looked at his patient's thumbs again — and suddenly the difference seemed more extensive than scale. He saw a pair of hammerhead sharks, devouring with a sharkish hunger the space around them. He blinked, and in the blinking the sharks were replaced by a couple of pears, full and luscious, swaying there in their outsized sweetness as if Cézanne had painted them on a canvas of air. Again he blinked, and . . .

Sissy noticed his blinking; perceived the unsatisfactory comparison. "Maybe, Doctor," she said, "my thumbs have known poetry and yours have not." She paused. "Or maybe it's simply this: you *have* thumbs; I *am* thumbs."

The shade shot to the top of the window, wrapping itself noisily around its roller.

"During those three days of lovemaking," resumed Dr. Robbins, the stubborn bastard, "the hermit obviously talked to you. He told you about his background and something of his philosophy. You've graciously shared his words with me . . ."

"I *needed* to talk about him to somebody. I need to talk about Jellybean, too."

"Right. Right. We'll get to her. But I'm curious. Did he say anything else? Did he say anything about uh, well, about life, anything further about, anything that I might . . ."

Sissy smiled. A skinny bumblebee with Con Edison soot on its fur cruised her psychiatrist's mustache (perhaps a few of the hairs were still sticky with wine), but Robbins paid it no mind. Dr. Goldman was standing in the French doors (perhaps gathering courage to finally interrupt this interview), but Robbins ignored him, too. Sissy's smile broadened. "The Chink said that some people run after sages the way others run after gold. He said we've produced a generation of spiritual panhandlers, begging for coins of wisdom, banging like bums on every closed door. He said if an old man moves into a shack or a cave and lets his beard grow, people will flock from miles around just to read his NO TRESPASSING signs.

"Is that why you're so interested in the Chink, Doctor? Do you think he knows something that the rest of the world doesn't? Something that can contribute to our salvation?"

Turning loose the shade, letting it hang any way it damn well pleased, Dr. Robbins retorted, "No, no, a thousand times no! In the first place, I distrust completely any man who holds himself up as an answer to those who can't find the inner resources to overcome their own sense of time-entrapment and loneliness. In the second place,

I'm not the least concerned with salvation because I'm not convinced there's anything to be saved from. My position is this: I'm a psychiatrist who has been betrayed by the brain. That's akin to an astronomer betrayed by starlight. Or a cook betrayed by garlic. Nevertheless, I have developed an outlook on life that amounts to both a form of wisdom and a means of survival. It isn't perfected yet, but it gets me by — and to those very rare patients who possess the guts and imagination to pick up on it, it might set a helpful example. Any psychiatrist or psychologist whose own life isn't happy and whole enough to be exemplary isn't worth the hide it takes to upholster his couch. He ought to be horsewhipped and sued for malpractice. But, to return to the point, as soon as you began to speak of the Chink, I sensed a rapport, an overview similar — perhaps — to my own. Maybe he has notions about the ebb and flow of the cosmic custard that are improvements upon mine. Maybe not. If not, *c'est la* frigging *vie.* If so, if might be beneficial to both of us, you and me, to rap about them. It sure as hell beats talking about 'inverted compensation.' "

"In that case," said Sissy, obviously pleased, "I'd be pleased. To be honest, I don't know whether the Chink has anything of value to offer or not. He didn't claim to, but that could have been a coverup. I'll tell you as much as I can remember of our conversations, such as they were, and you can judge for yourself. Fair enough?"

"Let 'er rip," said Dr. Robbins, as if speaking of the window shade that hung in tatters from his upper lip.

71.

PRAIRIE. Isn't that a pretty word? Rolls off the tongue like a fat little moon. *Prairie* must be one of the prettiest words in the English language. No matter that it's French. It's derived from the Latin word for "meadow" plus a feminine suffix. A prairie, then, is a female meadow. It is larger and wilder than a masculine meadow (which the dictionary defines as "pasture" or "hayfield"), more coarse, more oceanic and enduring, supporting a greater variety of life.

If the prairie may be compared topographically to a rug, then the Dakota hills are prairie with bowling balls under the rug. The flora and fauna of the Dakota hills are much the same as those of the prairie that adjoins them. From a cliff high above, the Chink was pointing out to Sissy some of the organisms that choose to live in those hills. He pointed out different kinds of grasses: wheatgrass and little bluestem, June grass and dropseed, needlegrass and side-oats grama. He pointed out flowers: asters and goldenrod, snakeroot and cone flowers, prairie roses and purple clover. He said clover was delicious; he ate it often for breakfast, grazing in it like a goat. He pointed out prairie dog villages and badger rathskellers. He pointed out where they could find a coyote or a golden eagle if they needed one. He pointed out where his meadowlark traps were set, and the rocks where the best frying-size rattlesnakes hung out. The Chink pointed out the habitats of rabbits and burrowing owls, weasels and grouse. Although the millions of little eyeballs certainly could not be seen from Siwash Ridge, the hills were micey and the Chink told Sissy of mice, too: deer mice, meadow mice, harvest mice, pocket mice and kangaroo rats. The Chink must have spoken, intimately, of every creature that lived in the Dakota hills (not to mention those that, like the whooping cranes, were just passing through) except one. Cowgirls.

"What's the problem with you and the cowgirls?" asked Sissy eventually. They were perched directly above the Rubber Rose. It looked like a toy ranch from there, a miniature that might have been carved by Norman the pastry chef, had he but toes enough and time. "Why aren't you more friendly to them?" The Chink only shrugged. His gaze was focused on Siwash Lake, where several more whooper flights had joined the early arrivals.

"You obviously get along with Jellybean, that horny little sneak. And poor Debbie thinks you're some kind of god. But most of the girls agree with Delores. Delores says you're a god, all right. She says the way you sit up here so high and mighty is just like our big daddy macho God: paranoid, ill-tempered and totally aloof."

The shaggy Jap snickered. "Delores is right about God," he said. "He's best known by his absence. Judaeo-Christian culture owes its success to the fact that Jehovah never shows his face. What better way to control the masses than through fear of an omnipotent force whose authority can never be challenged because it is never direct?"

"But you aren't like that."

"Of course I'm not like that. I'm a man, not a god. And if I *were* a god, I wouldn't be Jehovah. The only similarity between Jehovah and me is that we're bachelors. Jehovah almost alone of the ancient gods never married. Never even went out on a date. No wonder he was such a neurotic, authoritative prick."

"But look at you," Sissy insisted. "People come from all over to seek your help and you won't let them within forty yards."

"What makes you think I have anything helpful to give them?"

Sissy wheeled on him, turning her slender back to the hills and prairie. "You've told me lots of wonderful things. Don't be coy! You may not be an oracle — I don't know — but you're wise enough to help these people who seek you out, if you chose to."

"Well, I don't choose to."

"Why not?" By then Sissy was so full of Chink semen she squished when she walked. She felt she had a right to probe his personality.

The old hermit sighed, though the grin never left his lips. "Look," he said, "these young people who seek me out, they're wrong about me. They're looking at me through filters that distort what I am. They hear that I live in a cave on a butte, so they jump to the conclusion that I lead a simple life. Well, I don't and I won't and I wouldn't. Simplicity is for simpletons!" The Chink underscored that remark by tossing a fair-sized chunk of limestone over the cliff. Look out deer mice! meadow mice! harvest mice! pocket mice! kangaroo rats! Look out below!

"Life isn't simple; it's overwhelmingly complex. The love of simplicity is an escapist drug, like alcohol. It's an antilife attitude. These 'simple' people who sit around in drab clothes in bleak rooms sipping peppermint tea by candlelight are mocking life. They are unwittingly on the side of death. Death is simple but life is rich. I embrace that richness, the more complicated the better. I revel in disorder and . . ."

"But your cave isn't disorderly," protested Sissy. "It's neat and clean."

"I'm not a slob, if that's what you mean. Slobs don't *love* disorder. They're ineffectual people who are disorderly because they can't help themselves. It's not the same. I set my cave in order knowing that life's disorder will only mess it up again. That's beautiful, that's right, that's part of the paradox. The beauty of simplicity is the complexity it attracts . . ."

"The beauty of simplicity, you say? Then you do find value in simplicity. You've contradicted yourself." Julian had taught Sissy to sniff out contradictions.

"Of course I've contradicted myself. I always do. Only cretins and logicians don't contradict themselves. And in their consistency, they contradict life."

Hmmm. Sissy wasn't getting anywhere at all. Maybe she ought to back up and come in from a different angle. Thumbs were of no help here. "How else do the pilgrims misjudge you?" It was the best question she could muster at the moment.

"Well, because I've lived in wilderness most of my adult life, they automatically conclude that I am gaga over Nature. Now 'Nature' is a mighty huge word, one of those sponge words so soaked with meanings that you can squeeze out interpretations by the bucketful; and needless to say Nature on many levels is my darling, because Nature, on many levels, is *the* darling. I was lucky enough to rediscover at a fairly early age what most cultures have long forgotten; that every aster in the field has an identity just as strong as my own. Don't think that didn't change my life. But Nature is not infallible. Nature makes mistakes. That's what evolution is all about: growth by trial and error. Nature can be stupid and cruel. Oh, my, how cruel! That's okay. There's nothing wrong with Nature being dumb and ugly because it is simultaneously — paradoxically — brilliant and superb. But to worship the natural at the exclusion of the unnatural is to practice Organic Fascism — which is what many of my pilgrims practice. And in the best tradition of fascism, they are totally intolerant of those who don't share their beliefs; thus, they foster the very kinds of antagonism and tension that lead to strife, which they, pacifists one and all, claim to abhor. To insist that a woman who paints berry juice on her lips is somehow superior to the woman who wears Revlon lipstick is sophistry; it's smug sophistical skunkshit. Lipstick is a chemical composition, so is berry juice, and they both are effective for decorating the face. If lipstick has advantages over berry juice then let us praise *that part* of technology that produced lipstick. The organic world is wonderful, but the inorganic isn't bad, either. The world of plastic and artifice offers its share of magical surprises."

The Chink picked up his candy-striped plastic transistor radio and kissed it — not as passionately as he lately had been kissing Sissy, but almost.

"A thing is good because it's good," he continued, "not because it's natural. A thing is bad because it's bad, not because it's artificial. It's not a damn iota better to be bitten by a rattlesnake than shot by a gun. Unless it's with a silver bullet. Ha ha ho ho and hee hee."

"But . . ." said Sissy. Sissy said "but" while sitting on her butt on a butte. The poetic possibilities of the English language are endless.

"But," said Sissy, "how can you criticize the misconceptions of your pilgrims when you do nothing to correct them? People are eager for the truth, but you won't give them a chance."

The Chink shook his head. He was exasperated, but continued to grin. His teeth caught the sunlight like spurs. He would die with his boots on.

"What kind of chance are they giving me?" he asked. "A chance to be another Meher Baba, another Guru Maharaj Ji, another bloody Jesus? Thanks but, no thanks. I don't need it, *they* don't need it, the world doesn't need it."

"The world doesn't need another Jesus?" Sissy had never felt much craving for Jesus, personally, but she assumed that for other people he was ice cream and pie.

"Most definitely not! No more Oriental therapists."

Rising and stretching, pulling some of the tangles out of his beard, the Chink motioned with his head. "See those short sunflowers growing way over there near the lake? Those are Jerusalem artichokes. When properly prepared, the roots taste a bit like yams." He smacked his lips. Obviously, he had tired of their dialogue.

Sissy's curiosity, however, had suffered pique. She persisted. "What do you mean, Oriental therapists?"

"Oriental therapists," repeated the Chink, uninterestedly. He reached into his robe, pulled out several juniper berries and began to juggle them expertly. Too bad the Ed Sullivan Show was off the air.

"What does Oriental therapy have to do with Jesus?" Sissy asked. "Or with you?" She smiled at the cascading juniper berries so that he would know she wasn't indifferent to his talents.

In group formation the berries followed the rock over the edge of the precipice. Mice, don't forget to wear your hard hats! "Well, if you can't figure it out for yourself . . ." said the Chink. "Meher Baba, Guru Maharaj Ji, Jesus Christ and all the other holy men who amassed followers in recent times have had one gimmick in common. Each of them demanded unquestioning devotion. 'Love me with all your heart and soul and strength and do my bidding without fail.' That has been the common requirement. Well, great. If you can love someone with that completeness and that purity, if you can devote yourself totally and unselfishly to someone — and that someone is a *benevolent* someone — then your life cannot help being the better for it. Your very existence can be transformed by the power of it, and the peace of mind it engenders will persist as long as you persist.

"But it's therapy. Marvelous therapy, wonderful therapy, ingenious therapy, but *only* therapy. It relieves symptoms, ignores disease. It doesn't answer a single universal question or put a person one step closer to ultimate truth. Sure, it feels good and I'm for anything that feels good. I won't knock it. But let nobody kid himself: spiritual devotion to a popular teacher with an ambiguous dogma is merely a method of making experience more tolerable, *not* a method of understanding experience or even of accurately describing it.

"In order to tolerate experience, a disciple embraces a master. This sort of reaction is understandable, but it's neither very courageous nor very liberating. The brave and liberating thing to do is to embrace experience and tolerate the master. That way we might at least learn what it is we are experiencing, instead of camouflaging it with love.

"And if your master truly loved you, he would tell you that. In order to escape the bonds of earthly experience, you bind yourself to a master. Bound is bound. If your master really loved you, he would not demand your devotion. He would set you free — from himself, first of all.

"You think I'm behaving like a cold-hearted ogre because I turn people away. Quite the contrary. I'm merely setting my pilgrims free *before* they become my disciples. That's the best I can do."

Sissy nodded in appreciation. "That's fine; that sincerely is fine. The only problem is, your pilgrims don't know that."

"Well, it's up to them to figure it out. Otherwise I'd be dishing them the same precooked and packaged pap. Everybody has got to figure out experience for himself. I'm sorry. I realize that most people require externalized, objective symbols to hang on to. That's too bad. Because what they are looking for, whether they know it or not, is internalized and subjective. There are no group solutions! Each individual must work it out for himself. There are guides, all right, but even the wisest guides are blind in *your* section of the burrow. No, all a person can do in this life is to gather about him his integrity, his imagination and his individuality — and with these ever with him, out front and in sharp focus, leap into the dance of experience.

"Be your own master!

"Be your own Jesus!

"Be your own flying saucer! Rescue yourself.

"Be your own valentine! Free the heart!"

Upon the sunny rock on which she sat in her semen-stained panties Sissy was very quiet. She supposed she had been given a lot to think about. There was, however, one more question on her mind, and eventually she asked it. "You use the word 'freedom' fairly regularly," she began. "Exactly what does freedom mean to you?"

The Chink's reply was swift. "Why, the freedom to play freely in the universe, of course."

With that, he reached out and grabbed the elastic band that moored Sissy's underpants to her hips. She raised her legs and in one smooth motion, he pulled her panties off — and flung them over the edge of the cliff. In the Dakota mouse world, it was quite a day for aerial phenomena.

72.

MAYBE the clouds just got sick of all the publicity. Posing for Ansel Adams's big camera had been okay; the landscape artists who had painted them had been sympathetic and discreet; even their appearance in occasional movies, floating unobtrusively in the background while cowboys and soldiers did their manly deeds, had less offended the clouds than amused them. But now these weather satellites, these *paparazzi* of outer space, following them everywhere they went, photographing them constantly, giving them no peace or privacy, their pictures in the papers every single day! They knew how Jackie felt. And Liz. Maybe the clouds just got sick and tired of it. Maybe they ducked under the South Pole, in dark glasses and wigs, for a well-deserved vacation.

At any rate, not a cloud had been seen over the American plains in about two weeks. The seasonette known as Indian summer persisted. A sky as open and dry as the brain is wrinkled and goopy stretched above the Dakota hills, permitting sunlight to warm, uninterrupted save by night, the long feathers of resting whooping cranes, the jubilant faces of postrevolutionary cowgirls and the rectal tissues of Sissy Gitche.

Although her mind was aware that Marie Barth, not to mention millions of Arabs, enjoyed it regularly, Sissy's body had not yet decided whether the unfamiliar pleasure of anal intercourse compensated for the unfamiliar pain. The Chink, with yam oil as a lubricant, had just performed for a half-hour in Sissy's fundamental orifice, and now she rested belly-down on a blanket in the sun.

So quiet was she that her host finally looked up from the snakeskin belt he was stitching (He would trade it in Mottburg for water chestnuts and yams) and asked what she was thinking. Flattered that such a self-contained man was interested in her thoughts, she answered quickly, "About the cowgirls." It was true; she *was* thinking about cowgirls. It was only her gently throbbing rectum that was paying attention to her gently throbbing rectum. "You've managed to avoid telling me how you feel about the cowgirls."

Returning his attention to the slender, squamous hide, every sun-fired scale of which reflected for Sissy a bad memory of Delores, the Chink kaff-kaffed and hawked, muttering through the last hurumph, "They certainly have improved the view from up here. Umm. Kaff."

"They're just cute little things for you to ogle, eh?" said Sissy. There was an accusatory note in her voice. She wondered from where it had come.

"I would think that a woman who worked as a professional model would be cautious about how she criticized ogling." The Chink looked up long enough to ascertain that he had made his point, then went back to the elegant epidermis of the creepy-crawler. "They're cute, all right. Although all of them aren't so little." Perhaps he was recalling the day he'd seen Big Red wrestle a steer. "There are other reasons for watching them, however."

"Such as?"

"Ah, well, Sissy, you see, a lot of noisy rain has fallen on our people in the past few years. Riots and rebellions, needless wars and threats of wars, drugs that opened minds to the infinite and drugs that shoved minds into the mushpot forever, awesome advances in technology and confusing declines in established values, political corruption, police corruption and corporate corruption, demonstrations and counterdemonstrations, recessions and inflations, crime in the streets and crime in the suites, oil spills and rock festivals, elections and assassinations, this, that and the other. Well, you and I, we separated ourselves from all those happenings, they haven't touched us. You passed right through them; I let them pass right through me. You practiced the art of perpetual motion; I practice the art of stillness. The result has been much the same. We've maintained a kind of strange purity, you and I; you too mobile for current events to infect you; me too immobile, too remote.

"But those young women down there on that ranch . . ." The old man took one hand off the rattler hide and gestured toward the Rubber Rose. "Those young women have been dipped in the events of our times, immersed from head to toe. You were born with your trauma and you survived it magnificently, but they've been shuttled from trauma to trauma most of their young lives. Their parents' culture failed them and then their own culture failed them. Neither drugs nor occultism worked for them; neither traditional politics nor radical politics lived up to their expectations. A whole banquet of philosophies has been nibbled at and found tasteless. Many of their peers have surrendered: jumped back with broken spirits into the competitive System or withdrawn into a private mushbowl — 'spaced out,' they call it, though 'ambulatory catatonia' might be a more accurate description.

"These ladies, however, they're making another attempt at something honorable, another try at directing their own lives. Jellybean . . . ha ha ho ho and hee hee . . . yes, that incomparable Bonanza Jellybean, has taken a fiction and turned it into a reality. She has given form to a long-lost childhood dream. This is nurturing them. And that is why I watch them with such interest. To see where it leads them, and if they will be free and happy there.

"Of course, I also watch the way their rowdy buttocks punch at the bags of their jeans. And speaking of such, my dear Sissy, how is your sweet brown opening convalescing?"

Sissy ignored the indelicate query. "Isn't there something you could do to help them?" she asked.

"Help them? Ha ha ho ho and hee hee. There you go again. Help them, indeed. In the first place, they've got to help themselves. By that, I mean each individual one of them has got to help herself. In the second place, I thought I'd made it clear that I cannot help *anyone.*"

"But . . ."

"No buts about it. Spiritually, I'm a rich man. Because of my Asian ancestry, I've inherited a certain amount of spiritual wealth. But — and you and Debbie and the pilgrims and would-be pilgrims have got to understand this — I cannot share this wealth! Why? Because Eastern spiritual currency is simply not negotiable in your Western culture. It would be like sending dollar bills to the pygmies. You can't spend dollars in the African jungle. The best use the pygmies could make of dollar bills would be to light fires with them. Throughout the Western world, I see people huddled around little fires, warming themselves with Buddhism and Taoism and Hinduism and Zen. And that's the most they ever can do with those philosophies. Warm their hands and feet. They can't make full use of Hinduism because they aren't Hindu; they can't really take advantage of the Tao because they aren't Chinese; Zen will abandon them after a while — its fire will go out — because they aren't Japs like me. To turn to Oriental religious philosophies may temporarily illuminate experience for them, but ultimately it's futile, because they're denying their own history, they're lying about their heritage. You can hook a rainbow to a goofy vision — Jellybean is doing that — but you can't hook a rainbow to a lie.

"You Westerners are spiritually poor. Your religious philosophies are impoverished. Well, so what? They're probably impoverished for a very good reason. Why not learn that reason? Certainly that's better than shaving your noggin and wrapping up in the beads and robes of traditions you can never more than partially comprehend. Admit, first of all, to your spiritual poverty. Confess to it. That's the starting point. Unless you have the guts to begin there, stark in your poverty and unashamed, you're never going to find your way out of the burrows. And borrowed Oriental fineries will not conceal your pretense; they will only make you more lonely in your lie."

Sissy elevated herself on her elbow, keeping her anal compass pointed into the sun. "But what can a Westerner do, then, in his or her poverty?"

"Endure it. Endure it with candor, humor and grace."

"You're saying it's hopeless, then?"

"No. I've already suggested that the spiritual desolation of the West probably has meaning and that that meaning might be advantageously explored. A Westerner who seeks a higher, fuller consciousness could start digging around in his people's religious history. Not an easy task, however, because Christianity looms in the way, blocking every return route like a mountain on wheels."

Sissy's sphincter was a tiny fist, pounding on the table of love. For the moment, the pounding suited her mood. "I don't get it. I thought that Christianity *was* our religious heritage. How has it blocked . . . ?"

"Oh, Sissy, this really is tiresome. Christianity, you ninny, is an *Eastern* religion. There are some wondrous truths in its teachings, as there are in Buddhism and Hinduism, truths that are universal, that is, truths that can speak to the hearts and spirits of all peoples everywhere. But Christianity came out of the East, its origins highly suspect, its dogma already grossly perverted by the time it set foot in the West. Do you think there was no supreme deity in the West prior to that Eastern alien Jehovah?. There was. From earliest Neolithic days, the peoples of Britain and Europe — the Anglos and Saxons and Latins — had venerated a deity. The Horned One. The Old God. A bawdy goat-man who provided rich harvests and bouncy babies; a hairy, merry deity who loved music and dancing and good food; a god of fields and woodlands and flesh; a fecund provider who could be evoked through fornication as well as meditation, who listened to songs as well as to prayers; a god much loved because he loved, because he put pleasure ahead of asceticism, because jealousy and vengeance were not in his character. The Old God's principal feast days were Walpurgisnacht (April thirtieth), Candlemas (February second), Lammas (August first) and Hallowe'en (October thirty-first). The holiday you now call Christmas was originally a winter revelry of the Old God (all historical evidence points toward Christ's having been born in July). These feasts were celebrated for thousands of years. And veneration of the Old God, often disguised as Jack-in-the-Green or Robin Goodfellow, continued surreptitiously long after Christianity closed its chilling grip around the West. But the Christian powers were nothing if not sly. The Church set about to willfully transform the image of Lucifer, whom the Old Testament informs us was a shining angel, one of God's chief lieutenants. The Church began to teach that Lucifer had horns, that he wore the cloven hooves of the lecherous goat. In other words, the leaders of the Christian conquest gave to Lucifer the physical traits — and some of the personality — of the Old God. They cunningly turned your Old God into the Devil. That was the most cruel libel, the greatest slander, the worst malicious distortion in human history. The President of the U.S. is a harmless carnival con man compared to the early Popes."

From somewhere down the mountainside, there came the vibratory drumming of a grouse. It was precisely the sort of noise Sissy's anus might have made were it wired for sound. There was a time, her rectum chaste then except for the occasional probing finger, when Sissy had had a minimum of curiosity about the matters she and the old hermit now discussed; she had established, in motion, her relationship to the universe, and it was concrete and thrilling and whole; in gloriously articulated stops and starts she embodied its life/death rhythms and was one with them, riding high, riding free, riding out on the crazy edge of it All, scooping up with her own two thumbs life's ecstasy and its terror. Things change. Perhaps now that she no longer strongly *felt* the universe, she had to *know* the universe. Sissy asked another question.

"If I — if we Westerners dug back into our heritage, what would we find there? Something valuable? Something as rich as your Oriental inheritance? What would we find?"

"You'd find women, Sissy. And plants. Women and plants. Often in combination.

"Plants are powerful and harbor many secrets. Our lives are bound up with the plant world far more tightly than any of us might imagine. The Old Religion recognized the subtle superiorities of plant life; it tried to understand growing things and pay them their due. One of the most highly developed orders of the Old Religion, the Druids, took its name from the ancient Irish word *druuid,* the first syllable of which meant 'oak' and the second syllable, 'one who has knowledge.' So a druid was one who had knowledge about oak trees — and about the allegedly poisonous mistletoe that grows on oaks and that was sacred to the Druids.

"Every village in olden times had at least one Wise Woman. These ladies had profound expertise in botanical matters. Mushrooms and herbs were their intimates. They used plants to heal the body and to free the mind. These women, of course, were nurturers and nurses. Many of their herb remedies, such as digitalis (from foxglove) and atropine (from belladonna) are still in use today.

"Yes, if you scratch back past the Christian conquest into your true heritage, you will find women doing wondrous things. Women were not only the principal servants of the Old God, women were his mistresses, the power behind his pumpkin throne. Women controlled the Old Religion. It had few priests, many priestesses. There was no dogma; each priestess interpreted the religion in her own fashion. The Great Mother — creator and destroyer — instructed the Old God, was his mama, his wife, his daughter, his sister, his equal and ecstatic partner in the ongoing fuck.

"If you can look beyond Christianity, you will find legions of midwives, goddesses, sorceresses and Graces. You will find tenders of flocks, presiders over births, protectors of life. You will find dancers, naked or in greenery gowns. You will find women like the women of Gaul, tall, splendid, noble, arbiters of their people, instructors of their children, priestesses of Nature, the Celtic warrior queens. You will find the tolerant matriarchs of pagan Rome — what a contrast to the Caesars and Popes! You will find the Druid women, learned in astronomy and mathematics, engineering Stonehenge, the premium acme apex top-banana clockworks of its era, bar none.

"So there is plenty of treasure in your antiquity, if you could get at it. How it compares to mine is another matter. Maybe where it is lacking is in the realm of light. Buddha and Rama and Lao-tzu brought light into the world. Literal light. Jesus Christ also was a living manifestation of light, although by the time his teachings were exported into the West, Saint Paul had trimmed the wick, and Jesus' beam grew dimmer and dimmer until, around the fourth century, it went out altogether. Christianity doesn't even have any warmth left; it probably never was very calorific. The Old Religion, on the other hand, was profoundly warm. It decidedly was not lacking in heat. But it was a heat that generated very little light. It warmed every hair on the mammal body, every cell in the reproductive process, but it failed to switch on that golden G.E. bulb that hangs from the loftiest dome of the soul. There was enough pure sensual energy in the Old Religion that had it been directed toward enlightenment it surely would have carried its followers there. Unfortunately, it was subverted and enervated by Christianity before its warmth could be widely transformed into light. Maybe that's the path that needs to be completed, that's the logical goal for Western man. As individuals, of course; not in organized groups. And the United States of America is the logical place for the fires of paganism to be rebuilt — and transformed into light. Maybe. I could be wrong. But I can say for sure, there is plenty of treasure in your antiquity if you can get at it."

"But we can't go back," said Sissy. "We can't dwell in the past."

"No, you can't. Technology shapes psyches as well as environments, and maybe the peoples of the West are too sophisticated, too permanently alienated from Nature to make extensive use of their pagan heritage. However, links can be established. Links *must* be established. To make contact with your past, to re-establish the broken continuity of your spiritual development, is not the same as a romantic, sentimental retreat into simpler, rustic lifestyles. To attempt to be a backwoods homesteader in an electronic technology may be as misguided as attempting to be Hindu when one is Anglo-Saxon. However, your race has lost many valuable things along the road of so-called progress and you need to go back and retrieve them. If nothing else, to discover where you've been may enable you to guess at where you're going.

"If anywhere. Ha ha ho ho and hee hee."

Sissy lowered her arms and cradled her blond head in them. The Chink might be right, she thought. Her pre-Christian ancestry might bear looking into. Her race, the poor Scotch-Irish, had produced nothing of note, spiritually *or* materially, in modern times, but perhaps there had been a day . . . Yes, it was worth investigating. But what of that part of her that was Indian; where did that fit in?

For as far back as she could remember, she had felt apart from her neighbors and kin. Oh Lord, South Richmond! There once was a neighborhood, its name was South Richmond, and it let numerous frame houses peel, fade and sag along its gritty streets. It allowed numerous cars — clunkers and junkers — to be parked in front of the houses, even though the cars dripped oil into the grit and even though they had to be pushed to get them started on frosty mornings, sometimes on warm mornings, too. What a constant puff and grunt and goddamn, pushing those cars! And South Richmond permitted numerous people to occupy the houses, even though the people chewed Juicy Fruit gum so hard they cracked the wallboards, and even though on Saturday nights husbands exhaled bourbon fumes through those cracks, and frequently, if the week had been mean enough in the cigarette factories or the unemployment lines, stuffed their wives' heads into those cracks, pin curlers and all. There once was a neighborhood called South Richmond, where women sported bruised jaws and men purchased bleacher seats for the stock car races and children never learned that James Joyce invented the tape recorder, that Scarlet O'Hara had a seventeen-inch waist or that the original Frankenstein monster spoke fluent French; a neighborhood where dogs and preachers whined and hillbilly vocalists sang mournfully of somebody running off with somebody else's little darling, and toy Confederate flags fluttered over everything and a girl grew thumbs so big they made rolls of baloney swoon in their casings, and she didn't care, because those thumbs meant that she was something her neighbors and kin were not, hallelujah.

When Sissy had learned she was one-sixteenth Siwash, she thought that maybe her thumbs were the Siwash part, that the ancient Indian spirits had sent her the thumbs as a sign that she was not made of South Richmond stuff, that circumstances more glorious and heroic lay in her past and her future.

That was naïve, of course. Now, she was not sure that those sparse Siwash cells made any difference at all. Look at Julian — he was full-blooded, and look at him. Yet she remained curious about it, and finding herself upon real estate holy to the Siwash, in the company of a man, Japanese though he be, who was an ordained Siwash shaman, she had been waiting only for the right moment to begin her inquiry. This moment seemed as right as any.

Before she could speak, however, there was heard a noise so sudden and loud it made her sit up straight with no thought to her bottom. It must be told that the Chink was startled, also, running a needle through the snake's skin into his own. But he quickly relaxed and sniggered, "Ha ha ho ho and hee hee." And Sissy realized that it was the clockworks that had chimed — there it went again!

Bonk! went the clockworks, and then it went *poing!* and unlike the chimes of a regular clock, which announce, on schedule, the passing — linear and purposeful — of another hour on the inexhorable march toward death, the clockworks chime came stumbling out of left field, hopping in one tennis shoe, unconcerned as to whether it was late or early, admitting to neither end nor beginning, blissfully oblivious of any notion of progression or development, winking, waving, and finally turning back upon itself and lying quiet, having issued a breathless, giddy signal in lieu of steady tick-and-tock, a signal that, decoded, said: "Take note, dear person, of your immediate position, become for a second exactly identical with yourself, glimpse yourself removed from the fatuous habits of progress as well as from the tragic implications of destiny, and, instead, see that you are an eternal creature *fixed* against the wide grin of the horizon; and having experienced, thus, what it is like to be attuned to the infinite universe, return to the temporal world lightly and glad-hearted, knowing that all the art and science of the twentieth century cannot prevent this clock from striking again, and in no precisioned Swiss-made mechanisms can the reality of this kind of time be surpassed. *Poing!*"

73.

....
....
....

. . . .
. . . .
. . . .
. . . .
. . . .
. . . .
. . . .
. . . .
. . . . *Bonk!*

74.

YAM OIL seeped into her pores. Her thumb pores, this time. The Chink was anointing them. He waved burning twigs of juniper around them. He shook a little bell at them. Hung garlands of goldenrod 'round them. Serenaded them — his instrument was a cigar box across which was pulled tight a single wire, which he bowed furiously. It made the worst music Sissy had ever heard. It made her want to turn on the all-polka radio.

They were in the entrance chamber of the cave, protected from stone by Japanese matting. Just outside, a small campfire flickered on their third and last night together.

At dawn, the Chink would go down into the hills and plains to harvest. There were foodstuffs that he must gather and add to the supply that he already had stored in the lower level of the cave, where he would winter.

Sissy would leave before he returned next day. She had a husband waiting. She had a cowgirl to see, a Countess to appease. She had questions to answer and maybe to ask. For example, "Where did all this lust come from!"

It is important to believe in love. Everyone knows that. But is it possible to believe in lust?

Sissy wasn't positive what she believed anymore. Once it had been simple. She had believed in hitchhiking.

She asked the Chink what he believed. Just like that. She interrupted thumb-worship, parted the meat curtains of lust, stared at his teeth and asked, "What do you believe in? I mean, really, what do you really believe?"

"Ha ha ho ho and hee hee." He laughed at her, saying nothing. His laughter and his silence made her weep. Tears, however, did not dampen her lust.

Lust lasted late, and when in midmorning she awoke, the Chink was gone.

Sunbeams galloped through the cave mouth, following the same route firelight had taken. Something was different about the cave. Trying to determine what it was brought her fully awake. With the sun's help, she saw that an inscription had been freshly scrawled with sumi ink across the right wall. Then her eyes were drawn to the left wall, where another graffito was dripping.

On the right wall had been written:

I BELIEVE IN EVERYTHING; NOTHING IS SACRED.

And on the left wall:

I BELIEVE IN NOTHING; EVERYTHING IS SACRED.

75.

Dr. Goldman caught up with Dr. Robbins shortly after the intern submitted a report requesting that Sissy Hankshaw Gitche be discharged immediately from the clinic. The confrontation between the two psychiatrists came to be known in psychology circles as the Gunfight at the I'm O.K./You're O.K. Corral.

"Am I to understand," asked Dr. Goldman, "that you regard Mrs. Gitche a stabilized personality unneedful of treatment?" His voice had an incredulous tone.

Dr. Robbins chinned himself on the saggy bars of his mustache. "Stabilized schmabilized," he said. "What could this clinic possibly treat her for?"

"What indeed," snorted Dr. Goldman. "Here we have a woman more than thirty years of age, who, though unusually intelligent and lovely to look at, has failed to transcend a slight, albeit bizarre congenital deformity . . ."

It was Dr. Robbins's turn to snort. Although a younger man, less experienced at snorting, Dr. Robbins's snort made up in bravura what it lacked in finesse and was the match of the older fellow's. "Transcend, you say. What a pompous word! The very idea of transcending something smacks of hierarchy and class consciousness; the notion of 'upward mobility' with which this country attracts greedy immigrants and chastises its poor. Jesus, Goldman! The trick is not to transcend things but to *transform* them. Not to degrade them or deny them — and that's what transcendence amounts to — but to reveal them more fully, to heighten their reality, to search for their latent significance. I fail to detect a single healthy impulse in the cowardly attempt to transcend the physical world. On the other hand, to transform a physical entity by changing the climate around it through the manner in which one regards it is a marvelous undertaking, creative and courageous. And that's what Sissy has done since childhood. By erasing accepted standards of perception, she transformed her thumbs while affirming them. In her affirmation of them, she intensified the vividness and richness of associations they might arouse. To paraphrase a remark she made to me, she introduced them to poetry. I would think that Sissy is an example for every afflicted person, which is to say, *Doctor,* an example for each of us."

Snort time again. The pig war was on. Inspired by his junior colleague, Dr. Goldman's latest snort was issued with a certain boldness, although the dignity of the snorter was carefully uncompromised. "Pardon me, but the concept of introducing a deformed thumb to poetry is one I find rarefied and imprecise, one that most people, afflicted or otherwise, would consider utter nonsense. Nonsense is of no help to anyone . . ."

"It isn't? Are you sure?"

"Nonsense, if you'll let me speak, Robbins, is of no help to anyone except as it might manifest itself in a neurotic fixation upon which one's stability depends."

"Stability, schmability."

"Centering her life on her handicap rather than overcoming that handicap; building, if you will, a mystique around that handicap might seem a poetic undertaking to Mrs. Gitche. It might even seem such to you, God forbid. But I am not convinced, nor is Mr. Gitche, who cares for her most and knows her best. Mr. Gitche . . ."

"Mr. Gitche is a flaming asshole."

"Hardly a professional evaluation, Robbins."

"Oh no? I thought you Freudians were really big on assholes. I recall entire lectures devoted to anal expulsion, anal retention . . ."

"Don't be cute. We haven't got all day." Dr. Goldman glanced at his office clock the way an insecure husband glances at his flirtatious wife at a party. The clock went right on batting its big eye at eternity. "To return to the point, Mr. Gitche contends, with apparent justification, that his wife is immature . . ."

"Growing up is a trap," snapped Dr. Robbins. "When they tell you to shut up, they mean stop talking. When they tell you to grow up, they mean stop growing. Reach a nice level plateau and settle there, predictable and unchanging, no longer a threat. If Sissy is immature, it means she's still growing; if she's still growing, it means she's still alive. Alive in a dying culture."

Dr. Goldman stirred a half-amused little chuckle into his snort, much as a splash of red Burgundy might be stirred into a pot of lard. "We could have an interesting argument about that sometime," he said. "For the present, however, let's appreciate Mr. Gitche's viewpoint. Mr. Gitche told me once that what bothered him the most about his wife's devotion to hitchhiking was its obviousness. She was afflicted with enlarged thumbs, ergo she hitchhiked. Now, had she decided, instead, to become a fine seamstress or to excel at tennis or to take up painting . . ."

Speaking of painting, there was a Julian Gitche watercolor on the wall above Dr. Goldman's desk. It was a landscape, a Central Park scene, rather free and airy, like a hose spray of green Easter-egg dye in which some sprite or minor deity was taking a bath. One wondered what would happen to the artist's protoromantic style were he to set up his easel in the Dakota hills. And one suspects that the experience of the Dakotas is too strong for any established aesthetics to withstand. At any rate, the painting quivered a bit on its hanger when Dr. Robbins boomed:

"There you go again! Transcendence! Wishing her to deny her thumbs by compensating for their limitations instead of affirming them by exploiting their strengths. Jesus!"

"But *hitchhiking,* Robbins. What kind of affirmative activity is that? Mrs. Gitche wasn't even interested in travel. It seems to me that fairly early in life she seized upon hitchhiking as a means of coping with an understandable anxiety, and that what began as an ill-chosen defense mechanism gradually evolved into a pointless and somewhat grotesque obsession. *Hitchhiking,* of all things . . ."

Dr. Robbins grasped his mustache, as if to prevent it from turning and leaving the room without him. There is a point where even hair can become exasperated. "Hitchhiking, schmitchhiking. Don't you see that it doesn't matter what activity Sissy chose? It doesn't matter what activity *anyone* chooses. If you take any activity, any art, any discipline, any skill, take it and push it as far as it will go, push it beyond where it has ever been before, push it to the wildest edge of edges, then you force it into the realm of magic. And it doesn't matter what it is that you select, because when it has been pushed far enough it contains everything else. I'm not talking about specialization. To specialize is to brush one tooth. When a person specializes he channels all of his energies through one narrow conduit; he knows one thing extremely well and is ignorant of almost everything else. That's not it. That's tame and insular and severely limiting. I'm talking about taking one thing, however trivial and mundane, to such extremes that you illuminate its relationship to all other things, and then taking it a little bit further — to that point of cosmic impact where it *becomes* all other things."

A flicker of comprehension lit up Dr. Goldman's heavy orbs the way a flash of heat lightning might light up the nocturnal droppings of a well-fed mule. "I see," he said. "You're referring to Gestalt — or to some far-fetched interpretation of Gestalt. Are we leading into a confrontation between Freudian and Gestalt psychology?"

"Gestalt schmagalt," growled Dr. Robbins. "What I'm referring to is magic."

Dr. Goldman shook his head wearily, even sadly. After a while he said, "In your rather abbreviated report" — he held up a single page of paper against which some rude sentences had been smacked as if slapped there by the nasty tail of a barnyard animal — "you recommend only that Mrs. Gitche be discharged and that she be encouraged to divorce her husband. Surely you're aware that there is no way in which we can therapeutically, ethically or legally encourage a patient to divorce her mate. Our business is preserving marriages, not ending them . . ."

"Our business *should* be liberating the human spirit. Or if that's too idealistic for you, if that strikes you as the business of religion — which it should be, too — then our business should be assisting people to function — crazily or not isn't our concern; that's up to them — helping them to function on whatever level or levels of 'sanity' they choose to function on, not helping them to adjust and locking them up if they don't adjust."

Past the point of snorting, Dr. Goldman removed his horn-rimmed glasses, rubbed his eyes and said evenly, "Dr. Robbins, our fundamental differences are greater than I had imagined. I'll have Miss Waterworth schedule a conference for us next week and we can give them an airing and decide if they can be reconciled. For the present, however, my concern is for the patient. Encouraging her to divorce is, of course, out of the question. Mr. Gitche is a talented, educated sympathetic man who loves his wife a great deal. Mr. Gitche . . ."

"Mr. Gitche has pulled his wife away from the edge and into the center. In here with the rest of us. I don't mind the center. It's big and mysterious and ambiguous — perhaps as exhilarating in its soft, shifting complexity as the edge is exhilarating in its hard, stark terminations. But the center can be a harmful place for one who has lived so long on the edge. Normality has been a colossal challenge for Sissy and I think she's met the challenge bravely and well. However, normality is a neurosis. Normality is the Great Neurosis of civilization. It's rare to discover someone who hasn't been infected, to greater or lesser degree, by that neurosis. Sissy hasn't. Yet. If she continues to be exposed, she'll eventually succumb. I think that would be a tragedy akin to sawing the horn off the last unicorn. For our sake as much as for her own, I believe Sissy should be protected from normality. Freed from the center and left to return to the edge. Out there, she's valuable. In here, she's just another disturbing noise in the zoo. Julian Gitche may be, as you say, kind and sympathetic, but he's a threat to Sissy, nonetheless. He's seduced her into a situation that is the mirror-opposite of what she believes it to be. Julian is driven by material ambitions; narrow, insatiable, intense, systematic, egocentric. In other words, he's a settler. Broad-based, timeless and dreamful, *Sissy* is the *Indian.* You're aware, Doctor, of the destruction met by the Indian when the settler lands on his shores."

A sigh, not a snort, was what Dr. Goldman issued next: a soft sigh like a trade wind blowing its nose against the sail of a toy boat. "Robbins, you're introducing concepts that are intriguing but, to my mind, irrelevent. Let me ask you one direct question. Do you honestly feel there is no disturbance in the personality of this woman, this woman with these . . . these *thumbs,* except the effects of a bad marriage?"

"No, I never meant to imply that." The younger man flicked the end of his mustache as if he were knocking the ash off an impotent cigar. "Sissy is suffering a bit of confusion."

"Ummm. And to what do you attribute this confusion?"

"To the fact that she's simultaneously in love with an elderly hermit and a teen-aged cowgirl."

Dr. Goldman got his snort back. He almost choked on it. "Mein Gott man! Are you joking? Well, why didn't you mention that in your report? Surely you don't regard it lightly? You don't think it's all right?"

Flicking the other end of his mustache, Dr. Robbins answered, "For many people, maybe for most people, being in love simultaneously with an old hermit and a teen-aged cowgirl might be a horrendous mistake. For other people, it might be absolutely right. For most people, having oral sex with anteaters may be the wrong thing to do; for a few people it may be perfect. You see my point? As for Sissy, she's finding the situation a bit confusing. I'm not sure that it's doing her any real harm."

The senior psychiatrist slapped his forehead. Had there been a mosquito there it would have vanished as completely as Glenn Miller, leaving only the memory of its music behind. "Mein Gott: I mean, my God. So. Well. I'd say that this evidence of homosexuality in Mrs. Gitche's libido rather firmly substantiates the fact of her emotional immaturity. You *will* agree with that?"

"Nope. Not necessarily. Lesbianism is definitely on the rise. I can't believe that the many who practice it are all suffering from preadolescent fixations. No, I'm more inclined to believe that it's a cultural phenomenon, a healthy rejection of the paternalistic power structure that has dominated the civilized world for more than two thousand years. Maybe women have got to love women in order to remind men what love is. Maybe women have got to love women before they can start loving men again."

Once more Dr. Goldman was rendered snortless. "Robbins," he said softly, as if drooping from a cross, "never in my career have I encountered anyone, neither psychiatrist nor psychiatric patient, with such a hodgepodge of confounding ideas."

"Well, Doctor," said Robbins, "The Chink says if it gets sloppy, eat it over the sink."

"The Chink? Oh, you mean Mao Tse-tung?"

Dr. Robbins laughed so abruptly he frightened his mustache. "Yeah, yeah, right. Mao Tse-tung."

"Heaven help me. It's not enough I've hired a kook. He's a Communist as well."

Robbins laughed again. This time the mustache was ready. "So you think I'm a kook, do you? Maybe you're right, Doctor. Maybe you're right. I've never mentioned this to anyone, but as a child . . ."

"Yes?" There was a sudden gleam in Dr. Goldman's tired eyes.

"As a child . . ."

"Yes? Go on."

"As a child, I was an imaginary playmate."

Dr. Robbins escorted his grateful mustache out of the room.

76.

YOU'VE HEARD of people calling in sick. You may have called in sick a few times yourself. But have you ever thought about calling in well?

It'd go like this: You'd get the boss on the line and say, "Listen, I've been sick ever since I started working here, but today I'm well and I won't be in anymore." Call in well.

That's what Dr. Robbins did, exactly. The morning following his consultation with Dr. Goldman, he called in well and he wasn't faking. You can't fake a thing like that. It's infinitely harder to pretend you're well than to pretend you're sick.

After telephoning, Dr. Robbins donned an electric yellow nylon shirt, and when he tucked it into a pair of maroon bell-bottoms, it was like lightning striking a full wino. Before he left his apartment, he fed both his alarm clock and his Bulova to the disposal unit. "I'm passing out of the time of day and into the time of the soul," he announced. Then, when he considered how pretentious that sounded, he corrected himself: "Strike that!" he said. "Let's simply say that I'm well today."

Out on Lexington Avenue, Dr. Robbins strolled leisurely. He sat on a park bench and smoked a Thai stick. He ducked into a phone booth and looked up Gitche in the directory. Didn't call; just looked at the number and smiled. Sissy, on her own insistence and with Julian's hesitant permission, was, indeed, being discharged from the clinic that day.

On Madison, Dr. Robbins went into a travel agency and asked to see a map of the western United States. He stared at the Sierra range of California and at Dakota and not much in between. A travel agent, who looked like Loretta Young and who appeared as if she feared Robbins's mustache had sneaked into the U.S. in a bunch of bananas, was obliged to be of service, but there was little she could do for a traveler with clockworks on his mind.

Dr. Robbins strolled on. Without knowing it, he strolled beneath the laboratory windows behind which the Countess was pitting the full ray of his genius against that furtive deep-swimming mammal whose sea breath escapes in sultry condensations from the dank lungs of the cunt.

In a glass display case in the lobby of the Countess's building lay a handmolded red rubber syringe — the very first Rose, the awkward prototype, the blushing original, the progenitor of the line of sensationally successful squeeze-bags whose name still adorned the largest all-girl ranch in the West. In innocence, Dr. Robbins passed it by.

Dr. Robbins wasn't certain where he was going on that May morning. As to his eventual destination, however, he was clear. He would go to the clockworks. And to the Chink. What's more, Sissy would lead him there. You see, the healthy and unemployed psychiatrist had recently arrived at a twofold conclusion: (1) if there was any man alive who could add yeast to the rising loaf of his being, that man was the Chink; (2) if there was any woman who could butter that loaf, that woman was Sissy. Dr. Robbins was quite convinced, quite determined, quite excited, quite in love. He faced the future with a sparkling mind and a silly grin.

However, there was a force at work that Dr. Robbins had not reckoned on, a force that Sissy had not reckoned on, a force that had not been reckoned on by anybody in North America, including the Clock People, the Audubon Society and that man who, due to someone's calling in sick (not well at all in this case) at the White House, was soon to be the new President of the United States. That force was: the whooping crane rustlers.

Part V

This is a bird that cannot compromise or adjust its way of life to ours. Could not by its very nature, could not even if we allowed it the opportunity, which we did not. For the Whooping Crane there is no freedom but that of unbounded wilderness, no life except its own. Without meekness, without a sign of humility, it has refused to accept our idea of what the world should be like. If we succeed in preserving the wild remnant that still survives, it will be no credit to us; the glory will rest on this bird whose stubborn vigor has kept it alive in the face of increasing and seemingly hopeless odds.

— Robert Porter Allen

77.

It was about two minutes on the tequila side of sunrise. So early the bluebirds hadn't brushed their teeth yet. Homer referred in *The Odyssey* to "rosy-fingered dawn." Homer, who was blind and had no editor, referred over and over again to "rosy-fingered dawn." Pretty soon, dawn began to think of herself as rosy-fingered: the old doctrine of life imitating art.

Fingers — and thumbs — of rose were drumming gently, like a Juilliard professor at a jazz club, on the table top of early morning America.

First light ventured through the windows of the bunkhouse. Softly, cowgirls turned in their beds. They made sleepy little noises, like the love cries of angel food cakes.

Heather was dreaming about her diabetic mother, who was forever threatening to commit suicide with Hershey bars if Heather didn't come home. Almost inaudibly, Heather whimpered into her pillow. Jody was dreaming she was back in high school, taking a math exam. She remembered that she hadn't studied, and she began to sweat with embarrassment and fear. Mary was dreaming she was ascending to Heaven in a rubber life raft. In the dream, Mary wore flippers on her feet. Mary would wake up puzzled. Elaine was dreaming about the source of her bladder infection. Her nipples were erect. She was smiling. LuAnn was dreaming the dream she dreamed nearly every night, the one in which her boy friend, his dilated pupils as black as Muslim golf balls, approached her with a dripping needle. In real life, she had awakened a few hours after the fix. Two years later, her boy friend still had not come to. LuAnn was on the verge of screaming. Debbie was dreaming she could fly, and Big Red, snoring mightily, dreamed she had found a lot of money lying around on the ground. Linda was dreaming she was in bed with Kym. She woke up and discovered that it was true. She scampered back to her own bunk.

Just in time. The sack of peyote buttons beneath Delores's head was singing her awake, as it did each morning. The forewoman stretched and rubbed her eyes. Soon she would stride down the aisle cracking her whip. No alarm clocks were necessary at the Rubber Rose. Besides, a clock radio would have played nothing but polkas.

From the main house there floated the voodoo smell of perking coffee. Donna, whose turn it was, had already begun breakfast. Up, pardners, up. There were goats to be milked and birds to be . . . watched over.

Plap. Plap plap plap. Bare cowgirl feet began to hit the linoleum. Feet with painted nails and feet with blisters, clean-smelling feet and feet fermenting in toe jam, tender feet, flaking feet, feet that had fidgeted indecisively in shoe stores and feet that had fallen in love with the gym floor at the prom, go-go feet, ballet-lessons-on-Saturday-mornings feet, pink feet, yellowish feet, arched feet, flat feet, massaged feet, neglected feet, beach feet, sneak feet, tickled-by-Daddy feet, feet pinched red by too-tight boots, feet that attracted glass shards and splinters and feet that imagined themselves to be clouds. *Plap plap.* Bare feet kissed the linoleum and pattered girlishly to foot lockers (in which there were no spare feet), to windows (to see what kind of weather was afoot) or out to the shitter (exactly ninety-two feet from the bunkhouse).

Plap. Plap. Listen. There were other *plaps* to be heard upon that summer's dawn. *Plaps* sounded in cities and towns where no barefoot cowgirls trod. The author is speaking now of the *plap* and *plap* of morning newspapers, rolled and tucked, *plapping* against porches as newsboys demonstrated their careless aim.

Countless newspapers landed with countless *plaps* on countless porches, bringing to countless readers the ball scores and comics and horoscopes and, on that particular morning, the first public notification of what many would consider a shocking ecological disaster. Different papers played the story in different ways. Perhaps the headline in the St. Louis *Post-Dispatch,* succinct as it was, told it best. It read: OUR WHOOPING CRANES ARE MISSING.

78.

Some five hundred thousand years ago, the North American continent finally got up enough nerve to kick the last of the glaciers out of its parlor. Ice gone, the North American continent called in the decorators and ordered them to create an environment worthy of some classy new wildlife. "Grass is in," the decorators announced, and they began to assemble a landscape of vast prairies, inland seas and wet savannas. A primitive pre-Pleistocene swamp bird cast a yellow eye upon the endless acres of marshy vegetation, waving grass and shallow waters and decided it liked the new décor well enough to move in. In fact, this bird liked the new décor so much it let out a whoop. Thus, inspired by its surroundings, it evolved into the whooping crane.

The whooper was classy, all right. It combined great size with majestic beauty and a kind of shy arrogance to produce a total effect that no bird before or since has equaled. The satiny black markings on its dazzlingly white body were economically and perfectly placed; its ruby crown and cheek patches (which were, in fact, red skin bare of all feathers) provided a certain flash without being vulgar; its tapered silhouette and graceful curves were to excite artists and designers not yet born; its powerful voice could spook the spine of a predator from a half-mile away; the aloof pride with which it conducted its daily business invented the word *dignity* for animal dictionaries. Ranging coast to coast and from the Arctic to central Mexico, the whooping crane was surely El Birdo Supremo in North America during the Golden Age of Grass.

Things change. Even grass goes out of fashion. In the later Pleistocene, trees became a hot item. Forest gradually encroached on the grasslands and the water table subsided. The crane habitat, un-Sanforized, began to undergo a relentless shrinking. The sandhill crane, the whooper's smaller, plainer cousin, made the necessary adjustments, adapting good-naturedly to a less grassy, less watery world. But not our bird. The whooping crane practiced the science of the particular; it enacted the singular as opposed to the general; it embodied the exception rather than the rule. To hell with compromise! It knew what it wanted and that was that. Unlike those integrity-short teemers, including man, the whooper opted for quality instead of quantity, rejected the notion that anything is better than nothing. It would survive on its own terms or not at all. And, indeed, it retreated in numbers as well as range, clinging defiantly to ever-narrowing confines. The whooping crane population had dwindled to fewer than two thousand even before civilization set its hard, polished shoes upon our shores.

Still, two thousand whoopers were two thousand whoopers — enough sheer feather power to stop every show in the nightclub district of birdland — and the crane census might have remained at that approximate figure had not civilization decided to do North America a favor by inviting itself to dinner. Between civilization and whooping cranes there was an immediate and lasting personality conflict. In the luggage of the civilizing process there came farming, shotgun sport, egg collecting, industrialization, urban sprawl, polluting, aviation, oil drilling, military operations, grass fires and the Army Corps of Engineers, those busy little khaki beavers who have set out to turn America's natural waterways into industrial ditches. Added to predators, climate changes and hurricanes, it was a bit too much for the super duper whooper. After 1918, when a Louisiana farmer named Alcie Daigle shot twelve cranes that were feeding on rice fallen from his threshing machine (Alcie Daigle, may sharp beaks scissor your testicles daily in the fried ricefields of Hell!) there were but two flocks of wild whooping cranes left alive in the world. Soon there was only one. By September 1941, this flock, incessantly harassed, was down to fifteen birds. Fifteen, count 'em, fifteen. Extinction music swelled in the background.

Ever since its founding in 1905, the conservationist Audubon Society had taken a special interest in whoopers. It knew an extraordinary bird when it watched one. The Audubon's little old ladies and mild gentlemen in galoshes pecked at the government so tirelessly that finally the politicians, in a weary outburst, decreed, in 1937, that the wintering grounds of the last remaining whooper flock would henceforth be a refuge. Like most prolife gestures on the part of the government, the Aransas National Wildlife Refuge on the Gulf

Coast of Texas was not much more than a token. Aransas offered the cranes winter shelter from hunters and egg collectors, to be sure, but the U.S. Air Force was allowed to maintain a bombing range right off shore, and the major oil companies continued to drill and dredge and diddle and daddle all along the edges of the preserve. Also, the flock, though illegal game, had no real protection on their long migratory flights between Aransas and their summer nesting and breeding grounds in the northern Canadian wilderness, and each year several cranes fell to the merry pow-pows of drunken sportsmen. The flock hung on to life by its toenails, although it hung with aplomb.

In the early fifties, however, a hero cometh, a Batman — or Craneman — winging into the arena on a cape of white quills, goosing the government and causing extinction to duck. The hero's name was Robert Porter Allen, research director of the Audubon Society and no galosh-wearing dispenser of birdseed, he. Allen liked whooping cranes more than he liked statesmen or movie stars or Our Father Who Art in Heaven; he was brilliant, thorough, tough, persuasive and, most important, he had a way with the press. When only nineteen whoopers returned to Aransas in October of 1951, he managed to get the media concerned. And after numerous news reports and editorials were broadcast and published, the government magically began to make a more conscientious effort on behalf of those untamed monsters it had declared its official wards.

The government ran some crane-cheek-colored tape through its red tape machine, and after a few years civilization began to go a mite easier on the whooper, not that the whooper gave a high-circling damn. In 1956, there were twenty-eight cranes wintering on the Aransas preserve. In 1957, the flock decreased to twenty-four. In 1959, the number was up to thirty-two. And so it went. Like scores from the ballpark of the Absolute. And each spring and fall, at times of crane departures and crane arrivals, the media dutifully reported the crane scores, giving them space alongside accounts of the international situation, which was desperate, as usual.

When, in 1969, the whooper population hit a big fat fifty, the media cheered wildly. In 1973, there were fifty-five birds wintering at the Texas refuge, a figure that, when announced, caused hardened cons to smile in their slammers. Or so some folks would have us believe.

At any rate, as sometimes happens in this malleable but not self-malleable curious cultural consciousness of ours, a kind of mystique grew up around the whooping crane, around the drama of its survival. Nonfeathered backs were patted all around, and the whooper was called "a symbol of both this country's new-found concern about its wildlife and of its opportunity to atone for its destructiveness in the past."

It did not set the national thyroid to pumping happily when it was learned that this symbol, the entire last existing flock of whooping cranes, had vanished without a trace.

79.

"IT WAS a routine flight," said the official of the Canadian Wildlife Service, as if there was any such thing as a routine flight. The people who see miracles are the people who look for miracles, the people who open their eyes to the miracles that surround us always. The people who have routine flights are the people who believe they are on routine flights . . . but now, what with our whooping cranes AWOL, now is not the time for digressions upon the obvious. The official was as skinny and nervous as the last snake out of Ireland as he fumbled with his pipe and tried to make an important mission sound as if it had been a routine flight.

The flight in question had been made in a two-seat, single-rotary helicopter. The pilot was an employee of the Canadian Wildlife Service, as was the passenger, field biologist Jim McGhee. This May, as every May for the past fourteen years, McGhee had made a "routine" flight over the desolate marshes south of Great Slave Lake, near the Alberta–Northwest Territories border, to count whooping cranes. McGhee would compare his count with the number of birds reported to have left Aransas, Texas, to see how the cranes had fared on their twenty-five-hundred-mile migration. Rare was the year when they didn't lose one bird, but conditions certainly had improved since the fifties, when Canada filed formal protests with the U.S. in an attempt to protect the cranes from American hunters, oilmen and bombers. Yes, whooping crane stock was up a half-million points on the big board, and an investor such as McGhee, who had bought cheap, had every reason to feel smug and to fancy himself on a routine flight when he churned in low over the marshes to check the Dow Jones averages that May.

Back in 1744, a French explorer made the following entry in his journal: "We have [in Canada] cranes of two colors; some are all white, the others pale gray, all make excellent soup." Well, it was as if some fiendish French fatso from the gluttony wards of Hell had cooked up a cauldron of Campbell's Cream of Whooping Crane, for squint as they might, Jim McGhee and his pilot could not spot a single whooper that day.

McGhee was puzzled, a trifle alarmed, maybe, but not freaked-out. The cranes must have moved, he reasoned. Their nesting grounds had been threatened twice by forest fires since 1970, and despite the Canadian government's maneuvers to bar sight-seers from the area, there had been increasing air traffic over the whooper nurseries in recent years. The five-hundred-square-mile enclave in which birds of this solitary flock chose to build their nests of heaped grass, deposit their mushroom-colored eggs and hatch their sparrow-sized chicks was a mere postage stamp on a vast package of forbidding terrain. It was part of a region that was as rugged and remote as any on the North American continent. Dotted with shallow, muddy lakes separated by narrow zones of spiky black spruce and twisting rivers too choked by fallen timber to be navigable, it had been trod upon by neither white man nor Indian. In fact, the whooper domain was so well hidden it had taken airborne searchers from both U.S. and Canadian Wildlife agencies ten years to find it. As McGhee theorized over a bottle of Uncle Ben's malt liquor in Fort Smith that evening, the cranes could have transferred their nesting area to a different part of the wilderness. Since the birds live in isolated family groups, often separated by as much as twenty miles, it didn't seem likely that the entire flock might have rejected the traditional nesting grounds as if of one mind, but McGhee knew that wild creatures sometimes did the unlikely. McGhee liked wild creatures. He had once elbowed his wife awake in the middle of the night to tell her, quite factually, "Wild animals don't snore." That was a month before the breakup. Ah, well. McGhee ordered another Uncle Ben's, deciding not to sound a crane panic until he and his pilot had looked further.

The following day, the two men applied closer scrutiny to the usual whooper habitat. They flew so low they were practically sodomized by cattails. No birds. The day after that, they surveyed the area south of the traditional nesting grounds, whirring above the banks of the Little Buffalo River and its marshy tributaries, the logical (?) places for a whooper relocation. Not so much as a snowy pinfeather tickled their eyes. That evening, Jim McGhee radioed Ottawa.

From the capital came the skinny, pipe-smoking official of the Canadian Wildlife Service. He was not yet showing signs of nervousness, but he was soon to be rattling like the muffler on a hula girl's convertible. The official enlisted four additional helicopters in the search. For a week they went through the wilderness the way the Errol Flynn Memorial Panty Raid Society went through the coed dorms at Kansas State University that terrible night in 1961 — but with nowhere near the success.

At last the official — O champagne of trembles, O waterfall of bones — had no choice but to notify the insufferable Americans. Both the U.S. Fish and Wildlife Service and the Audubon Society responded at once. It was ascertained and ascertained again that fifty-one whoopers, in groups of one to three families, had left the Aransas refuge during the third week of April. Aransas's superintendent testified that the cranes' mating dances had been unusually athletic that year, but there was no reason to believe that they were having a last fling.

About midway in migration, the whoopers normally stopped for several days of rest and recreation along Nebraska's Platte River. There the stiff-legged birds would stride in agitated dignity, like so many Prince Philips pacing outside the quarters of the queen, as they hunted the river banks for frogs, scratched in the sandbars for mollusks or stalked grasshoppers in the open stretches of high grass. It was standard procedure for governmental agents to take inventory of the cranes during the Platte River stopover, but thereafter to rely for migration information upon voluntary reports from citizens until Jim McGhee made his annual nesting count. This year was no exception, and the wildlife wardens who monitored the cranes in Nebraska now reiterated their reports that the big birds had been all present and accounted for and looking as healthy as rich men's children before the ennui sets in. A farmboy and a telephone lineman had reported seeing separate whooper flights over southwestern South Dakota. After that, nothing.

Between Murdo, South Dakota, and the Alberta–Northwest Territories nesting grounds, the cranes had disappeared. Canadian officials eyed the Americans suspiciously. American officials eyed the Canadians suspiciously. Was the highest card in the Deck of Birds up somebody's sleeve?

An American plane traced the whooping crane flyway from Nebraska to the Saskatchewan border. A Canadian plane followed the migration route from the U.S. line to the nesting grounds. *Nada.*

"We're scheduling daily flights along the flypath," announced the Americans. "We're scheduling daily flights along the flypath," announced the Canadians. The first American flight passed just out of view of the Rubber Rose, where tiny Lake Siwash was shimmering like a pool of cowgirl tears.

The calendar had dipped its muzzle into late May — nearly two weeks after Jim McGhee's infamous "routine" flight — when the craneless news was broken to the public. A terse, unemotional press release from the Department of the Interior, an announcement that urged citizens to cooperate by reporting any and all sightings of tall white birds, hit the media like a ton of human interest bricks. Every TV network and most of the nation's papers gave the story major play. The scope of the coverage caught the government off-guard, as did public response. Interior's switchboards were flashing like a lightshow gone stoned mad at the Fillmore, and every ecology-oriented organization from the Sierra Club to the Girl Scouts wired pledges of assistance. The following day the Secretary of the Interior himself was obliged to call a press conference (It made the six o'clock and eleven o'clock news). "Umm, ah, er, hum," said the Secretary. "No cause for extreme concern." Although the cranes constitute a single flock, they travel in smaller units of one to three families, the Secretary explained. And the families nest miles apart. There was no probable way the entire flock could have met foul play ("Ahem. No pun intended") either from humans or the natural elements. The whooper flyway passes almost entirely over isolated regions, and the Canadian wilderness is vast. Sooner or later these splendid birds will turn up. Even should they remain incommunicado all summer, they would certainly be back in Texas come fall.

The Secretary believed his remarks, as men of his station sometimes do. His underlings in the Fish and Wildlife Service believed them, too. Up in Canada, the skinny, pipe-puffing official shook like the icecubes in a fire-eater's highball and was not so sure. As for field biologist Jim McGhee, he sucked on a bottle of Uncle Ben's, signed another alimony payment, stared at aerial maps of the terrain he would search next day and muttered to no one in particular, "Wild animals don't snore."

80.

DESPITE HIS TITLE, the Secretary of the Interior was a shallow man. He was given to surfaces, not depths; to cortex, not medulla; to the puff, not the cream. He didn't understand the interior of anything: not the interior of a tenor sax solo, a painting or a poem; not the interior of an atom, a planet, a spider or his wife's body; not the interior, least of all, of his own heart and head.

The Secretary of the Interior knew, of course, that there was a brain in his head and that the human brain was Nature's most magnificent creation. It never occurred to the Secretary of the Interior to wonder why, if the brain, with its webs and cords and stems and ridges and fissures, with its glands and nodes and nerves and lobes and fluids, with its capacity to perceive and analyze and refine and edit and store, with its talent for orchestrating emotions ranging from eye-rolling ecstasy to loose-bowel fear, with its appetite for input and its generosity with output; it never occurred to the Secretary to wonder why the brain, if it is as awesomely magnificent as it purports to be, why the brain would waste its time hanging around inside a head such as his.

Maybe some brains just like the easy life. The Secretary of the Interior did not put many demands on his brain. Mainly, he wanted only to be informed if this or that action would be politically expedient. For example, the Secretary went to his brain there where it was lolling lazily in its cerebral hammock, sipping oxygen and blood, absently humming some electrochemical folderol culled from two billion years of continuous biological chatter; a brain that bore no neon scars of love, that showed no signs of having ever been dazzled or crunched by art, that obviously was not staying awake nights puzzling over what Jesus really meant when he said, "If a seed goes into the ground and dies, then it will grow"; a brain that would have appeared preponderantly placid were it not for the skinning knife, the automatic rifle, the bazooka, the machete, the napalm, clubs, arrows and grenades that were piled under its pillow where they might be employed instantly to chop, gut, bludgeon, burn and blast the very first mouse squeak that might threaten it; the Secretary went to his brain, prodded it and asked it how he might end this whooping crane hubbub in a manner advantageous to himself.

His brain's immediate reaction (yawn) was that the problem should be passed up the line to some other brain to solve. That, however, was not feasible this time. The only person up the line was the President, and the President's brain, having been finally cornered after a lifetime of cheating, conning, lying, hustling and vampiring greedily on jugulars public and private, was rolled up like a sick armadillo at the moment and could not be enlisted. Should he get through to the President he could expect only that the President would yell, "Shove those fucking birds up your goddamned ass! What are you doing to protect me?" or something, and the Secretary did not wish to be yelled at by the President. Should he speak to one of the President's intimate advisers, he would be told in an aseptic German accent that the matter should be turned over to the CIA, and while the Secretary was not entirely opposed to the high aides' method of putting annoying problems in the hands of the secret police, he wasn't certain that it was expedient to have his own authority thus usurped.

No, sorry, brain, fat old pal, but you and the Secretary must work it out yourselves.

Under normal conditions, the Secretary might have donned the Pendleton wool shirt his wife had given him for their twenty-second wedding anniversary (Or was it the twenty-third? His brain couldn't remember), requisitioned a jet and gone out personally to lead a massive crane hunt. Now that would have been good politics. Ha ha! Then, when those kooky environmentalists got in a snit because his branch of government was allowing industry to develop the land the way God intended it to be developed, he could say, "Trust me, friends; I have proven myself an ardent conservationist. I am the man who rescued our whooping cranes!"

Alas, normal conditions did not prevail. The major oil companies were in the act of pulling off a daring economic coup, a brilliant piece of business, on the whole, but one that had of necessity created a simulated shortage of petroleum products, and the citizenry, not understanding what was best for it, was bemoaning what had been labeled an "energy crisis." The average working man was a helluva lot more concerned about the energy crisis than he was about a missing flock of goony birds, the Secretary reasoned quite accurately; the Secretary wasn't convinced the average working man gave a moldy tail feather about those missing birds. Were the Secretary to authorize a large-scale air search for the whoopers, there would most surely be adverse reaction to the quantities of fuel an expedition of that size would require. He simply could not justify such an expenditure of precious petroleum.

So he would do this: he would keep a single light plane plying the wide and capricious migration route; one plane, in the air daily. If the working stiffs complained, he could say, "We've got a little bitty economy-sized Cessna looking around for those birds, boys; that's it." If the conservationists bitched, he could say, "I've got a modern up-to-date reconnaissance aircraft with radar and all the latest equipment in the sky this very moment searching every inch of isolated territory for those marvelous herons, and I won't rest until they are safely back where they belong." Umm. Yes. Yes, indeed. All bases touched. Good work, faithful brain. You've earned a siesta.

Politics served, the Secretary reassured himself that the herons or cranes or whatever they were would turn up in the near future. Good Lord, there were hundreds of square miles of lowland marsh in Saskatchewan that hadn't even been peeked at yet. The birds were in there, probably, or nestled into some muskeg swamp in the Canuck boonies. They'd show up eventually, safe and sound. If only the media would let the matter drop, the public majority would forget it quicker than a Bufferin can dissolve in the cutaway belly of a TV doll.

Indeed, the media *might* have let the matter drop. And the masses *might* have forgotten the vanished birds. If it hadn't been for Jim McGhee.

One evening toward sunset, the Canadian field biologist stood up from his bottle of Uncle Ben's and walked away into the bush without pack or provisions.

On his third morning in the wilderness, after three chill nights among sleepers who do not snore, a bedraggled McGhee was sitting on a log when he saw a snake slink by. The snake was moving fast. It carried a card under its tongue. The card was the jack of hearts. "I must get to Delores del Ruby at once," hissed the snake. It slithered away toward the south.

Behind in Fort Smith, McGhee had left a note. There was no mention in the note of McGhee's ex-wife or of his two little freckle-faced sons. But the note made numerous references to whoopers, closing, in fact, with the line "I have gone to join them in extinction."

So, to the Secretary of the Interior's chagrin, the missing flock was once again warm copy. The flurry touched off by Jim McGhee was characterized, somewhat sensationally, by this Page One-filling headline in the New York *Daily News:* WHOOPING CRANE SUICIDE.

81.

SISSY. You darling. What's happening? You're holed up on East Tenth Street, growing pale. Pale as a phantom tangled in lace curtains. Pale as Easter. Pale as the foam on a maniac's lips. Even your thumbs are losing their cheery sanguine sheen.

What's happening, honey? Outside, it's turning warm. Folks in the less respectable tenements are beginning to take the evening air from their fire escapes. Down the street, below Avenue B, the Puerto Rican husbands have moved their domino games onto the sidewalks. The little bow-wows and woof-woofs are starting to pant again. Always a bad sign. Julian says you won't be using your air conditioner as much this summer. Energy crisis.

Sissy, the sun is making personal appearances daily, hamming it up in typical Leo fashion; but you, what do you think you are, a mushroom? Two mushrooms?

Unquestionably, you have a lot to think over. If you have lived your whole life in an unrealistic manner, as so many people have claimed, then you suppose that for the past year and a half you have been taking reality lessons. You've had some powerful teachers, too. Julian, Bonanza Jellybean, the Chink, Dr. Robbins.

From two of those teachers you have learned that in olden times everything was run by women. And that everything was better then. That is stunning information. You wonder what it should mean to you, personally. Julian says it's rubbish, that most anthropologists dispute the matriarchal theory. On that subject, Dr. Robbins has been silent.

Dr. Robbins does telephone you, however. About once a week. Just checking up on a former patient, he says. His style amuses you. He invites you to lunch, to opium dens, to a flea circus. You refuse. You think he wants to fuck you. It would be fun, but not worth it. Definitely not worth it. You may know next to zilch about reality, but you know a thing or two about magic. Your thumbs taught you. Magic requires a certain purity. Without purity, magic weakens. You still have hopes that you and Julian can create together a magical relationship. So you try now to keep it pure.

Julian has become quite understanding. He doesn't interrupt your thinking anymore. You sit on the bed by the empty birdcage, run through your exercises and let the cow of your mind eat its way out of the haystack that has collapsed on it. You feel that you will stay in this new life that is so much stranger to you than your old strange one. You feel that you will stay with Julian. In a year or two, when the time is right for both of you, you think you might have Julian's baby.

Oh Sissy! Have you forgotten, then, Madame Zoe's prophecy?

82.

SISSY, don't you believe you ought to go out for a hot dog? Or a wedge of pizza? You know, some delicacy that can be balanced between sets of fingers without involving thumbs. Up First Avenue, near Bellevue Hospital, there's a pushcart. The walk would do you good. The sunshine.

Couldn't you think just as well, if you must think, in Tompkins Square Park? On a wino-nourishing bench where pigeons pop their buttons? You have a way with birds.

Clever, isn't it, Sissy, the way the author turned the subject to birds? Have birds been on your mind lately? What was your reaction to the article in this morning's *Times?* The one that reported that Congress had given the Justice Department the authority to deal severely with any person or persons found to be interfering with the safety or free movement of the world's last flock of whooping cranes.

You say you aren't thinking about whooping cranes? Well, if you say so.

You aren't thinking about cranes this morning. You're thinking about . . . time.

The Clock People are waiting for the end of time. The Chink says it's going to be a long wait.

You wonder, as so many have wondered, did time have a beginning? Will it stop? Or are the past and the future manufactured by the present? Such questions are as important as they are unfashionable.

You read where Joe DiMaggio ordered that fresh red roses be placed on Marilyn Monroe's grave every three days, forever. Not for Joe DiMaggio's lifetime, mind you, or the duration of Hollywood, its films and its cemeteries, but *forever.* And you think, "If there is an end of time, Joe DiMaggio is going to have some money coming back."

83.

So. Sissy. You don't go out much. Only occasionally do you even look outside. From your windows, as from windows everywhere, nowadays, you can see the cake crumbling.

Julian says we're heading for a depression. Or worse. He mentions famines, plagues, purges. When he says these things, he cocks his dark head to one side, as if, like the Mohawk he ought to be, he can hear famine gathering its dusty forces, preparing to march over from the Sahara, India, Starving Armenia. He hears Panic in the dressing room, putting on its skeleton suit. He hears the sizzling silence of the energy crisis. "Here in America we are reverting to our native fascism," says this native American, ignoring twelve thousand years of his own people's history. The international situation is desperate, as usual.

Not overly optimistic, Julian feels, nevertheless, that if a liberal Democrat is elected President in 1976, a world economic poop-out can be avoided. As for Dr. Robbins, he just laughs into the telephone. "The cake is crumbling," he says to you in an awed whisper. "Isn't it *grand?*"

You don't know if it's grand or horrible. You only know that hitchhiking didn't bring it on. Hitchhiking can't stop it.

In the tub, you cause a thumb to plow through the scented water. How evenly the bubbles break before its sleek snout; how perfect its wake. Then you jerk your wrist in a special, staccato way, and suddenly the thumb is twitching crazily underwater, like a diver who contacted mercury poisoning sucking off a mermaid.

Thus you amuse yourself. You smile. But there are wrinkled tracks on your brow. Did whooping cranes make them?

What's that? Someone at the door. Julian leaves off his painting to answer. Well, surprise, surprise. You couldn't mistake that nasty drawl.

The Countess hasn't been around in quite a while. Julian painted ahead and has no more to do for him. And since your husband has begun to paint for a German account, it isn't likely he'll get any more calls for pastoral landscapes suffused with the luminous haze of Yoni Yum or silvered with dreamy drops of Dew. The Countess likes to be exclusive, if not unique. As for you, you haven't had a modeling assignment since the Dakota debacle. Your eyes, while still beautiful, have lost some of their innocence; your mouth, while still ripe, has lost some of its perk. Too, your little sojourn in Dr. Goldman's spa for half-rich fuck-ups couldn't have enhanced your career. Oh well. You dry and wrap yourself and patter in to see your old benefactor.

Powdered stubble pricks your face as you kiss. Upon his monocle are the dried deposits of sauces that no French chef will ever stir again. In a voice that sounds the way a can of cheap dog food would sound if a can of cheap dog food could speak, he tells you you are looking swell. "Domesticity, the male's meat, the female's poison, seems to become you," he says. A can of Skippy with a slight lisp.

And how is the Countess? "Shit O dear!" he exclaims. "Sales are down more than ten percent. Are things so desperate that women can't spend a few pennies to control their atavistic stench? I ask you. A samurai warrior, before going into battle, would burn incense in his helmet so that if an enemy took his head he would at least offer his beheader a pleasant aroma. Now, it appears to me that no matter how bleak a future a woman faces, she could at least face it with an inoffensive vagina."

"You're convinced, then, the future is bleak?" asks Julian. He had been painting a sprite beside a pellucid pool.

The Countess's store teeth clack compulsively. Rat a tat tat! Dental gangbusters. "Indeed," he says. "This country is in one hell of a mess."

"It all depends on how you look at it," you say.

Julian and the Countess pause and stare at you expectantly. They suppose that you are going to explain yourself, to tell them how national events may be viewed in a light that makes them seem less messy. But you have nothing to add. You meant only what you said, that it all depends on how you look at it, that *everything, always,* depends on how it is perceived, and that the perceiver has the ability to adjust his perceptions.

Conversation resumes. Julian and the Countess make small talk about small issues: the economy, politics. You are in postbath terry-cloth, feeling a bit drowsy.

Suddenly, the Countess whirls at you. He gets right in your face. His smile looks as if it had been rear-ended at an intersection. He cracks a question at you; it is like Delores cracking her whip. "Why haven't you spoken out about the whooping cranes, Sissy?" Crack!

"What . . . what do you mean?"

"You know very well what I mean. I've been working day and night in the lab and haven't paid attention to the news. But last evening I heard that the whooping cranes were missing. The whole bloody flock. Truman gave me the details. He was practically in tears. There's been a furor about it . . ."

"Yes, it's been in the papers incessantly," interrupts Julian.

"There's been a furor about it, and rightly so. My question is, why haven't you spoken out? I know where those cranes are, and so do you."

Julian gawks at you. Bewilderment widens his eyes.

"What do you mean?" Your voice is as soft and tremulous as a butterfly's good-by.

"Sissy, don't play dumb with me! You're a good model but a shitty actress. The cowgirls are involved in this whooping crane disappearance. You know perfectly well they are. Last seen in Nebraska. Didn't make it to Canada. Siwash Lake is between Nebraska and Canada. The cowgirls have possession of Siwash Lake. And who else but Jellybean's wild cunts could possibly conceive of doing something so diabolical as to tamper with the last flock of some nearly extinct birds? Of course they're behind it. Of course they are. How much do you know about it? Have they murdered those cranes the way they murdered my moo cows?'

"I don't know anything about it," you protest. You sense your pale flesh turning paler.

Julian continues to gawk, but now his eyes have been narrowed by suspicion. The Countess leans so far into your face that you are almost wearing his monocle.

"Sissy, you're either a liar or a fool," the Countess spits, "and you may be a weirdo but I've never known you to be stupid. You're trying to protect those scuzzy bitches. Well, let your conscience be your guide, as my mommy used to say, but it won't work. I have a call placed to the Secretary of the Interior, a simple jerk but a jerk who never forgets a political favor. I'll be speaking to him right after lunch. And I'm going to tell him where to find his whooping cranes. I'd tell the President directly, if he wasn't busy driving himself berserk trying to avoid stepping in his own shit. But the Interior Secretary will do. He's a law and order man, and he'll take care of it nicely. He'll also take all the credit for it, but don't think he won't find a way to reward me. Of course, it will be nearly reward enough just seeing those cowgirls get what's coming to them. Those stinking sluts are going to suffer . . ."

There is then a sound such as neither the Countess nor Julian

Gitche has ever heard. They do not know, are never to know, whether the sound issued from your throat or was produced by your first or most preaxial digit as it was thrown through air. In any case, that sound is quickly obscured by another, the sound of your right thumb striking — with astonishing force — the Countess's face.

Immediately, the thumb strikes again, this time shattering the Countess's monocle against his eye.

"Shit O dear," the Countess gasps. His dentures fall onto the shag rug, as if to graze there.

Then . . . O my God and Goddesses! . . . Can you believe it? . . . The *left* thumb strikes.

Thumbs that not once in a lifetime had been raised in anger; thumbs that had known risk often but never violence; thumbs that had invoked and mastered secret Universal Forces without acquiring the faintest stain of evil; thumbs that had been generous and artful; thumbs that were considered so delicate and precious that their owner would not so much as shake hands for fear of damage; those same thumbs, wound 'round with the glory of a million innovative and virtuoso hitchhikes, are now smashing the face of a human being.

What are you doing, Sissy? I'll tell you what you're doing. You're swinging them like ballbats, like the legendary swatters of Babe Ruth, socking flaming homers over the left-field fence of Hell. Beads of blood land noiselessly upon the keys of the white piano.

Julian is paralyzed. He cannot stop you. He cannot speak. You continue to swing and swat. The Countess is out on his feet. His eyes are closed. His legs wobble. He does a pathetic dance, like a drunken old fool trying to boogie with a chorus girl. Coagulating polka dots turn his linen suit into clown garb. He topples forward to meet your onrushing thumb (the thumb that once made the Pennsylvania Turnpike into a playground); the thunder of it straightens him up, sends him over backward. Motionless, he lies on the floor, a crimson part in his thinning hair, a bright ooze at each nostril.

The poodledog, Butty, short for Butterfinger, had been awakened by the commotion and had trotted into the living room to check it out. You notice he is growling at you now, baring his teeth at your unprotected ankles. You catch him broadside with a low swing, sending him flying to the opposite wall, where he flattens out with a breathless whimper against a Dufy lithograph. Poodle and print drop to the carpet together, a heap of broken glass, doggy curls and images of sailboats so fanciful they seemed suited only for lakes of lemonade.

Julian finds his voice. "Sissy," he says, each syllable an organ note of horror, pumped from the pipes at a Dracula matinée, "Oh Sissy. What have you done?

Of course, he knows *what* you have done; it is all too obvious. What Julian means is *why* did you do what you did, *how* could you have done it. And you are incapable of telling him. You emerge from your trance of fury, observe the aftermath with clear if disbelieving eyes, yet nowhere inside you is there an explanation dying to catch the next bus downtown. The word *cowgirls* starts to form in your mouth, but it dissolves.

Never mind. This is no time for explanations. Somebody had better call an ambulance.

84.

WHATEVER one's theory of time, one had to admit that the big clock in the hospital corridor moved unusually slowly. One could imagine its springs having been French-kissed by the junior jam-taster at Knott's Berry Farm.

Seated on a spotless wooden bench that had known neither pigeon nor wino, Sissy and Julian stared at the clock, waiting for its minutes to chase its hours around — but it was a warm day and the minutes were walking.

How many hours passed before the surgeon emerged from his operating room? Sissy and Julian didn't know. The clock could not be believed. When the surgeon finally did emerge, the Gitches rose to meet him. He addressed them with efficient gravity.

"Well, he's not out of danger, but I think we can safely say he's going to make it. I'd be pretty surprised if he didn't. However, there is evidence of injury to the frontal lobe, and I have reason to fear that this injury may be permanent. The patient may never again function as a normal human being."

"Brain damage," muttered Julian, shaking his head. Then, more distinctly, if somewhat hysterically, he asked, "You mean he's going to be a *vegetable?*"

Sissy, to whom abnormal function was old hat, could not prevent her mind's eye from focusing upon certain apparitions: a monocle-wearing asparagus, for example; turnip teeth clamped upon an ivory cigarette holder; a tomato made redder by Ripple; Veggie the Gay Cucumber. To drive these images from view, she re-examined her thumbs. They were sore and bruised, but essentially unimpaired. All those years she had underestimated their physical strength.

"Vegetable?" repeated the doctor. He closed his eyes momentarily, as if he, too, were visited by strange hallucinations from the produce stalls. "Vegetable? I wouldn't say that, no. We won't ascertain the extent of the injury for some days, but there is a genuine possibility of severe and lasting behavioral defects. I wouldn't classify it in the vegetable category, however." The surgeon didn't mention animal or mineral.

Julian asked a few more questions. The answers added little to what had been said. Preparing to take his leave, the surgeon spoke to Sissy. "Mrs. Gitche, this hospital had no choice but to report this matter to the authorities. You might appreciate being informed that a warrant for your arrest has been prepared. If I were you, I'd go down to police headquarters right now and, er, negotiate. Considering the circumstances, the, ah, unusual and personal nature of the, er, instrument that caused the injury, well, you wouldn't want the press to get wind of this, I wouldn't think . . ."

"Oh, we will, Doctor," blurted Julian. "We'll go immediately."

Julian was fibbing. He wanted Sissy to turn herself in, but not immediately. "Let's go home first," he said.

"But why?" protested Sissy. "Hadn't we best just get on down there and get it over with?"

"Sweetheart, you look dreadful. Dreadful. That old jumpsuit. It's even got blood on it. You haven't a trace of make-up. I want you to come home and let me help you into the dress I bought you, the party dress, the low-cut one. And make yourself up. You're a beautiful woman and there's no harm in taking advantage of it. We'll let the authorities know we're citizens of some standing. It's important to impress them. Cops are just as susceptible to physical charm as any other men. Turn them on a bit, if that's what it takes. It'll go easier for you. Here, you wait here. I'll duck into the gift shop" (They were now in the hospital lobby) "and get you some rouge. You never wear it, and you're looking pale." Julian headed for the cosmetics counter, where he found the selection extensive.

There is an animal called the water mongoose. It inhabits the swamps of Asia. The water mongoose has one grand trick up its sleeve (although up its sleeve is not exactly where the trick is at). It can distend its anal orifice until it (the anal orifice) looks like a ripe red fruit. Then the water mongoose stands very, very still. Sooner or later, a bird will come along and start to peck the "fruit." Whereupon the water mongoose whirls around rapidly and eats the bird. *Even Cowgirls Get the Blues* could find a parable in that, if it wanted to — but that might be too far-fetched.

85.

CARNIVAL SEASON rears its mad, masked head just before Ash Wednesday, the austere first day of the Roman Catholic forty-day Lenten fast. Carnival, whether lasting three days, as it does in most places, or two weeks, as it does in a few looser locales, culminates on Mardi Gras, or Fat Tuesday, with particularly riotous merrymaking.

The commonly accepted view is that carnival originated as a final fling on the part of good Christians before they commenced their forty days of fasting and penitence in preparation for Easter. It is written in encyclopedias and taught in universities that the word *carnival* is derived from the Latin *carne levare,* meaning "the putting away of flesh." Thus, it is thought to refer to some festive, last-minute, pre-Lenten carnivorousness, for during Lent none of the faithful may eat meat.

Poppycock. Balderdash. And flapdoodle. In other words, bullshit.

The carnival celebrated in Catholic lands is actually an adaptation of an ancient pagan whoopdedoohoo, the Festival of Dionysus, which in turn was adapted from the still older Haloa and Thesmophoria, two of the fertility festivals of the mother goddess Demeter.

(In Classical Greece, at the time when paternal rule began to ace out maternal, newcomer Dionysus was elevated to the Olympic Council, replacing the hearth goddess, Hestia, and taking over Demeter's festivals. For untold thousands of years, there had been no male deities in Europe. Dionysus, incidentally, was originally associated with psychedelic mushrooms, first the *Amanita muscaria* and later the smoother, more delightful *Psilocybe.* As the paternalistic Christian influence gained power, Dionysus was purged of his mushroom practices and was pronounced the god of wine. The Church, and the political and business interests who found Christianity a perfect front, much preferred the masses to use booze, which depresses the senses, instead of mushrooms, which illuminate them, just as they preferred that the aggressive logic of the paternal stereotype supplant the loving grace of maternalism. If kissing is man's greatest invention, then fermentation and patriarchy compete with the domestication of animals for the distinction of being man's worst folly, and no doubt the three combined long ago, the one growing out of the others, to foster civilization and lead Western humanity to its present state of decline. Cha cha cha.)

In truth, the word *carnival* is derived from *carrus navalis,* "cart of the sea." This was a boat-shaped vehicle on wheels used in the processions of Dionysus, and from which all kinds of witty and lust-inducing songs were sung. These ship carts, *carri navales,* making reference as they did to Dionysus' fabled underwater retreat in the grottos of the sea goddess, Thetis, from which he emerged at festival time, were accompanied by musicians and dancers of both sexes, skimpily clad or nude. They continued to be pulled through the streets in European festivals until the later Middle Ages, and today have their less nautical and less naughty counterparts in Mardi Gras floats.

The pagan festivals were deeply entrenched in the hearts and minds of the people, and they weren't inclined to give them up. Substitute the cross of guilt and suffering for the sea cart of joy and fecundity? Somehow that didn't seem like an A-1 good deal. They ran it up a flagpole and only a few paranoiacs and uncontrolled spastics saluted it. So the Church shrewdly compromised. It permitted carnival, but conspired to give it Christian significance, gradually succeeding in divorcing it from carefree fertility and associating it instead with self-denial and death (albeit, at three days, the shortest death in history, according to the *Guinness Book of World Records* — and as Jesus himself once said, "You're either for us or a Guinness").

Reader, the foregoing information concerning carnival is presented here merely as an example of the sort of facts uncovered by Dr. Robbins during his investigation of paganism. If Sissy was content to sit and think about the meaning of her pagan heritage, as described by the Chink, if she was as passive as a baked turkey in her consideration of the pagan potential in modern America (again, as suggested by the Chink), then Dr. Robbins took a more active approach. In the days since he had called in well at the Goldman Clinic, he had engaged in research. Unbiased data about our pagan past was not extensive — our Christian leadership had seen to that — but Dr. Robbins found enough to fascinate him. He had, as a matter of fact, just returned from a profitable morning of scholarship in the public library when his telephone broke a long silence, shrieking from its stationary pedestal as if it thought itself a flashy car being driven at high speeds over back-country roads. Well, even telephones can dream, can't they?

It was Sissy calling. She was upset. In distress. She had just ditched Julian at St. Vincent's Hospital and must see Dr. Robbins at once.

Naturally, Robbins was willing, but he pressed for further details. So Sissy blabbed the whole bloody thing.

"My, my," said Dr. Robbins. "My oh my. This is bad, this is very bad, but you mustn't think of it as a razor held to the Dali's mustache of your life. Violence stinks, no matter which end of it you're on. But now and then there's nothing left to do but hit the other person over the head with a frying pan. Sometimes people are just begging for that frypan, and if we weaken for a moment and honor their request, we should regard it as impulsive philanthropy, which we aren't in any position to afford, but shouldn't regret it too loudly lest we spoil the purity of the deed.

"Now. I don't really want you coming to my place, in case the cops trace you here. I've got half a kilo of grass stashed here, not to mention a couple of other embarrassing odds and ends. So, tell you what we can do. We'll meet at six this evening in my aunt's house in Passaic, New Jersey. My aunt's away and I have the keys. A safer place you couldn't find. You can get to Passaic, can't you? It's only twenty minutes from Manhattan. Here's my aunt's address.

"Say, Sissy, by the way. Did you know that Nijinsky once played tennis in Passaic, New Jersey? He did. Only time he played tennis in his life. And the only historical event I would like to have filmed. Nijinsky playing tennis in Passaic, New Jersey. Wow! Now that'd be a movie fit to be shown to Jesus, Dionysus *and* Demeter."

86.

AFTER TALKING with Dr. Robbins, Sissy felt better — but not much. To the knapsack of her guilt was now added another rock, this one flecked with running-out-on-Julian.

"Maybe it's just that my perspective is wrong," ventured Sissy. She thought that she would see if there wasn't some positive way to view her actions. It might take time (ah, time!) to arrive at such a vantage point, however, and urgency was running up her leg like a mouse.

After that thumping she'd given the Countess, the authorities would say she was crazy for sure. And one thing she did not want, could not tolerate, was to be committed to the Goldman Clinic or its state-funded equivalent. She felt guilt, she felt sorrow, shame and confusion, but she did not feel that she owed society any accounting for her behavior, as bad as her behavior might have been. Society had never looked upon her with favor. It had been eager to write her off when she was just a little girl. Society might have institutionalized her way back then if she had cooperated. Society had neither liked her nor believed in her, but luckily she had liked herself and believed in herself, and although she recognized that she had floundered in recent years, erred in recent hours, she still liked and believed, and the reckoning she must make was with herself, not with society, especially not with a society that was willing to put a matter as delicate as this in the kitten-crusher hands of the police.

Thus, Sissy Hankshaw Gitche, a self-recognized ongoing system of uncommon abilities and unexpected vices, headed for New Jersey; for options, alternatives, choices. And didn't it feel sweet to be up to her armpits in traffic again, to be dancing cheek to cheek with traffic, to be charming the deadly snake of traffic, to be sticking her thumb into the pie of traffic, Oh she could bouncy-wouncy baby Volkswagens on her knees and suck on Italian racing cars just to freshen her breath, traffic was her element, her medium, the vocabulary from which she snatched the words of her poem, Oh didn't her hands come back to life with a squeal! and wasn't it swee-eet?

So happy was Sissy to pick that conservative blue Econoline van out of the throng on Canal Street and draw it to her as if on a string that she failed to look over its driver until she was seated and he was stomping the gas-feed. It was with a sense of disgust at her own failure that she scrutinized his sweaty brow, his smug, hot leer, his eyes so starved for erogenous scenery that they did not register her thumbs. Her heart sank another twenty fathoms when she saw his gun and his knife.

87.

LAWS, it is said, are for protection of the people. It's unfortunate that there are no statistics on the number of lives that are clobbered yearly as a result of laws: outmoded laws; laws that found their way onto the books as a result of ignorance, hysteria or political haymaking; antilife laws; biased laws; laws that pretend that reality is fixed and nature is definable; laws that deny people the right to refuse protection. A survey such as that could keep a dozen dull sociologists out of mischief for months. (Ford Foundation, are you reading this book?)

The first laws prohibiting hitchhiking were enacted in New Jersey in the 1920s to keep city-bred flapper freeloaders away from selected resorts and rural paradises. New Jersey remains one of two states (Hawaii, the other) where hitchhiking is both completely illegal and the law strictly enforced. It was because of the Jersey ban, and the toughness of its state patrol, that Sissy had selected the blue van. She was on Canal Street, near the entrance to the West Side Highway. She had hoped to get a ride up the West Side Highway and over the George Washington Bridge, putting her as close as possible to Passaic, keeping her hitching — as much as she capital-A Adored it! — to a minimum once in Jersey. The blue van had Jersey plates. That's why she chose it.

It had been a mutual choice, for the blue van's driver had spotted Sissy a block away and had manuevered into the curb lane. He had started talking even before he braked, and once Sissy was aboard he was rapping away at such an amphetamine clip that had he died at that moment the undertaker would have had to beat his tongue to death with a stick.

He was also unzipping his pants.

"I'm going to give it to you like you've never had it before. Oh, you didn't know it could be this good. You're gonna like it. You're gonna like it. You're gonna like it so good. You're gonna love it so much you're gonna cry. You're gonna cry and cry. Do you like to cry? Do you like it when it hurts a little bit? Whatever happens to you, it'll be worth it. The way I'm gonna give it to you, it'll be worth anything. Everything. Go ahead and cry if you want to. I like it when women cry. It means they appreciate me." Etc., etc.

The van pulled off Canal, down a deadend street between warehouses. In the rear of the vehicle was a soiled mattress.

By then, the driver had his organ out in the late afternoon sunlight. It was erect and of Kentucky Derby proportions.

With a swift swoosh that gave the June air bad memories of winter, Sissy's left thumb came down hard on the penis top, nearly cleaving it to the root. The driver howled. His finger fumbled for gun trigger. Before he could squeeze it, however, the thumb splatted between his eyes. Twice. Three times. He lost control of the van. It lumbered into a street lamp, giving both van and lamppost a taste of what it's like to be organic.

Sissy lept from the vehicle and ran. Four or five blocks away, out of breath but safe in the neon aura of a just-closing working man's luncheonette, she stopped to rest. The tears the rapist had longed for made their appearance, heavy and hot, just the way he would have liked them. The thought of it made her stop crying.

She examined her thumb. Fresh bruises, like blue jellyfish, were floating lazily to the surface. Sore muscles twitched mechanically, as if typing an essay: "The Thumb As Weapon."

"Twice in one day," Sissy sobbed. "Twice in one day."

Abruptly, the sobbing ceased. With a look of determination that could have served as the dust jacket for any number of how-to-succeed manuals, Sissy announced in a clear, hard voice, "Okay! If they want me normal, then normal, by God, is what they're gonna get!"

She hailed a taxi. Rode uptown to the Port Authority Bus Terminal. Bought a one-way ticket to Richmond, Virginia.

As the southbound Greyhound hissed through the Jersey flats, she recalled that several centuries ago this fetid fairyland of oil refineries had been jumping with whooping cranes.

88.

THIS NOVEL now has as many chapters as a piano has keys (Eat your hearts out, ye writers of ukuleles and piccolos!), and in point of fact it would be but moderately trite to label this the "piano chapter." For as Chapter 88 rears its hastily typed head, Julian Gitche is sponging dried Countess blood from the keyboard of his white baby grand, sponging, gulping Scotch and going slightly bananas wondering what has happened to his wife.

And up in Passaic, New Jersey, where Nijinsky once played tennis in ballet slippers, there was another piano, this one a battered old upright in the parlor of an aunt. And there, another man was puzzling where Sissy might be.

Dr. Robbins didn't play the piano. In order to distract his thoughts from the fact of Sissy's lateness (if one's philosophy of time permits one to accept as facts such notions as late or early), he toked on reefers and outlined a movie. Not a movie of Nijinsky leaping twenty-five feet in the air trying to backhand a lob in Passaic, New Jersey: it was too "late" for that, time and brain being the odd couple they are. No, Dr. Robbins was thinking how it might be interesting to make a film from Adelle Davis's perennial best seller, *Let's Eat Right to Keep Fit.*

Representing a classic confrontation between good and evil — in this case, nutrition versus unhealthy diet — the story had definite box office appeal. The role of the hero, Protein, probably should be filled by big Jim Brown, although Burt Reynolds undoubtedly would pull strings to try to get the part. Sunny Doris Day would be a clear choice to play the heroine, Vitamin C, and Orson Welles, oozing saturated fatty acids from the pits of his flesh, could win an Oscar for his interpretation of the villainous Cholesterol. The film might begin on a stormy night in the central nervous system. Alarmed, the ever-watchful pituitary gland dispatches a couple of trusted hormones with a message for the adrenals. Even though it's all downstream, the going is rough because of boulders of white sugar and passageways dangerously narrowed due to atherosclerosis. Suddenly . . .

Oh come on, Robbins, that's enough! If you can't play the piano, why don't you just watch TV?

89.

SISSY'S BUS, transportation obtained with money instead of magic — alas, our heroine seems to be following in the footsteps of the modern world — rolled into a sleeping Richmond with the milkmen.

Dawn lay on the chops of the city like a washcloth: still, damp, heavy, warm. By the calendar, summer was more than a week away, but heat had caught up with Richmond; it had the seat of Richmond's pants in its teeth.

Pretty swell pants Richmond was wearing these days, too. In 1973, Richmond had moved ahead of Atlanta, the South's showcase city, in per capita income. Almost everywhere Sissy looked, there were signs of prosperity. New office buildings, factories, apartment houses, schools, shopping centers. It was a bit difficult, sometimes, to distinguish one from the other — the factories and schools were especially similar — but there they were, showing confident faces, one and all, to the rising sun, brighter, cleaner, more solid than any pine groves that had ever stood in their places. More permanent? Well, we'll see.

Industry in the city was much more diversified than in the Eisenhower Years. In fact, several major tobacco firms, including Larus Brothers and Liggett & Meyers had discontinued operations in Richmond, and only Philip Morris, with its mammoth new plant and research center, had ventured any notable expansion. Nevertheless, a golden effluvium still toasted the air of South Richmond. At least, it seemed so to Sissy. Maybe it was merely memory speaking into her nostrils.

Prosperity had not overlooked South Richmond. Only recently, the angel of economic visions had flapped its wings in Sissy's old neighborhood, knocking rickety houses to and fro with each vital beat. Every dwelling in her old block had been condemned and evacuated, in preparation for the demolition that, miraculously, fifty years of domestic brawls had not wrought.

The Hankshaw residence had been boarded up clumsily, like a box hastily readied for some funky Houdini's escape trick. It was a house dead on its feet. It looked like the shell for a termite's taco.

Sissy paid the taxi driver and walked to the front door. By pushing strenuously with her shoulder, she was able to separate boards from nails to the extent that the door opened four or five inches. She looked inside.

Sagging linoleum. Peeling wallpaper. Dust doing its dust dance in the morning light. Nothing to indicate that a man and woman had once lived here in love and hate, had conceived in one of these rooms or the other, three children; one of them a daughter distinguished by a certain anatomical slapstick that had caused the man and woman much embarrassment until the daughter had grown into a teen-ager, in this very house, here, dribbling jam on the floor, pee in the bowl and dreams on the pillows, had grown into a teen-ager and run away, never contacting her family again, sparing them further discomfort, forgotten by them, finally unknown to them except as a monster girl that sometimes crawled into their nightmares. Or so Sissy believed.

Just as she turned to leave, however, a widening shaft of sunlight illuminated a corner, instantly remembered as the corner where her mama's sewing table had long stood, and there, thumbtacked at eye level on the wall were six or eight bright pages ripped from magazines, advertisement pages, pages upon which a tall blond girl, hands mysteriously hidden, posed in various romantic settings, urging the women of the world to purchase a well-known feminine hygiene spray. None other.

90.

In Richmond, it was almost possible not to hear the cake crumbling, smell the bacon burning. A recent magazine article had stated, "Unlike most of the nation, Richmond is thriving." The economic and psychic depression that was sucking the smile off of the face of Western civilization could barely be noticed in this proud Southern town. Of course, Sissy seldom noticed such things, anyhow. What she did notice, on her homecoming day, was a lot of spiffy new cars, many of them British imports (Richmond being obsessively Anglophilic). She thought that the hitchhiking would be interesting here, perhaps more interesting than in her girlhood — but she wasn't hitching. It was inside another taxi that Sissy rode to the midtown medical building where she remembered that Dr. Dreyfus had had his office.

The office was still there, all right, but it had changed. Whereas on Sissy's first visit there had been two or three tastefully framed prints on the wall, the place now looked more like an art gallery than a doctor's office. Everywhere there were reproductions of Picasso, Bonnard, Renoir, Braque, Utrillo, Dufy, Soutine, Gauguin, Degas, Rousseau, Gris, Matisse, Cézanne, Monet, Manet, Minet, Menet, Munet and others. Many were not framed, but were pinned to the walls in such close proximity that they frequently overlapped, bumping each other like fish in a school. It was as if a survey of modern French painting had gotten mixed up with an aquarium.

The receptionist was away from her desk, so Sissy stared at the tanks full of Gauguin guppies and Picasso triggerfish. Eventually, a woman came in from a rear cubicle to inform Sissy that the office was closed. Closed? Yes. Permanently. Dr. Dreyfus had retired the previous week and the woman was there putting things in order, referring patients to other plastic surgeons, closing the books and so forth.

"I'd be happy to refer you to someone else," said the woman, who was short, juiceless and gray, like a village school principal's night on the town.

"Only Dr. Dreyfus will do," Sissy pleaded.

"I'm sorry," said the woman.

"But if he just retired last week, he could still do one more operation, couldn't he?"

"I'm afraid not," said the woman. "Not a chance of it."

"Is he ill or something?"

The woman didn't answer immediately. "That's a matter of opinion," she sighed at last. "You're not from around Richmond, are you?"

Before Sissy could answer, the woman snapped, "Ma'am, you're wasting your time and mine. Dr. Dreyfus will not be performing any more surgery, and that's definite. Now, if you don't wish a referral, please excuse me. I've got to start taking those fool pictures down. Oh Lord."

Like a bad habit, another taxi let Sissy fall into it. She gave the cabbie the address the telephone directory had given her. It was in the West End, in one of the better neighborhoods, although not the best. The best neighborhood in Richmond, as in Heaven, is reserved for those of the Christian persuasion.

Dr. Dreyfus himself answered the door. He hadn't changed much, and he remembered Sissy. Rather, he remembered certain parts of Sissy. If he hadn't, he wouldn't have let her in. He had been bothered by journalists, he explained. He didn't inquire why Sissy had called; he seemed to know. "I'm afraid I can't help you," he said. "Please, child, don't be dismayed. We all have problems these days. But as the painter Van Gogh said, 'Mysteries remain, sorrow or melancholy remains, but the everlasting negative is balanced by the positive work which thus is achieved, after all.' I don't suppose that means very much to you. Here, you read this while I get out of my dressing robe and into my puttering clothes. Some other physician can help you. This will explain why I cannot."

To his visitor he handed a clipping from a newsprint periodical. "There have been many other articles, but this one says it most objectively." He left Sissy alone to read:

FRUSTRATED ARTIST BLOWS MED CAREER THROUGH NOSE

As a boy in Paris, Felix Dreyfus had dreamed of becoming an artist. An older cousin who was a guide at the Louvre let him tag along on tours, where he acquired a precocious knowledge of art history. Alas, Felix's parents were philistines who constantly deflated the boy's artistic dreams, while grooming him for a career in medicine.

Young Dreyfus gave in, finishing med school with high marks. If his parents saw in his choice of plastic surgery as a medical specialty the remnants of the old artistic urge — plastic surgery is, after all, a rather sculptural, relatively creative discipline — they did not let on.

Emigrating to the U.S. in the Nazi years, Dr. Dreyfus developed a successful practice in Richmond, Va. There, he was fairly active as a patron of the arts, and accumulated an extensive collection of books on painters and sculptors. He married his nurse, and they led a quiet, comfortable life.

Then, last month, Dr. Dreyfus, 66, undertook to perform cosmetic surgery on a 14-year-old boy, Bernard Schwartz. A routine operation, it was to alter the size and shape of the boy's Semitic nose. Although he specialized in injuries to and deformities of the hands, Dr. Dreyfus had successfully completed many "nose jobs."

When the bandages were removed from Bernie Schwartz's proboscis, however, the boy's horrified parents were gaping at what has been called "the most scandalous incident of deliberate malpractice in the recent history of medicine."

Succumbing, maniacally, to his suppressed artistic drives, Dr. Felix Dreyfus, disdaining marble, clay and plaster to work in living flesh, had sculptured upon the face of little Bernie Schwartz the world's first Cubistic nose!

Bernie's new nose had six nostrils, two in front, two on each side, and three bridges, so that in either profile it looked as if you were seeing it frontally. According to the exuberant Dr. Dreyfus, Bernie's nose is "simultaneously viewed from several aspects, all the aspects overlapping, so that what we have is a nose in *totality*, and that totality manages to suggest motion, even when static; it shatters the classical idea of the face in which the nose is fixed and unchanging; it is a nose in a perpetual state of ultimate noseness, yet it is on the very verge of the abstract."

Dr. Dreyfus's enthusiasm may be short-lived. The Virginia Medical Board has suspended his license, and it is reported that the surgeon may be permitted to retire as an alternative to being barred permanently from practice. Bernie's parents, unconvinced by the creator's glowing aesthetic evaluation of his work, are suing Dr. Dreyfus for three million dollars. Moreover, the "masterpiece" is doomed. As soon as medically feasible, a team of plastic surgeons in Washington, D.C., will restore the world's first Cubistic nose to a realistic style that promises to please even devotees of Norman Rockwell. Meanwhile, Bernie Schwartz spends a lot of time indoors.

When Dr. Dreyfus returned, rather sheepishly, to the living room, Sissy rushed to embrace him. She was smiling for the first time in more than twenty-four hours. "Oh, Doctor!" she cried. "You've got to do it. You and nobody else should be allowed to take away my gift."

91.

"Ah the thumb," mused Dr. Dreyfus, yawning his small eyes so that they might take in the full length and breadth of Sissy's prodigious pucky-wucks. "The thumb, yes. The thumb the thumb the thumb the thumb the thumb the thumb. One of evolution's most ingenious inventions; a built-in tool sensitive to texture, contour and temperature: an alchemical lever; the secret key to technology; the link between the mind and art; a humanizing device. The marmoset and the lemur are thumbless; none of the New World monkeys has opposable thumbs; the spider monkey's thumbs are absent or reduced to a tiny tubercle; the thumbs of the potto are set at an angle of one hundred eighty degrees to the other digits, making them nonfunctional except as pinchers; the orangutan, which is humanlike to the extent that it is called the 'man of the woods,' has a thumb so tiny in relation to its extremely long curved fingers that its manipulation is only nominal;

the thumb of the chimpanzee opposes the bent fingers in a clumsy action, and the gorilla lacks a grip precise enough to hold small objects; the baboon comes close — its thumbs are fully opposable and it has a good precision grip — but have you ever observed the thumb of the baboon, how flat and splay-headed and crudely shaped it is; no, there is but one true thumb on this planet and *homo sapiens* has got it."

Pause.

"And so you are demanding at last the privileges of thumb that nature has perversely denied you?"

"I just want to be normal," said Sissy. "Give me that old-fashioned normality. It was good enough for Crazy Horse and it's good enough for me."

"Ah yes," said Dr. Dreyfus, smiling weakly, like a duck in dishwater, too embarrassed to quack. "Very well, my dear. Here is what we can do.

"Full normality, whatever that may exactly be, is out of the question. But out of the question comes the answer, so to speak. If your thumb bone — actually, two phalanx metacarpal bones — if your thumb bones were of normal size, then we could merely cut away the excess tissue and sew your thumb inside of your chest for a while, for a skin graft, you see. Then you'd have thumbs that were normal in appearance as well as in function. However, as I recall, your thumb bones are enlarged in proportion to the whole. That makes it more complicated. That calls for pollicerization. One thing a surgeon cannot do is reduce volume of bone. Bone can be shortened but not reduced in size. So. In pollicerization, we make a thumb out of your index finger. We shorten the bone of the index finger, alter its angle and move it over. After a time, it becomes a completely acceptable thumb. But your hands, you realize, would still not be quite normal, because they'd have only four digits a piece. Your present thumbs — there certainly is a peculiar glow about them — would, of course, have to be amputated."

What??? Feel faint. Ooooo, dizzy. Sick to the tummy. A startle of fishes in the seas of the abdomen. A thick black toxin spews from the heart to numb the teeth. Sissy suffers shortness of breath. The author's own fingers tremble on the keys. Amputation. A leaden word. A word with a built-in echo and a built-in ache. A word off Dr. Guillotine's workbench. A lump in God's gravy. Can thumbs understand the word "amputate" the way whooping cranes understand the word "extinct"?

Felix Dreyfus offered the shaken Sissy a glass of sherry. She declined. Probably not a dram of Ripple in the whole West End. In lieu of alcoholic stimulant, then, the good doctor administered the tonic of conspiracy.

"This will be a risky escapade," he confided, "but I'm old now and can afford to take risks. I'll not run from Nazis ever again. My brother-in-law is a surgeon. Ha! Some surgeon. He couldn't cut the pimento out of a stuffed olive. He ought to have a red and white striped pole outside of his office. He's employed by the Veterans' Administration. Only the government would hire such a boob. Well, as our luck would have it, he's in residence at O'Dwyre VA Hospital over in South Richmond. I'll have him schedule you for surgery. He owes me thousands; he'll do what I say. Then I'll show up to 'assist' with the operations. I'll use an assumed name. Nobody at O'Dwyre will be the wiser. They're understaffed, outmoded, incompetent and corrupt. The follow-up work I can do here at home. Faintly ingenious, yes? Against all rules, but as the painter Delacroix said, 'There are no rules for great souls: rules are only for people who have merely the talent that can be acquired.' But I don't suppose that means much to you."

92.

ONCE, a young woman was admitted to a hospital, and no birds sang.

Once, blood was analyzed in a laboratory, and no birds sang.

Once, powerful lamps were turned on in an operating room, and no birds sang.

Once, IV tubes were inserted in veins, and no birds sang.

Once, a young woman was wheeled into surgery, and no birds sang.

Once, an anesthesiologist stuck a needle into a curved and creamy ass, and no birds sang.

Once, an anesthesiologist stuck needles into a long, graceful neck, and no birds sang.

Once, a nurse scrubbed an arm for ten full minutes, and no birds sang.

Once, a body and a table were draped with sheets to create a sterile field, and no birds sang.

Once, a tourniquet was placed on a slender right arm, and no birds sang.

Once, an elastic rubber bandage was applied so tightly it squeezed most of the blood out of an arm, and no birds sang.

Once, a tourniquet was inflated, and not a single ornithological peep was heard.

Once, a surgeon outlined in iodine an incision around the base of a thumb, and still no birds were singing.

Once, pale smooth skin was incised along a premarked line and dissected down to the bone, while silence prevailed in treetop and nest.

Once, arteries and veins were divided and tied, and a nerve was separated and allowed to detract into a wound, without an accompanying warble or whistle or tweet.

Once, a joint was opened, and it wasn't a new roadhouse nor were any of our fine feathered friends chirping there.

Once, tendons were cut, snapped and allowed to retract like rubber bands, a sound that could not have been mistaken for a meadowlark or a thrush.

Once, a metacarpal bone was fractured with a saw, a task that, due to the unusual size of the particular bone, required such exertion on the part of the surgeon that he could not have heard any birds if they were singing, which they weren't.

Once, a drain was placed in a wound, and not so much as a sparrow opened its mouth.

Once, woman flesh was sewn shut with four-ought nylon suture, and the beaks of the birds must have been sewn shut, too.

Once, a pressure dressing was applied to a hand, but no amount of pressure could induce the birds to sing.

Once, a tourniquet was deflated, a bloody arm bathed, and a numb young woman rolled to a recovery room, four fingers showing from a bandage and not one of them pointing to the silent skies.

Once, a nurse and two surgeons, their attention directed by an intensifying pinkish glow, turned to stare into a metal pan, where a huge human thumb, disarticulated from the hand it had served (in its fashion), was now flopping about like a trout — no! not flopping aimlessly in breathless panic but, rather, arching and thrusting itself in a calculated and endlessly repeated gesture, the international gesture of the hitchhike, as if, to avoid troubling the world with its great white grief, it was trying to flag a ride On Out of Here.

And no birds sang.

93.

THE SKY was as tattered as a Gypsy's pajamas. Through knife holes in the flannel overcast, July sunlight spilled, causing Sissy's eyes to blink when she stepped outside the long, dark corridors of O'Dwyre VA Hospital. The air was so humid, she felt orchids growing in her armpits.

Masquerading as the pensioned widow of a Vietnam hero, Sissy had been in the hospital for three full days. On this, the fourth morning, the drain had been removed from her wound, a fresh dressing applied and a discharge granted.

On this morning, also, Dr. Dreyfus had learned that Sissy had spent the fortnight prior to her surgery sleeping on the warped linoleum of a condemned house, the rat-slobbered old Hankshaw residence in South Richmond. Now he was driving her to his own house, where his wife (who turned out to be the short gray woman from the office) was preparing a room for her. She was invited to stay with the Dreyfus family until the work on her hands was completed. Because of the magnitude of the wound left by amputating such large digits, Dr. Dreyfus had decided that four operations would be necessary. The first, just done, would remove her right thumb. The second would remove the left. The object of the third would be the pollicerization of the right index finger; the fourth, the left. They would allow six weeks between each operation. One doesn't get to be normal overnight.

Mrs. Dreyfus didn't approve of her husband's illegal ministrations to Sissy, but, like many native Richmonders, she was gracious to the point of agony. Margaret Dreyfus did her bust-a-gut best to make the convalescent feel at home. Meals were regular, cheerful and good. With air conditioning, showers and pitchers of limeade, Sissy's armpits were defoliated, fruit bats discouraged from hanging from her sex hairs. In the evenings, a portable TV was rolled onto the screened-in veranda, the programming left to Sissy's wishes. During late-night thunderstorms, discreet inquiries were made as to whether the guest was nervous. The latest magazines appeared on her bedside table.

If Sissy didn't feel completely at home, it was because Sissy wasn't completely at home; she wasn't completely anywhere, she wasn't complete. Part of her — oh such a part! — was literally missing. Even though it *felt* as if it were still there, it was gone, gone, gone; gone to her questioning eyes, gone to her fumbling touch, gone from all dimensions except the inexplicable dimension of bioenergy, where its heavy aura pulsated and practiced phantom poses just in case some psychic researcher should start taking Kirlian photographs with a wide-angle lens. Sissy was determined to feel no remorse, but shock showed on her eyeballs like a marmalade glaze.

"Lord!" exclaimed Margaret Dreyfus. "She acts like that big ol' thumb had been her child."

"No," corrected her husband. "She acts as if she had been the thumb's child."

Two weeks after the operation, on the day the stitches were removed, Sissy phoned Marie Barth in Manhattan. She learned that the Countess had survived, although some spots seemed to be missing from his dice. There was a warrant for Sissy's arrest outstanding, but as long as she kept away from New York State, she was safe: The crime was not serious enough for extradition; in fact, in the High Renaissance of crime that New York was now enjoying, Sissy's little assault was considered no more important than, say, the after-hours doodles of one of Botticelli's apprentices. By Marie, Sissy sent word to Julian that she was well and that she would be coming back to him some day, but first she had some changes to go through.

After the call, Sissy felt a bit more perky. Several times she accompanied Margaret Dreyfus on shopping expeditions — to Richmond Kosher Meat Market on West Cary Street and to Weiman's Bakery on

North Seventeenth. With Dr. and Mrs. Dreyfus and their son, Max, a law student at Washington and Lee University, she attended movies at the Colonial Theater and the Byrd. There had been few visitors to the Dreyfus home since the Bernie Schwartz scandal, and Sissy found the patio private enough for nude sunbathing. Once, she walked as far as Byrd Park, the weight of orchids and bats dragging her down, and fed the ducks. She returned home saturated, panting, her ears resonant with blessed duck music, and beat Dr. Dreyfus at chess. That night she seemed vaguely joyous.

For the most part, however, Sissy had joined the ranks of the Unhappy Waiters and Killers of Time. Oh God, there are so many of them in our land! Students who can't be happy until they've graduated, servicemen who can't be happy until they're discharged, single folks who can't be happy until they're married, workers who can't be happy until they're retired, adolescents who can't be happy until they're grown, ill people who can't be happy until they're well, failures who can't be happy until they succeed, restless who can't be happy until they get out of town; and, in most cases, vice versa, people waiting, waiting for the world to begin. Sissy knew better than to fall into that dumb trap — certainly the Chink had taught her enough about time so that she needn't ever mark it — but there she was, playing the zombie game, running in place, postponing life until normality was achieved — while simultaneously she mourned the decrease in personal magic that had occurred with the loss of that famous Airstream Trailer of digits, the thumb that had launched a thousand trips.

But one afternoon, some twenty days into July, word was flashed into the Dreyfus home, as it was flashed (impartially and regardless of whether the homeowner had ever turned a nice Jewish boy's nose into a six-sided museum piece) into the homes of all Americans, that . . . the whooping cranes . . . had been found. And Sissy was jostled awake, alive.

94.

Sissy One Thumb watched network news early and late, and Lone Thumb Gitche laid her ear to the breast of the radio, and Little Miss Nine Fingers was first person up mornings to retrieve the *Times-Dispatch* from the delivery boy's pitch. Scarcely anybody followed the whooping crane "story" more closely than Semi-Thumbelina, the single-minded seraph grounded in Richmond's West End.

As news, whooper developments were overshadowed by events in Washington, D.C., where the President was having a little hand trouble of his own. Which is to say, the President had been caught red-handed, hands redder than a travel poster sunset, pimp red, a red that could enrage bulls and stop locomotives, but not blood red, for blood is sacred and the red that ran off the President's hands was the red of lies and deals and greed and arrogant megalomania. The President's hands had been seen, coast to coast, in the till up to the elbows, and the public — hopelessly brainwashed about the true significance of movements — was more enthralled with the frantic scramblings of the President's crimson hands, wringing and jerking and shaking off bribery, diving for a safe pocket, trying to force their way into a distinguished pair of gloves, than it was by the graceful glidings of new-found whooping cranes over the hills of Dakota.

By no means did the media ignore the whooper saga, however; it was the number two news story in the land, rating for a while more time and space than the international situation, which was desperate, as usual. Thus did Our Lady of the Missing Digit, though she had to saw through cords of political punk to get at heartwood, stack the following facts:

The Countess had had nothing to do with it; his brain — and brains have their weaknesses, as we all know — had been involuntarily tuned to another frequency, perhaps to that channel that broadcasts to mongoloids, sleeping beauties and house cats. Nor, to the Interior Secretary's displeasure, had the government search plane located the cranes, although it had passed within an aeronautical whisker of them on several occasions. No, the Walt Disney Studios cinematographers had simply emerged one day from the Florida swamps, where they had been filming *Lunch Time in the Everglades,* learned of the whooper disappearance and sent word to the authorities: "Hey, why don't you have a look at little Siwash Lake in the Dakota hills; the cranes stop off there, and there're goings on around that place that you wouldn't believe."

Very next day, two area representatives of the Fish and Wildlife Service attempted to check out the lake. They drove to the gates of a ranch, where they were turned back by a teen-aged girl with a rifle.

The following morning, the Fish and Wildlife agents were flown over Siwash Lake in a U.S. Forestry Service helicopter. Before shots from a band of young women on horseback drove them away, they observed more whooping cranes than any humans had ever seen all in one place (that is, any humans except those crazy girls, and who in Jesus Jumping Hell were they, anyhow?)

That afternoon, the two representatives of the Fish and Wildlife Service returned to the ranch. With them were two Forest Service rangers, a state game warden, the county sheriff, four deputy sheriffs, Mottburg's town marshall, several of *his* deputies, the editor of the Mottburg *Gazette* (who doubled as regional stringer for the Associated Press), a couple of bird watchers and a run-of-the-mill thrill-seeker or two. This party was met at the gate by at least fifteen armed females, mostly between the ages of seventeen and twenty-one, in jeans, skimpy tops and Western-style hats and boots. One of the young women, described as extremely attractive, identified herself as Bonanza Jellybean, ranch boss, and told the authorities, "Yep, the birds are here all right. They're in fine shape, and as you musta saw from your f—— whirly machine, unrestrained, free to go as they please. But this is private property and you aren't laying a foot on it, none of you." The cops tried to bluff the cowgirls — for cowgirls were what they were — but it didn't work. "We'll be back with a court order and a fistful of search warrants," warned the sheriff. To which Ms. Bonanza Jellybean replied, "Just come back with a couple of people who know what they're doing and we'll let 'em on for a nice close look at the birds." Another young woman, carrying a whip and dressed entirely in black, added, "And make sure those two people are female." Ms. Jellybean amended that demand. "Make sure at least one of them is female," she said. "And you'd better do as we say or they may be trouble." The lawmen told the Wildlife agents they'd get them to the lake then and there if they wanted, but the senior federal representative, as level-headed as a chopping block, replied that force could endanger lives, crane as well as human, and he was sure the problem could be safely solved on the morrow. "Let's get to a phone," he said to his associate, and as if some Mottburg telephone booth was the last coffee break left in the universe, off all of them rushed.

When the rosy fingers of dawn next strummed the string of the horizon, there was gathered at the Rubber Rose gate the entire party from the previous afternoon, plus nine additional thrill-seekers, eight television journalists, seven newspaper reporters, six officials from the nation's capital, five more deputies, four Audubon Society members, three FBI agents, two well-paid consultants and a CIA man in a pear tree.

The cowgirls had gained in numbers, too; the wide-eyed editor of the Mottburg *Gazette* counted nearly twice as many as the day before. They were sipping cocoa, brushing one another's hair and rubbing the sleep out of their eyes. Bonanza Jellybean, in a leather skirt so short her crotch thought she hadn't dressed yet, advanced to negotiate with an Assistant Undersecretary of the Interior. She spun a six-gun on her tiny fingers as she talked.

Eventually, it was agreed that two observers would be permitted on the ranch. They were to be the man perhaps most familiar with whooper life, the director of the Aransas, Texas, Wildlife Refuge; and the extremely nervous Inge Anne Nelsen, a professor of zoology at North Dakota State University. Professor Nelsen wanted a cowgirl to remain outside the gates in temporary custody, as insurance against the possibility of the professor herself being held hostage. The request infuriated the Rubber Rose forewoman, the darkly dressed Delores (spell it with an "e") del Ruby. Snapped Ms. del Ruby, "One reason we wanted a woman for this job was so we wouldn't have to put up with that kind of male mentality paranoia provocative bull——." And Ms. Jellybean scolded the zoologist, "Don't be a traitor to your womb." At that point, a cowgirl known as Elaine scampered over the gate, volunteering to stay with the authorities. Elaine delighted the cameramen and infuriated the cops by proceeding to hug the Assistant Undersecretary flirtatiously about the neck.

The zoology professor and the Aransas director were given horses, and escorted by a half-dozen mounted cowgirls to the lake. After about two hours, a period during which the journalists unsuccessfully pumped Elaine for information and the lawmen ogled, with that mixture of desire and disgust peculiar to men reared in a Puritanical environment, the cowgirls guarding the gate, the Siwash expedition returned. The government's delegates reported in private to the Assistant Interior Undersecretary (whom Elaine persisted in calling the Inferior Undersexed Assistant), and he, in turn, issued an informal statement to his subordinates and the press.

"It will be my extreme pleasure to report to the President, who has been gravely concerned about the fate of our whooping cranes [hee ha hee, snigger snigger] and to the Interior Secretary and to the American people that the entire flock of cranes is, indeed, at Siwash Lake, and in apparently healthy condition. The cranes have built brooding nests around the whole circumference of the small lake, and have hatched chicks there. Counting the young birds, there are now approximately sixty cranes in the flock." (Loud cheers from the Audubon section and the free-lance bird watchers.) "While this is good news, it is also quite bewildering. Whooping cranes are territorially minded, militantly so. They have never been known to nest as close as a mile to one another, yet here they are virtually side by side. Furthermore, as long as man has been acquainted with this flock it has nested nowhere but in the wilderness of northern Canada. Why did this year it cut its migration short by over a thousand miles and choose to brood cramped up at this little lake, so close to human beings, when whooping cranes are notoriously shy of humans? Those are perplexing questions, which our best experts will attempt to answer in the near future. For now perhaps, it is good news enough to learn that our cranes are alive and [a furtive glance at the cowgirls] apparently safe."

On the morning after that one — and days do *seem* to follow days, don't they, students of time? — as the Assistant Undersecretary and his party pushed its way through the throng that milled outside the Rubber Rose, past writers, photographers, ranchers, loafers, mothers nursing babies, rural punks with T-shirt sleeves rolled up to show off the sum total of their personalities, Indians, tourists, bird-lovers, old men chewing tobacco, runaway daughters wishing to join the cowgirls and, of course, shootout enthusiasts from almost every branch of law enforcement; as the Assistant Undersecretary moved through this faintly festive mob, he was in a conciliatory mood. For one thing, his boss, the Secretary, had advised him to be conciliatory. For another, on the previous evening — and days do *seem* to antecede days — at the Elk Horn Motor Lodge, the Assistant Undersecretary had sounded out the citizens of Mottburg. He had heard that the cowgirls were tramps, lesbians, witches, dope fiends, that they fornicated with farm animals, subsisted on gook rice and flew funny kites. Yet the natives believed that these same cowgirls, trash as they were, had every right to keep "the government" off their land: prairie folk are decidedly opposed to federal interference. The Assistant Undersecretary paid the heed to local opinion that sailors pissing off bowsprits pay to the wind.

Thus was compromise born. Bonanza Jellybean agreed that Professor Nelsen and the whooper warden from Aransas could visit Siwash Lake twice each week to monitor the cranes. In return, the Assistant Undersecretary would see to it that low-flying aircraft were not allowed over the Rubber Rose. Moreover, he would seek the cooperation of surrounding landowners and the sheriff's department in keeping crowds of the curious away.

(Before the ban on aircraft was enforced, however, each major network filmed aerial footage of Siwash Lake and the cranes thereon. The sight of that pert pond, ringed round with cattail, reed and arrowhead, reflecting sweetly plump hills as a Tantric's eye might reflect his goddess's boobs, caused Sissy to squirm before the TV screen, as if being boiled by her own deep fires.)

Publicly, at least, the government was taking this position: the cowgirls seem to be innocent of any overt wrongdoing so far as the whoopers are concerned. The women admit to feeding the birds, but without apparent intention of interfering with their natural habits. Certainly they haven't tried to exploit the cranes in any way. The fact that they withheld information on the whoopers' whereabouts, and the fact that they fired upon federal agents, is suspicious, and in the latter case might result in charges' being filed, but for the time being, in light of the birds' multiplication and the fact that certain compromises have been reached, the ladies of the Rubber Rose would be extended courtesies and benefits of doubt.

Things went well enough for a week. Then Professor Inge Anne Nelsen requested permission — reluctantly, she professed — to kill a crane. Said she, "The birds' behavior is so atypical, their psychology altered so drastically and, I might add, suddenly, that I can only hypothesize that they are being drugged — unintentionally or otherwise. Ms. Jellybean has refused to allow us to inspect the feed with which they supplement the cranes' natural diet. Therefore, the only recourse is to perform an autopsy on a dead bird."

"Kill a bird that is on the verge of extinction?" asked the Assistant Undersecretary, and moaned. His ulcer came out of the closet. "Why, we'd be lynched on the steps of the Museum of Natural History." The noose was tightening around his ulcer already. Any last words, ulcer? Yes. *Wahwahwahwahwah!* it screamed.

"Consider this," countered Professor Nelsen. "The cranes didn't migrate to Canada for the summer. Suppose they don't migrate to Texas for the winter? You do know, don't you, Mr. Assistant Undersecretary, what winters are like in this neck of the woods? The flock wouldn't last until Christmas. Better one dead bird than sixty. Sixty is all there is."

"Permission granted."

When the professor attempted to carry out the deed, however, she was accosted by cowgirls. They called her a disgrace to the nurturing traditions of womankind. They threatened to paint a mustache on her and shoot off her nipples.

At this point, the government decided to apply a pound of pressure. What the hell, the President was on the verge of leaving the White House via the fire escape; what else could go wrong? The FBI uncovered that the cowgirls didn't have title to the Rubber Rose. They sought out the rightful owner so as to persuade him to evict the young women and/or grant the government unrestricted trespass, but that person proved to be a cosmetics tycoon who had recently suffered severe head injuries and now spent his hours making eyes at the figures on wallpaper while listening to distant winds whistling down the necks of ethereal Ripple bottles.

The authorities had better luck with their next ploy. It was discovered that the Rubber Rose was operating as an unlicensed dairy, selling quantities of goat milk to a Fargo cheese factory. One day, the very day the President ducked out the back door with socks and stocks exploding from his suitcase, an inspector from the county health department paid a visit to the ranch, noted sixteen violations and shut down the dairy operation. Ouch! Deprived of their sole source of income, the cowgirls, indeed, were pressed.

All this Sissy learned from the media, and if the media did not inform her whether or not Delores had had her third peyote vision, or whether Elaine's urinary troubles had cleared up or whether Debbie had yet reached, via one path or another, the peace that passeth all understanding, still it was a tall measure, and she carried it in her head when she was readmitted to O'Dwyre for her second amputation.

95.

STOP, SISSY! Stop, you can't do it. It's unfair and irresponsible. We appreciate your motives; we realize that your intentions are good; we can even detect a certain bravery behind your intransigence, an ennobling sense of sacrifice there; and God knows we are sensitive to the suffering that has sometimes broken loose to come billowing forth from your appendages like the pungent vapors of whales — often it appears that in this life of experience and accommodation we pay just as dearly for our triumphs as we do for our defeats. But Sissy . . . hold on!

To the extent that this world surrenders its richness and diversity, it surrenders its poetry. To the extent that it relinquishes its capacity to surprise, it relinquishes its magic. To the extent that it loses its ability to tolerate ridiculous and even dangerous exceptions, it loses its grace. As its options (no matter how absurd or unlikely) diminish, so do its chances for the future.

Sissy, the world *needs* those unflattering digits of yours, those dazed balloon snakes, those ruddy zucchini, those exclamation points that end with such force the understated sentences of your arms; needs your thumbs — one gone already! — the way it needs the rhino, the snow leopard, the panda, the wolf and, yes, the whooping crane; the way it needs headhunters and "wild" Indians and real Gypsies in horsedrawn carts; the way it needs some land without access by road or air, land with jumbo forests left on it forever and oil left in the ground to fulfill without interference its fossil destiny; the way it needs drunks and lunatics and old people with filthy habits; the way it needs the mirrors, hallucinations and metamorphoses of art.

Whether you need the solace of normality more than you need your unique powers is a personal matter, which only you may decide. But Sissy, don't let people such as Julian Gitche influence your decision. Julian needs your thumbs, huge and murmuring like the mouths of unexplored rivers—just the way nature made them—even if he isn't wise enough to understand that he needs them.

Never in history have there been thumbs to match yours, neither in size nor in deed. Answer this: what can replace them? Okay, yes, there are the children prophesied by Madame Zoe, but that's a gamble, like Heaven, the Eternity of Joy and the steady-state economy. Sissy, the mastodons are all gone; so are the Amazons. Timbuktu is now a roadside zoo and nobody ever found El Dorado.

Remember how the Chink venerated those biggies? Wouldn't it benefit others of us to do the same? Your thumbs were not metaphors or symbols; they were real. The one that remains, it still sings of the terror and ecstasy of flesh. Your thumb disorientates us, Sissy, and for the person courageous enough to see it out, disorientation always leads to

love.

Don't deprive us of an opportunity to love unselfishly that which, like Christ when he was alive, is difficult to love. Don't spoil our fun.

96.

DINNER was good that night and Dr. Robbins was again amazed by the purple cabbage, its color making him wonder where all the blue food is.

As he was indulging a genteel burp, the telephone rang. "I'll get it," he said, which was odd for he had dined alone. Perhaps he was talking to his mustache.

The caller was Sissy Hankshaw Gitche. Her call was two months late.

"I'm sorry I stood you up."

"Oh, that's all right," Dr. Robbins replied. "I'm cute when I'm mad."

Sissy was phoning from O'Dwyre VA Hospital. Her second surgery was scheduled very early the next morning, so Dr. Dreyfus had had her admitted overnight so that she might get a good night's sleep. People still used that phrase, "a good night's sleep." It was probably a quite old expression, although it seemed to suggest the Eisenhower Years. Before the sixties woke us up.

Cries for help are frequently inaudible. Even when drowning, some people are too shy or embarrassed to yell. There was something Sissy needed to talk about with Dr. Robbins, but she couldn't get it out. So, instead of poking his eardrum with an icicle word such as *amputation,* she found herself asking, "Well, Doctor, what do you think about the whooping cranes?"

"Oh, I'm pro-whooper," said he. "They go well with my blue sky."

"No, what I mean is, how do you account for their tenacity? Why are they holding on like this? I mean, they're out of place in the modern civilized world; if they're going to refuse to attempt to adapt to changed conditions, wouldn't it make more sense just to go ahead and go extinct and avoid the hassles and suffering? What are they trying to prove?"

"Maybe," said Dr. Robbins very slowly, "maybe they're waiting for us to go away."

97.

WHEN THE SURGEONS, their blades grinning like piranha in their cases, dropped in for a preliminary examination next morning, Sissy surprised them. "Just go ahead and polli . . . polli . . . polli wanta cracker my right index finger," said she. "I think I'm going to live with my left thumb for a while."

The brother-in-law was vexed, but Dr. Dreyfus understood: "As the sculptor Alexander Calder answered when asked if he'd be willing to make a mobile for the Guggenheim Museum out of solid gold, 'Sure, why not? And then I'll paint it black.' But I don't suppose that means very much to you."

Shortening the finger bone, moving it over, increasing its angle, was tedious precision work, requiring intense concentration, yet throughout the pollicerization the surgeons were aware of the singing of birds.

After the operation, an incision was made in the patient's abdomen and her new quasi-thumb sewn into it to begin the grafting process. The next day, when Dr. Dreyfus entered her hospital room, he found Sissy standing before a full-length mirror in only bikini panties, having a thorough look at herself.

"Well, what do you think?" asked the plastic surgeon, artist and three-million-dollar defendant.

"Criminey," said Sissy. "Looks like I was in such a hurry to masturbate I missed the hole by a foot."

98.

LET'S END this gossip once and for all: Richmond, Virginia, is not in love with England, no baby is expected, no wedding in sight. For its part, the internationally renowned England scarcely is aware of Richmond, Virginia's existence, and furthermore, has a Richmond of it's own living under its roof in North Surrey. As for prosperous, conservative, up-and-coming Richmond, Virginia, what it feels for England — many years its senior — is not romantic passion but envy. It admires England's centuries of respectability and wishes they were its own. It longs to wear England's knickers, not get in them. Remember, you read it here first.

One way in which Richmond demonstrates its admiration and envy is through imitation (Don't we all?). For example, Richmond has reproduced tons of English architecture and left it out in the weather, permitting it to be occupied by persons whose accents would drive a proper Englishman to stuff his ears with hasty pudding. In the West End, the most popular house style is the enlarged version of the traditional English cottage, with old beams and storybook roofs, but usually luxurized by such non-Anglo features as swimming pools, patios and porches enclosed with thermal glass.

It was in just such a posh cottage that Sissy waited for her new thumb to come out of the oven.

Meanwhile, she took refreshed delight in the old thumb, the monstrous left one, the one that broke the bank at Monte Weirdo. Sissy oiled it and perfumed it, sunned it and fanned it, flexed it and rotated it, made awful ovoid shadows with it on ceilings and walls, aimed it at stars and planets, let it splash in the tub, rolled it over her erogenous zones, flashed it at imaginary speeders on the Highways of the Heart and talked over old times with it. It was like a second honeymoon. The only occasion when the reconciliated appendage failed to thrill and cheer her was when she thought of it smacking skulls. Then she would shudder like the sanitation man who had to collect the garbage at Frankenstein's castle.

Mostly, though, Sissy carried the left thumb around grandly, a sight that befuddled Margaret Dreyfus, caused Felix Dreyfus to smile. Their reactions mattered little, however, because when Sissy wasn't absorbed with her thumbs — little new one baking, big old one basking — she was equally absorbed with following the whooping crane story in the news.

99.

ONE PRAIRIE NIGHT when the sky looked like a bowl of cream of moon soup, stirred by the long ladle of the wind, the vehicle known to the cowgirls as "the peyote wagon" and to the press as "the reptile-decorated camper" pulled out of the Rubber Rose and didn't return. Delores del Ruby was at the wheel. The media speculated that the departure of the "black-garbed, whip-cracking second-in-command" was significant, perhaps an indication that there was dissension at the "mystery ranch."

For the next few days, reporters watched for signs of disharmony, but as far as they could tell through their binoculars, and in occasional conversations with taciturn guards at the gate, solidarity prevailed. Indeed, the pardners were attempting to enjoy cowgirl life just as if the National Eye never interrupted its scrutiny of the new President in order to blink at them. To the director of the Aransas Wildlife Refuge, who observed them riding, roping, skinnydipping and flying Tibetan tantra kites, they had "every appearance of young girls on a lark."

In their bunkhouse meetings, however, a certain sobriety overtook their giggles, and as they cleaned firearms and analyzed their situation, no one would have mistaken them for Girl Scouts. Vivid and vulgar curses left their lips, directed at the elements that parched their vegetable garden one week, flooded it the next.

"The prairie gods were never friendly to agriculture," Debbie reminded her companions. "They were more into buffalo."

Big Red wasn't placated. "We don't have beans *or* buffalo," she complained.

"The goats are our buffalo," said Debbie. "As long as we got them we got milk, yogurt and cheese."

"We got milk, yogurt and cheese," agreed Jellybean, "but we aren't gonna have any Crosby, Stills and Nash — not when the power company cuts our electricity off, we aren't. So those of you that favor the stereo over my old Gibson, why don't you volunteer to work on the windmill this afternoon, even if this is a Sunday?"

"I must observe the Sabbath and keep it holy," objected Mary.

"Okay, Mary," said Jelly, "you can spend the afternoon praying for those podners who are out working their butts off. By the way, Billy West is giving us the windmill materials free of charge, bless his heart, bless all three hundred pounds of him; he told me this morning that he isn't gonna charge us. So what you say we get in high gear and get that baby built. Any questions?"

"Yes," said Heather, "What if every podner on the ranch wore one of those beanies with the little plastic propeller on top? The way the wind blows around here, would that generate enough extra electricity so's I could send away for a vibrator?"

"Vibrators run on batteries, honey," said Jelly, feeling guilty, perhaps, about her weekly yam sessions with the Chink. "Meeting adjourned."

A crew of cowgirls set out to build the windmill, singing as they worked. The official observers of the ranch found nothing alarming in that construction. But a short time later, the girls undertook some further building, the implications of which were to bring things squawling to a head at the Rubber Rose.

Oh yeah . . . Sissy, back there in Virginia listening to the news, Sissy guessed correctly where Delores had gone. The forewoman was off to New Mexico on a peyote run.

100.

WELL, here we are at Chapter 100. This calls for a little celebration. I am an author and therefore in the same business God is in: if I say this page is a bottle of champagne, it is a bottle of champagne. Reader, will you share a cup of the bubbly with me? You prefer French to domestic? Okay, I'll make it French. Cheers!

Here's to the one hundredth chapter! Hundred. A cardinal number, ten times ten, the position of the third digit to the left of the decimal point, a power number signifying weight, wealth and importance. The symbol for hundred is C, which is also the symbol for the speed of light. There are a hundred pennies in a dollar, a hundred centimeters in a meter, a hundred years in a century, a hundred yards on a football field, a hundred points in a carat, a hundred ways to skin a cat and a hundred ways of cooking eggplant. There also are a hundred ways to successfully write a novel, but this is probably not one of them.

Don't be so quick to agree. *Even Cowgirls Get the Blues* can still teach you a thing or two. "For example?" you ask snottily, while helping yourself to my champagne. For example, this: on a number of occasions this book has made reference to magic, and each time you've shaken your head, muttering such criticisms as "What does he mean by 'magic,' anyhow? It's embarrassing to find a grown man talking about magic in such a manner. How can anybody take him seriously?" Or, as slightly more gracious readers have objected, "Doesn't the author realize that one can't write about magic? One can create it but not discuss it. It's much too gossamer for that. Magic can be neither described nor defined. Using words to describe magic is like using a screwdriver to slice roast beef."

To which the author now replies, Sorry, freeloaders, you're clever but you're not quite correct. Magic isn't the fuzzy, fragile, abstract and ephemeral quality you think it is. In fact, magic is distinguished from mysticism by its very concreteness and practicality. Whereas mysticism is manifest only in spiritual essence, in the transcendental state, magic demands a steady naturalistic base. Mysticism reveals the ethereal in the tangible. Magic makes something permanent out of the transitory, coaxes drama from the colloquial.

All right, I'll try to expound, if you insist. And just to prove I'm no sorehead, I'll conjure up another magnum of Dom Perignon. Here. Say when. Mysticism is self-contained and beyond external control. Something either has a mystic emanation or it doesn't. It is present in a single entity, animate or inanimate, where it is known to those who have faith that it is there. Mysticism implies belief in forces, influences and actions, which, though imperceptible to ordinary sense, are nevertheless real.

Magic, on the other hand, can be controlled — by a magician. A magician is a transmitter just as a mystic is rather strictly a receiver. Just as love can be *made,* using materials no more ethereal than an erect penis, a moist vagina and a warm heart, so, too, can magic be *made,* wholly and willfully, from the most obvious and mundane. Magic does not seep from within of its own volition (or appear unannounced to someone in a state of heightened awareness); it is a matter of cause and effect. The seemingly unrealistic or supernatural ("magic") act occurs through *the acting of one thing upon another through a secret link.*

The key word here is *secret.* When the substance of the link is revealed, the magic fades or can be counteracted by rival magicians. Thus, *Even Cowgirls Get the Blues* may call your attention to some magic that results from, say, the acting of the smells of the female body upon the last surviving flock of wild whooping cranes, but it may never give away the secret link between them.

Hmm. The author can sense that Chaper 100 displeases you. Not only does it interrupt the story, it says too much and says it too didactically. Well, a book about a woman with sugar-sack thumbs is bound to be a bit heavy-handed.

Come on, now, that's enough champagne. Either give me a kiss or get out of here.

101.

EXPRESSIONS such as "chord factors," "frequency patterns," "strut lengths" and "A. B. S. plastic joints" began to be heard on the shores of Siwash Lake, where heretofore only the radio signals of froggies, excerpts from Chinese Crane Opera and an occasional girlish "yahoo" or "yippee" had been heard. In addition, there now were the chewing noises of hungry saws and the spock-spock of hammers taking the direct approach in trying to teach some impressionable young nails about the dangers inherent in a permissive society, spock-spock-spock.

On their next regular visit to the lake, Professor Inge Anne Nelsen and the Aransas Wildlife Refuge director were stunned by all this activity taking place practically in the midst of the whooping cranes. They made immediate inquiries.

"We're building a dome," answered Bonanza Jellybean.

"A dome?"

"Not just any old dome. A four-frequency, hemispheric, geodesic, *arctic* dome, triple-glazed against the cold. Of course, the very shape of a dome is a defense against cold. A mean mad icesnake of a wind will tend to glide over its rounded surface instead of picking up velocity in an exterior corner where on a rectilinear building it would be tempted to wiggle its way inside. The Eskimos knew that. There's also less surface area through which heat can be lost . . ."

"Aw, hell, Jelly, that ain't important," interjected Big Red. "Most of your heat loss takes place through doors and windows, anyways. Since we're only gonna have one good-sized door and a couple of little bitty windows, that won't worry us a whole hell of a heap. But we're triple-glazing the bastard, like Jelly said. It's gonna be a real arctic-type dome."

"Just like Santa Claus lives in, right, Red?" said Kym.

"Haw haw," Big Red laughed.

A foundation of 2 x 8 joists atop eight-foot beams had already been laid, and from its circumference the government observers could ascertain that the dome was going to be quite large. They were incredulous. "What is it for?" asked the man from Aransas. "Why are you building it so close to the lake?" asked Professor Nelsen.

"For the cranes," Jelly informed them.

"For the cranes??!" Their incredulousness became triple-glazed.

"Sure. It's almost the end of August, you know. Come winter, these birds are gonna need some shelter. On clear, calm days we'll break the ice for them and they can fart around in the lake. But when the blizzards and the big winds hit, they'll need shelter. This dome is gonna be their winter quarters."

"Impossible," gasped the Aransas warden. "They'll never bunch up in there, so close together, with a roof over their heads." As he looked around at the birds, however, so unusually serene in the vicinity of humans, and with only ten yards or so separating one crane family from the next, he was not so sure.

"This means," asked Professor Nelsen, pointedly, "that you don't expect them to migrate to their Texas wintering grounds?"

"Can't see as why they should," said Jellybean.

"Well, I can see many reasons why they should," stormed Professor Nelsen. Her hands were on her hips, as in the statue of the Ill-Tempered Red-Headed Scorpio Madonna. "Including their well-being and survival. You actually believe you're going to stick this flock of wild whooping cranes in some crazy building . . ."

"Not so crazy, ma'am," said Debbie, who had stopped sawing struts in order to wipe her sweaty brow with a Katmandu prayer cloth. "No, not crazy in the least. This is a *round* building; it's square buildings that are crazy. Drinks Water, a Dakota medicine man, had a vision back before the whites came that his tribe would be defeated and made to live in square houses. When this came true, the Dakota tribes were miserable. Black Elk complained that it was a bad way to live. 'There can be no power in a square,' he said. Black Elk said, 'You will notice that everything an Indian does is in a circle, and that is because the Power of the World always works in circles, and everything tries to be round.' You're a zoologist; you should know that there are no squares in Nature, not in macrocosm nor microcosm. Nature creates in circles and moves in circles. Atoms and galaxies are circular, and most organic things in between. The Earth is round. The wind whirls. The womb is no shoebox. Where are the corners of the egg and the sky? Look at the nests those cranes made over there. Perfectly round. The square is the product of logic and rationality. It was invented by civilized man. It's the work of masculine consciousness. Primitive tribes and matriarchal cultures always paid homage to what is round. Look at your belly, Professor, there under your girdle. Look at your tits. Woman is a round animal. The male, in his rebellion against what is natural and feminine in the universe, has used logic as a weapon and as a shield. The whole object of logic is to square the circle. Civilization is a circle squared. That's why in civilized societies woman's lot — and Nature's lot — has been such a sorry one. It's the duty of advanced women to teach men to love the circle again. No, ma'am, this won't be a crazy building; it'll be a sane one. Unless you're silly enough to identify rational logic with sanity. In which case, this structure — and everything else we do — will be as crazy as we can make it. The cranes won't mind taking shelter in our dome. It's a round building made by round animals. Yippee!"

Professor Nelsen and associate hurried back to Mottburg to report. A conference was held, in the middle of which phone calls were made to Washington, D.C. Late that afternoon, a federal judge (seated at a square table in a square chamber) issued an order. By sundown, it had been delivered to the Rubber Rose.

The court order called for the cowgirls to cease construction on the dome. It ordered them to move their equipment and themselves away from the lake, to remove guards and barricades from the gates and to make the ranch ready for unrestricted occupancy by government personnel, who would then take whatever steps necessary to restore normal conditions among the population of America's whooping cranes. The cowgirls were given forty-eight hours in which to comply.

102.

THE TUBE PEDICLE — the cylindrical flap of belly skin under which Sissy's pollicerized index finger lay three weeks a-grafting — was snipped at one end, and ta-ta-ta-ta-ta-dum! — a thumb is born!

Along came a thumb, but what kind of a thumb? Crooked and red (a thumb to greet flamingos, not whooping cranes), awkward and stiff, as scrawny as its predecessor had been gross. Sissy was exercising this petrified strawberry licorice whip, trying to teach it some simple thumb routines, when the news of the Rubber Rose court order was announced on NBC.

Sissy stood, little scarlet thumbkin dangling rigidly at her side. "How fast do you think I could get to the Dakota hills?" she asked.

Dr. Dreyfus looked up from the pad on which he was sketching thumbs in the manner of Seurat, dreaming, perhaps, of the first living Pointillist digit. "By hitchhiking, you mean? Well, you certainly couldn't make it within forty-eight hours."

"Ha ha ho ho and hee hee," said Sissy, and it was difficult to argue with that.

103.

SOME PEOPLE could not have been more stupefied had archeologists dug up a dinosaur wearing a flea collar. Some drivers thought that the tadpole that conquered Atlantis had escaped from a drive-in movie screen and was making its way to the sea. Others recognized it as a thumb, maybe the ultimate thumb, and accepted it with the same bewildered fatalism with which they accepted tornados and government.

Here it came, there it went, exerting a force with which few could cope, playing with speeding automobiles the way pre-Friskies cats had played with mice. It put new life in old clunkers and caused late model dreamboats to poot like go-carts. One flick of it and radios would blare on automatically, headlights would glaze over as if in shock. It could reach across four lanes of heavy traffic and draw the vehicle of its choice to its side. It could even cause cars that had passed it by to suddenly make illegal U-turns and circle back two miles to obey its wishes. It was Sissy's left thumb, getting its big chance at last, after more than a decade of understudying the right — and a lump inflated in the throat of Creation just to watch it do its stuff. Aw, well, maybe that's exaggerating, but honestly, had anybody ever been as good at anything as Sissy Hankshaw Gitche was at hitching?

There were favorite maneuvers to bring back and enjoy, and a few fresh tactics she wanted to try: in her mind's eye she conceived of intricate patterns that she would like to have weaved over the continent. Alas, she had set a deadline for herself: the Dakota hills in thirty hours. So, although she showed off and experimented more than she should have on a speed run, she actually stopped only once — at a telephone booth in western Pennsylvania.

Her intentions had been to call Julian. She was going to tell him of her compulsion to rush to the Rubber Rose, of the inexplicable longing she had to stand by the cowgirls in their time of crisis, and how she just had to see the Chink again to find out why the clockworks continued to beat so loudly in her blood. She would promise Julian that when she had done what she must do in Dakota, she'd hurry back and rest her new normal-sized thumb against his buzzer. After all, Julian needed her. As she was about to place the call, however, she thought, "Yes, Julian needs me. But I need me, too. And the world needs my need for me worse than it needs Julian's need for me." She called Dr. Robbins instead.

Dr. Robbins didn't answer. Neither did his mustache. They were both across town at the Countess's penthouse. When Robbins had read in one of the whooping crane stories in the *Times* that the Countess owned the Rubber Rose, the ranch adjacent to Siwash Ridge, he had called on the feminine hygiene magnate, and, having been informed of the state the poor fellow was in, volunteered his psychiatric services free of charge. The Countess's accountants accepted the offer, and from that day Dr. Robbins had scarcely left the Countess's side. At the instant of Sissy's call, in fact, Robbins and the Countess were propped up on satin pillows, playing cribbage and drinking Ripple. The young shrink was teasing the middle-aged tycoon about the damage his brain had taken from Sissy's thumbing, and the Countess was laughing good-naturedly. The Countess was also winning at cribbage.

Reminding the Countess of Murphy's Law, which states that if anything can go wrong, it will, the unlicensed psychiatrist then introduced him to Robbins's Law, which states that whatever goes wrong can be used to your advantage, providing it goes wrong enough. The Countess laughed some more and increased his lead. The phone that was ringing was a long way from here.

Sissy hung up and kept traveling.

While Sissy was still on the road, some eight hours before their court-ordered deadline expired, the Rubber Rose cowgirls issued a communiqué. It was sent to the federal judge, copies to the press. This is what it said:

> The whooping crane has been driven to the edge of extinction by an aggressive, brutal paternalistic system intent on subduing the Earth and establishing its dominion over all things — in the name of God the Father, law, order and economic progress. From men, the whooping crane has received neither love nor respect. Men have drained the crane's marshes, stolen its eggs, invaded its privacy, polluted its food, fouled its air, blown it apart with buckshot. Obviously, a paternalistic society does not deserve anything as grand and beautiful and wild and free as the whooping crane. You men have failed in your duty to the crane. Now it is women's turn. The cranes are in our charge, now. We will protect them as long as they still require protection — while working toward a day when the creatures of the world no longer have to suffer man's egoism, insensitivity and greed. We refuse your order. We say take your order and shove it. This flock of birds is staying with us. Get lost, mac.

Needless to say, all the hands did not agree on the text of this communiqué. Debbie, for example, thought the communiqué itself aggressive; she said it reeked of the same hostile sexism that the pardners disliked in men. She lobbied for a more enlightened resolution, one firm yet gentle; she said they should set a good example. Debbie was not alone. As for Bonanza Jellybean, she thought it pretentious to claim that she was working toward a day when the creatures of the world would be safe from man, when actually all she was working toward was a time when any little daughter who wanted to could grow up to be a cowgirl.

Had the Rubber Rose been organized as an anarchistic system, rather than along democratic lines, each cowgirl who chose to do so could have issued her own communiqué, each with equal weight. "Majority rule" held sway, however, and the communiqué — drafted mainly by the Delores del Ruby faction — was presented to the court, the press and the public as the collective opinion of "the whooping crane rustlers."

And the communiqué was not taken lightly. No, it decidedly was not taken lightly. Sissy made it through the gates of the Rubber Rose only minutes before Delores was arrested entering Mottburg with nearly a thousand peyote buttons in her truck — and only hours before two hundred federal marshals, reinforced by at least a dozen agents of the FBI, took positions outside the ranch, loaded guns trained on anything that shook feather, hoof or tit inside the kinetic confines of the largest all-girl ranch in the West.

Part VI

To live outside the law you must be honest.

— Bob Dylan

104.

THERE IS an unearthly glow. It comes from a dimension that we do not understand yet.

Meeting in this supernatural aurora are two animate things. Growing accustomed to the light that is the substance of this "landscape," we recognize one of the things as a human brain. The other proves to be a thumb.

The Brain rests placidly. The Thumb, which has only recently appeared on the scene, gives us an opposite feeling. It appears agitated.

"Why so glum, chum?" asks the Brain.

"I thought you'd never ask," snaps the Thumb. "I'm just sick and tired of it, that's all."

"Sick and tired of what?"

"Taking the blame. Being called 'the cornerstone of civilization.' Being treated by one kooky author as if I were a goddamned *metaphor* for civilization. I had nothing to do with it."

"Well, now, I wouldn't go so far as to say that. The civilizing process occurred as a result of advances in technology. Until man had tools, tools to save him labor as well as to give him the predatory edge over other animals, he hadn't the leisure to develop language or to refine his psychic and physical capabilities. You, Thumb, gave man the ability to use tools. If nothing else, you started him down the path to civilization. And were you not with him, helping him, every step of the way?"

"Yeah, I was, but I was innocent. I had no control. I wanted to help him lift shiny pebbles, to pick fruit, to hold flowers, to build bowls and baskets, to make music, to weave; I wanted to help him remove slivers and to caress the flesh of loved ones. I didn't want any part of that other stuff: that hardware, that killing and maiming, that overdevelopment, that subjugation of Nature and attempts to build monuments against death. I didn't want any of it, but I contributed to it because you made me do it, you prick!"

The Brain issues a short scornful laugh that undulates its folds. "The Prick had a lot to do with civilization, all right, but you'll have to take that up with the Prick. I'm the Brain. Remember?"

"How could anyone forget?"

"Nasty, nasty." The Brain wags its stem. "You're behaving rather irrationally, aren't you? Are you really blaming *me* for civilization?"

"Precisely. That ugly crumpled upper surface of yours, that cerebral cortex, is almost nonexistent in lower animals, but once you got the hang of evolutionary growth and a taste of the inflated abstract thoughts you could make with that cortex, you enlarged it and enlarged it until it became eighty percent of your volume. Then you started cranking out rarefied ideas as fast as you could crank them, and issuing commands to helpless appendages like me, forcing us to act on those ideas, to give them form. Out of that came civilization. You willed it into being because, with your cortex so oversized and all, you lost your common ground with other animals, and especially with plants; lost contact, became alienated and ordered civilization built in compensation. And there was nothing the rest of us could do about it. You were holed up in there in your solid bone fortress, a cerebrospinal moat around you, using up twenty percent of the body's oxygen supply and hogging a disproportionate share of nutriments, you greedy bastard; you had hold of the muscle motor switches and there was no way any of us could get at you and stop you from spoiling the delight of the world." The Thumb's nail was crimson with anger.

Slowly shaking its configuration of deep crevices and wide protrusions, the Brain sighed. "Yes, yes, there is some truth in what you say. I *am* the body's favored organ, but that's because my work load is so heavy and so vital. And I contributed enormously to civilization, as did you. It couldn't have happened without me, as it couldn't have happened without you. But I was just as innocent as you . . ."

"How could you be? You expressed the desires, you formulated the models, you issued the orders, you were in command."

Once again, the Brain sighed. It was the sort of sigh one might expect from a fat and rather affected grub: gray and wet and yukky. "You don't understand me, do you? You think you know me — all that semieducated blather about cerebral cortex evolution — but you don't really know me. Oh, I'm sure you're aware that I've an electrochemical network of thirteen billion nerve cells, and maybe you realize that in some of my nooks and crannies — you're fortunate to be smooth and holistic — these cell bodies are so densely packed that a hundred million fit into a cubic inch, every cottonpicking one of them humming, pulsing and flashing, and none of them exactly alike; yes, you may know that but you can never really know how hard it is to be electrochemical, to be, and I'm not boasting, the most intricate and effective thing in Nature . . ."

The Thumb gestures as if it were bowing a violin. "That's the saddest story I've ever heard," it says sarcastically.

"I'm not seeking your sympathy; just your understanding. Bear with me, and if I digress, remember, I'm not as tightly focused as you. Now, listen. There is a constant shower of incoming electrical pulses hammering at me like rain on a tropical roof. I'm subjected to a never-ending barrage of signals that cause my nerve cells — neurons, if you will — to fire in succession, like Chinatown firecrackers. During each of these pulsations, electrical charges are altered, chemicals are expelled, clefts are opened and closed, ions desert one neuron and invade another; it's unbelievably complicated, and the whole cycle takes place in about a thousandth of a second. A thousandth of a second — and man thinks he has a conception of time. Ha!"

"If I was the Mouth, I'd yawn," says the Thumb. "Get to the point before you bore me stiff."

"And nobody likes a stiff thumb, does he," teases the Brain. "Well, the point partially is this: the information that activates me, that sets my neurons to firing in chain reaction, is sensory and is sent to me by other parts of the body, including *you*. How I react to the external world is partly a result of the kind of data *you* send me as you go around touching our environment."

"This is getting specious," objects the Thumb. "In the first place, the data I give you are completely objective. I can tell you if a blade is sharp, but I can't advise you to have it stuck into another body (I never would) — and in the second place, you get such an infinitely greater supply of info from the Eyes, for example, that there's no comparison."

"Maybe not," agrees the Brain, "but you do contribute. And my point is, the commands I give you and the rest of the body are largely my natural reactions to the sensory stuff you're always feeding me. Largely. But not wholly. Because the truth is, my neurons occasionally fire spontaneously in the absence of a stimulating signal. I'm subjected to a fair amount of randomly generating currents. It isn't as orderly in here as you might imagine. Often I'm at the mercy of random forces."

In the eerie light of the indefinable dimension, the Thumb twiddles. At last, it says, "You're trying to tell me you aren't in control."

"Exactly! Jeeze, I thought you'd never catch on."

"Well, if you aren't in charge, what is?"

"I don't know," says the Brain, softly, solemnly. The blob seems genuinely sad.

"Oh come off it. Those thirteen billion cells that are cooking in you, you make use of no more than ten percent of them. Ninety percent of your resources lies dormant at all times. If you'd just bother to put that awesome mass to work, if you'd quit being so damn conservative — Christ, it's no wonder you're gray! — and stop worrying about survival all the time; if you'd start sifting through those vast regions of your slimy self that haven't been explored, then you'd find out rather quickly where Central Control is located, I'll bet, and you'd find the answers to the philosophical and spiritual questions that are driving you — and the rest of us — bananas, and that because they've been answered *wrongly* (by that ten percent of you that makes an effort) have fostered the worst features of civilization. You're holding out, that's all."

"Thumb, old buddy, you don't know the Ass from the Elbow. Sure, I'm a bit conservative; I have to be. It's my assignment to preserve and perpetuate the species . . ."

"Assignment from *whom*?"

"From the DNA, of course. But don't ask me from where the DNA gets *its* orders, because I honestly don't know. But the reason I don't know has nothing to do with the fact that about ninety percent of me is dormant. It's dormant because I inhibit it, and I inhibit it because if I didn't I would be swamped by insignificant information. I'd be reacting to so many signals from the external world that I couldn't think at all, and every time humans opened their eyes, they'd have something like an epileptic fit. You see, there is nothing in that dormant portion that isn't already in the rest of me. Just more of it, that's all. More of the same. There're no answers to the Great Mysteries hidden in there, no secret superior systems for evaluating experience; it's quantitative, not qualitative. I narrow the flow of input to keep us from being drowned in excitations, that's all."

After that, the Thumb twiddles for a long time. "Then it's hopeless," it says finally.

"What do you mean?"

"Well, if you don't have the answers to the Big Question and don't know who does, if you aren't in control and don't know who is, then we're right back where we started, and it's bloody hopeless; we'll never know What's What, and we'll never figure out how to overhaul civilization."

"Don't despair. It's bad form." Synaptic disturbances cause the Brain to vibrate gently. It resembles the gelatin salad at a banquet for trolls. "I suspect there may be other possibilities. You see, I'm a tool, of sorts, an instrument, an apparatus just as you are. I can be employed. Employed for thinking. Well, mostly I've been used clumsily and all too sparingly. Not that humans haven't thought deep thoughts with me; they have and they continue to. There are probably no deeper, greater thoughts left in me; the best of them have all been thought and rethought many times. But maybe what is needed is not more thinking or even better thinking, but a different kind of thinking. Over the centuries a handful of humans — poets, madmen, artists, monks, hermits, composers, yogis, shamans, eccentrics, magicians, anarchists, witches and rare bizarre subculturites such as the Gnostics and the Sierra Clock People — have used my thinking machinery in unusual and unpredictable ways, with interesting results. Perhaps if more of these 'off-beat' kinds of thinking were done, I might be more useful to the Universe."

"Hmm," murmurs the Thumb.

"And look here. I spend nearly as much time dreaming as I do thinking. Yet how many put their dreams to any kind of practical or enlightening application? Precious few, I'll tell you. Sleeping/dreaming may be what I do best. It may be my true vocation, and the time I have to spend tending to survival just chore time; taking out the garbage, as it were."

The Thumb seems amazed. "You know, Brain, what blows me is that you know yourself and don't know yourself at the same time, and you know yourself knowing yourself and you know yourself not knowing — oh, this is getting ridiculous."

"It's the old paradox," says the Brain, smiling with its many cracks and fissures.

"But what is the paradoxical force that lets you do that?" asks the Thumb. "What is it that permits you to think about thinking and feel about feeling?"

"Consciousness."

"Okay all right already. If you have all that consciousness, and consciousness is so almighty powerful, why can't you right things, put them in balance . . ."

"Because, dear Thumbo, I don't have 'all that' consciousness. I have a fair amount. But I certainly haven't a monopoly on it. Everybody assumes consciousness is the exclusive province of the Brain. What a mistake! I've got my share of it, to be sure, but hardly enough to claim special privileges. The Knee has consciousness and the Thigh has consciousness. Consciousness is in the Liver, in the Tongue, in the Prick, in *you,* Thumb. It's coursing through you, too, and you're acting it out. You're each a part of it. In addition, there is consciousness in butterflies and plants and winds and waters. There is no Central Control! It's everywhere. So, if consciousness is what is required . . ."

"I'm beginning to comprehend," says the Thumb.

Lo! the moment the Thumb recognizes itself as an agency of consciousness, various pieces of the Puzzle begin to fall into place for it, and though the picture they form makes little logical or literal sense, there is a correct and beautiful feeling about it. "Wow!" cries the Thumb. "Everything seems much brighter and righter. If only the other parts of the body realized that they are manifestations of absolute consciousness, then . . ."

"Maybe we can wake them up," suggests the Brain. "Only we must do it slowly, gradually, so it doesn't threaten survival."

The Thumb ignores the Brain's cautious qualifications. "Let's try to wake them up," it says, eagerly. "Let's try. Where's the Prick?"

"Uh, probably over bullying the Cunt around, as usual. Shall we look?"

In the realm of body light, there is movement, and that is the extent that can be said about it because nothing else can be said.

105.

THE RADIO was playing "The Day-Old Apple Strudel Polka." Kym was carrying the radio across the corral. She carried the radio as if it were a suitcase full of skunk lice. It was offensive baggage but Kym wasn't about to set it down. At any moment the song might end and the announcer say something about the siege of the Rubber Rose.

"Man, this is the stupidest music I've ever heard," said Kym. "This radio should have stayed in the privy where it belonged." But Kym roped the radio to her saddle horn and prepared to give it a ride across the Dakota hills, mice, meadowlarks and other auditorily sensitive creatures fleeing before it in the sunlight.

Kym was taking the radio to Siwash Lake. Hours earlier, the cowgirls had deserted the ranch buildings and withdrawn to the pond. There, where the rippling wheatgrass merged with marsh reeds, they had set up their barricades and prepared to make their stand. Except for Debbie, each of them was armed; except for Big Red, each of them was scared shitless; without exception, each of them was determined. At their backs were the last sixty whooping cranes left on Earth.

The deadline was up. The American Civil Liberties Union had requested an extension, which news commentators felt would be granted since the government, while it could not allow itself to be defied, was not longing for the kind of publicity that would follow another shootout. The government was aware that its marshals and agents were all too willing to uncork the bottle of blood. The government was not entirely sure its marshals and agents could be restrained. The government pondered the predicament; the marshals and agents throbbed with the lunatic lust of the law; the cowgirls dispatched Kym back to the outhouse for their radio so that they might tune in their fate.

In the outhouse, Kym found Sissy, peeing in polka time. Sissy had hitched up to the ranch with a TV crew and, in the midst of some confusion, had simply scrambled over the gate. Howdy.

Kym hugged Sissy so hard she didn't have to wipe herself.

"You know what you're getting into if you come over to the lake," warned Kym.

"Yes," said Sissy, "but I want to be there. I want to see Jellybean. I want to see the cranes."

"Okay," Kym agreed. "I'll go tell Jelly you're here. If she says it's all right, I'll bring a horse for you. Meanwhile, I'd stay in the privy if I were you. No telling when those goons might start something. Ta ta."

For nearly an hour, Sissy waited in the outhouse. A couple of flies and the photograph of Dale Evans kept her company. The flies kept trying to get familiar, but the photo of Dale Evans, like the bust of Nefertiti, was content to rule over its little niche of eternity. The photo of Dale Evans made America 1945 seem like ancient Egypt.

The outhouse was warm and rather dim. Sissy might have dozed except for the noise at the gates. The marshals and agents were forcibly ejecting persistent journalists, cowgirl sympathizers and bird-lovers, removing them to the checkpoint two miles down the road. The marshals and agents were deploying themselves militaristically. The noise at the gates sounded like Cecil B. DeMille's garage sale.

Sissy was not overly curious about the activity at the gates. Had she ignored Kym's warning and stepped outside, she would have looked not to the gates but to Siwash Ridge, hoping for a glance of a dirty bathrobe. We are what we see. We see what we choose. Perceptions are a hypothesis. In a noted experiment at MIT, a scientist outfitted two men with prismatic spectacles that grossly distorted their vision. One man was assigned to walk around, pushing the other in a wheelchair. The man who was active swiftly adapted to his new view of the world, but his passive partner made no adjustment at all. From this, the MIT scientist concluded that in order to perceive an object properly we have to establish some kind of pattern of movement in relation to it. Because Sissy had perceived the events of her lifetime always in relation to her pattern of constant movement, perhaps hers had been a far truer vision than many assumed. Maybe the fact that she would have looked at the crazy old coot on the ridgetop instead of at the besieging forces mounting around her is indicative of . . . well, maybe there is a lesson there.

At any rate, a cowgirl on horseback trotted up to the privy, and it was Heather this time, leading an extra steed. Heather helped Sissy into the saddle and they set out at a brisk trot. The hills received them. With its skinny million tongues of wheatgrass, the hills whispered to them the secrets it used to share with the buffalo. Like defeated prize fighters waking up after knockouts, asters were starting to open their violet lids all around them. Would prismatic spectacles have made any difference in the way the asters perceived September?

Swimming through grasses and flowers, the horses carried the two women to the crest of the hill overlooking the lake. From there, Sissy gazed on strange sights. The circular foundation of the aborted dome had been turned into a fort. Barricades of barrels and rusty reducing machines stood ready to perform grim services. Gun metal reflected the sun. Off to one side were hobbled horses and a few goats, chained. The rest of the goats had been left to wander, and even now some of them were grazing their way eastward across the prairie, perhaps heading for Dr. Goldman's clinic to teach psychiatry something about male-female relations. In the lake, and along its soggy shores, whooping cranes strode with primal steps. Although quiet, they seemed as charged with uninsulated electricity as if they had just sprung into life.

"We heard on the radio that the judge has set Delores's bail at fifty thousand dollars," said Heather. "Now she won't be here when we really need her."

Sissy could only nod and stare at the scene below.

As Sissy rode into camp, Kym, Bonanza Jellybean, Debbie, Elaine and Linda danced up to meet her. In homage, they had fashioned fake thumbs for themselves out of willow bark and reeds. At first, they waved these goofy appendages wildly, in unrestrained salute, but their antics lost considerable momentum when — what?! — they noticed that Sissy was only half the monster she once was.

106.

"I KNEW there was something different about you, but the light wasn't good in the privy and I didn't notice what," said Kym.

"I noticed it right away but I didn't know what to say," said Heather, who still didn't know what to say.

"What happened?" asked Linda.

Sissy shrugged. "Just another miracle of modern technology." It would have required still another technological miracle to have removed her eyes from Jelly's.

Before Sissy was completely on the ground, Jelly's tongue was in her mouth. She stumbled out of the stirrup into a wiggly embrace.

"It doesn't matter what happened," squealed Jelly, shaking off one of her own honorary thumbs. "Let's celebrate!"

"That's why I was so long in coming for you," explained Heather. "We had to get a little welcome celebration together."

Behind the barricades, in the center of the dome foundation, a floral display had been arranged. There were pots of tea, cheese sandwiches, honeyed rice balls, marijuana cigarettes and yogurt with fresh cherries on top. A daisy chain was looped over Sissy's left thumb as she was led to Debbie's Tibetan meditation pillow and seated there. Giggles, kisses and tea poured forth.

Facing an imminent battle with federal police, the cowgirls didn't hesitate to party, because, well, Sissy Hankshaw Gitche had returned and a party was only proper.

"Ain't that just like women," growled the ghost of General Custer, peering through the grass.

Yes, oh yes yes yes sweet yes.

Ain't that just like women, indeed.

107.

GHOSTS, because they can walk through walls, have a tendency to generalize. Your author, however, should know better. What should have been said was not "just like women" but "just like some women" or, better, "just like the feminine spirit." All women do not possess the feminine spirit.

Some of the cowgirls, for example, conspicuously refused to join the welcome party. They remained at the barricades, as the cranes can bear witness, shooting ugly glances at those who reveled. What was Sissy to them? A noncowgirl. A goofy-handed freak. An older woman who had starred in advertisements that had told them that their cunts smelled bad. Furthermore, what would the enemy think if through its binoculars it could spy this sipping of tea, this weaving of daisy chains, this puffing of pot? Of course, what the cowgirls couldn't have known was that no enemy was watching them, for every attempt the FBI had made to establish an observation post on Siwash Ridge had met with peculiar disaster (Could the brotherhood of Chink and rock have been responsible?). Between the girls and their adversary was a succession of hills, and in the other direction stretched an open prairie that offered no opportunity for concealment and therefore was of absolutely no use to government.

Ignoring the disdain that her party drew from the barricades, Jelly spooned yogurt and exchanged with Sissy loving expressions. "Looks like every time we get together things are in a mess," she said.

"So be it," said Sissy, who was a trifle giddy from marijuana and affection. "It really looks serious this time, though. All these guns . . ."

"Billy West got most of them for us. Did you ever meet him? Twenty-two years old and weighs three hundred pounds. Born and raised in Mottburg, every ounce of him. All during his childhood he had the suspicion he was being screwed. When he finally figured out who was screwing him, he decided to become an outlaw. Not for revenge but for purity."

"I never met him," said Sissy, doodling her new little red thumb down Jelly's bare arm. "But these guns . . . Are you actually prepared to kill and die for whooping cranes?"

"Hell no," responded Jellybean. "The cranes are wonderful, okay, but I'm not in this for whooping cranes. I'm in it for cowgirls. It's a rotten shame that things can get to the point of killing and dying being acceptable alternatives, but the script sometimes turns out that way. I mean, Sissy, I look around me and everywhere I look I see people, as individuals or in groups, conservative people, liberal people and radical people, who have been left crippled and soiled inside by their years of surrender to authority. If we cowgirls give in to authority on this crane issue, then cowgirls become just another compromise. I want a finer fate than that — for me and for every other cowgirl. Better no cowgirls at all than cowgirls compromised."

"Wow!" exclaimed Linda, who had approached to refill Jelly's teacup. "That's pretty heavy, but I reckon that's the way it is."

Sissy looked pleadingly at both Linda and Jellybean. "But you can't possibly slay this dragon." With her greatest of thumbs, she gestured across the hills, although she might just as accurately have gestured in any other direction.

"Jelly knows that," said Debbie, who had approached to replace Sissy's sandwich. "What she doesn't seem to know is that it isn't our job to slay the dragon. It's traditionally been the work of the hero to slay the dragon. It's the work of the maiden to transform the hero — *and* the dragon. I believe that it's not too late to accomplish such a transformation."

Jelly seemed to have joined the clouds in a vow of silence. "Shit, Debbie," she said, eventually (the clouds stuck to *their* vow). "I can't argue with you. The Chink says I shouldn't even try to argue with you. The Chink says I should follow my heart. And my heart tells me that I can't sit back and let a gang of politicians push cowgirls around."

Noticing that both Jelly and Debbie were collecting tears in their eyes, Sissy asked, "How did this business get started, anyhow? How did you end up with this flock of birds?"

Debbie blew her nose on her embroidered bandanna. "You were aware that we were feeding them weren't you? We fed them brown rice last fall and they stayed over a couple of extra days. This spring we decided to try something different. We mixed our brown rice with fishmeal — whoopers love seafood (minnows and crawdads and little blue crabs), and fishmeal is cheap. Then Delores suggested another ingredient, and we think that's what did the trick."

"You mean . . .?"

"Peyote!" said Debbie and Jelly together.

"Then that professor was right. They *are* drugged."

"Aw, come off it, Sissy," said Jelly. "What do you mean, 'drugged'? Every living thing is a chemical composition and anything that is added to it changes that composition. When you eat a cheeseburger or a Three Musketeers bar, it changes your body chemistry. The kind of food you eat, the kind of air you breathe, can change your mental state. Does that mean you're 'drugged'? 'Drugged' is a stupid word."

"You've been smoking pot," said Linda. "You're drugged. How do you feel? Could we make you do something you didn't want to do?"

Debbie joined in. "Look at them, Sissy. Do they look like they're drugged? They hunt, they eat, they crap, they preen, they roost; they laid eggs, hatched them and took care of their young. They dance and whoop from time to time, and every now and then they go up for a flight. Only thing they don't do that they've always done is migrate. Is that so drastic?"

Framing the flock in a hole in her cheese sandwich, Sissy had to say, "No, I guess not. One of the largest whooping crane flocks we know about, the one that once inhabited the yellow grass country of Louisiana, never migrated. So it must not be absolute to the species." She lowered her sandwich. "But the peyote is obviously affecting their brains. It's made them break a migratory pattern that goes back thousands of years. And it's made them less timid of people. Not even I could get this close to them before, and I have . . ."

"A way with birds!" Jelly and Debbie sang together. "A way with birds, a way with birds!" Their little song skittered shrilly over the pond, reminding neither bird nor bird watcher, one hopes, that early American settlers made flutes from the wing bones of cranes.

Sissy blushed.

Jelly kissed her.

"The way I see it," said Debbie, swinging her reddish brown pigtails from lakeside to hillward, "is that the peyote mellowed them out. Made them less uptight. They were afraid of bad weather and humans. That's why they migrated and kept to themselves. But the peyote has enlightened them. It's taught them there is nothing to fear but fear itself. Now they're digging life and letting the bad vibes slide on by. Don't worry, be happy. Be here now."

Did Sissy buy that? Not a feather of it. "Fear in wild animals is completely different from paranoia in people," she argued. "In the wilderness ecosystem, fear is natural and necessary. It's merely a mechanism for maintaining life. If the cranes hadn't had a capacity for fear, they would have disappeared long ago and you'd be having to get loaded with common old everyday meadowlarks and mallards."

"This here discussion is destined to become academic," said Jelly, "because we've got less than half a bag of peyote buttons left and Delores's run ended up in the Mottburg jail. So any day now we'll get a chance to see how the whoopers behave when they come down, to see if the peyote experience really changed them or not. But in the meantime, I want to say this about fear . . ."

As Jelly pronounced the word *fear,* it suddenly materialized around about them.

A noisy unstoppable churning wheel of fear that rolls out of the altitudes like the flat tire off God's Cadillac; an ear-filling, stomach-tightening busy beater of death-egg fear that has poisoned the dreams of Southeast Asia's children.

The helicopter came in low over the hills from the south, chopping the blue September sky into war meat. It headed straight for the tea party.

108.

"HOLD YER FIRE!" yelled Bonanza Jellybean. "Hold yer fire!"

Luckily, her cry was heard above the oxygen-slicing swipes of the helicopter rotors, above the fusillade that resounded from the panicky cowgirls at the barricades. The shooting stopped as abruptly as it had begun. The only casualty of the outburst was a horse that was struck in the temple by a ricochet. The horse died with fresh grass in its mouth. Even so, death is the last straw.

Jelly had detected in the amateurish stripes of black and red paint with which the copter was decorated the hand not of law but of outlaw. She was correct. When the machine, having blown the floral display into disarray, settled in the wheatgrass a few yards to the north of the dome foundation, out stepped Billy West. Dressed entirely in black, like Delores, he had all he could do to bend his girth sufficiently to allow him to pass under the whirling blades without being beheaded (The co-pilot, a young man with hair to his waist, remained at the controls).

Jelly jumped off the foundation into an elephantine hug. Held above the ground in Billy's arms, her six-gun clattered against his six-gun.

"Git some gals over here and help me unload," Billy said. "I brauch ya a few more boxes of ammo. And some Wonder Bread. And some beans. What ya think of my whirlybird? Got it in a deal over in Montana. Shit. Your trigger-happy chicks went and messed up my new paint job." Fat fingers pointed at a streak of bare metal where a bullet had grazed the helicopter. "Well, c'mon now, let's git unloaded; I gotta git loose and vamoose. The feds are gonna be on my tail for sure."

Boxes of ammunition, crates of bread, cases of beans were passed hurriedly from the chopper, then from girl to girl, finally to be stacked beside the chuck wagon. Then, blowing a chubby kiss, Bill West oozed back into the helicopter and off it flew for God knows where, its fearful churning agitating the hills.

The quiet that followed was overpowering. Manna from Heaven was never like this. Except for a few Trappist clouds, the sky was empty now. No use looking up there. Look instead at the new provisions. At the dead horse. At stunned and embarrassed faces. At the radio, which alone had the gall to infringe upon this contemplative moment.

Agreeing with the turning Earth that the "time" was now six o'clock, the radio was extracting news from the ether. More than one silent cowgirl heard the news announcer say that Judge So-and-So, at the request of the ACLU, had granted a forty-eight-hour extension of the deadline by which the Rubber Rose cowgirls must comply with his order. Negotiations between the cowgirls and the government were expected to follow.

Well, that development wasn't entirely unexpected. The next one was, though. The announcer informed his listeners that Rubber Rose forewoman Delores del Ruby was free on bond, her bail having been paid by the owner of the besieged ranch, Countess Products, Inc. The surprising and puzzling announcement that the Countess was going Ms. del Ruby's bail came from the tycoon's personal adviser, a certain Dr. Robbins of New York.

109.

THAT NIGHT, Sissy and Jelly lay under the same stars, under the same clouds, under the same blankets, under the same spell. Like political candidates, they frequently switched positions. In the campaign of 69, the polls didn't close until dawn.

As dawn's famous rosy fingers grasped the life preserver of the horizon, the early-rising cranes overheard Jelly say, "Every time I tell you that I love you, you flinch. But that's *your* problem."

Answered Sissy, "If I flinch when you say you love me, it's both our problems. My confusion becomes your confusion. Students confuse teachers, patients confuse psychiatrists, lovers with confused hearts confuse lovers with clear hearts." She chuckled at her awkward aphorism. "I think I need to see the Chink," she added quietly.

"I think so, too," said Jellybean. "We cowgirls got two days now with nothing to do but play word games with lawyers. Why don't you slip away for the ridge?"

"I will," said Sissy. And as the new day pulled itself onto the deck of the prairie, she did.

110.

SHE HADN'T intended it to go like this. When it had happened in her mind, it had happened differently. In her mind, there had been a fond embrace, a cool dipper of water to tame her thirst after the steep climb, a restful sitting in the shade of a rock and wise words filtered through a Sunday school beard, words that barked and snapped at the fleeing heels of confusion.

In her mind, he had kept his robe on, at least until bedtime. There had been no hand in her pants, not right off the bat. And certainly he had had more to say than "Ha ha ho ho and hee hee."

Expectations v. *Realizations*. We all remember that old case. In truth, he *had* spoken more than sniggerese. Immediately upon seeing her — only the rocks know how long he had been watching her climb — he had laughed "Ha ha ho ho and hee hee," but then he had nodded from thumb to thumb and said, "That's wonderful. I like that combination. Now you're balanced."

"Balanced?" Sissy had asked. "Balanced? but one's short and skinny and the other long and plump."

"Don't confuse symmetry with balance," he had answered.

In vain, Sissy waited for an elaboration. Instead of a discourse on opposites and paradox, however, there had been another snigger. Then it was off with jumpsuit and robe. The reader can guess what followed, although the reader probably couldn't guess with what frequency and duration. Were he obliged to do so, the author could describe it: each drip of sweat, each contraction of muscle, each pant, each moan, each slish of slippery tissue. Were he of a mind to, the author could make you hear slurps as plainly as if you were the briny Popsicle that was being licked; could make you smell the rising tide of toadstool musk as sharply as if he had pulled the funky blankets over your head. However, such descriptive passages might be misconstrued to be an appeal to your prurient interest. Moreover, the author has other data to impart, and the twentieth century is running out of pages. So, let what is sufficient suffice. Until Sissy and the Chink are on their feet again, the author is going to turn his back on them and read the newspaper. Here, I'll read it aloud. On page 31, we find

HOUSEHOLD HINTS

Dear Heloise: What does one use to polish rosebuds?

G.S.

Dear G.S.: Bluebird spit and sugar should do the trick. Apply with a bee muff.

Heloise

111.

OKAY, they're through now. They can barely walk to the cliff edge to watch the sunset, the naughty kids. In retrospect, though, we must consider that the Chink *was* trying to help Sissy chase her confusion. Having spent the night making love with Jellybean, had she not then spent the day making love with the Chink there could have been no accurate comparison. And the Chink might have thought a comparison necessary, although he would not have seen any necessity for a choice.

Love easily confuses us because it is always in flux between illusion and substance, between memory and wish, between contentment and need. Perhaps there are times when the contradictions of love are so intermingled that the only way to see the truth of love is to pit it against the irreducible reality of lust.

Of course, love can never be stripped bare of illusion, but simply to arrive at an awareness of illusion is to hold hands with truth — and sometimes the hard light of lust affords just such an awareness.

At any rate, it was a calm and satiated Sissy who stood on the parapets of Siwash Ridge, watching snowy specks of whooping cranes melt in the dusk. Neither Jelly nor the Chink occupied her thoughts; instead, a quiet ecstasy gathered around her immediate sense of awareness of her own illusions, and that ecstatic overview filled the spaces between her and the distant lake.

"What do you think of this business of the cowgirls and the cranes?" she asked. It no longer seemed absurd to her that it had taken an entire day for them to broach the subject.

Was that a sigh that elbowed its way through the tangles of the smoky beard, or was it the higher octaves of an exhausted snigger? "The cranes are beautiful. For that matter, so are the cowgirls. It's a shame they're relating to each other in such a compromising way."

"I think I share your feelings," said Sissy. "The cranes are still skittish — they insist on a certain distance and maintain some integrity — but I can't help seeing them as being rather like pets now. Domesticated. It was you who taught me . . ."

"I've never taught you anything."

"Oh, shut up, you old turkey!" Sissy laughed. It was almost a snigger. To keep the Chink from turning away and escaping the dialogue, she seized his limp member and held fast. She was learning how to deal with him. "It was you who made me aware that the domestication of animals was one of history's major mistakes, a devastating error not only in terms of ecology, but in terms of the psychological and philosophical consequences that are still being suffered. You know, I don't really hate dogs per se, or even dog owners; it's the idea of pethood that turns me off, the taming of wild things, the use of animals as surrogate children — or surrogate lovers." She pondered a moment, without loosening a fraction her grip on the Chink's dick. "It's ironic, isn't it? All the great agrarian cultures of old Europe were matriarchal; then along came the nomadic herdsmen from Central Asia with their love of the bull and their concomitant belief in penis power. The herding tribes gradually overran the feminist states, replacing the Great Mother with God the Father, substituting the Christian death trip for the pagan glorification of life, venerating beasts ahead of vegetation and oh, yeah, let's see, placing the notion of spirit ahead of the fact of matter — you first called my attention to this, you fart. The women who planted, cultivated, harvested and got high were crowded from their central position by men who drifted from worn-out pasture to virgin pasture, fighting and getting drunk. Well, it's ironic. Because cowgirls are, by their very name, herders. And these particular Rubber Rose cowgirls not only keep horses and goats, they've semidomesticated the grandest, wildest flock of birds in the world. Ironic."

The Chink shook his beard in the evening breeze. He was hairy inside and out. His beard sent out shocks of milkweed and mutton. "Yes, ironic, finding women who would be women imitating men. But there are other aspects of this saga that I bet you haven't considered."

"If you'll tell me, I'll turn you loose."

"Makes no difference to me. Actually, I was hoping you'd hold on, just in case I yield to this impulse to jump off the cliff."

She let go.

"Ha ha ho ho and hee hee," said the Chink. Then he swept his smirk under the rug. "I was merely thinking about the significance of the fact that there are *cranes* involved in this confrontation between girls and government. The crane is the bird of poetry. It was Robert Graves who pointed out that the crane has been traditionally connected with poetry all the way from China to Ireland. The crane is the national animal, the totem animal of Hungary — and as Graves wrote, there are twenty times more poems written and published in Hungary each year than in any other country. Obviously, cranes bring luck to poets, and vice versa. The only country in Europe where cranes are still breeding is Hungary. The last crane in the British Isles was shot in nineteen six. Russia's cranes are hiding in Siberia. Japan's, too. And we know the state of U.S. cranes. Graves says, 'While there are still cranes in Hungary, poetry is bound to continue.' He's right. And if poetry continues, Hungary will continue. Religion and politics are unnecessary to the culture — or the individual — that has poetry."

"You really don't believe in political solutions, do you?"

"I believe in political solutions to political problems. But man's primary problems aren't political; they're philosophical. Until humans can solve their philosophical problems, they're condemned to solve their political problems over and over and over again. It's a cruel, repetitious bore."

Sissy thought she had the old goat this time, and not just by the pecker, either. "Well, then, what are the philosophical solutions?"

"Ha ha ho ho and hee hee. That's for you to find out." She didn't have him. "I'll say this much and no more: there's got to be poetry. And magic. Your thumbs taught you that much, didn't they? Poetry and magic. At every level. If civilization is ever going to be anything but a grandiose pratfall, anything more than a can of deodorizer in the shithouse of existence, then statesmen are going to have to concern themselves with magic and poetry. Bankers are going to have to concern themselves with magic and poetry. *Time* magazine is going to have to write about magic and poetry. Factory workers and housewives are going to have to get their lives entangled in magic and poetry. As for policemen and cowgirls . . ." The Chink wagged his beard at the ranch below. It was a beard that a nesting crane might enjoy.

If Sissy failed to comprehend completely, at least she no longer felt confused. Through a pinhole in the peace that dropped like the dusk around them, she squeezed one last question. "Do you think such a thing can ever happen?"

"If you understood poetry and magic, you'd know that it doesn't matter."

The moon rose.

The clockworks struck.

A crane whooped.

She understood.

111a.

POETRY is nothing more than an intensification or illumination of common objects and everyday events until they shine with their singular nature, until we can experience their power, until we can follow their steps in the dance, until we can discern what parts they play in the Great Order of Love. How is this done? By fucking around with syntax.

[Definitions are limiting. Limitations are deadening. To limit oneself is a kind of suicide. To limit another is a kind of murder. To limit poetry is a Hiroshima of the human spirit. DANGER: RADIATION. Unauthorized personnel not allowed on the premises of Chapter 111a.]

112.

BREAKTHROUGHS on Siwash Ridge notwithstanding, there was precious little communication down on the Rubber Rose. All day, attorneys from the ACLU tried to build bridges between the government and the cowgirls, but each bridge was burned before it was crossed.

As their final and most generous offer in a series of overtures, Justice Department spokesmen at last promised that no charges would be filed against the cowgirls were they to withdraw peacefully and allow the Interior Department to take whatever steps it felt necessary for the present well-being and future preservation of the crane flock. As a sort of bonus, the Assistant Undersecretary of the Interior said that if a bird was killed for an autopsy, it would be later mounted and presented to the Rubber Rose Ranch as a symbol of that place's concern for America's vanishing wildlife.

"Just what we've always needed," snapped Delores del Ruby. "A stuffed whooping crane."

Yes, Delores was back. And with her return there disappeared any hope for settlement. Many of the pardners, concerned for the safety of themselves and one another, concerned for the birds, concerned, even, for the men at the gates, were growing increasingly willing to accept the government's terms. Bonanza Jellybean herself conceded that the cowgirls had made their point, had made it repeatedly, had made it before a worldwide audience — so there might be little additional to gain by pushing it any further.

Ah, but Delores. A dark shadow of a woman. With nocturnal eyes. And a midnight voice. A smile like a hiss of asps in the rain. It is said that a long ebony hair curled from the nipple of each of her perfectly formed breasts. Delores was adamant.

"It isn't for ourselves that we take this stand," she said, her voice as heavy and slow as the lids of a crocodile. "It isn't for cowgirls." She flicked her arrow tongue at Jelly. "It's for all the daughters everywhere. This is an extremely important confrontation. This is womankind's chance to prove to her enemy that she's willing to fight and die.

If we women don't show here and now that we aren't afraid to fight and die, then our enemy will never take us seriously. Men will always know that, no matter how strong our words and determined our deeds, there's a point where we'll back down and give them their way."

Cracking her whip to obscure Debbie's gentle protests, Delores paraded proudly before the barricades. "I'm prepared to battle!" she cried. "Furthermore, I'm prepared to win! Victory for every female, living or dead, who's suffered the temporary defeats of masculine insensitivity to their inner lives!"

A few of the cowgirls cheered. Donna said, "I'll fight the bastards." Big Red was opening a can of beans with a bowie knife. "I'll fight 'em with bean gas, if necessary," said Big Red.

Delores and her whip shared a grin. Said the forewoman, "The sun's going down. Let's those of us not standing watch get some sleep. In the morning we'll plan our fight. Tomorrow afternoon those of you who'd like can join me in the reeds, where the cranes and I will be sharing the last crumbs left in the peyote sack."

113.

If you want details of the secret White House whooping crane meeting, you'll have to read the exposé Jack Anderson will write as soon as he can get his hands on the tapes. If there *were* any tapes. Seymour Hersh says the conference wasn't taped; says that, after the taping experiences of the prior President, nothing will ever be taped in the White House again, not a Mantovani concert or an Xmas package or a sprained ankle — and that is why Seymour Hersh plans no in-depth article on the subject. Face it; you may never get the details of the secret White House whooping crane meeting. Are you positive you want them?

The author knows *generally* what took place in the conference room off the Oval Office that morning in late September, and although he's been warned to keep mum, he is going to divulge it here. It ought to satisfy you. Many small streams empty into these pages. I never promised you the Potomac.

One thing that is certain is that the President, the *new* President, was an uncertain man that morning. In the salts of his bile, he felt lumpy. Somehow, he had a nagging suspicion that the *last* President wouldn't have allowed himself to be called into a meeting on whooping cranes and cowgirls. The last President, thought the new President, would have ordered his aides to take whatever action was most politically expedient in regard to the cranes, while he, the last President, never one to relish the intimacy of social problems, jetted off to Peking or Moscow or Cairo to make historical hay from the international situation, which was desperate, as usual. The new President felt cheapened, felt wimpy about being expected to preside over a meeting on long-legged birds. Indeed, he would have refused had he not been informed that Pentagon and Petroleum wished him to confer. New on the job though he was, he sensed that as President he could no more ignore Pentagon and Petroleum than he could as congressman, but he sensed, too, in the bubbles of his bile, that he would regret that goddamned meeting on whooping cranes.

The interest of the military and the oil lobby in the Rubber Rose affair was recent. Heretofore, the matter was the concern of the Justice Department, which sought to end (in its usual fashion) what it regarded as defiance, subversion and criminal misappropriation of federal property, and of the Interior Department, which sought to get the cranes back on the job and out of its hair. When the generals and oil men suggested a different approach, however, Justice and Interior were, for the most part, in accord.

The meeting opened with the director of the FBI explaining to the new President how the cowgirls had set up their barricades directly in front of the crane flock. "A devilishly shrewd tactic," he called it, for were federal agents to fire on the young women, the lives of the cranes would be jeopardized. "They're holding the cranes as hostages, as it were," the FBI chief said. "They've got us over a barrel."

He yielded the floor to Pentagon, represented by a four-star general from the Air Force. The general, with facts and figures pulled from a blue plastic folder, explained to the new President that this flock of whooping cranes had been a thorn in the flesh of the military for more than thirty years. Since 1942, by far the finest and most-used bombing range in America had been the one on Matagorda Island, off the Gulf Coast of Texas. The majority of the B-52 crews that served in Vietnam had trained over the Matagorda range, for example. In addition, helicopter gunships had made frequent and effective use of Matagorda target runs. Because these whooping cranes winter on Matagorda, or on the nearby mainland across San Antonio Bay in what is known as the Aransas National Wildlife Refuge, the Air Force and Army had been frequently blamed by conservationists for the threatened extinction of the birds. Under pressure, even the Interior Department had begun to harass the Air Force about the bombing range. Naval and Coast Guard operations in the area had also been criticized and curbed, said the general. He told the new President that Pentagon considered the cranes detrimental to the best interests of America's defense.

The new President was not a thing of beauty, though, in truth, he was fairer to look upon than his predecessor. The new President possessed a face that might have comforted a lonely orangutan. One could draw a good likeness of the new President with a weenie dipped in fingerpaints. There was something close to farce in the manner in which the new President nodded his head quasi-sagely at the conclusion of Pentagon's testimony and in the way that head jerked to exaggerated attention when the oil lobbyist, pulling facts and figures from a black leather briefcase, began his spiel.

It was hardly necessary to remind the new President of the energy crisis, but the petroleum-pusher did so. Then he proceeded to inform the chief executive of large quantities of oil that lay wasting in the seabed because off-shore drilling in the Matagorda-Aransas region had been disallowed due to this one lousy flock of birds, birds that contributed not a copper to the Gross National Product and that held not a feather's weight in negotiations with the Arabs. You get the picture? The new President did. Maybe it was an overstatement to say the whooping cranes were crunchy granola in the bedsheets of the economy, but they were certainly one more obstacle to smoothing out that badly rumpled bed.

Once again, the FBI director took the floor. It was almost certain, said he, that there would be a showdown on the Dakota ranch. He described the so-called cowgirls as fanatical subversives violently opposed to the American way of life. These women wanted bloodshed, he said. They had mocked a court order, had refused to negotiate, were at that very moment pointing firearms, possibly of Communist origin, at government agents.

It seemed inevitable to the FBI director that federal lawmen would be fired upon. This did not worry the top cop, for the vastly superior firepower of the U.S. marshals and FBI agents would quickly and thoroughly prevail. Furthermore, there might be positive benefits from a shootout. Suppose that, in returning the cowgirl's fire, the marshals and agents should "accidentally" pepper the whooping cranes with shots? Suppose that canisters of extrastrength tear gas ostensibly lobbed at the cowgirls were to land in the midst of the birds, who were known to be fatally susceptible to tear gas? In the process of routing the rustlers, the crane flock could be so decimated that the government would be obliged to capture the few survivors and place them in zoos. Thus, in one fell swoop, the U.S. could rid itself of a band of troublemakers and the whooping crane nuisance. Could the President — in secret, of course — support such an action?

The new President wished he was on the golf course, wished he had a glass of whiskey, wished an aide would hand him a statement to read, wished this and wished that, but no fairy godmother attended the new President. It was September 29, Brigitte Bardot's birthday; perhaps all the wish-granters were in France waiting for Brigitte Bardot to blow out the candles on her cake.

At last the President opened his banana-biters to concede that the plan had merit, but that he did not believe the public would stand for federal agents shooting teen-aged girls.

The half-dozen others in the conference room disagreed. They pointed out that these girls were lawbreakers, armed, dangerous, immoral, disruptive influences, enemies of the public good — not unlike the young women who had been annihilated in Los Angeles. There would be no more of a public outcry than in the L.A. executions, and much less than in the suppression at Kent State. Moreover, with a little help from the press, the government should have no difficulty in blaming the tragic fate of the whooping cranes on the violent, lawless actions of the cowgirls. The fair-minded majority would believe the girls had gotten their just deserts.

"Besides," said the man whom the new President had nominated to be the new Vice President, "it doesn't make any difference politically.

The bleeding-hearts raked me over the coals for permitting the rioters at Attica Prison to be, ah, severely dealt with, but it hasn't hurt my career one iota. Mr. President, maybe you underestimate the moral sense of the American people."

It was a convincing argument, though the way it was phrased did nothing to cream the texture of the presidential bile. The new President rolled his eyes from Pentagon to Petroleum. He was trapped and knew it. Narrowing the beam on his monkey lamps, to suggest that he was both thoughtful and independent, he said, "I'll have to give it some consideration." He stood with an amateur actor's interpretation of dignity, banging his thigh painfully against the conference table. Expensive handtooled shoes, which he remembered now as having been a gift from the oil lobby, bore him from the room.

As soon as possible, he exchanged those shoes for golf shoes. Before he left for Burning Tree Country Club, the new President called in his most trusted aide. "In two hours — no, better make it three — I want you to tell FBI that I have decided to approve Operation Whooper Pooper."

The new President went out on the green Earth and knocked a little ball around.

114.

Sissy Hankshaw Gitche never made it back to Siwash Lake. No thumb was large enough, no mastery of movement so perfect, no will over landscape and its travelers of such strength as to get her there.

She was turned back by U.S. marshals and FBI agents, who had parked armored vehicles on the hilltop and now squared off against the cowgirls from close range. The federal forces had held her for questioning, and when she was released, it was in the sour custody of a marshal who escorted her to the Rubber Rose gates and pointed her toward Mottburg.

It took more than that to stop her, of course. She doubled back along the base of Siwash Ridge and into the southern hills, intending to approach the lake from the eastern or prairie side, the only side that was not now guarded by the government. With every step she took, however, the wind increased by some large fraction of a knot. By the time she began to angle onto the prairie, Dakota had its dust up. Like a fog of knife tips, like a hurricane of harsh ants, the dust enveloped her, bit her, choked her, blinded her. She fought the storm, but it would not stand still. She hitchhiked it, but it would not take her with it.

The storm had no sense of humor. There is little in Nature that does. Maybe the human animal has contributed really nothing to the universe but kissing and comedy — but by God that's plenty.

The storm reminded Sissy of that creature that is simultaneously the most dangerous and most pitiful thing on Earth: a scared old man with a title. It was more frustration than fear that drove her back to Siwash Ridge, a refuge whose frenzied heights occasionally showed themselves through the dust. It took her hours to get there, and when she finally crawled, exhausted, into the cave, she felt as if she'd been sandpapered in the hobby shop of Hell.

The Chink sought to apply some varnish — yam oil, to be exact — but Sissy pushed him away. "Not now," she said. "I'm sending all my energy to Jellybean. I want her to feel that I'm standing with her in this crazy thing that she does."

Love grew thumbs. And hitchhiked unmolested through storm and stormtroopers to the lake. It arrived at about the same instant as Delores's Third Vision. About the same time as a very battered, very skinny, very pooped-out snake with a card — the jack of hearts — under its tongue.

115.

WE HAVE a reptile in our totem. It has been there since Eden. It lives at the base of the brain and has a special relationship to women. It is associated with the dark world, dark consciousness, the necessary opposite of light. However, it does not function as a symbol because it is too unpredictable. In a male, its venom can cause violence or art. In a female, it produces a peculiar madness that men do not understand. In children, it is the little red wagon painted blue.

Delores ate seven peyote buttons, after cutting away their poisonous tufts. She gave three apiece to Donna, LuAnn, Big Red and Jody. That left only four buttons in the sack. Not enough for the cranes, who already were showing signs of coming down — restlessness, wariness, noise — and none of the other cowgirls wished to get high. So Delores ate the last four plants herself. Peyote is ugly to look upon (the "buttons" resemble grungey green Naugahyde hassocks for the splayed feet of malevolent gnomes) and horrid to taste. Its seven alkaloids produce seven varieties of abdominal cramps (Within an hour, five cowgirls were puking) and dirty burps of bitterness.

Nauseated, Donna, Big Red, LuAnn and Jody wandered around the lakeshore, batting their eyes at everything that moved, which was everything. Their faces were hot, their legs rubbery, their thoughts soaring. The armored cars on the hill seemed ridiculous, childish. The way the wind kept accelerating, never content with this speed or that, struck them as funny, too. But the wind has no sense of humor, and when billows of dust began to rise, the stoned-out cowgirls took refuge in the barricades, huddled together in an anxious stupor, perhaps reliving the dusty moments of Creation.

But Delores . . . Delores lay in the reeds at the water's edge. Asleep yet awake, she had sunk so deeply into the hole in her mind that gale and dust could not follow her. Jellybean gave up on trying to rouse her and lead her to shelter, leaving her there, spattered with green vomit, to communicate with her totem. Delores moaned. Her hand opened and closed on the handle of her whip. She seemed about to crawl on her belly, to slither into the wind-whipped waters of the pond.

It was there in that state that they found her. "They?" Niwetúkame the Divine Mother and the snake from the message service. Had they come together? Were they in cahoots, the serpent and the goddess? What was said? How was the playing card dealt? Was Delores shown jewels or hummingbirds or strikes of lightning? Did she meet her double? What business was transacted? Was it stunning and frightful, or was there an air of show biz about it? Delores has never said.

Long after the vision of St. Anthony and Paul's epileptic flashes on the Damascus road, long after the voices spoke to Joan of Arc and Blake had his eyeballs seared with heavenly wonderments, long after Edgar Cayce's prophetic trances and Ginsberg's glimpse of the hip angel, there came the three visions of Delores del Ruby, the third of which sent her stumbling into the barricades, in the dark of night, at the end of a Dakota dust storm, to snatch the rifles from the hands of her cowgirl sisters.

Her black eyes were shining like the wet crowns of drakes; her face had softened into a sweet mask of electric blood. In the moonlight, she stood out like a city surrounded by flames. She walked as if in sleep. With a slow underwater strangeness, she threw guns into the dust-covered grass.

No one dared question her actions; no one so much as *thought* to question her actions. She obviously was operating under divine authority. She had abandoned her whip.

When she spoke, it was as if someone had filed the burrs off her consonants and fluffed out her vowels. She spoke simply, but with intensity.

"The natural enemy of the daughters is not the fathers and the sons," she announced.

"I was mistaken.

"The enemy of women is not men.

"No, and the enemy of the black is not the white. The enemy of capitalist is not communist, the enemy of homosexual is not heterosexual, the enemy of Jew is not Arab, the enemy of youth is not the old, the enemy of hip is not redneck, the enemy of Chicano is not gringo and the enemy of women is not men.

"We all have the same enemy.

"The enemy is the tyranny of the dull mind.

"There are authoritative blacks with dull minds, and they are the enemy. The leaders of capitalism and the leaders of communism are the same people, and they are the enemy. There are dull-minded women who try to repress the human spirit, and they are the enemy just as much as the dull-minded men.

"The enemy is every expert who practices technocratic manipulation, the enemy is every proponent of standardization and the enemy is every victim who is so dull and lazy and weak as to allow himself to be manipulated and standardized."

The cowgirls gathered around Delores in a tight circle. None was missing. Many were transfixed. Their eyes had begun to glow in pale approximation of their forewoman's orbs.

"It is woman's mission to destroy as well as to give birth," Delores told them. "We will destroy the tyranny of the dull. But we can't destroy it with guns. Or whips. Violence is the dullard's Breakfast of Champions, and the logical end product of his or her misplaced pride. Violence fertilizes that which we would starve. But Debbie, we can't love the dull away, either. We only pollute our own waters when we try to extend our true affection to those who don't know how to accept love or to give it. Love is very powerful, but it has limits and it's a costly mistake to spread it too thin.

"No, we will destroy the enemy in other ways. The Peyote Mother has promised a Fourth Vision. But it won't come to me alone. It will come to each of you, to every cowgirl in the land, when you have overcome that in your own self which is dull.

"The Fourth Vision will come to some men, too. You will recognize them when you meet them, and be their steady sidekicks in equal and ecstatic escapades of poetic behavior and romance." Delores held up a card. The prairie moon illuminated its tattered edges. It was the jack of hearts.

The forewoman seemed to be tiring. Fumes of weariness streamed from her black hair. Her voice was leaning against the wall of her larynx when she said, "First thing in the morning, you must end this business with the government and the cranes. It's been positive and fruitful, but it's gone far enough. Playfulness ceases to serve a serious purpose when it takes itself too seriously. Sorry I won't be with you at the conclusion. As you know, I've been sick and stupid for a long time. I have a lot to make up for, a lot to accomplish, and there's someone important that I've got to see. Now."

As graceful as a ballet for cobras, Delores turned and walked away into the dry Dakota night.

116.

The cowgirls didn't sleep a wink. They felt intoxicated. The ideological tensions that had divided them had called in well. Purposes had been redefined. Right around the next corner, mysterious Fourth Vision destinies were singing. Whole new aspects of existence beckoned, like stupendous . . . thumbs. The pardners were ready for more of everything, and even that might not be enough.

When life demands more of people than they demand of life — as is ordinarily the case — what results is a resentment of life that is almost as deep-seated as the fear of death. Indeed, the resentment of life and the fear of death are virtually synonymous. Does it follow, then, that the more people ask of living, the less their fear of dying?

Or was Dr. Robbins merely being cute when, explaining how such a cowardly concept as "Theirs not to reason why, theirs but to do or die" could gain popular favor, he said, "Some people would rather die than think about death"?

Well, we can observe only that so elated were the cowgirls, so expectant, so immersed in magic, that it was difficult for them to concentrate on the menace facing them from the hill. They knew merely that they no longer wished to battle with the authorities — on the authorities' terms — and they had faith that no battle would ensue.

Behind the shield of the armored cars, however, the U.S. marshals and agents of the FBI shared no such notions. The men hadn't slept a wink, either. The storm had left them dirty, pink-eyed and irritable, but as dawn neared they trembled with the ancient power of the hunter. When they thought of the soft young game they would bring down, they trembled the more. They chewed gum furiously. Many of them had erections.

Neither camp was prepared for dawn when it did appear. Like the hands of a cat burglar, those famous rosy fingers suddenly slid over the window ledge of the hemisphere and with silent efficiency began to jimmy the lock of the day. Before their excited minds could fully cope with the idea, the cowgirls and the G-men were staring at the faint outlines of one another's barricades.

"Well," said Jellybean, "what we got to do is one of us has got to go up that hill and tell them boys that America can have its whooping cranes back. Since I'm the boss here, and since I'm responsible for a lot of you choosing to be cowgirls in the first place, it's gonna be me that goes."

"But . . ."

"No buts about it. It's getting lighter by the second. You podners keep your heads down. Ta ta."

"Jelly! Please!"

The cutest cowgirl in the world stood up and stretched. For a moment, her rigid arms resembled wings. The goose flesh on her bare thighs drew taut. Her breasts vibrated in her gaudy Western shirt. Had Francis Scott Key observed such breasts in the dawn's early light, he might have gone below deck and written quite a different anthem. (Or maybe Francis Scott Key would have ignored the erogenous mammaries — mere sexual trappings where men are concerned — and commented instead on the more universal example of a lone human being bravely accepting a dread responsibility. Let us not judge the composer unfairly nor confuse his sensibilities with those of that awful roller derby performer, Francis Skate Key.)

Jellybean vaulted over the carcass of a reducing machine and planted her Tony Lama boots in the dewless grass. "Nothing to be scared of," she told herself. "I'll just get this message delivered as fast as I can and head for the butte to see Sissy." Jelly had no idea what was going to happen to the Rubber Rose now, but she had never felt more like a cowgirl.

About halfway up the hill, her dimpled knees knocking dust puffs off aster heads, she remembered that she was still wearing her six-gun. Delores had overlooked that one in her disarmament spree. "Better get rid of this," Jelly thought. "Might give those greenhorn dudes a fright."

Rubber-doll fingers reached into the holster and drew the gun. She had been pulling pistols out of holsters since she was three years old. Play. Just play. She started to fling the toy away, but before her pinkies could release the pearl handle, a shot rang out from the top of the hill.

Jelly felt a blow to her tummy. Something was stinging her baby fat. The six-gun slipped from her fingers as she lifted her satin shirt tail and pulled down the waistband of her skirt. Bright red blood was running out of her scar; she could see it in the dawnlight, could see the warm brightness pouring from that exact spot where she'd fallen on a wooden horse when she was twelve.

"I wasn't *really* shot with a silver bullet," she confessed to no one in particular.

"Or was I?"

She smiled the deliciously secretive smile of one who instinctively recognizes the reality of myth.

Twenty or thirty more sweaty triggers were squeezed on the hilltop, and Bonanza Jellybean was blown into a bloody mush.

Down by the lake, the cowgirls screamed and cried. They hugged one another in horror. A couple of them, LuAnn and Jody, leaped from the barricades to retrieve their weapons, and were immediately riddled.

A voice bellowed over a bullhorn, "You've got two minutes to come out with your hands over your heads." But it was obvious there would be no opportunity for surrender. Random G-men already were starting to snipe, and at any second there would erupt an orgy of gunfire intended to seduce with death every cowgirl in the Dakota hills.

Funny no one paid any attention to the helicopter. Those G-men who heard it at all must have assumed it was one of theirs. Its red and black markings would not have been conspicuous in the dim morning. At any rate, nobody took a shot at the chopper, even though it was flying extremely low. It was so weighted down with explosives it couldn't have climbed another inch.

By the time it floundered to a landing, dissolving the semicircle of federal cops, nothing could be done about it. There wasn't enough "time." The fat boy in the cockpit — it was impossible to tell whether he was laughing or crying — pushed the detonator and a mighty blast took the top off the hill — wheatgrass, asters, little bluestem, dust, mice, armored cars, G-men and all.

In the hush that followed the echoes of the explosion, the whooping crane flock rose in one grand assault of beating feathers — a lily white storm of life, a gush of albino Gabriels — swarmed into the waiting sky, and after circling the pond one time — either a limbering exercise or some primordial ornithological farewell — flapped south toward Texas.

Leaving human friends and human foe to clean up their respective human messes.

117.

AMONG the casualties of the whooping crane war was the Chink.

Sissy had been so worried about Jellybean that she couldn't sleep. The Chink had told her stories, massaged her feet, poured yam wine down her and played a sort of screech owl lullaby on his one-string cigar-box violin, to no avail. At last, she let him seduce her, and sparing no muscle, tendon, ligament or joint, he gave her a real workout: she had four orgasms and by the time the last one had boiled away, her aristocratic nose was packaging little *z*'s and shipping them all over. Then the Chink couldn't sleep.

The Chink sensed disaster. Well, so what? Survival, his own or anybody else's, was not a top priority with him. To a man who "kept time" by the clockworks, there were far more interesting and important things. Yet some silly sense of responsibility nagged at him. And nagged. Until he said, "All right, all right, I'll go out and play, just this once. Might as well; can't sleep anyhow."

He had descended Siwash Ridge after moonset, a feat no one else could have duplicated. There are burros that could not walk down that trail by blaze of noon without ruining their reputation as surefooted beasts. There are some mighty round beer barrels that could not roll down the Siwash trail, and some mighty twisted pretzels that could not do a decent imitation.

At the end of the trail, he had met Delores del Ruby.

Neither of them seemed surprised, but it must have been an act.

They stared one another down, she trying to appear cool, he cooler. He wanted to ask her what she was doing there, but he wouldn't. She wanted to tell him she was on her way to see him, but she couldn't. She anchored her hands on her hips; he wrinkled his nose. The harder they tried not to smile, the more the little mouth muscles struggled to get free. The force of suppressed grins caused their ears to wiggle in the dark.

"So you're the great boohoo, eh?"

"Maybe I am and maybe I'm not. No big deal either way."

"I suppose I owe you an apology. I've bad-mouthed you from asshole to elbow . . ."

"No big deal."

"Well, I just wanted you to know that I'm starting to appreciate you. Some of your ideas are not half-bad."

"*You* like them? I must have been misquoted."

"Aren't all big boohoos misquoted?"

"Misquoted, distorted, diluted and deified. In that order. At the hands of his worshipers, Jesus suffered a far worse fate than crucifixion. You have a lovely ass."

"You're not much like Jesus."

"How do you know?"

"Talking about my ass."

"You don't think Jesus would have admired your ass?"

"Not the Jesus I've read about."

"Exactly. Misquoted, distorted and diluted. Actually, if Jesus *had* admired your ass, he probably would have kept it to himself. So you're right; I'm not much like Jesus. I'm not much like Hubert Humphrey, either. Hubert Humphrey can chew two hundred forty-six sticks of gum at one time. I can't do that."

"Your cute little mouth was probably meant for finer things." She leaned over and slapped a kiss on his chops. First time she'd kissed a man in a snake's age.

"You're not half-bad yourself. When you leave your whip at home."

"I don't play with whips anymore."

"Oh yeah? What *do* do you play with?"

"I'm learning that there's a whole universe of things to play with. Including big boohoos."

"Boohoos can play rough. What do you want from me? The key to the treasure?"

Delores reached into her black shirt, among the dark nipples, hairs and moles, and drew the jack of hearts.

"Oh, you do card tricks, too. You're a hell of an act."

"I've had a vision tonight. I didn't come here to solve anything. I came here to celebrate, and for you to celebrate with me."

"In that case, you can stay for a while. It's a wise woman who doesn't come to the master for solutions."

"No big deal."

"Yes, um. It's going to be light soon. I've got to go see some men about some birds. When it gets so you can see, would you mind going up to the cave and keeping Sissy company until I return?"

Delores agreed, and the Chink trotted off through the wheatgrass.

Perhaps he had had a plan, a magic trick to play. He must have had something up his baggy sleeve. But whatever the Chink was going to pull on the G-men never got pulled. When he saw Bonanza Jellybean cut down, the old geezer made a beeline for the government barricades. Nobody heard his shouts. They were obscured first by gunfire, then by bullhorn, next by helicopter and finally by explosion.

The blast threw him back down the hillside, beard, robe and sandals flying, as if the blast was the toughest bouncer in Jerusalem and he a gatecrasher at the Last Supper. His left hip was shattered.

118.

AND so it came to pass that Sissy Hankshaw Gitche and Delores del Ruby spent a sorrowful day in Mottburg.

Midmorning, about the time the sun popped above the grain elevators, the two women (one in disguise) hurried past the Sears-suited coffee-breakers in Craig's Cafe; past the plump young mothers, hair in curlers, jawing in the self-service laundry; past the Chevrolet agency and the blank-faced American Legion Post. They arrived at the railroad station just as the casket was being loaded in a baggage car. Bonanza Jellybean (alias Sally Elizabeth Jones) had a one-way ticket to Kansas City. Her father, a short, balding man, had come to accompany the body. Jelly's mom had stayed home out of shame. Chugging out of the station, the train dissolved in teardrops that fell upon the tracks like silver bullets.

Later, while Delores sipped Irish coffee in a dim corner of the Bison Room of the Elk Horn Motor Lodge, Sissy tried to visit the twenty-six cowgirls who were locked up at the Mottburg Grange hall because there wasn't room in the jail. The pardners were being held without bond, awaiting trial. Sorry. No visitors.

At two o'clock, Sissy and Delores joined a curious crowd at the Lutheran Church cemetery for the funeral of Billy West. There was a token coffin, but no corpse. You would think that out of 300 pounds there would be a spoonful left, but there wasn't. The family was tense, the preacher embarrassed, the rites perfunctory. The mourners, if you could call them that, were mostly Billy's peers, who still couldn't believe that the butterball they'd teased in school had become a famous killer outlaw and had learned to fly a helicopter in one afternoon. As the crumbly prairie sod was being shoveled onto the uninhabited casket, Granny Schreiber said in a loud voice that Billy West was the only hero Mottburg had ever produced, and that she wished to hell she'd joined up with the cowgirls. Her grandsons spirited her away.

The next stop for Delores and Sissy was the small hospital. The Chink was plastered like a wall. You could have hung a picture on him, and a mirror, too. Beware the butterfly that could bust out of that cocoon. He was in pain, but winking. The eyes he winked with were as cloudy as semen. The women were too depressed to do him any good. Sissy sobbed on his bedside. "Is everything getting worse?" she cried. "Yes," answered the Chink, "everything *is* getting worse. But everything is also getting better."

And so it came to pass that the Rubber Rose Ranch was officially deeded to the cowgirls who had worked it. Each of the surviving hands was made an equal partner. Until the girls were free to do with it what they would, Sissy Hankshaw Gitche was asked to oversee the ranch, at a salary of $300 a week.

Giving away the Rubber Rose was the last piece of business conducted by the Countess before he dissolved his corporation and went to work as an orderly in the maternity ward of a charity hospital, on the orders of his psychiatrist and personal adviser, one Dr. Robbins.

"Get thee back to the aroma of birth," Dr. Robbins had told the Countess, "for the smells of the female body, the smells you have sought to kill with your totalitarian chemicals, are the very smells of birth, the strong odors of the essence of existence. The nose that is offended by the hot perfume of the cunt is a nose unsuited for this world, and should be sniffing gold on the scrubbed streets of Heaven. The vagina reeks of life and love and the infinite et cetera. O vagina! Your salty incense, your mushroom moon musk, your deep waves of clam honey breaking against the cold steel of civilization; vagina, draw our noses to the grindstone of ecstasy, and let us die smelling as we did when we were born!"

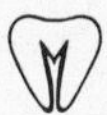

And so it came to pass that, as soon as possible, Sissy and Delores brought the Chink to the ranch to convalesce. They fixed up the master bedroom for him, the room that had slept Jellybean, and Miss Adrian before her. The ranch house held a minimum of charm for the old fart, but he was well aware that the two women couldn't carry him up Siwash Ridge. Delores put the stereo in his room, so he could pass the autumn days listening to rock 'n roll while meditating, chanting, eating deep-fried yams and leafing through *Oui* magazine.

Sissy served him faithfully, and most of the time cheerfully, but she was subject to fits of depression. Once, in a particularly grim despondency, she had turned to him and assigned him partial fault in Jelly's death. "You should have done more!" she charged.

"I did all I could."

"What was that? I never noticed you do anything — until it was too late."

"I set an example. That's all anyone *can* do. I'm sorry the cowgirls didn't pay better attention, but I couldn't force them to notice me. I've lived most of my entire adult life outside the law, and never have I compromised with authority. But neither have I gone out and picked fights with authority. That's stupid. They're waiting for that; they invite it; it helps keep them powerful. Authority is to be ridiculed, outwitted and avoided. And it's fairly easy to do all three. If you believe in peace, act peacefully; if you believe in love, act lovingly; if you believe every which way, then act every which way, that's perfectly valid — but don't go out trying to sell your beliefs to the System. You end up contradicting what you profess to believe in, and you set a bum example. If you want to change the world, change yourself. You know that, Sissy,"

Of course Sissy knew it. Hadn't the world's greatest hitchhiker always operated on that premise? It's just that she had a brain and our brains are forever having fun with us by making us learn over and over what we've known from the beginning. The brain may have been unjustly criticized in this book, but you've got to admit, the brain has a weird sense of humor.

And so it came to pass that Delores and Sissy became lovers.

They shared the room adjacent to the Chink's, keeping close in case he needed anything during the night.

In time, they found themselves needing something during the night.

Delores slept on the left, Sissy on the right. Before long, there wasn't any middle.

The bed never grumbled beneath them. Even the springs, tattle-tales by nature, resisted all temptations to squeak. The walls and ceiling auditioned each new position, apparently approving, for nothing cracked or fell. The little squeals that Delores's serpentine tongue pushed and pulled from Sissy's pipes, that Sissy's hitchhiker fingers beckoned from deep in Delores's throat, attracted no more attention from the hills beyond the fluttering curtains than the squeals of rabbits and mice. Sometimes four sets of lips would be smacking at once, but the edition of Amy Vanderbilt that Miss Adrian had left on the mantlepiece never once corrected them or turned up its nose. It was as if the world was absorbing their love, offering no resistance, but was lightly, softly breathing it in. Sighing "ah!"

Or "ha!"

But certainly not "ma!" Girl-love may have its place in the world, but as the bedsprings, walls, ceiling, hills and even Amy Vanderbilt must know, spit doesn't make babies.

And so it came to pass that when Sissy discovered she was pregnant, her thumb pointed at the Chink. Figuratively speaking, to be sure, for she told him nothing of it, nor did she mention her condition to Delores or write of it to Julian (whose drinking problem had become so acute that the "beautiful people" now shunned him, leaving him to wheeze out the effects of civilization in the posthippie hangouts of the East Village).

She concealed her morning sickness by pretending it was emotional, a physical manifestation of worry and grief, and no one was the wiser — except for a certain middle-aged woman who read palms and suffered trances in the drive-in movie outskirts of Richmond, Virginia.

And so it came to pass that the Rubber Rose cowgirls were acquitted on all counts. They rode out of Mottburg in a horseback processional, triumphantly waving their hats at the townsfolk, among whom was Granny Schreiber, cheering.

Back at the ranch, a meeting was called. In the bunkhouse, just like the old days.

Big Red read the hands some literature from the Girls' Rodeo Association. "All-girl rodeoing is enjoying the greatest period of growth in its history. Only five all-girl rodeos were held in 1973 — this year there were eleven." The GRA poop sheet went on to tell how Gail Petska, twenty-five, of Tecumseh, Oklahoma, had earned $19,448 in 1973, bull-riding, calf-roping, barrel-racing and goat-tying.

"I aim to cut into that pie," announced Big Red. "And I wish the rest of y'all would consider coming with me. We'll work outta Texas, just like the whooping cranes."

"Goat-tying as a sport is a new one on me," said Donna, "but with our experience us Rubber Rose podners ought to be damn good at it. You can count me in, but only if you'll help me agitate to end all-girl rodeos and get us back to competing with men again, equal, like it ought to be."

"Exactly what I had in mind," said Big Red. "But we'll do it gently, like the Peyote Mother told us to."

Seven cowgirls in all agreed to move to Texas and hit the rodeo circuit. Kym and Linda had already decided to winter in Florida, working as waitresses, saving money for some new adventure. Six cowgirls had made up their minds to give college a try, including Mary, who was going to study archeology to put her Christian faith to the test of historical fact. Some of the hands thought they'd just knock around for a while, trying different lifestyles on for size — preparing themselves for the Fourth Vision.

Outside the bunkhouse, two men were sitting on the corral fence. One was Elaine's sidekick, a thirty-five-year-old poet from San Francisco, who had been paying Elaine clandestine visits off and on since she'd been in Dakota. The other was an old friend of Debbie's from her Acid Atom Avatar days, a reformed LSD dealer who'd started reading the complete works of Albert Einstein and was learning to think (not reason, but think). Elaine and her sidekick, and Debbie and hers, wanted to run the ranch together. They planned to cultivate sunflowers and market the seeds.

It was agreed. Elaine and Debbie would be granted trusteeship of the spread, but the place was also to be permanently maintained as a haven for the twenty-six cowgirls, should any of them ever need a safe place to retreat from the slings and arrows of outrageous whatever.

Finally, the women voted to change the name of the Rubber Rose to El Rancho Jellybean. And that is how it is known to this day.

There *was* one more item of business. Heather wanted to know who stole the picture of Dale Evans out of the shitter.

119.

ONE MORNING the prairie dogs looked out of their cellars and saw that Indian summer had skipped town. It hadn't even left a good-by note. The prairie dogs shrugged, shivered and ducked inside, hoping to get to sleep before winter began stomping around upstairs in its hobnailed boots. That very same day, the Chink left, too.

Sissy and Delores returned windblown from a walk to find him hobbling on a cherry stick, his belongings tied in a skin. Out in the chill, Sissy had confessed her pregnancy to Delores, and the two of them had agreed that the Chink ought to be informed. Now, here he was, his second day on his feet, preparing to flee the ranch. And not for Siwash Ridge, either.

"I'm going to go back with the Clock People," he said. "I kind of miss those fool redskins and wonder what they're up to. Besides, they need somebody like me to needle 'em and keep 'em honest. Anarchy is like custard cooking over a flame; it has to be constantly stirred or it sticks and gets heavy, like government."

"I just can't believe you're going to leave the butte," said Sissy. But she could believe it. His bone had healed much more quickly than the physicians forecast, yet seeing him leaning on a cane, so drawn and pale, it was difficult to imagine him ever scurrying over the unpredictable architecture of Siwash Ridge again. What Sissy really meant was that she couldn't believe he was leaving *her*.

"Easy come, easy go," said the Chink.

"Wow, you sure have a way with words," said Delores.

The Chink actually blushed. "I can't help it if I grew up in an antipoetic culture," he said. "Language will be different when I'm with the Clock People, though. They're from an oral tradition. And I'm not talking about what you horny hop toads do in bed every night."

It was Delores's turn to blush. Sissy's turn, too. The walls had betrayed them after all.

"Well," sighed Sissy, trying to make her teardrops stay in their seats, "if the Clock People give you any inside information on the end of the world, drop us a postcard."

"The world isn't going to end, you dummy; I hope you know that much." He grew uncharacteristically serious. "But it *is* going to change. It's going to change drastically, and probably in your lifetime. The Clock People see calamitous earthquakes as the agent of change, and they may be right, since there are a hundred thousand earthquakes a year and major ones are long overdue. But there are far worse catastrophes coming . . ."

"Inevitable?" asked Delores.

"Unless the human race can bring itself to abandon the goals and values of civilization, in other words, unless it can break the consumption habit — and we are so conditioned to consuming as a way of life that for most of us life would have no meaning without the yearnings and rewards of progressive consumption. So I'd say yes, inevitable. It isn't merely that our bad habits will *cause* global catastrophes, but that our operative political-economic philosophies have us in such a blind crab grip that they prevent us from preparing for the natural disasters that are not our fault. So the apocalyptic shit is going to hit the fan, all right, but there'll be some of us it'll miss. Little pockets of humanity. Like the Clock People. Like you two honeys, if you decide to accept my offer of a lease on Siwash Cave. There's almost no worldwide calamity — famine, nuclear accident, plague, weather warfare or reduction of the ozone shield — that you couldn't survive in that cave."

"Okay for us," said Sissy, "and okay for the Clock People, but what about the rest of the world, the millions who aren't even aware of the dangers, let alone the alternatives? We should probably be working full-time educating the masses and trying to mobilize them for survival."

"No, no," said the Chink. He was leaning heavily on his cane. "Survival isn't important. What matters is *how* you survive. Every long-term survival plan conceived by our think tanks and scientists and social strategists involves variations on totalitarianism — anthill- or beehive-type societies. Well, insects are good at survival; better than any other creatures, for sure. That's because in the insect world there's no individualism whatsoever. Insect life is rigid and predictable; the bug psyche is concerned with absolutely nothing *but* survival: survival of the colony, the hive, the swarm. I think it's better that mankind dies out than resorts to a totalitarian survival lifestyle. We should take as our model the whooping crane rather than the termite. Let's go extinct if we must, but let's go with some dignity and humor and grace. Antmen and beewomen aren't worthy of survival."

The Chink reached out and caressed Sissy's thumb. The left thumb. The transcontinental whopper. So slow was his movement that she didn't even flinch. "Survival itself is of no concern to me, but here's something I do find interesting. Suppose that in the next twenty to fifty years a series of overlapping natural and manmade disasters wrecks our social structure and eliminates most of the human race. The probability of this is high. Only small, isolated groups would survive. Now, suppose that you, Sissy, were among the survivors — and if you exercise your option to reside in Siwash Cave, you *would* be among them. And suppose that you bear children . . ."

With that, he removed his wrinkled yellow hand from Sissy's perpetually pregnant appendage and began to caress her temporarily knocked-up belly. His eyes were smiling. My God? Did he know about that, too?

"Suppose that Madame Zoe's prophecy comes true and you bear five or six children with your characteristics. All in Siwash Cave. In a postcatastrophe world, your offspring would of necessity intermarry, forming in time a tribe. A tribe every member of which had giant thumbs. A tribe of Big Thumbs would relate to the environment in very special ways. It could not use weapons or produce sophisticated tools. It would have to rely on its wits and its senses. It would have to live with animals — and plants! — as virtual equals. It's extremely pleasant to me to think about a tribe of physical eccentrics living peacefully with animals and plants, learning their languages, perhaps, and paying them the respect they deserve. It's just fun to consider, that's all."

Sissy squeezed his hand. It felt like a wedge of stale cheese. "Fun is fun," she said, "but how am I going to be the progenitor of a tribe when I'm living on an isolated ridgetop with Delores?"

"That's your problem" said the Chink. "Actually, I'm not much more concerned with tribal situations than I am with mass populations. Most groups are herds and all herds are a mess. Debbie and those other misguided kids try to pigeonhole me as another Oriental boohoo. They couldn't be more wrong. The various Oriental philosophers have at least one thing in common: they take the personal and try to make it universal. I hate that. I'm the opposite. I take the universal and make it personal. The only truly magical and poetic exchanges that occur in this life occur between two people. Sometimes it doesn't get that far. Often, the true glory of existence is confined to individual consciousness. That's okay. Let us live for the beauty of our own reality."

Abruptly, the Chink pulled his hand from Sissy's stomach. He cleared his throat. "Kaff." And rolled his eyes until they looked like a couple of beans that had just got the word they were being transferred to Boston. "Listen to the way I'm babbling. That dynamite must have loosened one of my transistors. Don't pay any attention to me. You've got to work it out for yourself. The westbound choo-choo leaves Mottburg at one-forty. I want to be on it. Will you drive me to the station?"

When the authorities dropped charges against Delores — apparently seeking to wash their hands of cowgirls forever — they had returned the peyote wagon. The women decided to take it to town; after all, the new jeep (a gift from the Countess Foundation) belonged to the ranch and the ranch was now in the control of Elaine and Debbie. Delores drove, Sissy and the Chink beside her holding hands.

Fighting a nasty wind all the way, the serpent-encrusted camper made it to the station with only five minutes to spare. The train was already in. "Schedules!" said the Chink. "Ironic how I have to follow timetables in order to get back to the clockworks." His expression was one of admiration. "Don't ever bet against paradox, ladies. If complexity doesn't beat you, then paradox will."

Inside Sissy's burning ducts, teardrops were running, not walking, to the nearest exit. "But what about *your* clockworks?" she asked, sniffling.

"My clockworks? Why, I'm carrying it with me. Aren't you?"

He gave the women kisses of equal duration, although Sissy got a bit more tongue. Then he turned and limped across the loading platform.

Watching him hobble onto the train, Sissy was struck by how small and frail he had begun to look. Delores was weeping now, too.

In the doorway of the railroad car, the Chink suddenly spun, tore open his robe and shook his pecker at them. "Ha ha ho ho and hee hee," he sniggered.

The old goat.

120.

WITH SISSY AND DELORES snug in the cave, the ranch in good hands, the Chink rewinding the Clock People, the Countess carrying out pans of afterbirth and Jellybean roping clouds on the prairies of Paradise, things seem to have settled down for those entities whose adventures this book has chronicled.

We might conclude that *Even Cowgirls Get the Blues* has reached maximum entropy, were it not for one unexpected ongoing unsettling phenomenon: the behavior of the whooping cranes.

Following its flight from Siwash Lake, the crane flock stopped at its Aransas wintering grounds but briefly. Hours before the commencement of a gala celebration to welcome the big birds home, they took to the air again, leaving the Secretary of the Interior, the Governor of Texas, the Corpus Christi Chamber of Commerce and thousands of patriotic bird-lovers in the lurch.

Continuing southward, they rested in Yucatán for a while, then flapped on down to Venezuela and lunched on leopard frogs in the swamps of the Orinoco. In Bolivia, their droppings fell on a revolution. Over Paraguay, they stained the cathedrals of Asunción. Attempts by Latin-American scientists to get close to them invariably resulted in their moving on. They veered into Chile, maybe to pay tribute to the assassinated poet Pablo Neruda; next stop, Patagonia.

In the U.S. and Canada, many people were aghast. The head of the Audubon Society began to make noises that his fellow birdmen identified as loon and cuckoo. Was it the aftereffects of the peyote diet, or something at once more mysterious and more ominous that was making the cranes act so? Naturalists argued in laboratories and conference rooms — and the whoopers, crossing the Atlantic toward Africa, paid a call to the South Sandwich Islands.

After several of them were shot down by Congolese poachers, the United Nations passed a unanimous resolution making harming the cranes a prison offense in every country in the world. Just in time, too, for soon the great white flock was traveling through heavily populated regions. The whoopers ruined a beach in the south of France, upstaged the famous pigeons at St. Mark's in Venice and are said to have looked picturesque wading in the Thames.

The birds moved on — and are still moving. Nobody knows where they'll turn up next. Their whoops, greeted with religious fervor along the Ganges, could barely be heard above the horns and squealing tires of Tokyo traffic. At this writing, they are believed to be somewhere in the interior of China, where poems about cranes (non-whoopers, of course) once were produced at the rate of a thousand a day. But precious few crane poems are written in China anymore.

Is the most spendid and sizable American bird searching for a new home, scouring the globe in quest of a place where it can be private and free? That is one theory. Naturally, legends have sprung up around the travels of the whooper. In Burma, a woman claims to have had sexual intercourse with one of the cranes. Shades of Leda and the Canadian Honker.

Perhaps the whooping cranes carry a message, bearing it far and wide. A message from the wild to the wild-no-more. Is such a thing possible?

All's possible. And all's well. And since all's well that ends well, are we to conclude that this is the end?

Yeah, almost. Except to pass along the news that the cranes have just crossed the border into Tibet. Whooping.

Part VII

Flapping your arms can be flying.

— Robert K. Hall

121.

TIME HAS PASSED. Months. Seven to eight months, by the size of Sissy's belly.

It is midnight at the clockworks. A June midnight, warm enough for sleeping on the cave's upper level. Sissy and Delores are dreaming, and oddly enough, for they have grown apart in recent weeks, they share a similar dream.

Delores has told Sissy that she wants to go away. She won't go until after the baby has come, until Sissy is able and well; she loves Sissy, after all, but she doesn't feel complete with her. It is of completeness that Delores now dreams — of the two opposites of One that, in balance, enable It to both exist and live. A woman without her opposite, or a man without his, can exist but cannot live. Existence may be beautiful, but never whole. Beneath Delores's pillow is the card, the jack of hearts.

The swell of Sissy's belly forces her to sleep on her back, the ideal position to attract the dream. Sissy, too, dreams of the opposite that can complete her, that she can complete. Having a way with birds, Sissy knows that the spirit cannot soar with only one wing. From the Chink, she has learned how a thing's opposite holds it together. In Sissy's dream is a man who does not deny himself, as Julian did, but who is himself to the full limit of himself, as she has been.

The two women are restless. Delores tosses and squirms like a postcard with an illegible address. Sissy mews like a kitten with vodka in its milk dish. Their lids flutter but do not open.

In the cave, a third person is sleeping. Since birth is completion as well as beginning, perhaps that person, too, dreams of being complete. It wakes and gives Sissy a good jolt. Not with its foot but with its . . . In embryonic life, digits are formed as radiating ridges on the lateral surfaces of the hand and foot segments. Since these ridges grow more rapidly than the bodies of their segments, they soon project beyond the margin as definitive fingers and toes. Sissy has known for quite a while that the baby has her characteristics. It will come into the world half-Japanese, one-thirty-second Siwash and all thumbs. So be it. The moving finger writes, and having writ, moves on. The moving thumb beckons, and having bect, moves us with it.

The fetus hitchhikes Sissy's cervix. Her lumbar region. Her bladder. Even that does not wake her. What finally causes her to abandon her dream is not a gesture but a noise.

A strange noise, loud though far away. Possible sources of the noise are considered by the generals in her brain. It was a rumbling noise. Could it have been a long-awaited earthquake, breaking off the edges of the continent and propelling the Clock People into the Eternity of Joy? Could it have been the first nuclear firecracker of the war that is in the back of everyone's mind: the international situation *is* desperate. Sissy considers waking Delores and moving to the lower level of the cave.

She hears the noise again. It sounds closer this time, and the rumble less apocalyptic. It is, in fact, followed by a higher, more organic sound. Are the whooping cranes coming back? she wonders. Or is some cowgirl caught in another cowboy jam?

The noise is closer . . .

Maybe it's the clockworks. Beating out an entirely new rhythm, measuring unexpected developments in the continuum — such as a fit of laughter on the part of the collective unconsciousness, or sudden cosmic vibrations that defy the more sophisticated measuring devices of science because they are tender and obscene.

The noise is closer yet . . .

Sissy sits up in her bedroll. Delores is awake now, also.

And out on the Siwash Trail, following by flashlight a map hand-drawn in minute detail by the only person who could have drawn it (Chink!), comes stumbling, crashing, falling, cursing and sniggering, Dr. Robbins, your author.

Having gathered all of the material for this book, Dr. Robbins waits not even for light of day, but plunges, mustache first, into dangerous Dakota darkness to reach Siwash Cave. For what purpose?

Does Dr. Robbins actually believe he will mate with Sissy, that it is his seed that will next ignite her egg, he who will be called daddy by the prophesied brood of big-thumbed babes? Does he believe that he will share the pagan stewardship of Siwash Ridge — and that he is the agent of Sissy Hankshaw's special destiny?

Dr. Robbins won't say what he believes. Except:

I believe in everything; nothing is sacred/I believe in nothing; everything is sacred.

Ha ha ho ho and hee hee.

Special Bonus Parable

In a place out of doors, near forests and meadows, stands a jar of vinegar — the emblem of life.

Confucius approaches the jar, dips his finger in and tastes the brew. "Sour," he says. "Nonetheless, I can see where it could be very useful in preparing certain foods."

Buddha comes to the vinegar jar, dips in a finger and has a taste. "Bitter," is his comment. "It can cause suffering to the palate, and since suffering is to be avoided, the stuff should be disposed of at once."

The next to stick a finger in the vinegar is Jesus Christ. "Yuk," says Jesus. "It's both bitter and sour. It's not fit to drink. In order that no one else will have to drink it, I will drink it all myself."

But now two people approach the jar, together, naked, hand in hand. The man has a beard and woolly legs like a goat. His long tongue is slightly swollen from some poetry he's been reciting. The woman wears a cowgirl hat, a necklace of feathers, a rosy complexion. Her tummy and tits bear the stretch marks of motherhood; she carries a basket of mushrooms and herbs. First the man and then the woman sticks a thumb into the vinegar. She licks his thumb and he hers. Initially they make a face, but almost immediately they break into wide grins. "It's *sweet,*" they chime.

"Swee-eet!"